LOU'S
DIRTY DOZEN

Ranny Brady
PS.
150:6

LOU'S
DIRTY DOZEN

RANNY GRADY

TATE PUBLISHING & *Enterprises*

Published by Tate Publishing & Enterprises, LLC
127 E. Trade Center Terrace | Mustang, Oklahoma 73064 USA
1.888.361.9473 | www.tatepublishing.com

Tate Publishing is committed to excellence in the publishing industry. The company reflects the philosophy established by the founders, based on Psalm 68:11,
"The Lord gave the word and great was the company of those who published it."

Book design copyright © 2009 by Tate Publishing, LLC. All rights reserved.
Cover design by Kandi Evans
Interior design by Jeff Fisher

Published in the United States of America

ISBN: 978-1-60799-634-7
1. Fiction, Family Life
2. Fiction, Christian, General
09.07.08

Dedication

This author wishes to dedicate this book to Jessie Almeta (Crandall) Grady, my mother. *Lou's Dirty Dozen* is her life's story, as seen through the eyes of a ten-year-old girl who grew up to become a married woman with children.

While I never had the privilege to know my grandmother—the main character of the story—I do know her daughter, Jessie, has her indomitable spirit, her love for Jesus Christ, and unwavering trust in God's Holy Bible. She possesses her mother's clear, clean, spiritual "possibility vision" that motivates people to achieve excellence.

This story would not have been written without her unfailing love and her constant encouragement for me to follow my heart and my dream.

Thank you, Mother!

Also, my prayers were answered when God sent me what every writer needs: professional editors. Larry and Mary Wilson have been godsends to help me fulfill my dreams of having my stories read by the world.

Last, but not least, I want to thank my wife, Denise, for her constant encouragement, her willingness to listen to my progress while writing this story, and for her observations, particularly from a woman's point of view.

Table of Contents

The Ranti Crandal Family

Ranti Crandal

Louise Mae

Napoleon

Earl

Sammy

Rose

Pauline

Naomi

Howard

Charlie

Jessie

Deannie and Gracie (twins)

Arthur

Introduction

The Birthday Celebration

When my children told me they were planning a big celebration for that red-letter day in my life, my ninetieth birthday, I was pleased.

The children, grandchildren, and even great-grandchildren came in from Virginia, Florida, Indiana, Texas, Kentucky, and, of course, Oklahoma to help me celebrate a milestone in my life.

I walked into my one-bedroom apartment, completely tuckered out by the evening's activities. The comfortable rocker, where I spent most of my time reading, seemed to hauntingly and mystically call to me. *Jessie, where have you been? I missed your warm body.* Just the sweet thought of my old rocker missing me made me laugh; so I plopped down to take a load off my feet. I unbuckled the straps on my high heels and kicked them off. My feet seemed to yell, *It's about time!*

As I sat down, a warm, fuzzy feeling crept up inside my heart. A sense of satisfaction made me want to laugh with joy. A smile came across my face. *You show'd 'em good, gal. They didn't believe you could stand on your feet in those three-inch heels, let alone kick your heels up,* I mused.

"Ninety, and Jessie can still do the Charleston!" several people at the party remarked.

"There's nothing like an old fool acting like an old fool." I chuckled. *It was therapeutic showing my children and grandchildren that the "old gal" still had a little life in her,* I thought. "Though there was a time or two, out on that dance floor, when I was doing the Charleston, that I thought I might slip and break my arsarotomy (my momma's word for rear end). For a few fleeting seconds I was back in the dance hall in Tampa, Kansas, cutting quite a rug on the floor with some boy or my Pete," I mumbled.

The apartment was quiet, and my bones sagged. I was weary, and I must have dozed off for a minute because my mind's eye had taken me back to my birthday celebration.

The church fellowship hall was gaily decorated with banners, and the tables were decorated with bright colors, flowers, and balloons, most of which were black and gold (my school colors). Pieces of memorabilia from the Paul Leo Grady clan were on each table. A sparkle came into my eyes, not of tears, but of sweet remembrances of past achievement. On one table was a picture of me with my girls' high school basketball team wearing my varsity letter. It was the year I earned my varsity letter, and I was the second freshman to do so in the history of our school. I allowed myself a bit of a laugh. Our uniform bloomers were quite a sight! My, how I loved putting on that gold and black uniform. I thought we were quite the fashionable ones, with our large black T letters, which stood for Tampa High, on the front of our uniforms, our black bloomer pants, cut and tucked at the knee, and gold stockings with our gold and black basketball shoes.

On another table, decorated with a patriotic flare, was the picture of me shaking the governor's hand. *Now, who dug that out and put it on display?* I thought. "In recognition of selfless service to others, let it be known that Jessie Almeta Crandal was named one of Oklahoma's ten most outstanding volunteers." The governor signed it. Accompanying the picture was another picture and story, first published in the *El Reno Tribune*, detailing how Jessie won this coveted award. *It's better to wear out than rust out, huh, Momma?* I mused. "You were right!" I said, and I looked to the heavens where I knew Momma was residing.

On another table, in addition to the black and gold balloons, was my old Pink Lady uniform. Evidently, some creative person placed it on the table to serve as a tablecloth. It was pink and white, had a matching apron, and included the pin I wore on it each week to signify forty-nine years of volunteer service at the hospital. I'm still irritated that they decided to change that uniform—need to modernize. *In a pig's eye!* I thought. The card was sweet, and doctors and staff, wishing me well on this grand day of celebration, had signed it.

On the family table were photos and mementos of a lifetime of achievements spanning several generations. The center of attention was my lion, Paul (Pete) Leo Grady. The old heart still aches when I reflect about the nearly half a century of marriage, save one year, we had. *And our five children, successful beyond my wildest dreams, are all dedicated to Jesus Christ,* I reflected, and tears sprang to my eyes.

The First Christian Church was ready to shake, rattle, and roll tonight! I reflected.

I recalled the weight and the peculiar noise the plastic grocery bag, filled with over one hundred fifty cards, made as I placed it on the table marked "Jessie's cards." Its contents made my heart jump as I read the sweet, delicious words that conveyed the tender thoughts people wanted to express to me in celebration of my birthday. It made me want to jump for joy and cry like a baby, all at the same time.

The kids hired a band to play music of the thirties and forties. They weren't as polished or talented as my old Salina Moonshine Band, but it was so pleasant to hear the familiar strains of melodies from the wonderful songs of yesteryears.

"Pride goeth before destruction, and a haughty spirit before a fall." *I hear you, Momma,* I thought, and I could feel her presence as I basked in the warmth of knowing all of those cards meant that those people cared about me.

Maybe it was a dog barking, because something broke my sleep reverie, and I awoke. I recalled hearing one of the gentlemen, an elder at our church, tell my oldest son, "Your mother is the most remarkable woman I've ever known."

Funny how certain items or phrases can carry one back to another time and place. I remember staring at one of the shoes I had kicked off my feet when I first walked in the door. It was bright Kelly green; it had landed in a corner of the room and was propped against the wallboard.

I yawned, which I couldn't seem to keep from doing. *I need to get this old woman to bed.*

I was very, very tired, so much so, I evidently never made it out of my chair. I must have fallen into a deep dream sleep because I kept hearing my friend tell my son, "Your mother is the most remarkable woman I've ever known."

Remarkable! You think I'm remarkable? Let me tell you about the most remarkable woman God ever put on this earth. I found myself tugging at his shoulder and insisting he sit down and listen to my story.

Jessie, no one can be more remarkable than you, he kept insisting.

Just sit down and listen. When I'm done telling you about my momma, you'll stop tooting my horn.

Piss and Vinegar

I was filled with what Poppa called "piss and vinegar." Momma scolded him when he said that about me. "Jess is just right," she would counter. Like life itself, it took me a while to figure out the meaning of his crude comment. But as I grew older, I came to appreciate it.

I was ten in the fall of 1926 a.d. I was the ninth child in the Ranti Crandal clan of twelve children. I was old enough to taste some of life's better things, yet not old enough to be burdened with a lot of responsibility.

When a girl finds herself fourth in the pecking order of twelve, it behooves her to learn how to blend in and yet establish a place for herself. If not, she'll be a number lost in the shuffle of life. I was too young to demand my space and respect, so I used my moxie and wiles to compete with my siblings.

Even though I was one of the youngest in our family, Momma relied upon me to be her "right-hand man." My older siblings said I was her "step-and-fetch-it" girl. I didn't care. If Momma allowed me to spend more time with her, for any reason, I was sure the good Lord had chosen me to get an extra blessing.

Large families weren't uncommon in our town, though families with a dozen kids were unusual. Being a young lass, betwixt and between being a young woman and a girl, I was all jumbled up inside. I wished I had the answers to all of the mysteries of life, all gathered up in a little, bitty thimble; then I wouldn't walk around feeling and looking like a fool all the time. One day, Momma gave me an education about how large families were created.

One summer morning, when the morning cool was just starting to fade and the first edge of the stifling heat of the day was ready to make its appearance, Momma and I were in the kitchen snapping beans and preparing them for canning. Our easy conversation turned to a particular Lutheran farm family that had eighteen children.

"Momma, why did you and Poppa have so many kids?" I sheepishly glanced at her.

She looked up from her mess of beans, which were in a large, wooden bowl.

"Jess, honey, what makes you ask that question?"

I felt embarrassed. I shrugged my shoulders. "I…I don't know, just curious, I guess."

"What do you know about babies?"

"Not much." I hemmed and hawed. "You know…some girls say things. But it's true that nearly every time the doctor visits, I get a new baby brother or sister."

Momma laughed; it was more of a chuckle.

"And you've only been here for half of them. Honey, sometimes it was a mystery to me. All your poppa had to do was throw his overalls on the bedpost"—she winked—"and bingo, I was having another baby." She put her hand up to hide her mouth because she told me a secret.

I'm not sure if Momma ever knew, but I used to sneak into their bedroom and check to see if Poppa's overalls were hanging on the bedpost. I never did find them hanging, but I'd made up my mind if I ever did, I was going to snatch them off the bedpost to save Momma a lot of pain and grief.

Now that I'm old and gray, I can really appreciate the gift I was given by the good Lord when I was allowed to experience being reared in our large family.

My father, Ranti, was a man who was unable to find a way to be contented with his lot in life.

He had a peg leg. He held a number of jobs: he was driver for a fuel wagon, the town cobbler, and a sharecropper. My momma, Louise (everyone who knew her called her Lou), often said that my daddy was a fair- to middling farmer but a great dreamer. She teased him about being inoculated with the "wander-lust bug" when it came to life. He lived as if his pants didn't fit him, and he was always searching for a better fitting pair. Even when he found a comfortable fitting pair, he took them off as soon as he could. Poppa usually took her ribbing good-naturedly, but sometimes he would lash out at her and say mean things to hurt her. In hindsight, I suppose that Poppa's mean times far outweighed his good-natured times. All I know is that I used to hide under the bed every time he was in one of his mean moods.

When the great harvest of 1926 came in, I suppose Poppa found a pair of pants that fit him just fine.

The summer harvest of '26 was an especially prosperous one.

"It is like a land of milk and honey," my poppa often crowed with the anticipation of what those golden wheat fields were about to produce.

"If Mother Nature—"

"If the good Lord in heaven," Momma corrected him.

"—keeps those terrible storms away, we are going to have a bumper crop!" Poppa would nearly shout.

As we watched those fields turn from dark green to golden, signifying that the harvest was at hand, our excitement knew no bounds.

During the early summer of '26, some good friends of Poppa's and Momma's spent a few days visiting with us. They knew each other before Poppa married Momma. They lived in Missouri and operated a very successful business growing strawberries. Eddy and Horace Bosch were their names. He was a large and stockily built man with a full black beard. He had a very dark complexion from being out in the sun, and he had a prominent nose. He was not handsome, but he had a wonderful laugh that filled our house with joy.

"As the Good Book says, 'Laughter is medicine for the soul,'" he would say and let loose with a big belly laugh.

His wife, Ethel—he called her Eddy—, was a woman with dark eyes and flaxen hair. Her frame was willowy. She took pride in her appearance. Though barren, she mixed well with our passel of kids. She could tell the most interesting stories. Evidently, she was reared in a home with the finer things, because she knew all about famous and enchanting places: the Chicago World's Fair, New York's theaters, and Vaudeville theaters—places average folk just dream about.

One evening, as the sun was bidding the day adieu and the moon was on the horizon, the Boschs' and my parents sat on the porch sipping a cold drink. I overheard a private conversation between them.

"Ranti," Mr. Bosch declared, "I am telling you, if you can raise a few hundred dollars, you can make it big yourself."

"Now, don't you go filling his head with another rainbow and a pot of gold," Momma admonished Mr. Bosch teasingly.

"Woman, hush up! If I want your two bits, I'll ask for it," Poppa said. She glared at him but said nothing.

"Now, now, Lou, Horace didn't mean to meddle," Eddy butted in, acting as a mediator, "but Missouri has much to offer. This may be the Lord's way of helping Ranti stop living as a sharecropper. Isn't that something you desire?"

"All in God's good timing," Mr. Bosch declared. "It's something to think about."

Poppa proved to me that some ideas are more profound than others. Mr. Bosch's suggestion changed our family's life.

That fall, when that bumper crop came in, in no time at all we found ourselves loading up two Ford touring cars to move to Missouri. Somehow Poppa arranged to buy a second car for our move. All of our household goods were shipped in railroad cars on the Rock Island Railroad, to be picked up at the Humansville's depot Freight Department. Jenny and Jack, Poppa's two mules, and a prize Rhode Island rooster were also shipped on the train.

In the early part of November, the Ranti Crandal clan headed for Humansville, Missouri, to become strawberry and chicken barons. We kids were willing adventurers; it could be said that Momma came along kicking and screaming every inch of the way.

While we kids hated to leave Tampa, Kansas, and our wonderful school and friends, most of us were ready to jump onto Poppa's dream.

"Don't you want to live in a bigger house? Why, you might even have a bedroom where you have to sleep with only one of your brothers or sisters, not three or four. Wouldn't it be great to have our own farm so your poppa wouldn't have to be a slave to another man's sheep? One day your poppa will be an important man in this community. Wouldn't that make you proud?" He peppered us with many questions to encourage us to want to leave Tampa and move to Missouri.

He weaved his story so well about how great it was going to be when we moved, some days I was positive we would be magically transformed into rich people who had servants. I reckon my poppa was a gifted salesman.

If we had only recognized the portent foreshadowing the events that lay ahead.

AN UNEXPECTED GIFT

Sadie Moon was the owner of a nefarious saloon. She was a bawdy woman with a reputation no decent woman would covet, Momma didn't allow others to talk about her. She had a soft spot in her heart for Sadie's plight.

"Sadie's not a bad person; she just makes bad choices."

Momma's soft spot for Sadie came because she went out of her way to try to be neighborly. It happened during the time my family was preparing to move from Tampa to Missouri. In reflection, I think my befriending my friend Fancy (a high school girlfriend) was akin to Momma's treatment of Sadie. I guess "kindred spirits" travel the same road of kindness.

Poppa had decided that we were moving to Missouri so we could get rich. Momma and all of our family were busy packing and getting ready for the move. Sadie picked that time to make a call on us.

There was a loud knock on the door.

"Will someone answer the door?" she yelled. "Jessie, answer the door, please."

I came running from the kitchen and ran to the door. I opened it. There stood Sadie.

"Is Lou home?" she asked.

I nodded and ran to tell Momma.

"Sadie Moon is at the front door," I said in a low voice.

Momma lifted herself up from her packing. She pushed back some of her hair and rubbed her hands on her apron.

"What in the world is she doing making a call on me?" She brushed past me and went to the door. "Why, Sadie, what's the special occasion?" she said with a smile.

We kids gathered around Momma and peeked out from behind her.

"I probably shouldn't have come, with your packing and all," she apologized. "But I didn't want you all to get away before I had the chance to tell you that Tampa is going to miss the Crandal family." She scratched her nose nervously.

"Why, Sadie, that is one of the kindest things anyone has ever said about us, isn't it, kids?" Momma turned and looked at us. We nodded our heads and giggled.

"I can remember when I was a kid and my parents moved around a lot, leaving my friends…" Her voice trailed off, and it was easy to see she was getting emotional.

She started to unbutton her blouse and pulled out a tiny puppy.

"Lucky had more pups. I thought one of Lucky's pups might help cheer your kids up and help them make an easier adjustment to their new home."

The pup fit into Momma's hand.

"It's a mix of Mexican Chihuahua and Rat Terrier." She looked at us kids for approval. "It will be a good mouser, and you won't have any problems with rats."

"Look, kids. Sadie has given us this cute puppy." Momma turned and showed us the puppy, followed by one of her looks, which told us we should show Sadie our appreciation for her kindness, and we had good manners.

"Thank you, Sadie," we all said.

"You're quite welcome." Sadie laughed a little and tousled Arthur's hair before turning to leave.

Momma had been busy making sure we showed good manners. When she turned around, Sadie was about out through the gate.

"Wait, Sadie." Momma walked out to her. She stuck out her hand. Sadie put her hand in Momma's, and Momma put her other hand on Sadie's. Momma looked in her eyes. "Sadie, I want to thank you from the bottom of my heart," she said as she looked back at us kids on the porch, where Gracie was holding the new puppy. "You have a kind heart and a good soul."

I thought I saw a trace of a tear in Sadie's eyes as she walked away.

"Lordy, Lordy, what in the world am I going to do with a puppy that will pee all over everything, and in the midst of all this packing?" She pointed to me, as I was holding the puppy. "You kids are in charge of that thing, and don't bother me with it anymore. Sadie gave it to you, not me."

We named the puppy Susie. Susie made it to Missouri okay. Momma trained her; she was her master. She was soon house-broken. She never caught mice or rats, but she loved to cull chickens. Momma became her mistress and her master. She loved Momma best.

"That dog doesn't even know it has legs," Momma would say as we kids fought over who Susie would sleep with each night.

Momma raised some chickens for our family to eat. It seemed that she killed and dressed chickens nearly every day. When Momma got out her whetstone and sharpened her knife, Susie came running. There wasn't anything she liked doing better than helping Momma fetch the chickens. She'd prance around on the linoleum floor, and her toenails almost sounded like she was tap dancing. She barked to show she was ready to catch a chicken. Momma would hold out her knife and say, "Are you ready to get those chickens?"

Momma opened the door, and Susie flew out to the coop. When she arrived, she sat quietly, waiting for Momma to catch up. She never barked; it was as if Susie knew she shouldn't because it would rile the chickens. When Momma opened the gate, Susie stepped into the coop. All Momma had to do was point to the one she wanted, and Susie would cull it out and hold it until Momma came to get it. Momma would wring its neck, and its head would soon be in her hands. After she wrung the chicken's neck, sometimes Momma allowed Susie to stay in the coop. Susie would see that headless chicken, and she would attack it, thinking it wasn't dead. Before she could get back into our house, Momma would have to wash Susie, and she didn't like to be bathed.

Susie lived nearly as long as Momma lived. Even when Momma was really sick, sometimes she would get out her whetstone and rub her knife against it. Even though Susie was nearly blind and stove up with arthritis, she'd come from any place she might be in the house. As well as she could, she'd prance around and bark. She loved chickens.

Moving: More than an Adventure

Our family learned that moving is as much a spiritual adventure as it is an emotional and physical adventure.

We must have been some sight. There we were, packed to the gills, ten children of various ages, shapes, and sizes squeezed into two rather stately looking touring cars that Mr. Henry Ford had so graciously designed for such an occasion. The black Model Ts were convertibles, which had canvas tops that were used in inclement weather. Of course, this limited the amount any one family could haul. Momma earned her stripes as a packer and household mover as she found ingenious ways to compactly arrange items in and around people and machines to carry our goods to our new home. Poppa had his own ingenuous ideas about packing: he assigned seat assignments according to how much each one weighed. He worked on estimates, I guess, so the cars would travel easier. When Momma saw his figuring, she laughed loudly at his details, which ticked him off.

"Won't make any difference how you stack them," she declared. "When you have to make a stop for a pee, or worse, every half hour or so, it won't make a whit of difference how that brood is seated," she snickered, and she used her hand to shield her mouth to ensure Poppa didn't see her smirk.

"Why don't you just get your fanny back to the house?" Poppa snarled. "Try to do something constructive." He glared at her.

Momma didn't move fast enough to suit him.

"Now, woman! We need to get this show on the road."

Stinging from Poppa's harsh words, Momma scurried into the house. Once inside, she lingered.

Oooogah, ooogah. Poppa sat in the driver's seat and laid on the horn. It made a piercing sound as the Model T Ford's horn signaled the impatient attitude of the Ranti Crandal clan.

"Jessie, hightail it in there and tell your momma to get out here P.D.Q.," Poppa ordered.

A shack becomes a home to a woman if she has fond memories of the family who inhabited it.

Louise Mae, the wife of a surly peg-legged man and a mother to twelve children, including twins, stood in the room that was now bare. It had been her kitchen for many years. Just a hint of tears was in her bright, hazel-green eyes. She turned and stared d at me as I stepped into the kitchen.

"Oh, honey, I can just close my eyes and remember all the good times we had in this run-down house. In spite of the hard times, we sure had good times, didn't we?"

I had an urge to run to her and give her a hug, but I didn't want to get on Poppa's bad side.

"Momma, Poppa sent me to fetch you. He's getting mighty irritated."

With her right hand Lou dabbed at her eyes and softly brushed a lock of hair away from her face. She found a way to sweep it back into place. Her hair was a mixture of a few hints of gray and the evening's sunset glow of red. She wore her hair in a bun and secured it with a bright yellow ribbon. Ranti didn't like her style. He liked her to wear her hair down; he said it made her look less manly. She was not beautiful; her frame was a bit too boxy and short. She did have nice-looking legs, which men always seemed to admire as she passed by. Her face was a bit too rugged for one to classify her as pretty, yet her carriage and overall appearance had turned many a man's eye in her heyday.

"You go tell your poppa not to have a heart attack and to

stop blowing that blasted horn." She shooed me back out to the car.

Since Momma wasn't ready to leave, I wasn't about to return to the car to deal with Poppa's wrath. I stepped halfway out the door and stopped.

Momma stooped and slowly wrapped the hot bricks in the old blanket Poppa'd told her to bring. She noticed that I hadn't left.

"Jessie, my heart's breaking. Do you hear me?" she mumbled. "Not having Napoleon go with us is one thing, but moving without Sammy, not knowing if he's dead or alive . . ."

Napoleon, my oldest brother, had a good job and chose not to move with the family. Sammy and Poppa had a real disagreement, and when all of the smoke cleared, Sammy had left a terse note on the kitchen table and was gone.

Suddenly, I sensed I was watching a drama; Momma was playing all the parts. I was an audience of one.

"Sometimes I just ache to know if he's all right." She emitted a soft sigh. "Next thing you know, Satan will hire a sadistic herald who will have a seventy-six-piece band from hell to tell the world what a terrible mother I am."

I was getting antsy because I was sure Poppa was.

"I don't know. If I were a momma, I'd probably feel just like you do."

"Do you know why Sammy left? Did your brother Charlie tell you?"

I shook my head.

Her husband had refused to dwell upon it. He rebuffed her queries, and anytime she dared to pry it out of him, he became impatient and mean.

"What in tarnation is keeping you, woman?"

Momma and I were startled. She quickly did her best to brush away the tears from her eyes because she knew Poppa couldn't stand the sight of women crying.

"I . . . I'm coming," she assured him. "I was just—"

"Well, just do your damn crying on your time, not mine." He slammed the screen door and thumped his way down the porch stairs. "This old, worthless sharecropper's shack is all there is," he muttered. "And she has to be all weepy about leaving it."

I ran to the car where Poppa was sitting and jumped in behind the driver's seat. In a few seconds, Momma came out carrying those heavy bricks wrapped in the blanket. My second oldest brother, Earl, who was driving the second car, saw Momma struggling with the load and ran to her rescue. Momma opened the car door and got behind the wheel. Sometimes I think those suffragettes could have used Momma as one of their recruits because I am quite certain there weren't many women who did all the driving for the family like she did for ours. We kids teased Poppa about not driving when he was in an especially good mood, but that day wasn't one of them.

"I need the time to clear my mind," he'd offer as an explanation. "It takes a lot out of a body to use brain power. It's a damn fact that too little is used with this bunch!" Then he'd add, "Besides, someone has to navigate. If it was left to your momma, we'd always be lost." He'd throw back his head and laugh as if he were the only one who knew why it was the proper thing to do.

Momma didn't mind it. She always told us that she was a better driver anyway. "Your poppa likes to daydream way too much for our family to be safe when he is behind the wheel."

Most of the time he would accept her needle without saying too much.

"Time's a wasting," Poppa declared. "It's over two hundred miles to Humansville. I aim to get there today. Good-bye, Tampa! Good-bye, old 'Slave Driver' Joseph P. Hunt. Your sharecropper is never coming back. Good-bye, old cobbler shop. Someone else can put leather on folks' shoes." Forward, wagons!"

It was a long, dreary trip to Humansville. Because the touring cars' tops were up to try and keep us from freezing, we used hand signals from one car to the next to signify when we had to make a potty stop.

We stopped for a picnic lunch by a clear, running creek in a grassy spot just off the road. Momma had planned for this. She'd packed cold fried chicken, potato salad, homemade dill pickles, and some bread and butter. Poppa had splurged and bought us all Coca-Colas. Momma asked Earl to say the blessing; Poppa didn't believe in a blessing.

The road to Humansville, if one wanted to call it a road, was dusty and narrow. Charlie, my younger brother, did his best to entertain us transporting us back to the days of the covered wagons that made the trips out West.

"Let's pretend that we're all pioneers traveling west to strike it rich in the gold mines of California."

"Charlie, why don't you just shut up?" Poppa said. "Your constant jabbering is driving us all nuts."

"I have a better idea," Momma interrupted. "Let's sing some of our favorite songs."

"Charlie," Poppa immediately said, "your kind of jabbering may be preferable to your momma's."

"*Oh, the B-I-B-L-E, yes that's the book for me. I stand alone on the Word of God, the B-I-B-L-E ...*" That was the first of many songs Momma led our family in as we traveled. As soon as the car behind us could recognize the song we were singing, they'd join right in. Poppa acted as if he wanted to crawl into a hole and hide; it didn't matter to the rest of our family. We had a wonderful time whiling away the long hours, performing our own choir concert, which was mostly for any of God's creatures, large and small, that happened to be within earshot.

The November sun, which had appeared just for lunch, hid the rest of the day in a dank mist of gray clouds touched with just a hint of black. The clouds threatened to brew up a storm any minute. By the time our family arrived in Humansville, way after dark, we were so nearly frozen we had to gingerly stomp the ground with our feet to get the blood running and the feeling back into our bodies.

We pulled up in front of a large, stately looking building. The Emporium Hotel was lit up like a Christmas tree.

"Wait here." Poppa commanded. "I'll go in and get the message Mr. Bosch said he would leave for us." He slowly got out of the car and gimped his way into the hotel. In a few minutes he came back. He had a puzzled, yet pleased look on his face. He handed a note to Momma. She read it by the light provided by the lamppost in front of the hotel.

"Just received word today that your household goods haven't arrived yet. Railroad promised they would be here tomorrow. I have arranged rooms for family and food from restaurant for breakfast. In His service, the Boschs'.

"Now doesn't that beat all," Momma whispered. She was near tears. "Children, Poppa has an announcement."

Poppa stood a bit taller and straighter on his peg leg. He thrust out his chest as he announced with pride, "Young'uns, the Ranti Crandal family will be staying the night at the Emporium Hotel." We children looked at each other in surprise and disbelief. Even though we were in different cars, as if by some secret code, all of us broke out in whoops and hollers of happiness. As the commotion quieted down, Poppa, with a smile on his face, added, "We will be dining in the hotel restaurant for breakfast."

"Now you children mind your manners. Even if you've never been inside a fancy hotel, let alone stayed in one, act as if you have," Momma admonished as we traipsed into the lobby.

The lush carpet was a dark red like I had never seen before. It seemed as if our shoes sank into it as we walked. Momma told me later it was called burgundy. There was an incredible fountain spewing up streams of running water, sounding as though an ocean was nearby. Of course, I had never seen the ocean either, but I imagined it to be similar to the sound the waves would make as they rolled gently along the beach. On the ceiling were large fans to move the air. In the center of the lobby, above the fountain, was a very large, shining crystal chandelier with so many lights they were uncountable.

"Close your mouth. You're going to catch flies," my brother Howard teased me.

When we finally assembled ourselves in a military line formation, eldest to the youngest, as Poppa liked, we approached the front desk. The man behind it gave us a look we had become accustomed to seeing every time our family went somewhere together. It wasn't unusual to see families with a passel of kids; nearly a dozen stretched the idea of a "normal family." *Look at this rag-tag outfit,* I imagined him to be thinking. *Better check the silverware when they leave. Probably never slept in a bed with white sheets.*

"May I help you?" the short, stubby clerk, dressed in a fine-looking navy blue coat, inquired. He wore thick glasses that sat on the bridge of his nose.

Better to look down on folk he considered unfit to stay at the hotel, I thought to myself. Our Crandal outfit sure fit that bill.

Before any of our family could respond, in a voice tinged with contempt, he said, "I'm sorry, but we don't have any accommodations available, particularly for such a large family."

"I ought to punch him in the nose," Earl said through gritted teeth.

Poppa handed him the note Mr. Bosch had left. In a disdainful manner, he casually glanced down at the note. When his eyes focused on the note's message, it was as if some electrical shock had entered the clerk's body and jump-started his mind and heart. With a wide, cheery grin he hit the rather large bell sitting upon the lobby desk.

"Bellman!" he shouted. He turned the brown leather registration book around. "Mr. Crandal, will you please sign the register?" He coughed nervously.

"My wife handles all that petty stuff." He motioned for Momma to come and sign the register.

"So, you're Horace's good friend from Kansas?" The clerk pushed his glasses back in place on his nose.

"You know Horace?" Poppa asked.

"Oh, yes indeedy." He turned the registration book around and pointed to Hiram's name. "Mr. Bosch is a regular. He and Missus dine with us frequently. Plus, he often has guests stay with us whenever he is conducting business."

In a near whisper, Poppa said, "So you are aware of this arrangement for my family?"

The clerk winked at Poppa. "Don't worry about a thing, Mr. Crandal. Mr. Bosch has arranged *everything*. He reserved four rooms for your family."

Four rooms! For a family that was used to sleeping three or four to a bed, the idea of our family having four rooms for ourselves in the fanciest hotel in the world was more than we children could believe. In a few seconds, the level of excitement rose to a roar.

"Hush!" Momma commanded. "The poor man won't be able to think straight."

"One of these days I'm going to stay in places like this every week," Charlie announced to our family.

"In your dreams." Rose, the oldest girl in the family and Poppa's favorite, belittled his remark. "But I'm going to marry a rich man, and he will pay for me to stay in places like this all around the world." She trumped his bravado.

Several times in my short lifetime, I remember Momma declaring, "Now, I'm ready to die and go to heaven," after something truly wonderful happened to her, like getting a washing machine with a wringer. That night, in that hotel, with clean, fresh-smelling white sheets on the bed, with only two children in a bed, our family slept the sleep of the most blessed. There were even additional cots in each room for the youngest and smallest. Momma and Poppa had a room just for themselves.

I didn't sleep much since I was wide-awake and wondering how our family was, all of a sudden being treated as if we were important and rich. How could I sleep? I was atwitter just thinking about eating breakfast in that fancy restaurant.

At seven o'clock sharp our family was already "spit polished," as Momma always called it, to march down to breakfast.

"Now, you kids mind your manners," Momma said. "Your poppa told me to tell you that if any of you act up, for any reason, he is going to wale the daylights out of you with his razor strop. I'm going to root him on!"

Our family entered the dining area and was soon shown to a set of tables that had, evidently, been reserved for us. Two waitresses, wearing neatly starched white dresses, approached

RANNY GRADY

us; one was a short blonde, and the other a taller dark-haired woman. They both had lovely smiles.

"Good morning! How did the Crandal family sleep in our hotel?" the blonde waitress asked warmly. Her questions made me feel important and elegant.

They handed us menus; there were so many choices, it made a body dizzy thinking about all the delicious smells and tastes one could enjoy while eating in the restaurant.

"Now, let's keep it simple," Poppa declared.

"I don't care how simple it is," replied Earl, "as long as they bring plenty of it." He winked at me. "Steak and eggs—how much simpler can it get?"

"Just because something might be lawful doesn't necessarily make it expedient," Momma said. She didn't want her children to order what they wanted just because they could.

"Lou, just don't make a big deal about it. Relax. Let the children enjoy this."

I didn't know at the time that Mr. Bosch was footing the bill, so I was surprised and very happy that Poppa was telling Momma he thought it was appropriate for us to eat what we wanted, regardless of the cost.

Steak and eggs, eaten by the men, huge piles of waffles, my particular choice, and syrup, large glasses of milk, freshly squeezed orange juice, hot oatmeal, and toast were consumed in near record time, I think. Momma later said she was embarrassed because most of us acted as if we hadn't eaten before the way we ate that breakfast. I think she may have been a little bit hurt because several times during breakfast someone would comment, "Best breakfast I ever had." That did nothing to make Momma proud of all the many, many breakfasts she had slaved over a hot stove to please us with.

We traveled to the Rock Island depot the next afternoon and retrieved our household goods from the railroad cars they were shipped in, and Mr. Bosch was there to greet us and help us find our new home.

Our new home, Humansville, Missouri, was geographically situated in Polk County in the Ozark Plateau in the state's largest land region. Forested hills and low mountains gave it scenic beauty. The plateau rose five hundred to one thousand feet or more above sea level. The river valley was about its only flat land. Polk County sits on the Springfield Plateau. The Pomme de Terre River runs through the center of Polk County. Humansville was named after James Human, who located the first settlement at the Big Spring.

The mountain scenic views were breathtaking. It was a welcome sight after seeing nothing but flat wheat fields all my life.

When our family first saw the beautiful Ozark Mountains on the horizon as we approached the city, my brother yelled, "Golly, aren't those hills pretty!"

Our new house was a large white wooden-sided house with green shingles. It was two stories with four bedrooms and a large wraparound porch we kids loved to play on. Poppa put up a porch swing, and we all fought over whose turn it was to swing. Poppa said we had fifty acres, and it soon would be much more. He planned to buy more land and plant more strawberries, and he was going to use his prized Rhode Island Red rooster, Solomon. Momma gave him that name because, like the biblical king Solomon, who spent all his time managing his harem of women, with little success, our Solomon did the same with our henhouse. I had my doubts that Poppa was going to be able to accomplish all that, but I did know that his prize rooster was one mean fowl.

For a time after we moved to Missouri, it was as if a fairy had come and sprinkled fairy dust on our family. It seemed as though Poppa had turned over a new leaf. He was much gentler with Momma, and he whipped us kids less.

"The stars were all aligned just right," Poppa said.

"The good Lord up above has just chosen to hand out an extra portion of blessings," Momma said and would continue when describing how good fortune suddenly showed up at our doorstep.

The strawberry crop that came in was one of the best Mr. Bosch could ever remember. He had been in the business for over two decades. It allowed Poppa to purchase more land and plant more strawberries the next year. He started drawing up plans to build some large chicken coops so he could raise chickens and sell eggs.

For the first time in my life, it seemed as if Poppa had found a gold mine, not out West where Charlie said everyone who wanted to find gold had to go, but right outside our front door. Poppa's strawberries were a cash crop. At least I heard him say they were, and he was ready to buy more land. We had our own milk cow, and we had some sheep and a goat or two. Poppa traded a neighbor some strawberries for a butchered hog.

"We were eating high off the hog," Momma used to tell us as she laughed.

In late August of 1929, Poppa and the boys had just finished building two chicken coops. The family was gathered around the dinner table that night when he announced, "Next year, we are going to have two crops."

"Chickens aren't a crop," Rose corrected him.

A hush fell upon the room. Poppa did not cotton to be corrected any time, especially by one of his children.

Poppa glared at her. "I'm not that damn stupid! Do you think that I'm that damn stupid?" We had all nearly stopped breathing, and we waited for Poppa to get his strop. In a few seconds, the veins of his neck softened and the intensity of the moment lessened. "Rose, honey, I think you need to spend some more time with your poppa." He looked at her with fire in his eyes. "Evidently, you need to get to know me better."

All of us kids looked at each other with shock. We knew that if we had said that to Poppa, our butts would have felt the terrible sting of his leather strop.

"In fact, I have to make a business trip tomorrow. Why don't you come with me?"

"Why don't you take Howard and Earl?" Momma quickly asked. "Rose can't be much of a help to you."

"Maybe so"—Poppa looked at Rose in a strange way—"but she is much better company."

Rose looked up at Momma and gave her an odd look. Rose moved her body in a manner that indicated she had won a personal struggle over an adversary, a struggle I would later associate with two women seeking the favor of one man. Though Rose was barely fourteen, she had already "gotten the curse," as Momma often said as she taught sex education in her own unique style to us girls. Rose had developed large breasts, especially for her age.

When we would go to the mercantile to buy supplies, I noticed grown men gawking at her. It frightened me to know that she liked them looking at her. She would often take her hand and casually flip her long auburn hair into the breeze and walk with a swing to her hips. I accused her of openly flirting with the men, but she denied she ever did such a thing.

From that day forward Momma and Rose shared a different type of relationship: cordial but distant. It seemed as if they were in competition for Poppa's attention. It didn't make any sense to me at the time. I attributed the problem to Rose having the "curse."

When one of us children would start telling about our woes and the unfairness of life, Momma taught us that life was nothing more than a series of hills and valleys.

My prayer for my children is that you learn—whether you are climbing or sliding—the only way you are going to handle life successfully is with the aid of your Creator.

In just a short time, I learned how profound her wisdom was.

Driver's Education

Shortly after our family moved to Humansville, Missouri, and we had settled into our new and larger home, my education was taken to a much higher level. The summer of my eleventh birthday, just after school was out, I began to learn about the importance of driver's education. By the time I graduated from high school, I discovered that there was more than one kind.

Momma said, "Jessie ..."

I hated it when Momma said my name in that familiar tone of voice. It meant that she wanted something from me, which would require my time and a lot of effort. I never did understand how I came to be Momma's "step-and-fetch-it" girl. But out of a dozen, I was. I did my best to convince Momma that she had several other choices to do her bidding; after all, she had twelve choices. "After we get the breakfast dishes done and the house tidied up a bit, I want you to come with me."

"Yes, Momma," I said, dreading another errand she was going to send me on.

After we finished cleaning up, Momma told me to follow her. We went out the door and past the front gate and marched right up to Poppa's car.

"Get in," she said, opening the passenger's side door.

I started to sit in the passenger's side seat.

"Move on over," she said as she slid in the seat I had just vacated. I was behind the large steering wheel.

"I think it is time you learn how to drive." She looked into my startled eyes and grinned.

"Really? Do you mean it? You're not just joshing me,

"I'm dead serious."

I bounced up and down in the seat. I had my hands on both sides of the steering wheel, I was giggling uncontrollably.

"Me, a driver! Watch out, world. Here comes Jessie Crandal," I yelled.

Momma laughed.

"Now, your Poppa isn't too happy about what I'm doing, so you'd better mind your p's and q's, or we'll both get a whipping." She gave me a wink.

"Why doesn't he want me to learn how to drive?"

"He's worried that you'll wreck his car. I told him that since he refused to drive, because he could still drive even though he has a wooden peg leg, it would be best that you know how to drive because I get drowsy sometimes. He's really not for it, but he's not stopping it."

"I promise I won't wreck Poppa's car. I'll be the best driver there ever was," I bragged brashly.

"This isn't something I'm going to be able to teach you to do in a day or two. It's going to take some time and a lot of patience—on both our parts."

"I'll have the patience of Solomon," I promised.

"You mean Job," she corrected. "Well, I suppose the first thing we need to do is to find out if you're big enough in the breeches to do this job."

"I'm big enough in the breeches," I assured her.

"Let's see. Sit up tall and put your hands on the wheel. Now, try to put your foot on the right-side pedal; that's the gas."

I reached out my foot, and it touched the pedal.

"Good. Now put your left foot on the pedal next to the gas; that's the brake." I did as she told me. "Put your foot on the far left pedal; that's the clutch.

"An inch shorter and you'd be too short in the breeches." She laughed. "It's going to be a bit of a struggle, but I believe you'll do," she teased laughingly and gave me a hug.

"Okay, Jessie, before we even think about trying to drive this car, you must master how the gears are shifted," Momma instructed.

"I know. I already know. I've watched you and my brothers when they are driving."

"We'll see," she said skeptically. "For now, you watch your

momma as I demonstrate how to do it." She placed her hand on the knob and rattled it back and forth. "Right now it is in neutral. The car's motor will run or idle in this position and won't die on you. Now, pretend that you are driving, okay? In order to drive the car, you will need to know how to shift the gears. It works like this. You start in neutral, and you pull the knob down and to the left, and it will shift into first gear; then you shift the knob up and over to the right a bit, and it will shift into second gear. When you get the car moving well, you will pull the knob down, and it will shift into third, or running gear. If you need to back up the car, which I only do in an emergency, you will need to pull the knob down to your left and way back." She looked at me and knew I was hopelessly confused.

I pulled my hands off the gearshift knob.

"Maybe I'm not old enough to do this after all."

"Nonsense! Honey, it's no different than anything else you've ever done. Just remember, 'A brave man only dies once—a coward dies a thousand times.'"

"I'm not concerned about the thousand times, only the once."

Momma laughed loudly.

"Really, Jessie, you'll get the hang of it once we do this a number of times."

For the next fifteen or twenty minutes, Momma schooled me again and again how to shift the gears correctly.

"Now I'll shift those gears as smooth as butter," I bragged, laughing as I regained my confidence.

The next day, Momma drilled me about the use of my feet and the three pedals: gas, brake, and clutch. By the end of the second day's lesson, I was itching to drive, not just pretending to drive.

On the third day of lessons, Momma quickly ran me through my paces.

"I think you're ready," she said and she patted my knee. "Now for the hardest part." She motioned for me to follow her to the front of the car. "If you can't start the car, all of those instructions won't mean a thing." She directed my head downward and pointed to what looked like a specially designed compartment just below the radiator. She put her hand in it and pulled out a funny-looking piece of iron.

"So, is that what you use to start the car?"

"That's it, and if you don't have this little thingamajig, you're not going anywhere." Momma put it in its place. "Here, Jessie, feel how it fits in there nice and snug."

I reached down and put my hand on the crank.

"Try to turn it."

I did my best to turn it; I couldn't.

"Get up behind the wheel, and I'll see if I can get this started. Just make sure the knob is in neutral," she hollered.

Momma cranked it a few times and it never started. She was starting to sweat under the sun's late morning heat. She wiped her forehead with her hand. "Whew, this is turning out to be work." She winked and grinned at me. "If I don't get it started in the next couple of cranks, we're not going driving. I can't afford to put too much strain on my hernia." She gave it one bigger crank, and it started up. Momma signaled for me to put my foot on the gas pedal. I pushed down too hard, and the motor raced wildly.

"You can't do that! You'll ruin the motor." She slid into the passenger's seat. "Let me catch my breath." She leaned back and drew a long, deep breath. After resting a few seconds, she reached over and lovingly patted my shoulder. "Are you raring to go?"

I nodded vigorously and smiled.

"Now, before we give it a try, you must learn about the clutch. You have to have gas to keep the car going, but you have to work the clutch in order to shift the gears so that the car can move. Put your foot on the clutch pedal and push down on it."

I followed her instructions. I had a rude awakening because I discovered that it was much harder to do than I ever imagined. After a few tries it became more comfortable.

"Jessie, remember, you have to have gas to keep the car going, but you must push the clutch in all the way to shift the gears. If you let the clutch out too fast, the car will die. If the gear isn't in the right place, it will grind and make a horrible noise."

I pushed on the clutch and pulled the knob into first gear. I pushed down on the gas pedal and let the clutch out too fast, and the car bucked and died.

"That was a good start for your first time."

I knew she was lying, but it made me feel better.

Momma climbed out of the car to once again turn the crank. I went through all the checkpoints, did all I was supposed to do, but I didn't work the clutch right and the car died again. Momma looked over at me. "Well, this is a little more difficult than we thought, right?"

I was embarrassed and frustrated.

"Why can't they make a car that doesn't have a clutch? I'm never going to get this."

Momma saw my frustration as one of her golden teaching moments; therefore, she decided to tell me a story.

"One day I was in town and this man had a friend visiting him. He said he was a famous sailor. Said he had sailed nearly around the world. I can hardly believe the story is true, but he swears it's true. Anyway, he said, 'In Japan there is this very unique tree. The people plant, water, and dress it each year. They do that same work for five years, and the tree doesn't grow one inch higher. During the sixth year that tree grows ninety feet.'"

"Sound's like a big whopper to me."

Momma laughed. "Me too. I also know the Good Book says, 'Through Christ all things are possible.' It'll come. Just give yourself some time. Besides, maybe the good Lord has chosen a new way for your momma to lose a few pounds." She winked at me and went to start the car.

I managed to keep it going for a few bucking, snorting feet, grinding the gears, or stripping them.

"Jessie, sometimes you have to settle for the will instead of the deed in order to allow yourself to imagine that your success is just on the horizon."

Momma spent time with me nearly every day, in spite of Poppa's dire warnings of horrible consequences.

"That girl hadn't better put one scratch or one dent in my car, or I'm going to whip both of you," he bellowed.

Momma was right. It came slowly, but it came. After a couple of weeks, I was able to drive the car and not make it die. I was able to maneuver the car just about any way I wanted it to go, driving it just inside our property line.

I wanted to drive all the time, but I was only able to when Momma was with me because I couldn't start the car without her.

Several times a day I would go out to the car, insert the crank, and try my best to start it. I was just too "weak in the breeches," Poppa said any time we kids couldn't do something that required a lot of strength.

I'm not sure if it was good fortune, divine intervention, or stronger muscles because of those failed attempts to get the car started, but one day I was able to move that handle. With a lot of effort, I cranked it fast enough to start the car.

The first time I did it, I couldn't believe it happened. I deliberately made the car die just so I could try again. When I was able to do it again, I jumped up and down for joy. I ran around the car a few times, pumping my arms up and down as I ran. I did a couple of halfhearted cartwheels. I ran around and got in behind the wheel. I sat up tall behind the large steering wheel. I extended my right arm straight out and pretended I was like Poppa whenever our family piled into the car and we were ready to take off.

"Westward ho!" I hollered. Then I sat back down and started driving. It was about midmorning when I drove the car up as close to the house as I could get it. *Ooooagah!* I laid on the funny-sounding horn until Grayce and Deannie came out of the house. They saw me in the car and ran back into the house. In a few seconds, Momma appeared in the doorway.

When I saw her, I waved wildly. She put her hands on the sides of her red apron, my favorite, then smiled and waved back at me. I motioned for her to come and ride with me. She held up one finger to indicate that she needed a minute. Soon, she came out hurriedly, walking to the car with Arthur in tow.

As she approached the car, laughing at me, she asked, "How in the world did you do that?"

I flexed my right arm and showed her my muscle. "I don't know. The good Lord just let it happen."

We both laughed.

Momma put Arthur in the backseat and said, "Now, you sit down and don't you dare stand up, do you hear me?" Momma slid into the passenger's side and shut the door. She looked at me and shook her head a bit. "How am I going to live with you now?" We both laughed.

"Mrs. Crandal, your driver, Jessie Crandal, will take you anywhere you care to go," I said as I teased Momma and flaunted myself at the same time.

"Wait." She stood up and took off her red apron. She held it in her right hand and thrust it straight out the window. She turned and looked at Arthur and me. "Westward ho!" she hollered, and we all laughed. I took off, smooth as butter, and never stripped a gear. We had a wonderful time. I was driving, Momma was playing like the captain of a ship, and Arthur was yelling.

"Momma, it's like a red sailboat."

I was full of myself, laughing and thinking about how great I was as a driver. Suddenly on the horizon, I couldn't believe my own eyes. A huge black bull was heading right for Poppa's car. Momma saw it a split second later than I did.

"Jessie!" she screamed.

I turned the wheel as much and as fast as I could. The car leaned my way so much that it felt as though two wheels were off the ground. The sudden turn of the car's direction caused her to nearly fall out, and she grabbed the side of the window brace and clung on for dear life.

"Arthur," Momma screamed, "get down in the seat!"

I was too busy to see if he'd heard her or obeyed. Somehow I managed to right the car, and I felt the two wheels, which had been off the ground, hit with a heavy thud. I once again had control of the car. Momma had managed to hold on to the car's door window; then she was able to sit back down and reach back and pull Arthur onto her lap.

"Great jumping Jehoshaphat!" Momma cried out. By then the blood had started to return to my system. I had been too busy to be scared, but then the reality of what had happened hit me. My hands were shaking so badly, I had a hard time keeping them on the steering wheel.

"Where in the world did he come from?" Momma asked breathlessly. "Jessie!" she yelled as she glanced back.

I looked behind me when I heard her frightened voice. I saw the bull running full speed at our car. I looked down for Momma's apron; it was missing. I lifted up a bit in my seat and took a good look behind us. Momma's red apron was flying in the wind. It had caught on one of the rear reflectors. The bull saw our car as a challenge, and he knew he was up to it.

"It's your red apron!" I shouted.

"Mercy me!" she screamed and turned to see her apron blowing in the wind. Arthur thought it was funny and laughed uncontrollably. "Head for the house!" Momma yelled.

I made a fast turn, and we made a straight line to the house.

I am sure the Lord sent a blessing as the red apron dislodged and flew backwards at the bull. I hoped that apron would deter him because his red adversary was no longer a threat; it did not.

"Momma, you grab Arthur, and I'll do my best to put the car between us and the bull," I said as I drove as fast as I safely could. When we made our turn, I was hoping the bull would just stop. He didn't.

I pulled the car up next to the house, and we all made a mad dash for it. We made it inside safely and parked ourselves in front of the windows. The bull was raging, and he came galloping at full speed. I waited for him to recognize that his adversary in red wasn't another animal, but a piece of tin and steel. At some point, it must have registered in his brain—as pea-sized as it probably was—he dug his hooves into the turf and did his best not to run into Poppa's car. While he did do a decent job of slowing down, he couldn't stop soon enough. At the last second, he lowered his head, and one of his large horns pierced a hole in the back part of the driver's-side rear fender. It was a wonder he didn't puncture a tire.

"Lordy, Lordy, I thought that beast was going to demolish the car," Momma said, and she let out a sigh of relief.

There was one tiny problem, though. The bull's horn was stuck in the hole he had made when he rammed the car. At first he couldn't get it loose. He shook his mammoth head. His brute strength amazed me as he shook the entire car. He must have managed to make the hole a bit bigger since he was able to extricate himself in a few seconds. The bull pranced around the car and made a full revolution. Then he went about twenty paces behind it and turned to face Poppa's car.

"Oh, sweet Jesus," Momma whispered. "Don't let him ruin Poppa's car." She was already in praying mode.

I sat there, holding my breath. The bull used his hooves and scattered dirt and dust. He lowered his head and showed his massive horns. I just knew he was going to charge Poppa's car. *I'll never drive again as long as Poppa's alive,* I thought. Maybe our prayers were answered because suddenly the bull stopped, turned, and moseyed away.

It was about that time Poppa came around the corner and saw the strange bull on our land. We came out of the house and heard him holler.

"What the hell is going on here?" Poppa must have suspected something was wrong as he quickly ran to the car. When he saw the damage the bull had done, he took off his hat and threw it on the ground. He looked back at the porch where we were standing.

"Lou!" he yelled. "What the … How did that big—black—mangy"—Poppa focused his eyes on the hole in his fender—"get in our yard?" He bent down and put his finger in the hole the bull had made. He was enraged. He couldn't even spew forth a long list of profanities, which he was very good at. He walked over to where he had thrown his hat. Instead of picking it up, he dropkicked it.

We couldn't help ourselves; Momma and I started laughing.

Poppa looked at us with anger etched across his face and blazing fire in his eyes.

"I'm not sure how, but somehow"—he was pointing his finger at us—"you're at the bottom of this."

"Ranti Crandal! How in the world can you blame Jessie and me for a bull damaging your fender?" Momma asked as she fought with herself to keep from laughing in his face out loud.

"Who's the Jackass who owns that bull?" Poppa quizzed us.

"We don't know. Until a few minutes ago, none of us had ever seen it before. Just be thankful he didn't puncture a tire." Momma said and motioned for me to follow her back into the house.

"Wait until I get my hands on the dumb-ass who owns that brute!" Poppa yelled as we went into to house.

Once we were inside, safe from Poppa's ranting and raving, we looked at each other. We started with a giggle, and soon we were roaring out of control with laughter. We also offered up thanks to God that Poppa did not see the red apron lying harmlessly on the ground a hundred feet from where the car was sitting.

Poppa found out that the bull had escaped from a farm several miles down the road. By the time Poppa tracked down the owner, the bull was back in his home pasture. Poppa never did get any compensation, and he couldn't prove we had done anything to cause the bull to put a hole in his car. So he was left to "grind his teeth on a sharp edge," Momma said.

From that summer on, I drove more than Momma did.

The Changing of the Guard

On that fateful day in late August of 1929, the Ranti Crandal family was about to slide down off that mountaintop, the one Momma told us no one could ever stay upon except for a short time. We would fall into a valley none of us ever imagined existed, leastwise Momma.

Poppa, Howard, Charlie, and I had gone down to the south side of our acreage to mend a fence. We had taken Jack and Jenny, Poppa's two mules, and a wagon with wire for mending the fence.

"Please, Poppa, let me go with you. I want to drive the mules." I begged Poppa to allow me to go with him and my brothers.

"You won't be more than a pissant's worth of help." He looked at my hangdog eyes. "Oh, all right. Get in the wagon."

I jumped in the wagon and grabbed the reins. I tried to get the mules to go. At first they didn't move; suddenly, they took off fast.

"Whoa, Jack; whoa, Jenny. These mules are being more that just a little bit cantankerous," Poppa said as he quickly took the reins from me and did his best to harness the energy and direction of the team of mules.

"They are just a pair of 'dumb asses,'" Charlie hollered as he laughed loudly at his funny.

"Couldn't be any dumber than you are," Howard teased.

Poppa maneuvered the wagon to where it would do the most good to mend the fence.

"If you two goof-offs will get off your butts, we might get this job done today," he growled at them.

I crawled into the back of the wagon with my brothers to lend a hand. We had barely started unloading the wagon when a sudden wind began to whip up, and the atmosphere suddenly cooled.

"Seems we are about to have a change in the weather," Poppa said as he kept focused upon the job at hand. "Get some of that wire from the wagon so we can get this mending done."

Suddenly the wind came roaring, and it blew and forced my brothers and me to crawl underneath the wagon to take cover. Then, the wind died down, and suddenly there was a calm stillness. It was too calm.

"I have a funny feeling about what is happening with the weather," Poppa mumbled loudly.

"Look, look!" Howard shouted. In the distance, we could see a huge, black cloud filled with bolts of lightning. It was easy to see that it was churning.

"Get in the wagon, kids!" Poppa yelled. "We're headed for home. Now!"

We quickly climbed into the wagon, but the mules were frightened by our loss of the emotional composure, especially Poppa's. Instead of following orders, they reared up and stalled out, nearly turning over the wagon. Poppa managed to get them straightened up and headed for the house. Suddenly, a lightning bolt struck, and a large tree toppled over near us, blocking our path.

"Howard, Charlie!" Poppa yelled. "We will need to cross on the side of the road." Poppa handed Howard the wire cutters to cut the fence. "You will have to cut the wire wide enough so the mules and the wagon can pass. Once the fence is cut, Charlie can stand on one side and you on the other. Bend and mash that fence down low enough so the wagon can pass. Do you understand me?"

The wind was so strong and so loud; it forced Poppa to yell as loudly as he could. My brothers jumped out of the wagon, and Howard used the cutters to cut the path. The boys were not very strong or very heavy, so it took both of them working on one side at a time to the cut the fence and mash it low enough.

"Hurry up!" Poppa yelled. It took only a few minutes to get the fence cut and mashed down, but in the midst of the howling storm, and with the anxiety of not being home with the family to help them find shelter, it seemed as if it took all day to complete the job. Poppa motioned for Howard and Charlie to quickly take their places and stand on the fence.

"Jessie, you make sure I've got clearance on the other side. Git! Giddyup, Jack and Jenny!" Poppa hollered, and he put the whip to them. The mules, startled by the harsh treatment, reared up and quickly pulled ahead.

"As I pass by, you two jump on; I'm not slowing down!" Poppa hollered at my brothers. Just about the time the wagon had a full head of steam, a bolt of lightning struck. The mules bucked and reared up, and the wagon swerved and nearly rolled over. I held on for dear life.

Howard and Charlie, with frightened looks on their faces, got ready to jump off the fence and board the moving wagon. When the lightning bolt struck, it was as if they had been offered up as two Fourth of July rocket candles, exploding into air for the amusement of the crowd. But they weren't rocket candles; they were boys with a high probability of being fitted for funeral garb. The power of the bolt hurled them a few feet backwards from the place they were standing. They landed with a thud; they were like dead men.

"Sweet Jesus," Poppa said. He had seen his two sons fly through the air like pillows thrown effortlessly during one of their many pillow fights. My thought was that they were dead. The trauma of what we saw made my stomach churn. Poppa, not thinking very clearly, jumped off the wagon onto his peg leg.

"Ohh!" he hollered, and I could almost feel his pain. He did his best to ignore it and moved as rapidly as he could to try to rescue them. I jumped off the back of the wagon and reached the area where they had fallen before Poppa could get there. I turned back to see if Poppa needed some help. I could see he had a pained look on his face, and his breathing was short and labored. Suddenly, he acted as if someone had shot him from the bushes, and he grasped for his heart. It seemed to me he was trying to compress his chest so that it would force out the pain.

"Jess," he said, loudly. "*Jess!*" he screamed in pain, and he fell down at my feet.

"Poppa!" I screamed in fear. My mind and my body were in a dizzy pace, and it seemed that neither could function properly. Tears flowed down my face, and I desperately wanted someone to rescue me, not be in a situation where I had to rescue someone else.

Poppa rose up a bit on his side. "Go on," he said. "They need you more."

I reluctantly did as he ordered. I left him and ran to see about my brothers.

Howard and Charlie must have been knocked unconscious because by the time I reached them, they had started to come to and stir a bit. Neither knew what had happened.

"I'm coming! Don't die! I'm coming! I'm coming!" I shouted as I ran to them.

My eyes frantically searched for any sign of life, and a flood of emotional relief ran through my entire body as I saw Howard and Charlie sit up and try to get to their feet.

"It's a miracle!" I shouted as I laughed through my tears of joy.

Howard and Charlie, still groggy from the lightning strike that turned them into dead men for a short time, tried to run but found that they could not keep their balance or bearings.

"Poppa!" I yelled. "He's fallen, and he's hurt badly," I screamed.

"Poppa, Poppa, what's wrong?" Howard shouted and crawled to Poppa's unconscious body.

Howard tried to stand up. With a little help from me, they both managed to upright themselves.

"Is he dead? Poppa can't be dead!" Charlie shouted tearfully.

"I don't know," Howard replied. "But if we don't get him to a doctor soon, he probably will be." He motioned for Charlie and me to help him get Poppa's body into the wagon as soon as possible. We managed to get him in the wagon, and somehow the mules complied enough with Howard's pleading that they broke into a full trot.

As the mules pulled the wagon and Howard used the whip to urge them to move faster, Charlie and I rode in the back of the wagon. I moved up to the front of the wagon closer to Howard. Charlie was near the back where we had laid Poppa. Charlie looked down at Poppa's pale, weak body. His face was tear streaked, and he was waging a war to keep his emotions in check. Poppa moaned.

"He's alive!" Charlie shouted. "He moaned!"

With that encouraging news, Howard used the riding whip. "Jack and Jenny," he yelled, "your master needs your best! Do you hear me? Not some second-rate effort but your best!" He talked to them as if they could understand the dire circumstances we were in, and it was up to them to save Poppa's life.

Charlie lifted Poppa's right hand. Poppa gave it a slight squeeze. It was enough to signal he was alive. A flood of tears streamed down Charlie's face, and snot ran out of his nose. I felt chill bumps run all over my body, and even the hair on my head had a funny sensation as I watched Charlie do his best to comfort Poppa.

Later, after the trauma passed, in a quiet moment we shared, Charlie told me what he experienced riding in that wagon with Poppa near death.

"Jessie," he said, "in the midst of that horrific trauma, my mind suddenly faded away, and I closed my eyes and everything became crystal clear. I was back in a pasture, tending the sheep. I heard a bell in the distance. 'Where are you? There you are,' I said as I made my way to gather the lead sheep for the flock.

"When Poppa gave Sammy and me the responsibility of bringing in the sheep every day, he admonished us harshly. 'When you two peckerwoods are gathering in the sheep, you must always find the lead sheep. If you're too stupid to remember which one is the lead sheep, find the one sheep that is wearing a bell. I expect you to count them when you take them out, and you'd better have the same number when they come in or there's going to be hell to pay.' He threatened us with his razor strop every day."

Charlie said that he kept switching from past memories to present horrors. "Jessie, my reverie broke for a second, and I was suddenly looking into the pale face of Poppa, and I reached out and softly stroked his hair near his widow's peak. My eyes slowly surveyed his body, and I moved his wooden peg leg so that it was better aligned with the rest of his body. Poppa moaned again. 'Hold on,' I whispered.

"Just as quickly, I was in the past again," he said. "'Where can it be? How can a sheep get lost?' My voice possessed anger. I spent some time looking intently in the various crevices, crooks, and crannies where I often found wayward sheep as I was gathering them in for the night. The longer I spent searching, the angrier I grew. My frustrations started to increase, so I began to lose my temper.

"'That smelly piece of dung is going to get me killed,' I muttered. 'If I had a gun, I'd shoot that old man Schmitt,' I raged. 'He's got more money than he can use; why does he need a bunch of smelly, old, good-for-nothing sheep too?' I continued to shift blame for the missing sheep.

"'Did you find it?' my brother Sammy asked as he was hollering from a different section of the pasture where the sheep grazed.

"With the emotions of anger, rage, tears, and fear tingling in my voice, I replied, 'I have looked everywhere, and I can't find it.'

"'Our butts are in the sling, again,' Sammy said in a loud voice as he drew near to me. 'Maybe he won't notice one is missing this time,' he added in a tone of voice that indicated that he knew we weren't going to get a pass on another whipping.

"As we herded the sheep back home from the pasture, we discussed the whipping we knew we were going to get for losing one sheep. Once again, we were going to feel the deadly sting of the razor strop, which we were convinced Poppa loved to use.

"'How do you stand it?' Sammy asked me. 'I don't get it.

You're smaller, younger, and yet you don't cry when Poppa beats you. You don't even allow Poppa to see that you are suffering.'

"'I'm right, and he's dead wrong,' I snapped. 'He's got power; he's got no control!' I told him as I looked into my brother's eyes. 'If I can show him he can't hurt me, he loses.'

"'But it hurts so damn bad,' Sammy said. 'I swear, if he hits me with that strop again, I'm going to kick his worthless leg and tear him apart.' His remark surprised me because it possessed a tone of bravery I had never heard from him.

"'Poppa may have a peg leg, but he is one tough, mean S.O.B.' I warned Sammy not to underestimate Poppa's physical abilities. 'Besides, you're all talk and no show!' I teased him.

"'Not this time!' Sammy said as we brought the sheep into the pen.

"Poppa had already moseyed out to the sheep pen. We saw him standing in front of the barn, lazily, swinging his razor strop with a pendulum motion. He pulled out a piece of paper that held the exact number of sheep we had taken to the pasture. He spent a few minutes counting them.

"'You two numbskulls just can't do anything right, can you?' he sneered. 'It don't make a tinker's damn how much it costs me.' His facial features began to change. His voice became grittylike, and it was easy to see the anger rise in his being. He stood as tall as he could, and he swung the strop from one hand to the other in a menacing manner. 'How many more of these beatings are you two going to get before you learn to do your job right?' His eyes bulged, and his face broke into a nasty sneer.

"Then, Jessie, honest to God, I was back again in that wagon, and Howard was driving to beat all hell to get home. Poppa moved his right arm and moaned a little. He blinked his eyes as he tried to open them up and found it difficult to do. He reached over and touched my hand. This movement startled me, and Poppa jumped back.

"'He's really alive!' I shouted to Howard. Do you remember me shouting about Poppa being alive?"

"I sure do; I thought it was going to wake the dead." I teased him. "Poppa motioned for me to move closer to his face. He began to mumble, and I tried to lean closer to hear him.

"'Don't know if…time,' he whispered. 'Don't forget the toolbox,' Poppa said more than once.

"Tears were flowing down his cheeks. Jessie, I hadn't ever seen Poppa cry. I thought he was incapable of it. He just welled up in tears. I adjusted his body so I could remain very close to him. Poppa evidently mistook my movement for pulling away from him. His eyes opened wide. He reached out and grasped my shirt. He looked deep into my eyes.

"'Sorry,' he softly said. More tears welled up and poured out of his eyes. 'Sorry, Charlie.'

"I looked intently into Poppa's eyes, and for the first time in my young life, I detected softness in his tone of voice. It struck me he was trying to nurture me.

"*Now you're dying, and you want to tell me you love Sammy and me?* I thought.

"'Charlie, Sammy.' His whisper grew weaker. 'Sammy, wrong, Sammy,' Poppa said. I took it that he was trying to convey another message. He then slipped back into unconsciousness.

"'Hurry! Hurry!' I screamed. 'I think he's dying,' Charlie continued to shout.

After the family came out of the root cellar, safe and sound from the storm's fury, I asked Momma what she was doing while Poppa, Howard, Charlie, and I were away trying to mend the fence.

"I don't have time to tell you now, but after things settle down, I'll tell you the whole story." When things did settle down, this is the story she told me.

"I was in the midst of hanging out some wash on the line when that terrible storm came out of nowhere on that fateful day. I was oblivious to the approaching storm. Folks used to say that most women have a particular day for washing. When you have the Crandal brood, you need more than one day. The younger children were busy at play, and the boys who didn't go with Poppa to mend the fence were working in the garden.

"The wind had whipped up, and that just made me more

determined to finish the job. Even though the wind was wild and kept blowing my skirt up, which I had to pull down several times, and made my hair stand out on its end, I was determined it would not keep me from hanging my clothes to dry in the sun. "When the wind died down and the air suddenly grew deathly still, I sensed something was terribly wrong.

"'Earl,' I hollered, 'go fetch the babies!'

"Earl was working in the yard. He put down his hoe and came running. He looked over his right shoulder.

"'Momma! Look behind you! In the sky!' he screamed.

"It was an enormous, angry black cloud, and it was shaped like Poppa's oil can funnel. It had a loopy tail that seemed to swing to-and-fro. It reminded me of a poison snake looking for something to kill.

"'Children, boys!' I screamed. I waved my arms madly with a come-hither sign. In a few seconds, they came running.

"Jessie, the wind became so ferocious that no one could stand up alone. In only a few seconds, we were out in a little circle in the midst of that terrible storm. I had the children form a human chain, and each child was responsible for the safety of the person next to him.

"'Get down, and hold onto each other and stay low; move as fast as you can. We must make it to the cellar door before the storm hits our yard.'

"Our human chain moved at a turtle's pace. The wind was so strong it blew our entire human chain over two or three times. Each time it happened, I motioned for the children to get back up and continue to trudge forward. When we finally reached the cellar, I had Earl and Rose crawl around to open the doors; they opened on both sides from the middle. We had to secure them so they remained open for our family to get inside. Once inside, we could keep low and pull the doors shut. In a few minutes, we managed to get into the cellar. We were all exhausted, dripping wet, and suddenly very cold. We huddled in that dank, cool place, very thankful to be safe.

"I got busy counting noses, and I realized that Arthur, the

baby, was in his crib. I had left him in his crib to take a nap in order to give me a chance to finish hanging out the clothes.

"'Arthur! My baby! Arthur's in the house!' I screamed.

"'Where is he?' Earl asked as he looked directly at me.

"'He's in my bedroom; he is taking a nap.'

"Earl motioned for Rose and Pauline to get to the cellar doors.

"'I will need you to man the doors. If you don't keep a firm hold on the doors, they will blow away. Do you think you can manage to do that?' he asked them. They nodded. They opened up the doors just enough for Earl to slither out.'"

Earl told his side of the story in this manner.

"The wind was so ferocious, and I heard loud sounds all around me, as if things were being broken and wood was being hammered by other pieces of wood. I crawled on my belly through the muck and mire the storm was bringing. Slowly, I made it to the steps of the porch. I gradually forced my body up those few steps and made my way into the house. I could tell that some of the house was under attack, and parts of it were coming loose.

"'Arthur!' I screamed as I continued to crawl on my belly toward Poppa and Momma's bedroom. 'Arthur, Arthur!' I called even more loudly in desperation. I entered into the room, and the crib was empty. *What in God's name could have happened to him?* I thought. 'Arthur!' I screamed with a sense of fear for the life of my baby brother, who was just a little over two years old.

"Even above the roar of the storm, I heard a thumping. Then a voice cried out, 'Momma, Momma!' Arthur had crawled up into the wardrobe and had managed to pull the door shut. He certainly didn't know what was happening concerning the storm, but evidently he had previously tried out the wardrobe as some type of personal hiding place; so he moved to a place he was familiar with when he was frightened by the storm.

"I quickly made my way to where the crying was coming from. I gently opened the door, and there was Arthur, scrunched up with his back against the side of the wardrobe, his two little legs pulled up, and his head on his two knobby knees When he saw me, he grinned from ear to ear, despite the frightened tears that stained his cheeks. He reached out his arms, and I pulled him out of the wardrobe and clutched him very close.

"'There you are, little man.' I breathed a sigh of relief. I hugged him tightly.

"Arthur had managed to take his blanket with him. I wrapped him in it. The storm was still raging, and I knew I wouldn't be able to crawl with him on my belly. Before the storm hit, I was not wearing a shirt. I seldom do when I work in the garden, but I spied a work shirt hanging in the wardrobe. I grabbed it. I motioned for Arthur to get on my back for a piggyback ride, which he loved for me to do for him every day.

"'Hold on and squeeze me tight,' I told him.

"In the midst of the storm, Arthur was very contented to play games. 'Giddyup!' He laughed as he climbed up on my back.

"'Now stay still,' I told Arthur. I put the work shirt on but left the tail open. I helped Arthur get on my back but under the shirt. Arthur thought it was fun crawling up under the shirt. When he managed to get under the shirt, I put the tail of the shirt inside of my trousers. I took my knife and cut a strip off the bed sheet and used it to wrap around Arthur and me. I secured it in a knot tied in the front.

"'Don't let go, Arthur. Don't let go,' I told him.

"Now I was free to crawl on my belly. I made my way out of the house. I managed to retrace my path down the porch steps and inched my way back to the cellar. I pounded on the doors. For a few seconds, no one responded. I pounded some more.

"'Open up!' I hollered."

While Earl was absent from the rest of us in the cellar, Momma had managed to light the oil-burning lamp Poppa had put in the cellar for just this sort of frightening occasion.

"Pray, children; pray without ceasing, as the Apostle Paul taught us." Momma encouraged us to be brave. The children all saw their brother slip out of the apparent safety of the cellar to try and rescue Arthur. As the minutes slipped into what seemed an eternity, she had them sing a hymn: "What a Friend We Have in Jesus."

"Come on, kids. I know you are scared. I'm scared too, but we will feel better when we sing."

"We didn't sound too good, but it did help," even Rose admitted.

"What a friend we have in Jesus, all our sins and grief to bear!

What a privilege to carry everything to God in prayer!

O What peace we often forfeit, O what needless pain we bear,

All because we do not carry everything to God in prayer."

The storm raged on. The longer Earl was gone, and the fact that none of them knew what had happened to Poppa, Howard, Charlie, and me, the more their choir became discouraged, and the singing sounded more like whimpering. Tears were mixed with the mouthing of the song's words.

"Our God is an awesome God," Momma said in a loud, strong-sounding voice, doing her best to reassure them that they were going to remain safe. "He will see us through."

"Momma," Grayce said as she tugged at Momma's skirt. "Momma, I hear something."

The half-hearted singing ceased.

"Quiet!" Pauline shouted. "I hear something too."

Earl pounded again on the cellar doors.

"Let us in," he hollered. "Don't let go of those doors when you open it. Just open them enough so we can crawl in."

They opened the doors just enough for Earl to slide in and make his way down the steps. When he was finally inside, Momma and the children weren't able to immediately see that Arthur was with Earl since he was halfway hidden inside the shirt.

When Momma saw Earl and not Arthur, she shouted, "Couldn't you find Arthur?" Panic filled her voice. "Is he dead?"

About that time, Arthur said, "Giddyup, giddyup, horsey," and kicked his legs.

Momma saw that Arthur was indeed safe. When our family finally figured out how Earl had managed to transport our baby brother, they all started laughing and crying from the relief they felt, knowing that Arthur had been rescued and Earl had made it back from the terrible storm.

"What about Poppa?" Earl asked.

"And Howard, Charlie, and Jessie?" one of the twin girls, Gracie, said with tears in her eyes.

Then all of the kids started crying and calling out for Poppa.

"The good Lord's going to take care of Poppa and the boys and Jessie." Momma did her best to quell their fears.

Momma later said to me: "Unless a body has actually lived through a tornado, one just can't appreciate its horror. It seemed as if we were trapped in that cellar for a month of Sundays. It was about an hour. We heard very loud noises that made us believe the world had come apart above the cellar doors. When the worst of the storm ran our direction, and it must have been very close, it seemed as if a freight train was going to just run right through our cellar and kill every one of us. If a person were to stand in the middle of a railroad track, and the train was moving a hundred miles an hour, and it just ran through you, it surely couldn't have been more terrifying or louder. When it whooshed through, we just screamed at the top of our lungs. It's a wonder more people aren't killed just from the noise since one is nearly frightened to death!"

My sister Naomi said, "Momma did her best to abate our fears. She had us sing some more songs. We were a reluctant choir."

"Jesus loves me this I know," Momma started to sing. "Come on now," she urged us to join her. "Jesus loves me this I know, for the Bible tells me so."

Pauline was singing, and Momma motioned for Naomi to help get the rest of the family singing. "I was nearly too afraid to speak. Momma gave me a reassuring nod, and I started to sing with her. Soon we all were singing, even if it was halfheartedly," Naomi later told me.

It seems no one can tell how a tornado chooses its path or its victims. Every time a storm comes and goes, its quilt-patch pattern mystifies most people when it comes to figuring out why it traveled in a certain path. The storm that came upon our place and forced our family into the cellar wasn't a direct hit, but rather a glancing blow. Just as it arrived at our house, it veered off to the right. While we didn't get the worst of it, we did receive the torrential rain and the damaging hail. Some hailstones were as large as baseballs. Even so, the storm's course still took a portion of our roof, and it clean blew away Poppa's two new chicken coops that he had just finished building. Except for a few pieces of wood lying around, it was impossible to tell that there had ever been two chicken coops sitting there just a few short minutes before Mother Nature arrived in her fury of destruction.

The sounds of wind and heavy rain finally dissipated enough that Momma allowed the doors to be opened. She could see rays of sunlight prior to opening the doors, so Momma knew the storm was over. After everybody crawled out, Momma had all of them gather together, much like they did when they formed their human chain that allowed them to make it into the cellar when the storm struck. In the midst of the wet grass and mud, they all knelt down and prayed.

"Sweet Jesus, we can see that we lost our roof on the north side of the house," Momma prayed. . "We are just very thankful that you spared us."

"Momma, Momma!" Charlie and I screamed at the top of our lungs. The sounds of our shouts interrupted her prayer. As the children looked up, on the horizon they saw Jack and Jenny moving as fast as they had ever run. Howard brought the wagon and team of mules to a sudden stop, though I was certain he was going to run over our family before he could get the mules stopped. He jumped off the wagon and ran to the back of it.

"It's Poppa!" he yelled. "He's dying." He pointed to him lying unconscious in the wagon.

Momma would have made a great nurse, another Florence Nightingale, the way she took command of the situation.

"Get your poppa out of the wagon and into the house," she said in a calm but commanding voice as she instructed the boys.

"Jessie, you fetch the doctor. Tell him it's a matter of life and death."

If that storm had continued to move straight forward, at least that is what Mr. Bosch would say later, our strawberry crop would have been spared. But when it made an abrupt right turn, it headed right for our strawberries, and we lost the crop.

Poppa didn't die that day. He moved in and out of consciousness for a few days. When he did say something, Momma said he never really was able to make much sense with his communication. One time he asked about the strawberry crop. Momma refused to answer, because the doctor told her his heart couldn't stand much more. She was certain that he knew the truth.

"His dreams had been dashed, and his heart was crushed. His old ticker just stopped ticking," was the way Momma explained his death.

Life has a strange way of coming down that mountaintop. At least Momma said so. The day before the storm, the mailman gave Momma a letter. She read it and then stashed it in her apron pocket. She never mentioned it to Poppa or to anyone else. Ever since she read that letter, she was humming "Bringing in the Sheaves." Momma seemed to hum hymns whenever she was feeling happy.

After Poppa died, I tried to stay particularly close to Momma. I figured she needed all the loving a body could get. The night Poppa died, I saw Momma and Earl in a private conference in the kitchen. Momma was crying, and my brother was doing his best to comfort her. I suppose it wasn't the right thing to do, but I eavesdropped.

"What are we going to do?" I heard Momma ask Earl. "I . . . I mean, what is a widow with a dozen kids"—she paused and wiped a few tears away with the edge of her apron—"and an old woman, who's not in the best of health"—she looked up at Earl with a perplexed glance—"going to do?" She ran her fingers through her hair and scratched the top of her head, as a body is want to do when a mess of life has piled up on them, and it has reached a point of no return with its frustrations. It must choose to either remain sane or just go crazy.

"Where are we going to live? How are we going to live?" Her voice grew louder. The burden of all this weighty matter was just too much for her. I was crying with her as I watched the scene from a distance.

"Do you want to live in Humansville?" Earl asked in a soft voice.

That question jolted her. She stopped crying and sat up straight. She allowed a few seconds of silence to pass.

"No! That was your Poppa's dream, not mine."

"Well, do you mind cluing me in on your plans?"

"We are going home!"

"And how is a widow with a dozen kids going to afford to live back home? Momma, right now our situation looks bleak, but we can have a good crop next year. We can rebuild those chicken coops and start an additional business. If we move home, how will we earn a living?" He reached out and caressed her hands. "The crop's ruined, and we don't have money. We have to have a place to live." He continued to play the grim reaper bearing bad news.

"I heard a man say the other day, 'All this country's prosperity is just one major disaster from everyone being put in the poorhouse.'" He challenged Momma to do a better job of thinking. "Did he have any insurance? Well, did he leave a will?"

With a sigh of resigned frustration in her voice, she said, "I know that he once talked about a will, but I never knew him to follow through. As for insurance, as far as I know, Poppa didn't believe in insurance."

Momma stopped talking and put her head in her hands and bowed them down just above the table. She remained silent for a few minutes. She raised her head, and her countenance changed.

"I don't care what we have or don't have; the good Lord will provide all that we need." She had a wild-eyed look as she glanced at him. "Like manna from heaven, he will provide us with his blessings, and we will make it through this, so help me God, or my name isn't Louise May Crandal." She stood up and gave Earl a big hug.

"First thing in the morning, I want you to go down to the telegraph and send a wire to Napoleon. Tell him that we need him here. He can bring his car to help us move."

She then handed Earl the letter she had kept in her apron pocket.

Earl slowly opened the letter. He had a puzzled look on his face.

"What's this for?"

"Open it and see for yourself," she replied with an impish grin. Earl read the letter, and his teeth showed as his lips spread and his joy became evident. "Sammy!" He laughed.

When I heard Earl say, "Sammy," I couldn't believe it. I almost shouted, "Sammy's alive!" It would have undone me as a snoop.

"Send a second message to Sammy, and tell him I need him," Momma said as she reached out and touched Earl's face. "I need all of my boys."

Momma let our family read the letter from Sammy. The letter Sammy sent to Momma was postmarked from Chicago, Illinois. He was working for the Rock Island Railroad, living in a boardinghouse. He indicated that he did not intend to return as long as Poppa was alive; he had no intention of coming home, yet he didn't want Momma to fret and worry about him, so he sent her a letter. Momma had kept it from Poppa.

Momma always said, "Even in the midst of the darkest times, God often has a grand celebration waiting just around the corner."

After Momma sent Earl to send those messages to Napoleon and Sammy to come running as fast as they could, she had an errand for Charlie. Talk about the bearer of good news, little Charlie was soon to be the man of the hour. Shoot, he was Momma's man for her life!

"Charlie, come here, son," Momma said. "I want you to fetch Poppa's toolbox. We aren't going to be here long, but we have to find a way to patch that roof with something. Maybe some tar paper will do. Perhaps we have some tin lying around in the barn? Well, anyway, get Poppa's toolbox, you hear?"

Poppa's toolbox was made of wood, and it was very heavy to carry. Charlie drafted me to help him with that chore. Charlie and I had a wonderful relationship. I thought he was more than just my brother; he was my hero. I guess it was the interesting way I thought he handled life. Even though Poppa picked on him and brutally beat him with his razor strop, Charlie never seemed to be without a big grin and an impish look as if he were "up to something." He usually was, a joke or a prank of some kind. He teased nearly everyone in our family, except Howard. I always liked to believe that Momma liked me the best, but there wasn't anyone more fair-haired for Momma than Charlie. He was the only boy who really paid attention to Momma. He was always bringing her flowers, and half the time they were stolen from some other lady's yard. But he gave her hugs and bragged on her cooking, especially her pies. Looking back, maybe that was why Poppa treated Charlie in the cruel way he did; he certainly never showed much attention and affection toward Momma. I think it was a jealousy thing between them. Poppa understood it; I'm sure Charlie never did.

Charlie and I made our way out to the old, run-down barn. The storm had removed a few shingles, but it hadn't been damaged much. It was in need of some paint. He and I made our way over to the workbench, and he picked up the toolbox.

"Jessie, as we were riding in the wagon, Poppa whispered something to me over and over. Just now, when I touched his toolbox, I swear I could hear that whispered voice of Poppa's nearly dying breath as clear as if he were standing next to me in the barn."

It gave me goose bumps that ran up and down my arms, and it made my head tingle the way Charlie talked about the encounter.

"Jess, when I was riding in the back of the wagon with Poppa, he said the strangest thing. 'Charlie,' he said, and he looked into my eyes."

"Strange how?" I asked.

"He said, 'Don't forget the tool box.'"

"Maybe he has some hidden treasure or a map of some kind

where he buried some money. Let's open it and see." I encouraged him to seek an answer to our puzzle.

"Charles Crandal! What is taking you so long?" Momma hollered as her voice broke into our conversation.

"Coming, Momma," he said as he motioned for me to get a grip on the other end of the toolbox. We quickly ran to the house.

It had been a busy day. Earl had sent the messages and had received replies to them. Both boys were on their way to Humansville. The rest of the family had done their best to patch the hole in the roof with the tar paper. Momma and we girls prepared a meal from the leftovers some of the neighbors were so kind to bring to us when they heard about Poppa's death, even though he didn't have services in Humansville. I suspect that Mr. Bosch had a hand in all of that kindness.

Somehow, Poppa's toolbox found its way to our kitchen instead of out back in the barn by the workbench. It sat near the entrance to the back door.

"Charlie, why didn't you take the toolbox out to the barn?" Momma asked in a tone of voice that expressed a bit of exasperation. Charlie sent a glance over to me, and I could almost read his thoughts. *Because Jessie wasn't there to help me carry it,* his quick glance said.

"Momma, I have been meaning to tell you something," he said, and his reply didn't offer any explanation for his failure to take the toolbox to the barn. "When Poppa was in the wagon and Howard was driving the mule team, Jessie and I were in the back of the wagon with Poppa. Howard was doing his best to get us home as soon as he could; I was riding in the back closest to Poppa. One time when he came to, he kept mumbling something about the toolbox. 'Don't forget the toolbox,' he said, and he repeated it more than once." Charlie looked at me, and he motioned for me to come and help him. We picked up the toolbox and started to open the door so we could put it back into the barn.

"Bring it here," Momma said. We picked it up and set it down on the kitchen table in front of her. First, she took the top tray out and set it aside. Poppa always prided himself that he was clever enough to have fashioned a toolbox that had a top tray for easy access to heavily used tools; most of them were lighter in nature. Slowly, she took the tools out and placed them on the table. When it was empty, she searched for any sign of a treasure or secret type of message Poppa may have left, which he knew was important but about which she knew nothing prior to his passing away. She was searching for something that tied in the importance of the message her husband had given to his son in a near-death situation. It offered no clues. She then took the top tray and began to take the tools out of it. Once again she searched fruitlessly. Charlie helped her put the tools back into the box. Then she put the tools back into the top tray. Momma lifted it and was in the midst of placing it back into the toolbox.

"There is something on the bottom!" little Deannie, Momma's oldest twin girl by five minutes, yelled.

Rose spent most of the days after Poppa's death in her bedroom or in some secluded place as she mourned his death more so than any other member of our family, including Momma. She was the last family member to join our family in the kitchen while Momma searched Poppa's toolbox. Her face was puffy, and her eyes seemed as if they had been set back some into her face because she had rubbed them too often. Her light reddish hair was matted a little from lying in her bed. When she finally joined us, she forced her way into our kitchen meeting area, directly across from Momma. Momma casually glanced her way.

"Glad you decided to join us," Momma said.

"You all were making so much racket out here." She paused to look at everyone sitting around the long table on the matching benches that Poppa had fashioned. "No one would ever guess that Poppa just died." She looked directly at Momma with anger in her eyes.

Rose's remarks caused silence. Her caustic comments startled us, and no one was able to focus on what Deannie had discovered: an envelope nailed to the bottom of the top tray of Poppa's toolbox. Rose reached out and pulled the envelope from the toolbox's bottom. It tore from a corner, where evidently Poppa had nailed it. She started to open it and read it.

Earl was seated next to Momma and across from Rose, and he ripped the envelope out of Rose's hands and handed it to Momma. Rose jumped up and fled the room.

Momma took the paper out of the envelope and read it silently. For a few seconds, the room grew deathly silent. Suddenly, tears started to flow out of Momma's eyes. When she started crying, nearly all of us kids did too, even though we didn't know why we were crying. Momma started laughing. She threw back her head and took the paper and crushed it against her head, and her laughter continued to grow louder as she giggled and whooped.

"Praise the Lord! Poppa had a secret!" She flipped the paper to Earl.

He opened it and read what it said.

"'Pay to the beneficiary, upon the death of Ranti Horace Crandal, one thousand dollars, guaranteed by the New York Life Insurance Company.' That old fart," Earl said. He became embarrassed, and he looked at Momma. "I'm sorry; I didn't have the right to say that."

Momma ignored his crude comment. We kids said nothing.

"He believed in insurance after all. Can you beat that?" Momma got up and started dancing and jumping up and down. When she did, most of us kids joined in, and we had a merry time acting foolish for a few minutes. Earl sat at the table and grinned from ear to ear.

"We are going home, and we are going to buy a house," Momma shouted with joy. "Kids, we are going back to Tampa, our wonderful little hometown. Isn't that just wonderful?"

When we discovered we were moving home, all of us formed a circle around Momma. We celebrated with great happiness. We sang "Ring Around the Rosy, Pocket Full of Posies."

I turned to Howard. "Now you can become the Kansas

Flyer." I gave him a hug. "At least the Tampa High School Flyer," I teased.

Rose was right! Our family seemed to demonstrate little sorrow, certainly no wailing and public weeping over Poppa's death. Even after many years of being able to reflect upon that turn of events in our lives, I admit that I have a difficult time providing a plausible explanation for why we didn't show a more public display of sorrow for our poppa dying, other than that we were scared to death of him and he was mean to Momma. Even though we were just children, we were able to understand that Poppa spent a lot of time trying to publicly humiliate Momma, and she spent her time defending him and his mean ways so that we children wouldn't disrespect him privately, which we did, or publicly, which we never did, out of fear. We had heard and actually witnessed some of the terrible beatings Poppa had given to my brothers with his razor strop, especially to Charlie and Sammy. I usually ran and hid under the bed and cried as much as my brothers.

At the time, I could not understand why. Now, I am quite sure it had to do with Momma and Poppa's marriage being one of convenience. Poppa's relationship with Momma was a bit of a power struggle. Poppa did his best to subjugate Momma, so she lost her identity, and Momma did her best to make sure Poppa couldn't do it.

With the exception of Rose, after Poppa died, the atmosphere in our home changed from a place filled with tension and fear to a place filled with peace and love. While Poppa was alive, it seemed our house had been fitted with some type of mystical, invisible covering that encased a balloon filled with a great deal of angst, like a bunch of hungry lions roaring, looking for prey. It was constantly being filled with evil air, and it spewed forth meanness and cantankerous talk. It was the kind of talk that proves the folly of the old saying "Sticks and stones can break my bones, but words can never hurt me." My Poppa never actually hit me, but his words made my soul whimper and my bones raw from grinding out, whether it was true or not that "I looked too much like my mother" and was "too stupid to be worth more than teats on a bore hog" or just cursed because I was a girl.

"'Whatever is true, whatever is noble, whatever is right, whatever is pure, whatever is lovely, whatever is admirable—if anything is excellent or praiseworthy—think about such things.' Philippians 4:8," Momma said as she did her best to teach us what to say or do whenever we were wont to pay back someone for suffering an injustice, inside or outside our home. "As much as it depends upon you, keep the peace," she drilled us over and over.

Even as a girl of ten, right before my eyes, in the light of how Poppa treated Momma, she became a more remarkable woman each day.

Momma would often tell us that God always answers prayers. His timing seldom matches ours.

"It just might be the unanswered prayers that make the biggest impact in your life."

I suspect that Mr. Alfred E. Smith could be marked down as being in Momma's corner. He lost the presidential election of 1928 to Mr. Hoover, and Momma was elated.

"The worst scoundrel Republican is far better than any ole Democrat." She never hesitated to let anyone know what she thought about those "dumb-butts," as she called them, when she really got wound up about politics. Poppa was a staunch Democrat, so that was another thing for them to disagree about every four years.

My older sisters would chat about "flappers, gin, and men," but for a few years, when I entered into their space, they would clam up and tell me to get lost.

For a spell, prosperity was everywhere. I must admit, before Poppa died, even our lives had been changed quite a bit. Our family enjoyed many more things, one being a radio, a magical box from which one could hear music. It came from somewhere out of the air and was the best of all our changes.

Mr. Hoover, the winner of the election, who would become our nation's thirty-first president, campaigned with a slogan: "A chicken in every pot and a car in every garage." Once in a while,

Momma would mimic the speech we heard on the radio. We all laughed at her, and Poppa glared at her with disgust.

When one of us would get antsy about a future event that we couldn't wait for, or we would be so scared about it we'd all just lie down and die, Momma would say, "If'n the good Lord allowed his children to see the future, most of us wouldn't believe it."

If he had been able to see the future, just seven months into his presidency, Mr. Hoover probably would have decided to just live off his wealth, do more fishing, and maybe not just read a detective story, but write one, because he too fell off the mountaintop.

When we wanted to know how future things would turn out, we sought Momma's wisdom. It was as if she was a medium, or she had a direct pipeline to God's answer center. She often would say, "How many angels can dance on the head of a pin? Since they can't be seen nor counted, why worry about events that you will only be able to know about once they have arrived?" We often would finish her sentence, letting her know we had heard her answer too many times. We knew she was right; we refused the logic of her teaching.

It's for sure Mr. Hoover and the rest of our nation couldn't tell you how many angels could dance on the head of a pin because we all couldn't foresee the imminent financial disaster looming upon our nation's horizon.

Even in the midst of the aftermath of our poppa's death and the decision to move back home, none of us considered it a burden to pack up our household goods and make a new beginning, once again in familiar territory.

"At least we won't be going home as sharecroppers," I whispered to Momma at the breakfast table.

She gave me a big hug. "Won't that be wonderful?"

A couple of days later, our house was filled with so much joy and excitement that it was a wonder we all didn't just die and go to heaven right then because Nap and Sammy arrived from Tampa.

I remember asking Momma one time, when I was seven or

eight, "Why did you choose all those funny-sounding names for my brothers?"

"Jessie, honey,"—I just loved for Momma to call me that; it sounded like some refrain from some great piece of music, which just made a body feel good, like something warm and fuzzy that just melted your innards—"just because I'm the wife of a sharecropper and may always be one doesn't mean that my children won't become famous one day," Momma said. She reached out and tousled the hair on the top of my head. "I'm positive the Lord and I are rearing a future president of these United States!"

"Just because one of my brothers is going to be a president, you gave them all funny-sounding names?" I asked.

"No, not just because one of my boys is going to be president." She allowed her face to contort with her eyes growing, and she gave that big silly-nilly look. "I am expecting great things from them. So, I gave my boys names from history, of men who did become famous. I figured it would encourage them to become great men."

"But Momma, why'd you pick such funny names?"

"They aren't funny. They are names of importance. Now you take your brother's name, Nap. He was named for the famous emperor of France, Napoleon Bonaparte. He was a great leader of men, until he met his Waterloo." She laughed.

"What's a waterloo?" I asked.

"Never you mind. I'll let you read all about it when you are a bit older," she replied. "Now, your brother Sammy was named after the prophet Samuel in the Bible. When Samuel was just three years old, his momma took him to the temple and dedicated him to the service of the Lord. She left him there, and he was reared and trained by the priests, who served God, and he became famous as a prophet for the children of Israel. Do you remember about Moses and the children of Israel?"

I nodded my head. "Well, what about Earl?" I asked.

"Smarty pants." She gave me a quirky smile. "Trying to stump me, are you? Earl's name was in honor of the famous English Duke of Earl, who served the kings of England, such as

Henry VII. Charlie was named after Charles II, a king of England. Howard was named after the twenty-seventh president of the United States, William Howard Taft."

I knew he was a Republican, which Momma thought was the only kind of politician worth a tinker's damn. He was also Chief Justice of the Supreme Court.

"And your baby brother, Arthur, was named after the famous King Arthur of England and the knights of the roundtable. He was involved with a guy you may know something about—Robin Hood."

Since I experienced the crowded indignities of being the fourth child in a dozen, I was sure I would never have any children, especially after hearing the frightening, gory details that came from Momma and Poppa's bedroom every time the "baby doctor" showed up at our house and I got a new brother or sister. I resolved that if by some miraculous chance or a change of heart on my part I ever did have children, I would endeavor to give them names from famous people of history. I mean, I would do that if I were going to get fat and have a permanent tummy like Momma's from having children, leastwise it's what she said caused it. After all my sacrifice, I'd want them to make something out of themselves.

I can't recall just why I never did get around to asking Momma what ingenuous system she had for naming us girls, because we had ordinary names. After some quiet reflection, I just figured Momma's brain was all tuckered out, so she gave us girls any ole name she could think of. But Jessie Almeta! The only famous Jessie I ever heard tell of was a thief and a robber: Jesse James. Almeta! I wouldn't give a dog such a name, let alone a girl. And I don't care if she was Momma's favorite aunt.

There wasn't a dry eye in our household as we watched Momma and Sammy's first embrace. It was as if some Hollywood director had choreographed the scene. Sammy stood in the middle of the front door; the sun silhouetted his frame, and it made his face seem comely and even more handsome than he already was.

"Sammy," Momma whispered. It seemed more to herself,

as if she needed her soul to be comforted and reassured that her prodigal son had come home. "Sammy, Sammy, my boy, my darling boy." Her voice was choked up with tears. She held out her arms, beckoning him to fill them.

He hesitated a second, then he rushed to meet her, and they hugged and squeezed each other.

"I'll squeeze the packing right out of you," he said as they enjoyed the warmth and comfort of each other's caring. Tears were flowing down from Momma's and Sammy's eyes.

After a while, Momma pushed away from him. "Let me look at you." She gave him a look of approval. Sammy had been away from the family for nearly three years. It was easy to see he had grown some, and he now had a muscular build. Sammy had changed from a boy's frame to that of a man. His handsome face, framed by dark eyes and hair—the darkest hair in our family—and his dark tan, which all of us kids envied, made him look like a guy all the girls would surely swoon over.

Decades later, I can still close my eyes and recall their embrace and how utterly delicious it felt watching them hug each other, swaying from the awkwardness of a taller body trying to fit with a much shorter one, while they made a futile attempt to wipe tears from their eyes.

"If only you could," she teased. "If the packing could come out that easy, I'd have a group hug with each child every day," she added in reference to the extra pounds she carried upon her short, stocky frame.

Napoleon stood just behind them. Momma released her arms from Sammy and immediately moved to where Napoleon stood. Nap had made a trip to visit Momma about a year ago, but they were overjoyed to see each other again. Momma gave him a big hug and a soft kiss.

"I'm so happy you were able to make the trip on such a short notice"—she pointed to Sammy—"and that you were able to bring Sammy with you."

"When I got Nap's wire, he sent me one at my work address," Sammy explained. "I considered taking the train the next morning. But I packed a few things and jumped into the old Ford.

Here we are. This made it possible to arrive a day earlier than first planned."

Horace and Eddy Bosch came to visit later in the day. These two good friends of Poppa and Momma "were cut from the cloth that made the celestial robes of the heavenly beings," Momma said after they said their good-byes. Momma told us they had offered to help her rebuild the business, even loan her the money, if only she would stay. When they realized no amount of coaxing would change her mind, they gave her a hug and a kiss and wished her and the family God's speed and blessings. Eddy, his wife, whispered in Momma's ear, "If you ever need me, let me know."

Sweeter the Second Time

Nap and Earl made arrangements to ship our household goods once again on the Rock Island Railroad. They sold Poppa's mules, Jenny and Jack, to a friend of Mr. Bosch's. None of us children wanted to sell them. Since we didn't know where we were going to be living, we didn't have any choice.

"I am absolutely positive I'm not going to worry myself about a couple of mules, regardless of whether my children consider them family pets," Momma said loudly as she laid down the law.

The railroad required a family member to accompany the coffin and ride in the car with the body.

"I'll ride with Poppa," Sammy said.

"You sure you want to do this?" Momma asked.

Sammy remained silent for a few seconds as he stared down at the ground, as if he were in deep thought, then he lifted up his head. His voice possessed a noticeable bit of emotion. He struggled a bit to clear his throat.

"I'm sure," he said in a half whisper. Sammy looked up at the coffin inside the railroad car. "Someone has to do it; might as well be me. Perhaps Jessie can ride with me?" He looked at me and then at Momma.

"I...I don't know about Jessie," Momma said. "I think she's a bit too young."

"I'll go. Besides, Sammy needs some company," I said boldly.

Once the train started for Tampa, Sammy moved some of the mailbags and made a place for me to sit, which was more comfortable than the railcar's hard floor. The baggage car man had a chair for Sammy to sit on.

The *click clack* of the railcar's wheels passing over the rails, which were cinched together tightly, yet still left a gap that made the noise each and every time the railcar's wheels passed from one rail to the next, soon produced a rhythmic beat. It seemed to cause a body to relax and become drowsy. We were soon catnapping.

Something startled me. It may have been a sudden jostling of the car on the train tracks. I rubbed my eyes and looked over at Sammy.

He was wide-awake and staring directly at Poppa's coffin. Suddenly, he jumped up and rushed to it. He put his hand on it.

"Oh no you don't! You're not getting out." He laughed softly.

"Sammy, are you all right?" I asked. He didn't answer, and I could feel myself growing frightened.

"You can't get me at the trough this time! See, my hands are free. I won't be putting them around anything—ever!"

I didn't know what was happening; I only knew it was scaring me to death.

"Made you eat that strop, didn't I?" He sneered. "Hit me; hit me first. I'm to blame! No more Charlie! You sorry...!" He turned around and looked at me.

I was trembling, and his crazed look made me turn my eyes away from his.

"Sammy! Stop it. You're scaring me, acting crazy." I felt more panicky because I could tell he didn't see me in front of him.

He quickly turned back around to the coffin. He jumped up and down a couple of times.

"Oh no, not this time," he growled.

All I could figure out was that Sammy was doing his best to keep the coffin lid closed, as if he thought Poppa was trying to get out.

"We're more than pissants. I showed you, didn't I? You crippled, one-legged wimp!" He let out a low, guttural laugh. "Think you're so bad!" He snarled at the coffin. He stood up as tall as he could, and he walked around the coffin very slowly.

"*Ring around the rosy...*" he softly sang as he circled Poppa's coffin. Suddenly, Sammy raised his hands as if he were fending off someone.

"Charlie!" he shouted. "Get away. I'm going to finish the old fart once and for all." His voice sent shivers up my spine.

"Sammy!" I yelled, tears welling up in my eyes.

He looked at me, lunging menacingly for me, though he never moved toward me. I backed away and did my best to crawl deep into the pile of mailbags that were stacked up inside the car.

Sammy turned away from me, and he thrust up his hands. He swung his right fist as though he was hitting someone with a right cross.

"Not so tough now, huh, lying on your backside? He needs killing." He talked like he had gone half mad. He acted as if he were fending off someone again.

"Charlie, would you like to finish him?" He laughed. He used his hands as if he were handing something to someone. He acted as if he had thrown something down. Then he left the coffin and sat on the baggage man's chair once again.

I wanted to try and comfort him, but I was afraid to. He looked as if he were wide-awake, yet he was acting too strange to be lucid.

Sammy stared at the coffin in silence. The *thump-thump* of the train hitting each rail raced nearly as fast as my heart's *thump-thump*.

He opened wide his arms and lifted them up. Slowly he let them drop and then pointed his fingers at the coffin. "Why couldn't you love me?" His voice was raspy and mournful. "All I ever wanted was for you to say, 'That's my boy, Sammy,' just once." His voice cracked with emotion. "Just one little ole crumb, huh?" He stood up and took a step toward Poppa's coffin, and then he sat back down.

My heart hurt as I watched my brother have a private encounter with his dead father. I wanted to run to him and give him a hug, to tell him that I loved him, our entire family loved him, but I did nothing.

Slowly, Sammy got up out of the chair and moved to the

coffin. He stood at the far end, which was facing me, and stared at it. After a few minutes, he slowly, gently, leaned down and pressed his body against the coffin. He draped his arms around it as best he could, and he cried like a baby for a few minutes.

His suffering forced me to turn my head away. I had unwittingly become a witness to a tragic, painful, and private event that not a living soul should know; but I had to carry the secret in my heart the rest of my life.

"Daddy, why was I bad?" he asked, moaning woefully.

I put my hand on his shoulder.

"Sammy," I said, and my touch startled him.

"What? What the—" He looked up at me. He recognized he was awkwardly draped across Poppa's coffin. He looked up at me, and he was embarrassed. He wiped tears away from his eyes.

I helped him off the coffin and steered him back to his seat and then sat down amongst the mailbags.

He gave me a sheepish look. I put my finger to my mouth and made the sign that said "my lips are sealed." Sammy's body shook, and he nodded as he wiped tears from his eyes. He then drifted off to sleep. I never told another living soul, not even Momma, what happened in that train car when Sammy and I accompanied Poppa's coffin back to Tampa.

We buried Poppa the second day we returned to Tampa. Poppa was buried, and the preacher's words were hollow. What can one say over the body of a man who didn't take to churching, mocking Momma and us kids for attending church every Sunday? Though the preacher tried to give Poppa a decent eulogy, as Momma often said, "You can dress up a pig just so far to make a silk purse," with his words from God's Book, it didn't get him to purgatory, let alone heaven. None of our family ever recalled Sammy mentioning Poppa's name again in a public setting.

Nap's Ford touring car matched our family's car, except that his was newer. He had taken it upon himself to paint the tire spokes bright red. The older girls teased him about fixing up his car so girls would notice him. He deflected their ribbing in a good-natured manner.

My brother, Napoleon, had a stuttering problem.

"I-f-f-f you've got a f-f-face like mine, a f-f-fella needs all the help he c-c-can muster," he stuttered, in a self-deprecating way.

"Diogenes, we found you another man," said Pauline, my second oldest sister. She was the tallest girl in our family. She had large dark brown freckles all over her body, which she absolutely detested, but she had beautiful auburn hair, which she wore long and spent half her life brushing. She teased Nap as she made a reference to the story Momma told us about the man Diogenes searching the earth for ten honest men. Diogenes had a very hard time finding that many honest men. This teasing sent all of us, including Nap, into a fit of laughter. My brother's willingness to admit he wasn't very good looking only endeared him to us. Momma told us that honesty revealed a man's character.

While we all nearly froze to death moving to Missouri in early November, our move back to Kansas was under the hot summer sun. While moving back to Tampa, we didn't travel like we were wild bats just let out of hell, as we did when we moved to Humansville. We stopped several times to relax and enjoy picnics. The weather was so nice; we were able to have the tops down, and we sang songs for hours to while away the time.

"There it is!" I yelled as I spied the familiar sight of the large grain elevators jutting out upon the horizon as we finally drew near Tampa.

Tampa, Kansas, sat on the uplands of the northwestern part of Marion County. A Santa Fe Trail marker, erected by the children and citizens of School District # 99 in 1908, marked the place where the trail passed through the east edge of town. Five miles south of town, trail ruts were clearly visible in unplowed ground.

History records that the Golden Belt Town Company was responsible for the town of Tampa becoming a reality. The company filed for a plat on April 25, 1887. It had nineteen blocks with the railroad right-of-way crossing the southern end of town. Its land speculation took a while to become a profitable real estate venture. After about ten years, the town began to take hold and grow.

The Chicago, Kansas, and Nebraska (Rock Island) Railroad provided daily freight and passenger service. Its importance to Tampa can't be overemphasized, as it had monthly receipts of over three thousand five hundred dollars.

Most of the people were Lutheran because of the German ancestry. Some were Catholic. And as Momma used to say, "All the rest, like 'muckle-de-dung,' were members of the Evangelical Church."

I guess to the rest of the world, a hamlet of less than four hundred people wouldn't be anything to write home about. For me, it was a pure slice of heaven.

My outburst focused the attention of our family, and we all started whooping and celebrating.

Momma said it sounded like a Chinese washroom on laundry day since the noises we were making sounded more like foreign language than English.

"Children!" Momma said in a commanding voice. "Settle down. One would think you all have lost your minds with this carrying-on. We don't want the townsfolk throwing us out before we even get there, do we?" She teased.

"Oh, Momma, they love us," Howard said, patting Momma's right arm.

Howard and I had taken turns driving most of the way. Momma decided she wanted to be the one driving when our clan actually drove the car into town. I was never sure why she did that. But later, when reflecting, I believe it had to do with making a statement to anyone who might see our family, and to all of us, that Momma was in charge; make no doubt about it.

For those of us riding with Momma, Howard's statement and his subsequent touching of Momma's right arm moved all of us emotionally, especially when a few tears trickled down Momma's face.

"I sure hope they still do," she mumbled through her tears.

Poppa's half sister, Emma Harrison, whom I had never seen before Poppa died even though she lived in Tampa and had a dairy farm, allowed us to camp out in their barn until Momma could arrange for us to have our own home.

Aunt Emma was short and plump. "She looked like a fart sack with two pigs trying to get out," Poppa often said about women who were a bit too heavy. Aunt Emma had dark hair mingled with some gray strands. She had smallish blue eyes and a hawklike nose. Her teeth were a little too large for her face, but that wasn't her worst feature. She had a mean disposition; at least, I never could recall seeing her smile.

Momma and our family appreciated her act of charity, but Aunt Emma had a way of communicating that all of her apparent kindness was out of frustrated exasperation. She felt trapped into offering us the milk of kindness because she was our blood kin, and what would the townsfolk think of her if she were to refuse to aid her brother's family in their hour of need?

I may have been young, but I sensed that Momma needed all the help she could muster to keep in the good graces of my aunt. I took it upon myself to see if I could be of some service to them both.

"Aunt Emma, may I help you in the kitchen or do some chores?" I asked. My initiative startled Momma but pleased her.

"Of course," Momma chimed in. "All of my children will be only too happy to pitch in."

Aunt Emma looked directly at me with a stern face, which frightened me some.

"Jessie can stay and work with me, Lou. You and the children who are old enough can help Clem."

Clem was her husband. He was the exact opposite of Aunt Emma. Clem, my uncle, was slender and quite tall. He had blondish hair and a cheerful countenance His voice was comforting, and he was easy to be around. Aunt Emma bossed him around, but he seemed to ignore her as much as he could when she barked orders. During the few days we stayed with them, he often winked at me whenever my aunt was firing off orders to everyone in sight, and he'd say, "Don't pay much attention to her," as he pointed in her direction. "I don't." Then we'd share a quiet laugh. I spent time cleaning her house, which was very large, and cleaning up after her three children, who were nothing but spoiled brats. I helped prepare the meals that were cooked to feed the two large families. Her family ate first, and then when they were done our family came in from the barn and had dinner. Uncle Clem made my aunt fix some wonderful meals with some of his best meat and dairy. I can still recall how delicious those meals were.

When they weren't working, Momma, Nap, Sammy, and Earl spent time searching for a house to buy.

Mr. Amos Tetson, the owner of the five-and-dime mercantile, owned a two-bedroom house just a few blocks off Main Street, and it was for sale.

"Although it's too small for our large family,"—Momma did her best to explain why she had bought the house that would be our homestead—"it's just across from the school, so it will be good for you children. It was all that we could afford.

"Poppa left us one thousand dollars. Now at least we have a house bought and paid for." Her face lit up with a pride-filled smile. "No one can come and take it away from us."

After having lived in a much larger house in Missouri before Poppa died, the prospect of living in the much smaller house was less than appealing. As if Momma could read our minds, she did her best to take those lemons and make some sweet-tasting lemonade.

"We will have to sleep three to a bed, but we all love to snuggle and be close, don't we?"

Realizing that her reasoning wasn't satisfactory for her children, she said, "Of course, Nap won't be living with us, and Sammy has informed me that he is bound and determined to return to Chicago, so there will only be eleven of us."

Momma made it sound as if ten children living in a two-bedroom house wouldn't be a challenge at all. "Jessie can sleep with me."

I heaved a big sigh of relief when Momma said I would be sleeping with her. I slept with Momma until I left our home. When you sleep three to a bed, everyone, including Momma, had to accept life's little indignities, as Momma told us when we found out about our cramped sleeping arrangements. Momma took pity on me, for she knew my two sisters: Naomi and Gracie, were pee-tails who wet the bed all the time. Momma wrestled with this thorny problem for some time; Momma finally filled gunnysacks with hay, and when they became too saturated with pee, she would change the hay and wash the sacks.

"The boys can have one bedroom, and the girls can have the other. The baby girls can sleep in the kitchen. Baby Arthur can sleep in a crib in my room." Her voice cracked with emotion. Momma did her best to make us believe that our large family, being forced into living as a bunch of sardines packed in a can, was going to be just hunky-dory. We realized the last thing she needed was a pack of kids showing that they were unhappy and dissatisfied with her level of ability to provide a home for her family.

"She'll do just fine, won't she?" Earl said, his tone of voice indicating that we had all better get with the program or he would get angry. We never wanted to get him mad!

As if by some secret cue, we all rushed to give Momma a hug. Tears were falling down her face.

"Three cheers for Momma!" Howard hollered, and he made sure we all followed his lead. We gathered around Momma, and we slowly moved around her in a circle, shouting, "Three cheers for Momma!" over and over.

She stood in the middle of our shenanigans and smiled, laughed at our welcomed silliness, and allowed large tears to continue to streak her face. She insisted upon giving each of us a warm hug and a wet kiss.

"S-s-see what you've d-d-done," Nap said in a joking manner as his turn came for a kiss and a hug. He feigned disinterest, but I'm positive he enjoyed it as much as I did because his face wore a huge smile.

Rekindling Kindred Spirits

Since the first second we arrived in Tampa, my heart ached, and I was antsy to be reunited with Angela Hopkins, my best friend. Until the family was settled, which required us to be in our new home and no longer living in Uncle Clem's barn, Momma would not hear of it. No amount of begging or pouting could dissuade her.

Angela lived in one of the nicest homes in town. Her father, Rex, was a man of letters and the law. People said he was too educated for his own good. I took that to mean that he was very intellectual and knew what was right and what was wrong, especially about the courts and such. He was respected and feared. At the time, all I cared about was my kindred spirit, Angela.

The summer before we moved from Tampa to Humansville, Missouri, was the first time I had met her. We became bosom buddies in a heartbeat. Even though I was the daughter of a sharecropper, she and I became closer than skin. Her parents welcomed me into their home, and oh, how I loved to go to her home. It always intimidated me a little bit, being so formal and so fancy. I have to admit that I spent some time reckoning why Angela lived in her house and I lived in mine. Her friendship made all of that reflection run downhill and out of my heart, so I seldom dwelled upon our differences.

I slept the "sleep of the tormented," as Momma would say when referencing someone unable to handle the consequences of their actions. She schooled us about the choices of life. It wasn't from my poor decisions; it was because I just couldn't wait until the night passed and I was able to call upon my friend. I was so deliciously invigorated, my innards churned, and my mind's reflections kept rerunning the events of our last time together. We stood facing each other, tears falling like a monsoon in the middle of low tide, and the smell of jasmine in the air. Angela liked pretty flowers. Her mother always had flowers blooming, so she liked to wear them whenever she could. We said our tearful good-byes on that fateful day my family moved away.

During the nearly three years I had been away, any time I wanted to bring Angela close to me, I'd just close my eyes and allow my smell memory to flesh out her wonderful smell, and she just came alive. Instantly, my heart received a much-needed dose of kindred spirits, which only she could supply. Momma knew how much I had yearned to reacquaint myself with Angela, so she took it upon herself to arrange my visit. When she told me what she had done, my poor ole heart just about stopped from pure joy. I had begged to go as soon as possible, that very same day, but she wouldn't hear of it.

That night I laid out my dress. I didn't have much to choose from, but it was one of my nicest.

"Could I wear my Sunday-go-to-meeting one?" I begged Momma.

"Why, child? Jess, you're going to play, not to have a fancy tea party." She gave me an impish, unsympathetic look.

"I know," I whined, "but I want to make a good first impression. I haven't seen her for so long. Maybe she won't like me the way she did before."

Momma quickly recognized that my heart was doing its best to play tricks on me by giving me thoughts of inadequacies.

"Oh, Jess, baby," she cooed as she moved around the bed and made her way to my side. "Everything is going to be just fine."

With just a hint of tears in my eyes, and with a shaky voice, I uttered, "Oh, Momma, I'd just want to die if it weren't so." I moved into her open, waiting arms. She gently held me and rocked me until I grew strong. With the biggest, brightest smile I could muster, I whispered, "Thank you."

The next morning, as I walked to Angela's house, I'm not sure how I actually arrived at her front porch. Possibly, I flew, because my feet never hit the ground as I walked the five blocks to her house. It was as if time had somehow been trapped in a vacuum and held hostage in order to be released back into

Angela's and my lives. The entire world could be maneuvered to meet our desires; we alone would be able to choose just how this precious commodity of time would be spent to enrich our friendship.

When we saw each other for the first time in three years, Angela and I stood in blissful giddiness, holding back screams of joy. In those fleeting first seconds, my mind played the devil's advocate as it sent messages of doubt to my heart that Angela wouldn't appreciate my friendship again. Her dark eyes flashed, she rushed to me, and we embraced and began to jabber, nearly unintelligibly, as we hugged, jumped up and down, and squealed with shrieks of pure delight. In an instant, my heart was at peace; it were as if our time apart had never happened.

She pushed me away. "Let me look at you Jessie," Angela said.

Angela wore a yellow jasmine flower in her hair. She wore a white play dress that complimented her tan from the summer sun. I wore a multi-colored feed sack dress, compliments of Purina Feed and Seed Company, that Momma had made for me to play in. I had a new batch of freckles, compliments of the sun. I did an impromptu curtsy, which made us break into loud laughter.

"For goodness' sake." We heard her mother's voice interrupt our celebration. "Get in this house before the neighbors think I have a couple of crazy people on my hands." She shooed us inside, and as soon as we stepped into the foyer, she gave us both a hug.

"Jessie, I'm so glad that you could come and see Angela." She smiled at me. "That girl has been driving me nuts with, 'When can Jessie come over?'"

Momma was right again.

"Jess, when it is true friendship, time won't mean a thing," she had said. "Friendship is about kindred spirits. Kindred spirits melt all boundaries between the essences that make up that special bond only God can truly understand. It is often unexplainable, like oil and water suddenly mixing. They become useful for their intended purposes, but everyone knows that oil and water don't mix or go together for any reason." Momma did her best to allay my fears about meeting Angela.

Decades have passed, and Angela is now with her Maker, but she is still my kindred spirit; she was from the first day we met; she will always be. She's in my soul's heart.

Getting Busy with Living

Looking back many decades later, I really do believe my momma should have been president herself. She gave her boys famous names so that when they became famous, it would be easy for the world to accept them. Mr. Lincoln could have used my momma to win those battles with the Confederates when that dillydallier, McClellan, sat on his rear and did nothing but organize and play at soldiering instead of taking his men to the battlefield and winning the war. Lincoln finally had to replace him with Ulysses Grant, a hard-charging and hard-drinking general. Momma didn't cotton to hard drinkers, but she admired him for what he accomplished for President Lincoln and our nation. The South was defeated. Grant later became president. Like Grant, Momma was a great strategist and an incredible motivator of people. She would have been a super general. In no time at all, Momma found a way to help us "keep the wolf from the front door," as she often remarked, by finding work for her and jobs for all of the kids who were old enough to work.

"Kids," Momma said, calling us to a family meeting. "Ralph Stanton, Mr. Stanton to you,"—she made sure we remembered as children that we hadn't earned the right to be too familiar with adults by calling them by their first names—"Mr. Stanton offered me a little space in his shop to set up a cobbler shop."

Mr. Stanton was the town barber. He was a short, stocky man with a beer-barrel tummy. He was nearly bald, and he had a hairline that made his head look like a billiard ball sitting upon a poorly built nest. He had a wide, short nose, but his nostrils were rather open. He had blue eyes that sparkled, which matched his cheery smile. He never knew a stranger, and he had a fine reputation among men. He was one of our civic leaders who didn't mind speaking his piece.

"How in the world did you manage that?" Earl asked.

Momma stood up taller, and for a short person, that's not easy. She put her thumbs just under her armpits, so her hands were free to move about. She kind of waved and wiggled her hands, and she thrust out her chest.

"You didn't think your ole momma could pull it off?" she asked as she looked straight at Earl. "Like I said, stand back." She did an impromptu curtsy and a two-step to show off and add some entertaining dramatics (which she often did). "Momma Crandal is coming to the rescue." She kicked her leg up a little and to the right side of her body. She laughed and winked to all of her audience.

My brother Earl stood there grinning.

"Now,"—he paused—"tell us how it really happened." He did his best not to allow Momma's version of the story to overly impress him.

"Okay, okay," Momma said. "It really did happen this way. I was walking down the street, headed toward town, and the good Lord just spoke to me." She preened and smiled as she talked.

"He said, 'Lou Crandal,' and of course I couldn't believe anyone was talking to me, let alone God Almighty," Momma said, and her eyes were opened very wide to show that she was frightened. "So, I just kept walking, and pretty soon his voice grew much louder. 'Lou Crandal, the widow woman with a dozen kids, the half-crazy woman who had a dozen kids.'" Momma paused and allowed herself a little laugh. "'I have seen your misery, and today you are going to get an extra special blessing,' he told me. Well, when I recognized that God himself was speaking to me, I nearly joined your poppa, right then and there." Momma feigned a death swoon. This brought forth collective giggles from all of us children, including Earl. "'You've blessed me enough,' I told him. 'I'm like the Old Lady in the Shoe, and I've got so many children I don't know what to do.'

"'When the quiver is full of arrows, it is a sign of a happy family,' God said in a very authoritarian voice." Momma made sure she used a deeper-sounding voice to heighten the suspense of her story. "'You need a haircut,' he said. 'The barber will help you,' he said.

"It was the last thing he said to me. Well, I didn't need a haircut, but when God says you do, who am I to argue? So I walked into Mr. Stanton's barber shop." Momma paused to allow us to show her we were giving her full attention.

"'Lou Crandal, just the woman I've been looking for,' Mr. Stanton said to me.

"'Now, Ralph, what will Valerie say?' I teased him." Momma laughed with us a bit. "You should have seen Ralph's beet-red face.

"'This town hasn't had a cobbler worth a tinker's damn since Ranti left to go to Missouri,' he said. 'I have this large room, and I was thinking that if we did a little jury-rigging, with that extra door in the back, it would be suitable for a shoe-repair shop.' He motioned for me to follow him to the back of his shop.

"'Lou, if you are willing to provide our town with some much-needed shoe repairs, because I know for a fact that you did a lot of the shoe repairing when Ranti had his little shop, I will rent that space to you for little more than a song and a dance.' He did his best to sell me on his business offer. 'Besides, you are going to need all the help you can find to keep that brood of yours fed.' He continued to press me about his business proposition. He motioned for me to follow him. In the back of his barbershop, where my shop could be, he paused and stooped down and picked up a rather large piece of signboard. 'Lou's Cobbler Shop' it read in bold, red letters against a white background. And there was a place where the business hours could be added. 'I was quite certain that you'd go for my idea, so I just went ahead and had this sign made up for your new business.' He smiled. I could tell he had a lump in his throat. His emotions started to get the best of him."

"What did you say, Momma? What did you say?" Charlie asked.

"I told him I would think about it."

"Really?" we kids asked in a sense of disbelief.

Momma allowed herself a slow, throaty laugh.

"In a pig's eye," she said. "All I could do was stand there with a big lump in my throat, and my eyes were glistening. I guess my emotions got the best of me."

"I said, 'I'd better sit down.' My legs suddenly felt weak. After Ralph helped me to find a seat in one of the shop's chairs, I thanked him through my tears.

"'This is a godsend, and I will be only too happy to take you up on your offer.'"

"Did God really talk to you, Momma?" little Gracie asked. She wanted Momma to authenticate her visit with God.

Momma glanced down at her and lightly pinched her nose.

"Well, I can't say that he really did, but he did send us a blessing, and that's good enough for us, right?"

Momma's story was exciting, as only she could make it, and we were comforted. It left us with a sense of awe and reverence because of the extra special blessing our family had received.

After Momma finished her story, she motioned for us kids to skedaddle. "Everyone can get busy with their chores. Rose, I want you to stay so we can have a talk."

Even outdoors in the yard, we were able to hear some of Momma and Rose's conversation emanating from the house.

"I have my own life to live!" Rose shouted. "It isn't fair!"

"Rose Edna Crandal," Momma said, and Momma's voice nearly became as loud as my sister's, "you will handle your responsibilities whether you like it or not, whether it's fair or not."

In the next few minutes, we heard a lot of muffled talking. Some of it we could understand; most of it was just bits and pieces of conversation from Momma and Rose in a huge disagreement.

"You never loved him!" Rose said as she screamed in anger. "I loved him!" She made a confession and hurled an accusation.

We could hear Rose bawling.

"What your father and I had is none of your business." There was silence for a few seconds. "You will do as your are told, or so help me God, even if you are in high school, I'll have your brothers use the strop on your smart-alecky backside." The next thing we heard was the unmistakable sound of a hand on skin, probably on Rose's face, then a loud slamming of a door as Rose ran out of the house.

RANNY GRADY

After a while, Momma reappeared, and she came out into the yard. I could tell that she had been crying.

Sometime later, I found out that Rose did not want to accept the responsibility for taking care of Momma's children and managing our home. She especially did not like taking care of the smaller children, Deannie, Gracie, and Arthur, while Momma tended the cobbler shop.

She told Momma that she could find another nigger maid to do her work. Momma slapped her face, and they had nearly gone to "fist city."

When that ugly confrontation took place, it heightened my suspicions about the unusual relationship my poppa had with Rose. When Poppa and Rose were together, I was too young to know how to assess what my eyes and ears were able to perceive. Ever since Rose came into puberty, started blooming and bursting at the seams, and was becoming a woman, Poppa began to pay special attention to her. I often saw him staring at her in a discreet manner. It was about that time that Poppa began to show favoritism toward her, even when it concerned Momma. Whenever he would go on a business trip, he wanted to take Rose, not Momma. I never did see anything tawdry, but seeing them together just gave me the heebie-jeebies. Something just didn't add up.

As time passed, Momma and Rose grew more distant and adversarial. Looking back, I guess Momma felt threatened by my sister's suddenly firm, well-endowed body. That made Momma's falling-apart-after-a-dozen-kids body seem unappealing to her and to Poppa. I don't remember a time when Momma didn't wear a truss and a girdle. When I asked her why, she used to laugh and do her best to make light of her predicament.

"When a woman has twelve kids, her bottom sort of just falls out," she teased. "The good Lord can do just so much to shore up the necessities; I'm left to help all I can." She would point to her girdle and the truss she wore for her hernia and her hemorrhoids.

To my way of thinking, when Poppa preferred to spend personal time with Rose every chance he got, even though she was his daughter and not his wife, Momma and Poppa's relationship deteriorated. He openly showed favoritism to Rose the more "ripe" she became; he even allowed her to show small amounts of defiance and disrespect to Momma and to him. I could detect the change in her behavior. When we were together in town and we met men or teenage boys, they made sure she knew she was being ogled She knew it, and I once remarked to her that I was aware that it was happening.

"You'll never have men undressing you like they do me," she bragged. "Your breasts won't be big like mine." She loved to use her wiles and words to hurt people. Her words shocked me.

"Who cares?" I did my best to deflect her attempt to hurt my feelings. I couldn't help but wonder if somehow she had caught me standing in the mirror, nearly naked, examining myself and wondering if I would ever have budding breasts, let alone large ones like Rose. "Pride goeth before a fall," I warned her as I sought a way to defend myself against her hateful barbs.

"Don't go quoting me a bunch of Momma's garbage, or I'll never take you to town with me again." She grabbed my left arm in a menacing manner. I pulled away from her.

"Why are you so mean?" I glared at her and rubbed my arm where she clutched it. "Just because you have to help Momma?"

Rose put her hands on my shoulders and looked right into my face.

"Don't you tell anyone what we have been talking about, especially Momma, or I'll make you wish you had never been born." She put the fear of God in me that day.

I guess she saw me as being in Momma's camp, and she considered me untrustworthy. If she did, she was dead right. That day, Rose's and my relationship took a turn for the worse and never reconciled.

Momma always said, "In this world there are two types of people: givers and takers." My sister was certainly numbered in the latter group.

Because this puzzling relationship existed between Momma and Rose, even though Poppa was dead, he was too much alive in our house. I figured that Rose believed that Momma hadn't loved or respected Poppa enough, and that may have been true. When a man is petty and denigrates his wife and causes her a type of suffering that seeps into the marrow of her soul, plus he's responsible for her being pregnant twelve out of the seventeen years they were wed, while showing little affection or appreciation for her help, no wonder Momma had a rebellious streak every now and then. Like Momma said, "Life comes at you like a freight train, and you'd better be ready to ride the rails or get off the tracks before you go and get kilt." She usually ended her little ditty using improper English to make her point.

My momma proved she could "ride the rails." In no time at all, she had opened the cobbler shop, found cleaning jobs for her girls, including me, and sent my brothers out to find jobs.

One day my brother Howard found a new job.

"Momma, Momma!" He came home breathless, yelling as he rushed in the door. Howard was slender, rather tall for men of that time in history, nearly six feet tall, and looked rather bookish. It was a term that we girls gave to boys who weren't muscular looking and spent too much time seeking learning. He had dark brown-auburn hair and blue eyes, which always seemed to be searching for something that would unravel the ninth wonder of the world.

Momma said that his mind was just too busy all the time, and he often missed the simple things right in front of his nose.

"Guess what?" he asked.

"Slow down. Catch your breath for a minute." Momma did her best to help my brother get to a low roar so he could communicate.

He giggled and emitted a few breathless laughs, all the while smiling from ear to ear.

"I just happened to pass by Mr. Jackson's newspaper office." He gasped for more air. "I don't know what possessed me to do it." He paused again to catch his breath because the more he divulged, the more excited his voice grew. "But I just walked into his newspaper office, and one of his employees was speaking in a loud voice."

"'How do you spell 'extraterrestrial'?' he asked his boss, so I spelled the word correctly.

"'Say, you're a pretty fine speller! What's your name?' Mr. Jackson asked me as he stopped what he was doing and looked up at me from behind his big desk."

Mr. Jackson was a man in his late fifties, one of the oldest men in town. He had silver-gray hair, which he wore slicked back. It made him look like he had more hair than he actually possessed. He had a tanned face and a prominent nose that matched his ears. Even so, he was quite handsome. He had a deep voice that commanded authority whenever he was in a company of men. His thick eyebrows highlighted his face. His ready smile and dazzling white teeth made him a favorite of the ladies in town. He was a confirmed bachelor, though many of the single ladies in town had laid their snare. None had been successful.

"'Howard Crandal,' I told him.

"'You're Lou's boy?' Mr. Jackson asked. 'Your momma's one fine lady.'

"I just stood there grinning. Mr. Jackson got up and came over to me. Suddenly, he got the strangest look on his face.

"'You want a job?' He looked me up and down as if that would help him assess whether I would be a good employee.

"Momma, it was just like you say, 'Divine providence comes around the corner just when inspiration and perspiration meet at God's appointed time,'" Howard said in a whisper. "Do you think that's what happened, Momma?"

"Well, I'd have to be God to say it was a 'divine' appointment." She winked. "What I can say is that those times you studied your spelling lessons has paid you a handsome dividend. Not many lads your age could spell 'extraterrestrial.'" Howard looked at Momma and me; he beamed with pride.

"'Well, do you?' Mr. Jackson's voice grew louder and a bit impatient.

"I guess what took place seemed too real to be true. It dazed me," Howard stated. Grinning widely, I said, 'I…I sure do,' Howard stammered, a bit embarrassed by his slow reply. 'What will I have to do?'

"Pointing to his employee who couldn't spell 'extraterrestrial,' Mr. Jackson said, 'For one thing, help him learn to spell.' He looked at me and laughed. 'I'll just bring you along, and I'll see how fast you can learn.'

"I reached out and shook his hand as hard as I could. 'Oh! Thank you, sir.' I kept pumping his hand.

"Momma, he wants me to work every day after school and on Saturdays."

"How much is he going to pay you?" Momma asked. A blank look settled on Howard's face.

"Gosh, I don't know. I never bothered to ask him. I was so happy to get a job." He laughed in embarrassment.

Laughter filled the room as Momma opened up her arms and motioned for him to fill them. As she gave him a warm embrace and patted his shoulders, she said, "Mr. Jackson is a fine man and a fair one; he'll pay you what you are worth."

My older brother Earl was able to get a job as a farmhand with one of the farmers. Mr. Amos Hudson was a man of few words, but he was successful with anything he turned his hand to. Earl wasn't the most talkative fellow, so they were very compatible.

My brother Charlie, on the other hand, got a job that Momma didn't wholly approve of at the local pool hall and domino center. When he told her where he wanted to work, Momma threw a fit. "Surely you jest. Are you standing in front of your Momma requesting I allow you to take a job where all the cussing, drinking, and the telling of dirty stories take place all hours of the day and night?" Momma asked.

My brother Charlie, who was named after King Charles II, never gave a hoot about royalty. Charlie was just a smidgen over five feet eight inches tall. He had reddish hair, which was fine like flaxen hay, and it always seemed to need some assistance to be kept in its proper place. He was constantly brushing it back. He had an incredible smile that could melt hearts, especially those of the female persuasion. He was a tough guy who was in one scrap after another, in spite of Momma's haranguing him to use his head instead of his fists to navigate his life.

"Why can't you get a good job like your brother Howard?" Momma asked.

"Because, I don't want a job like his," he answered in a curt manner. "Momma, I'm good at dominos! I'm gonna be the best pool player there ever was!"

"But Charles, that place has ..." Momma paused to make sure she used the right words to get her point across. "I ... I just think you can do better."

"What if I don't want to do better?" Charlie looked her in the eye. "Momma, I'm not like Howard! I need more excitement, and I aim to get it. Besides, with those suckers down there at the pool hall, even if I'm young, I can win more money than Howard will ever earn at the newspaper. We do need the money, right?" He pressed Momma to acquiesce.

Momma always said about my brother Charlie, "That boy could talk the coon down from the tree so that the dogs could play ragtag with it." She wasn't the only person who thought that.

"Oh, all right!" She lost another epic struggle with my brother. "But if I hear any gossip about your improper behavior,"—Momma lowered her voice—"I'll come down there and snatch you bald-headed and skin you alive and drag you back home, you hear?"

"I hears ya, Momma, yes, uh, Missus Crandal, ma'am." He teased her and mocked her by using the master-slave relationship tone of voice, which she detested, as he quickly moved in and gave her a big hug.

"Charles Crandal, you're going to be the death of me," she said with a hint of exasperation in her voice as she recognized deep down that he had bested her once again.

In no time at all, Momma had all of her brood working to help keep the "wolf off the front door," as she would tell it. For a while, things seemed to run like an eight-day clock.

Mr. Roosevelt's Armageddon

One day in late October of 1929, when I met Angela to walk to school, she told me she had heard on their radio that men were jumping out of windows in New York City. Angela's home atmosphere had suddenly turned sullen and quiet. Her parents did a lot of whispering, particularly in her presence. She told me it was spooky, and it had unnerved her so much that she had some fits of crying when she didn't even know why.

The minute I came home from school, I asked Momma, "Momma, why would grown men jump out of windows?"

"Who filled your head with such nonsense?" she replied. "Men jumping out of buildings. Child, you mustn't believe all that you hear. I don't want you believing half what you see."

"Angela told me she had heard it on their radio," I said.

"Perhaps she just misunderstood what the person on the radio was saying."

"No. She didn't mess anything up or get confused. She said her parents have been acting strange and whispering in front of her."

The front door opened, and Howard rushed in.

"Momma!" he shouted. "They say the world is coming to an end."

"Since the Good Book clearly states that only God knows when the end of the world will take place, I don't cotton too much to rumors and rumormongers."

"I don't mean the earth; I mean our financial world. Look for yourself."

He pointed to some copy Mr. Jackson was preparing for the paper. "Black Thursday: Stock Market Crashes" was the headline. In the body of the article were accounts of men who days before were wealthy beyond anyone's imagination. Realizing that their worlds had just come undone, some decided to tempt the laws of gravity. They jumped out of windows to see if the good Lord would rescue them. I guess the thought of having to live like normal poor people was more than they could take.

As she did every day, Momma used the opportunity to teach us a lesson about life.

"God seldom takes you out of your mess. He promises he will stay with you in the mess." He didn't rescue the men who jumped out of the windows.

Stocks crashed. I didn't know what a stock was, let alone know how it could possibly crash. The crash reached all the way from New York to our small town, Tampa, Kansas.

Whatever was behind all that crash, in a year's time, we went from poor to nearly starving to death. As poor as we were, evidently we were richer than some because a number of families had to move out of their homes. Angela didn't have to move, but even they changed the way they lived.

"Maybe the good Lord just got tired of seeing how some folks lived like kings and queens while the vast majority of other people lived like sharecroppers, so he saw to it that we all had a bigger taste of his sunshine and rain." Momma's comment was in reference to those unsettling times.

"Your poppa may not have been all that you kids wanted or needed before he died," Momma often said during those dark days, "but he left us a house that the bank can't come and get.

"We might be poorer than hungry church mice, but at least we have a roof over our heads, praise to the Lord of life," she'd say, and she'd break out singing one of her hymns.

Momma used humor to help us cope with being poor. She teased about not having money while the folks who had money did nothing but worry about theirs. She wiped her brow with her hand. "Worrying is for folks who have money. Since we don't, it sure won't affect us. Whew, that was a close call, wasn't it?" She'd smile and wink.

Momma was right about ninety percent of the time. She missed the mark by a country mile on this occasion because the Great Depression swooped down upon us like ravenous vultures seeking prey after a fortnight of starvation.

RANNY GRADY

Momma's shoe-repair business took a big hit.

"If a body doesn't have shoes, it doesn't need to repair them. One man's disaster is another man's opportunity."

She was ready to get out of the shoe-repairing business because she had taken a second job managing Rosie's Café, the local hangout for the farmers.

One morning, shortly after breakfast, a young man walked into her cobbler shop and asked if she would sell him her business. She told him that she was interested in selling. First, she had to clear it with Ralph Stanton because it was technically still a part of his barbershop. Ralph understood the need for Momma to focus her time and energy on earning money for her large family, so he readily agreed for her to sell her business. She didn't get more than a tramp would need to panhandle to get out of town. Still, she was satisfied with the deal.

She later found out that the young man wasn't interested in running a cobbler shop. He needed those special shoe-repair tools of Poppa's so he could open a business where he handcrafted boots and made custom-made shoes for people who always had money. Regardless of the circumstances of the economy, some people always had money to spend on luxuries.

Whenever anyone would inquire about why she sold her cobbler shop business, Momma would say, "I'm way better at slinging hash than I ever was at slapping leather." Momma's pies were sought-after delicacies, a real drawing card for the café. Since Momma didn't need to spend any time with the cobbler shop, and we still needed money, she soon found a second job at the dairy creamer, working as a laborer separating the cream from the milk. She only worked a few hours three days a week, but every little bit helped to keep the bills paid.

"Jess, honey, your poor ole momma is just a jack-of-all-trades; unfortunately, a master of none." She teased us with her lament. She was so dead tired; her body just didn't want to go anymore. Because of her heavy work schedule, Momma wasn't home very much. I never felt her absence deprived me of anything. Momma and her kids' hearts were knitted together, and even when we were apart, we knew she loved us.

The Arrangement

Memorial Day wasn't just an ordinary day in the life of our town or our nation. Since the warrior wounds were still quite fresh from our country's fighting and defeating the Kaiser in World War I, it wasn't unusual to see young men who were missing limbs out and about in society. The act of honoring the dead was very important to everyone. Our family was no different.

"Girls, will you make sure your younger sisters are all dressed and ready to visit Poppa's grave?" Momma shouted as she and our entire family scurried about to dress in our finest Sunday-go-to-meeting clothes.

"Make sure your sisters' hair is all done up with some pretty bows," she hollered from her bedroom dressing stool as she was got herself dressed.

I was already dressed, and I did my best to make sure Momma didn't have to be bothered with too many details. She had enough on her mind since it was our family's first visit to Poppa's grave.

"Are you nervous?" I asked as I looked into her eyes. "You know, paying respects to Poppa and all."

Momma stopped her dressing for a moment and looked at me.

"Does it show?"

"A little."

"The old coot, leaving me with this..." She never finished her statement, just dabbed at her eyes.

"We're doing just fine." I did my best to reassure her. I walked over and gave her a hug. Then I left the room so she could finish getting dressed and perhaps have a moment to mourn in private.

One thing can be said about the Crandal clan: we made an

entrance wherever we went. We must have been quite a spectacle, all gussied up and walking two by two, talking and laughing as we walked the nearly one mile to the cemetery at the edge of town. Many other townsfolk were already at the cemetery, paying their respects to loved ones. Flowers were abundant, as they adorned the many graves. The kaleidoscope of colors added beauty to the scene and enhanced the tone of reverence that we all did our best to offer.

Our family made its way to Poppa's gravesite. Momma motioned for all of us to kneel down. We did as she wished. We held hands, and we remained silent for what seemed to be a long time. Momma gently placed some flowers she had brought with her in a basket upon the grave.

"Ranti, Ranti, you left us too soon," Momma softly said. Her words brought up a swell of emotion in all of us.

Little Gracie said, "Momma, when Poppa died, did he go to heaven?"

"Only believers in Jesus Christ go to heaven, you ninny," Charlie said.

"Don't pay him any attention," Rose said. "Of course Poppa is in heaven."

"Well, Poppa never believed in God," Charlie protested. "Aren't I right, Momma? Only believers get to go to heaven; all others go to hell."

"Now is not the time to discuss the merits of heaven and hell," Momma said. "The Good Book tells that only God gets to judge who will be in heaven or hell. Let's not spoil the day."

She hummed "In the Garden," and we all grew silent. Then she sang softly, "I come to the garden alone while the dew is still on the roses, and the voice I hear falling upon my ear…" We joined in with her. We sang a couple of other favorite songs quietly and reverently as we concluded our first visit to Poppa's grave.

"You kids go on home. You probably have things you'd like to be doing on this holiday," Momma said as we ended our visit at the cemetery.

One by one we all left, but not before we stooped to give Momma a soft kiss on the cheek.

"I need every one of those," she murmured after each kiss.

I was the last to leave.

"Why don't you stay with Momma?" Earl suggested. "She may want some company." I looked up at the rest of my siblings, and they motioned for me to stay.

I stood as still as I could, and I allowed Momma her quiet time at the gravesite with Poppa. From time to time it looked as if she were talking to him, then it looked like she was lost in prayer. I'm not sure how long that went on, but she surprised me when she said, "Jessie, why don't you come over here and sit with me a spell?"

I suddenly felt awkward and out of place. It was as if she had found out that I was snooping in a place I shouldn't have been to start with.

"I ... I don't want to disturb."

"Nonsense, I'm glad you stayed behind." She patted the ground where she was sitting, and I sat carefully, as if I didn't want to disturb the dead.

"He's dead, and he can't hear a thing," Momma teased me, and she smiled at me.

"He may recognize ole piss and vinegar." I glanced into her eyes. "Jessie, that's *pith* and vinegar, not piss and vinegar," Momma corrected me, and she laughed.

"Pith and vinegar? What does that mean?"

"It means that you are full of substance and have the ability to command respect from people because of your smarts and how you use it." She warmed the cockles of my heart as she said such nice things about me.

"I swear that Poppa said piss and vinegar."

Momma chuckled. "He did, and in his own way, he was paying you an even higher compliment. It was just his vulgar way of doing it."

I lightly patted the grave. "Do you miss Poppa?"

Momma remained silent for a few seconds. "When a woman has a dozen kids with a man ... well, your backside certainly misses your man, especially in the winter." She sighed. "I do get droopy eyed from time to time, especially when you kids are out of control." She brushed my hair as I leaned back against her breast.

"Momma, how did you and Poppa meet and get married?" It was a question I had been dying to ask her for such a long time; until that day, I didn't have the courage to do so.

"You don't know?" Momma sighed. "I guess it's high time you hear the story.

"I was fourteen when my parents were both killed in a horse and carriage accident. We lived in Nebraska. My father was a sharecropper, and he drank too much. My mother often did too. I wasn't allowed to do much except stay at home and stay out of the way. I often dreamed of running away, but I didn't think I could survive on my own.

"One day, my parents went to town and left me to fend for myself until they returned. I remember saying a prayer that day that they wouldn't come home all liquored up, as they did sometimes. When they didn't come home for two days, I began to wonder if they had left me and just took off someplace, not intending to ever come back. I recall how scared I was sleeping in that rundown shack all by myself.

"After the second day by myself, I decided I would take a walk and see if I could get one of our neighbors to help me decide what I should do. I was getting mighty hungry, and just as I left to fetch some help, the sheriff came in his car. It all seems a blur now, but he informed me that he had made contact with my mother's sister in Tampa, Kansas. He was to put me on the train that same day. All he ever told me was that my parents were accidentally killed while they were driving a horse and carriage.

"I never went to their funeral, never saw their dead bodies, and never really knew for sure if they were actually dead. The sheriff took me back to the shack we lived in because I told him I wasn't going to leave the family Bible that my mother had sitting on a table. It was the only tangible legacy I had. Reluctantly, he granted my wish. Then he put me on the train and wished me good luck.

"I arrived in Tampa about dusk, and my aunt was waiting for me at the station. Aunt Hilda was a widow, and she had eighty acres of wheat land, which she rented out. She wasn't wealthy, but her land, with its wheat, allowed her to live comfortably.

"'Gracious, child, where are your clothes?' she asked me when she saw me get off the train holding nothing but a large book.

"'They're all on my back,' I said in an embarrassed manner.

"Aunt Hilda was a woman with a potbelly. She had a kindly face, round in shape, and tiny lips, which seemed to disappear when she smiled. Her blue eyes sparkled when the sunlight hit them. She was diminutive and dressed plainly. She had a quick wit, and her smile gave me a sense of feeling warm and toasty around a roaring, winter fire.

"She gave me a hug as best as she could since she had to maneuver around the Bible I was carrying.

"'You poor child. Life just jumped up and smacked you in the nose, didn't it? Well, maybe the good Lord prepared me just for you.' She hugged me. 'How did the accident happen?'

"'I don't know. The sheriff didn't say,' I replied as she motioned for me to follow her.

"The baggage man helped us into her carriage. My aunt Hilda took the reins.

"'Giddyup, Matilda, honey.' She coaxed her gray mare to move.

"Jessie, honey, as a girl growing up, I often fantasized about living in a fine house with my own room, even while I was living in a shack. I never really expected to have the fantasy come true," Momma said.

"Aunt Hilda's house was white with green shutters. It had a white picket fence and lovely flowers all around. The room she gave me to live in was so beautiful, I was afraid to touch anything for fear of breaking something. It took me several days before I felt comfortable sleeping on a soft, down feather bed. I remember that I woke up in the middle of the night many times for the first few months, thinking that all of this was just a dream and I would suddenly wake up and be back home in that shack with my tipsy parents.

"My aunt quickly discovered that I didn't have any book learning.

"'Lou, you are just too old to go to our school. Since you are already fourteen, you just can't enter the grade you really need to enter. We will just have to do the best we can to see that you get exposed to the three R's.'

"Aunt Hilda took me up to the mercantile and allowed me to pick out some material. She taught me how to sew and helped me make three dresses. One of the dresses was designated just for Sunday and church. Soon after I arrived home from the shopping spree with my aunt, a delivery boy from the mercantile delivered a box.

"'Oh good,' Aunt Hilda said as she gave the boy a nickel, and we opened up the box. In the box was a large book, plus a couple of much smaller ones. I had a very quizzical look on my face. She pointed at the large book. 'Lou, that book holds the answer to the meaning of any word that exists; those two smaller ones are books that will teach you how to read and spell.' She smiled and nodded. 'We may not be able to send you to school; it doesn't mean you can't be educated.'

"At first, I just didn't know how to react to my aunt's kindness and generosity of spirit. In my whole life, no one had ever treated me as if I had any value. I was suspicious of her motives because I didn't know that people did good things because they wanted to or because it was the right thing to do.

"In just a short time, her consistent nurturing disarmed my hardened heart, even in the face of my demand to keep my heart overly protected from being crushed. Aunt Hilda told me she had given some consideration to not allow me to come and live with her, especially since I was more than half grown; nevertheless, she was very pleased that she had made the right decision by taking me into her home.

"'I'm not sure how all this is going to work out,' she informed me on the first night I arrived. 'I'm an old widow woman, set in my ways. If you're not happy, or I'm not happy, I'll help you make other arrangements,' she had promised. 'I don't mind telling you, Lou, your mother and I weren't on the best of terms. It was mostly about how she chose to conduct her life,' she confided in me.

"I did my best to reassure her that I was different.

"'I'm nothing like my mother.'

"'Well, as they say, the apple doesn't fall far from the tree, so we will just take it one day at a time, okay?'

"Just the thought of being cast out and having to forge for myself, under any circumstances, frightened me to death.

"'I promise I won't be any trouble,' I said.

"True to her word, my aunt did her best to teach me how to be a lady, and she gave me the education I always dreamed of acquiring.

"'Lou, your mind is sharp as a tack,' she told me after we started learning phonics, which soon led to my being able to read and spell. Once I learned how to read, she had me open up the family Bible I had brought with me when I came to live with her. 'Reading from this book will not just improve your mind; it will feed your soul.'

"I had been attending church services from the first Sunday I arrived. Once I learned how to read and I began to understand more fully about God and his son, Jesus Christ, I discovered that my aunt was right; my soul was being fed. When I was sixteen, I told her I wanted to become a Christian and live for Jesus the rest of my life.

"I informed her of my desire to make my good confession and be baptized.

"'Oh, Lou, I have been praying that you would make that decision.' Aunt Hilda hugged me and cried a few tears with me. On my sixteenth birthday, I was baptized in the creek along with two other people from the community. That day, I officially became a member of the Evangelical Community Church.

"Once I became educated enough to suit Hilda, she helped me find a job. I was able to get a job at one of the restaurants. Hilda and I kept to ourselves, except for church and its activities. But I was a young woman discovering my womanhood, and I was filled with my yearnings and myself. I was lonely, and when I saw other girls flirting with boys, it gave me real hankerings for things I didn't know a thing about but wanted to.

"My aunt was wise and very intuitive. Unbeknownst to me, she was busy behind the scenes working on my future. Maybe it was providential, happenstance, or kismet, but my aunt was shopping in town when she met your poppa's half sister. They got to talking, and one thing led to another. Soon, they concocted a plan to have your poppa meet me.

"I'll be the first one to admit, I would never be mistaken for a beauty when it comes to women, but I never dreamt my knight in shining armor would show up at my door with a peg leg, smoking a stogie, and smelling of beer," Momma said laughingly. "Much later, he told me he had stopped to have a beer to calm his nerves and to give him courage before he met me.

"When I heard a knock on the front door, I was busy reading before I had to return to the restaurant for the supper rush. My aunt Hilda hollered, 'Will you see who is at the front door? I'm busy in the kitchen.'

"Unaware of the shenanigans that had been put in place, I opened the door. There stood a man, I guessed in his early thirties. He had rust-colored hair and a ruddy complexion. He was about six feet tall. He wore a dark blue suit, white shirt, and a yellow tie.

"'You must be Lou,' he said.

"I looked him up and down. I thought for a second that he might be one of those hobos who sometimes came to Hilda's door looking for a meal. But he was too nicely dressed to be a hobo. 'Who are you?' I asked.

"'I'm the guy that's gonna change your life,' he said in a brash manner, as if his last remark was supposed to thrill me. He quickly recognized his remark had unsettled me. 'I'm my half sister's brother, the one your aunt was expecting.' The tone of his voice showed that he was now rather embarrassed.

"About that time, my aunt came to the door.

"'Oh, I see you two have met.'

"I looked at her, and my eyes were filled with fury. 'What is this?' I asked through gritted teeth.

"'Gracious me, I must have forgotten my manners. Come on in, Ranti. It will give all of us a chance to get better acquainted,' she said as she pushed me aside and made way for him to enter the house.

"I noticed he had little trouble walking. He sat down, and we just kind of stared at each other.

"'Dear me,' my aunt said, 'I wasn't expecting you quite so soon.'

"'I thought I might as well cull the herd and see if she's a keeper,' he said.

"It suddenly dawned on me that he was referring to me.

"'Are you buying a cow?' I asked.

"'Women and cattle are about the same. A man can't be too careful when you're inspecting the goods, if you know what I mean.' He chuckled. 'How about standing up so I can see how broad you are in the beam?' He used his hands to indicate he wanted me to get up. 'A woman who is broad in the beam bears children well. I want a lot of children. I want the arrows to fill the quiver.'

"'I'm not sure at what temperature my blood boils, but whatever it is, I'm positive his last crude remark pushed it over the boiling mark.

"'Why don't we have a nice cup of hot tea?' my aunt offered as she attempted to diffuse and change the direction our conversation was headed.

"'Aunt Hilda! Why is this rude man in our house?' I asked.

"'Now, Lou, I didn't want this to be handled in this fashion. Oh! Ranti's sister, well, his half sister, and I got to talking about our two lonely people.' She looked at me and blushed. 'Oh, I didn't … I mean …' Frustration grew in her attempt to explain the situation we were in. 'The other day … and … well, she mentioned her brother had recently moved from Pennsylvania and was starting a new life.' She allowed herself a loud sigh. 'I just happened to mention that I had a niece who was a bit lonely.' She saw my eyes grow tiny and my face flush, as I was angry and was about to start crying. 'I didn't mean to hurt you, honey. I was just trying to help.'

"The pressure of all things gone badly just swamped her, and she stopped talking. Tears started coming, and she got up and ran out of the room. Ranti and I just sat there in silence.

"'I'd better go see after her,' I said as I left the room.

"My aunt had fled to her bedroom. She was lying across the bed. I moved to the bed and sat down. My presence caused her to cry a little louder.

"Through muffled tears she said, 'I've made a mess of this, haven't I?'

"'Not if you are selling a horse,' I said with a hint of a sly looking smile in my voice. My aunt Hilda peaked her head out from under her arms. She made a face indicating she was in pain. "'That man's awful,' she moaned. 'I need to have my head examined.'

"'So you are finally going to get rid of me.' I did my best to tease her. "'Oh, Lou, I don't want to get rid of you, but it's high time you start finding your own way in this world. I didn't have the faintest idea that he was so old.' She rolled over and looked at me. Hilda suddenly grew very serious in her demeanor. 'I have been meaning to tell you something that I have been dreading.' She took my hand and held it. 'The doctor says I have a bad heart, and my son in Abilene wants me to come and live with him. I hate the thought of leaving Tampa. Sometimes life doesn't give an old woman her heart's desire.'

"The thought of losing my aunt struck me like a dagger splitting sinew and bone. Tears welled up in my eyes. We looked at each other, and our eyes locked. We both enjoyed a trip down memory lane from the first time we saw each other when I debarked from the train.

"'So you had to go and die to get rid of me?' I tried to tease her in spite of my tears as I did my best to survive the imminent parting, not of our choosing. We enjoyed a warm embrace.

"'Regardless of my leaving, you don't have to agree to this arrangement.' She sat up on the edge of the bed and touched my face and wiped away a tear.

"'Well, I haven't had any better offers, have I? This may be the only offer an orphan will ever get.'

"Hilda and I returned to the parlor where Ranti was still sitting. I walked up close to him and turned around slowly. 'Is that beam wide enough?' I asked, as I looked him in the eye.

"'By God, red hair and full of piss and vinegar.' He laughed and flushed with embarrassment.

"'Now, don't think you are going to come over here and carry her away tonight.' Hilda gave him his instructions. 'I expect you to come a'courting all proper, you hear?'

"'Well, I'm not some man to have his emotions trifled with, but I will respect your wishes. I want you to know one thing: I believe in short engagements.' He smiled.

"'And just how do you expect to support my niece?' Hilda asked him. 'And all those kids you say you want?'

"'One day, I'm going to be a wealthy man,' he bragged. 'For now, I just got a job as a sharecropper on some great wheat land. It has a two-room house with real wood floors,' he bragged a bit more.

"Our courtship was short; we were married in our church within two months. Ranti didn't want to be married in the church. He didn't believe there was a God. But I insisted, and one of the agreements for our marriage was his promise to never interfere with my attending church or to keep our children from attending church with me. He remained cantankerous about my church doings to the very end, but true to his word, he never interfered with my worship."

"How awful! You married Poppa without really loving him!" I exclaimed.

"For some women, love is too expensive," Momma said. "I didn't have too many choices. Besides, look at the blessings the Lord gave me." She put her finger on my nose.

"Your old momma has learned a few things in life. We are all weaving a rug with our lives. Until we are face-to-face with Jesus, all we can see is the backside, where all of the strings of the different cloths can be seen. They don't make much sense, and it sure doesn't seem attractive or comely. But one day, we will be able to understand the intended pattern God always had for our lives and see and appreciate its beauty and rejoice in its results."

"Momma, you do have a way with words." I sighed.

"But when I do get to heaven, I want to know why some of those ugly threads were necessary to get home." She nodded her head up and down as if she were saying, "Yes, sir, I need to know." We both laughed.

"Momma, is it bad of me to have mixed feelings about Poppa?"

"Jessie, knowing your Poppa, what other type of feelings could you possibly have?"

"I wanted to love him; I was just too scared to try. The way he beat Sammy and little Charlie, sometimes I wanted to kill him myself." Tears came into my eyes.

"If thoughts could kill, your poppa would have been dead a long time before he passed." She smiled at me, and we laughed quietly.

"But how did Poppa end up in Tampa, all the way from Pennsylvania?"

"Happenstance, kismet, and possibly some providence played a role in your poppa coming to Tampa. It is a story that I didn't even know until we had been married for a couple of years, and Napoleon was already in my arms. One night, your poppa came home more than a bit tipsy. He didn't drink much, but once in a while he would stop off and have a beer or two on his way home. That night, he had overestimated his ability to hold his liquor, and he came home staggering drunk. He banged on the door, and I opened it. I figured I had two choices. I could be surly and show him just how disgusted I was with his making a fool of himself, in public and now with me, or I could kill him with kindness and see if he wouldn't decide to put a stop to his foolishness. I chose the latter. I can recall that night's happenings as clear as a bell on a windless night.

"'Lou Crandal, your poppa is a mite under the weather.' He slurred his words. 'Maybe you can tell. I stopped and had one little dinky beer.' He looked at me as he grabbed hold of the doorframe to help him keep his balance.

"'If you only had one, that must have been some big bottle,' I said, and I reached out to him and helped him into the house. He was as polluted as I had ever seen him. The weight of his body hurt my back, and I felt my trusses come under strain. I was sure his leaning upon me wasn't helping my hernias. I knew it was too much for me to get him all the way to the bedroom, so I settled for the overstuffed chair.

"'I feel light on my feet, and I'm dizzy as a loon.' He laughed.

"I helped him make a crash landing in the chair.

"He looked at me, as if he were trying to stare a hole through my head.

"'I came this"—he held up his two fingers on his left hand—"close to being a big shot.' He slurred his words, and a little drool slid down the right side of his mouth. 'I wouldn't be in this one-horse town and saddled with'—he waved his hand at me and all around the room we were sitting in—'all this.' His voice got a creak in it, and emotion poured out upon him. 'If it hadn't been for ole ...'—he hiccupped loudly—'he's a sorry S.O.B Did I tell you that? Lou, I'd been squiring all the pretty ladies in Pittsburgh. Yessiree bob, old Ranti could'a been a dandy.' He laughed, more for himself than me. 'Maybe sipping champagne from a slipper.' He looked up at me with glazed eyes.

"'Sure, sure, and I could be dancing with the king of Siam,' I said, and I worked to help him get his shoes off. 'A good night's sleep will get you strong enough to dance with all those pretty madams.'

"'Did I ever tell you why I came to Tampa?' he asked, and he burped a little. 'Excuse me.' He chuckled.

"'Not that I can recall,' I said.

"'Hammering Jack! The old fart,' he bellowed. 'Do you know I've thought about shooting him deader than a doornail?' He started giggling a bit. 'Then just hang him by his neck till his eye-balls pop out.' His voice deepened and became more guttural.

"'That's a terrible thing to say about anyone.'

"'He deserves it! I was a brakeman with the Baltimore and Ohio Railroad, did you know that?' he asked. 'Would've been an engineer one day, but no, old Hammering Jack took care of that!' He started to moan.

"'Perhaps this story had better wait for another day,' I suggested as I thought about how I was going to manage to get him out of the chair and into our bed.

"He suddenly jumped right up out of the chair. He started flailing his arms.

"'Come back, come back!' he shouted. 'He didn't wait for signal,' he said. 'Not Hammering Jack! He waits for no man.' He put his arms down. 'I was a good brakeman; gonna be a fireman soon.' He turned his head and looked at me by his side, struggling to keep him on his feet.

"I put his arm around my shoulder, and we both staggered to keep our balance.

"'You're drunk too?' he said and laughed.

"'If I am, it's from your breath,' I informed him.

"I managed to get him to our bed, and he plopped on it. With his face buried in the bedspread, he moaned.

"'I was warned! They said, 'Watch out for Hammering Jack; he's nuts." His voice was muffled. He turned his head a bit and uncovered his nose and mouth. He let out a long sigh. 'Didn't wait, didn't wait. My leg was just lying there, bloody and all, and *poof!* it's gone.' He whimpered.

"'So you lost your leg in a railroad accident?'

"'Accident my butt!' he yelled. 'Said they couldn't use a peg leg man. Accidents happen, boss man said.'

"'Sister had pity on a cripple.' He laughed in a self-deprecating manner. 'Bingo, here I am in Tampa.'"

"So Poppa lost his leg in a railroad accident, and then he came to Tampa. That's when your aunt Hilda and his sister made the arrangement for your marriage?" I asked.

"In a nutshell, that's pretty much the way it was. Goodness me, look at that sun," Momma said. "We had better be getting along. It's late."

I rose up off Momma's lap where my head had been lying

RANNY GRADY

while she told me that interesting story about her and Poppa's marriage arrangement.

"Time flies when you're having fun," I snickered.

"If we don't skedaddle, they'll be rummaging up a ransom by now," Momma said, and I chuckled.

For the rest of my life, from time to time, when certain events took place concerning marriage and family, my heart felt saddened because I could never forget my parents' marriage was arranged, spiritually void of love.

The Preacher

When it came to religion and the freedom for one to choose to worship freely or not to worship at all, Momma had her own "Crandal Constitution."

Momma said, "I'm tolerant about my kids getting religion and attending church. I don't force you all to go to church. It's optional." She would pause and look us straight in the eye. "Of course, you will have to find a different roof to live under!" Her edict ended all of our conversations about her expectations and her demands that we all attend church services every Sunday, come hell or high water.

Various factions of our clan often debated the merits of our regular attendance at church, but, more importantly, it was Momma's right to direct our decisions concerning this very personal matter in each of our lives. On one such occasion, she taught us her churchgoing rule.

"Let me see how I can help you understand why you should go to church, even if you don't feel like it." She bickered with Rose and Charlie on several occasions. "It is my belief that God is omnipotent (all-powerful) and in control of everything in all of creation. Because I accept his authority in my life, I do his will. Are you with me so far?" she asked. They remained silent and sullen under her gaze. "You should look at it like this: he who holds the power makes the rules." She smiled at them and looked down her nose. She put her right arm up and made a fist. "See, your momma's mighty right arm and even mightier fist?" She looked them square in the eyes. "Good! I'm glad we got that settled." She tousled Charlie's hair and gave Rose a look that revealed that Momma knew Rose had been the instigator for their inquisition.

"'Train up a child (even a hooligan like my kids)'"—she gave us her all knowing look—"'in the way he should go, and when he is old he will not depart from it' from Proverbs. 22:6 is God's promise to tired and worn-out mommas." As Rose and Charlie left the room, Momma added, "Praise the Lord for small favors!" She settled the matter.

Since our family didn't have any money to put in the church's collection plate, Momma volunteered our family's services as the church's sexton, a glorified term for a janitor. "Our Lord Jesus probably honors sweat equity more than coins in a collection plate." She did her best to help motivate us kids to clean the church with the proper spiritual attitude.

"Religion is something good people put on once a week, like the Hebrew nation did once a year when the high priest would offer a sacrifice to atone for the sins of the people." Momma continued, "The high priest's sacrificial offering made the whole Hebrew nation feel better about themselves; it just didn't do anything about their sins. When God sent his only son, Jesus Christ, to willingly die on Calvary to pay for our sins, then man's relationship changed, and it became personal from the inside. When this happens, people attend church, and this experience isn't just religion; it changes people from within."

"Momma, it sounds good, but it really seems outlandish," Pauline said.

"We don't wear sandals and togas, and it doesn't make much sense," Naomi interrupted Pauline. Momma was caught in the middle.

"I suppose it doesn't. How about all of us putting on our thinking caps and see if we can find a way to make some sense of this very important biblical truth?" Momma looked at us and smiled with excitement.

My momma loved nothing better than to find a way to use God's Word to teach us how to live more spiritually and responsibly.

Momma got out her blackboard. She put two columns on it. One was marked "Religion"; the other was marked "Personal Relationship." We kids always loved it when Momma got out her blackboard and chalk.

She put her left index finger to her chin. "Let me see…um…suppose a man had a mercantile shop, and he was married and had a bunch of kids." She began to develop a way for all of us to participate and learn what she wanted to teach us about our walk with the Lord.

"If we go on the assumption, as we have already marked on the board, and if we talk about a man having religion, what we really mean is that he is more interested in feeling good about having religion than actually showing that he has it. Therefore, if we talk about a man having a personal relationship with Jesus Christ, it means that he is less concerned about religion and how he feels about it than he is about how it has changed him from the inside."

"That's about a clear as mud," Charlie said, and we all laughed.

"Okay, let's get started. Can anyone think of an incident that would help us understand this biblical truth?" Momma asked.

"Well," I said, "suppose I went to the store and bought some coconut—"

"Imagine that," Howard said, interrupting me. Our family knew how much I loved coconut, and we all laughed.

"If the shop owner just had religion, he might put his thumb on the scales when he weighed my coconut. If he had a personal relationship with God through Jesus, he wouldn't," I said with a bright, beaming smile because I was positive I had nailed it.

"Outward versus inward," Earl said. "Hey, that's good!"

"And if his son were in school and taking an arithmetic test and didn't know the answer, he might look on a neighbor's paper to get it right. His neighbor is the class brain. If he didn't cheat, he would take a lower score on the test. It would be one versus the other," Charlie said.

"And Charlie should be the one to know all about that," I said as I teased him, and all of us kids chimed in.

"What if a man lost his billfold and you found it? You could give it back expecting a reward or give it back not wanting a reward since it was the honorable thing to do," Pauline said.

"Very good thinking," Momma said.

"How about if someone at church tells you some juicy gossip, and you refuse to spread it? Better yet, you tell the one spreading the gossip that she is committing spiritual murder," Howard asked.

"That's it! Now you've got it." Momma gave us a thumbs-up sign. "Remember, Jesus didn't die so people could have religion. He died so people could have a personal relationship with him. It's all inside, not outside. If attending church doesn't change how you live away from the church building, you might as well go fishing."

"See, Earl. I told you we might as well go fishing," Charlie said, and we all looked at Momma and laughed.

Momma reached into the pocket of her apron and pulled out a tiny skeleton key. She held it up for us to see. "This was given to me by my aunt Hilda before she died." Her voice softened, and we could tell she had been greatly influenced by that woman. "I carry it with me. 'It is easier for a camel to go through the eye of a needle than for a rich man to get into heaven,'" she told us. "It's the difference between having religion and having a personal relationship with Jesus. The rich man believes his goodness will be enough to earn him a spot in the heavenly choir. The poor man, who doesn't think he is good enough, doesn't know how he can possibly make it through the eye of the needle like that camel. He relies upon Jesus to handle it."

For the rest of my life, I never looked at a sewing needle or a skeleton key in the same way. Momma never failed to find interesting ways to mold our minds, direct our thinking, and narrow our paths. In reflection, I am sure my brother Earl was right.

He said, "Momma's better than any preacher." Looking back, I can proudly say she was our first preacher.

"Red-letter days are days that you will never forget!" Momma often used that term. Our family had one the first Sunday we went to the Evangelical Community Church since returning home to Tampa after Poppa died.

Parson Jeb Brown was a kindly, elderly preacher who had served our church for many years. He was an enigma because he was steadfast in his refusal to embrace any newfangled idea, such as the automobile or the typewriter. Because our church membership was so few, and money was very hard to come by, the preacher had to serve two congregations to earn a living. He had a perfectly plain black horse carriage and Balaam, his midnight-black-colored horse, who was very old. They made the eight-mile trip to Lost Springs every other Sunday so he could conduct church services. Pastor Brown always wore a black suit, white shirt, and a collar, which helped set a string bow tie just right. He wore a white Stetson and cowboy boots. It was said, "People didn't know whether he was going to preach a sermon, conduct a funeral, or ride in a rodeo."

He had been married many years ago, but his wife, Leah, had died, and he had never remarried. She had been barren.

"Lou's dirty dozen cleans up pretty well." Momma offered her opinion as we all laughed and looked at each other. We were all finally dressed and presentable enough for our family to walk to the church.

In our small church, our Crandal clan filled up two pews. Members who knew us before we moved to Missouri cordially greeted us. They seemed overly polite, and this made me feel more distant.

We soon discovered Parson Brown was away conducting services for the other church. A man in a brown suit that was too tight for him got up and started with some announcements. He acted nervous and was fidgety with some papers he had on the podium. He haltingly read some scriptures from Psalms 53.

Sitting in church was often a trial by fire for me under the best of circumstances. With this poor man struggling to conduct church services, I was ready to bolt and find some comfort and serenity with God under the old elm tree at home.

"Our organist has the flu, so we will just have to carry on," I heard him say. He smiled, and to me it was as if he were suffering from embarrassment. "Unless we have anyone here who might help us out?" he asked in a pleading tone of voice.

The words no more dripped out of his mouth and the church suddenly became a morgue. It was as if all had stopped breathing, lest someone drag them up front of the church to force them to perform in some manner, all except my momma, that is.

Momma stood up. "Well, if no else is going to volunteer, our family will." She turned and looked at us.

All of a sudden, we shared the sense of being uncomfortable and embarrassed along with the man in the ill-fitting brown suit. We were looking at Momma, glaring at her, shaking our heads. We weren't interested in being a part of her harebrained idea.

It had been nearly three years since we'd last been in that church. We were a lot younger then. We didn't know better because we used to sing and perform all the time in church before we moved.

Momma opened up her arms and pointed them toward us. "The girls and I will be happy to sing for you." She used her head and motioned for us to heed her demand and get our bony rears out of the pew and help her sing.

As we reluctantly moved from our pew seats to the front of the church, I couldn't help but recall Momma's words, "Get busy doing, then you can worry about how you're doing it when it comes to the Lord's work."

All but Deannie and Gracie were soon singing acappella. We harmonized a few songs and then finished with Momma's favorite, "Rock of Ages." It became great fun to sing for the people and the Lord. The people were genuinely appreciative of our singing, especially the man in the brown suit. All of our family walked a bit straighter and a mite lighter on our feet as we made our way home after services. It was a red-letter day, though it took a heap of prodding on Momma's part to be classified as one.

"Our God works in strange and mysterious ways," Momma said when Parson Jeb Brown's body was discovered. No one ever knew all of the particulars, just the fact that the bodies of him and his beloved horse, Balaam, were found dead in a ravine about three miles from Tampa. From all appearances, it looked like Balaam and the parson had died of natural causes. He was still holding the reins of the horse, and his body was slumped over the front of the carriage. Balaam was lying down on his right side, peaceful like. After Parson Brown had been dead and buried awhile, Momma found out that he knew he had a bad heart. Still, he had refused to change the way he conducted his life as a preacher.

Not to make light of death, but people did get a laugh out of Bessie Grimes saying, "Well, he did die with his boots on," in reference to the cowboy boots he wore.

"There's no such thing as an indispensable man," Momma taught us. "And if he starts to think he is one, God will teach him a lesson or two about who controls what."

Profound statements dripped from Momma's lips. Our church's new preacher proved that Momma was a seer and confirmed that God possesses a sense of humor.

Malachi Daniel Hawes, Pastor Brown's replacement, was met at the train station by several men of the church on a hot and dusty day in mid-July. He had recently graduated from Princeton University Divinity School. He had turned down several offers to pastor churches in the East because he had always dreamed of living in the West.

After our family befriended Malachi, Momma often joked, "He was a very educated man but evidently failed geography because only an eastern city slicker could think Tampa, Kansas, was west, since California had been settled for quite some time."

Momma and I had gone along with the welcoming committee. "To help the young man start fresh on the right foot with our church" was the reason she wanted to be there to greet him when he arrived in Tampa she told our family. I went along mostly out of curiosity.

Malachi Daniel Hawes was the exact opposite of Parson Brown. While his predecessor was stocky, short, rotund, and had a round, jovial face with a large nose and wide, flaring nostrils, Hawes was tall, gawky, thin, and had fine facial features. His mop of hair and his toothy grin disarmed people. His clothes drooped over his body while his predecessor's expanded to their limit as he wore them.

His easy style allowed him to disarm and befriend us all by the time we helped him get his luggage and trunk off the baggage car and into the parsonage behind the church. His Eastern accent was very different from that of the wheat lands of Kansas. His letters were more precise and a bit cryptic as spoke.

"He's not much more than a boy in a man's job," Momma said. She became his staunch ally. "He's preaching to men twice his age, and it takes some doing to earn their respect. And he doesn't need any of your bright assessment," she said as she defended him against all comers.

"He looks like an Ichabod Crane to me," Charlie said as he put him down for his looks and mannerisms.

"He may be young, but when he stands up behind that pulpit and begins to explain the Word of God, and he points those long, slender arms and huge hands and fingers directly at our congregation, I swear, sometimes it is as if the very finger of God is touching my soul," Momma said.

"That happens to me too," Pauline said. "Does that happen to you too?" Pauline asked, and we laughed.

"Considering his inauspicious beginning, I'd say Malachi has done pretty well for himself," Momma opined, and we all agreed. We smiled and were soon laughing because we knew exactly what Momma was referring to.

R. C. Harker had been a member of the Evangelical Community Church since it was founded. He was nearly a century old and was just about an institution all by himself. He was a wealthy, retired farmer and was known as a mean checkers player.

Shortly after Malachi arrived, R. C. died. The family came from miles around, and all of the prominent people from the surrounding areas came to pay their respects.

"The biggest funeral I can ever recall," Momma said when it was all done.

It was Malachi's first funeral. He was nervous, he confided

to Momma. He took pains to make sure everything was prepared and nothing was left to chance. The funeral was on Saturday afternoon, so it allowed kin and others to travel without missing a day of work. Many of them came in early that week. The wake and layout became a happy reunion.

"Can't expect kin and folk to get mournful when a man lives to be nearly one hundred," Momma said. "Especially if they know he is going to heaven."

Saturday morning the sun came up bright, and it looked like it was going to be a good day to pay our respects to the dead. But by midmorning the clouds rolled in, and it began to rain.

"There's something fitting about rain on the day of a funeral," Momma said as I lamented how the nice weather was gone, and the rain was gong to spoil the funeral.

By two o'clock in the afternoon, the rain had managed to dampen spirits and make everything seem drab. The entire funeral service had been shortened so that the undertaker and his helpers could finish the job in short order.

"It is unsettling when your plans are scuttled at the last moment," Momma said.

In spite of the inclement weather, a large crowd of people gathered around the gravesite. The wooden coffin was readied to be lowered into the grave. The people held up their umbrellas for protection from the pelting rain. Malachi stood just in front of the open, freshly dug grave to conduct his funeral service. The wind blew, and the rain got his Bible wet as he read from Psalm 103:

> As a father has compassion on his children, so the Lord has compassion on those who fear him; for he knows how we are formed, he remembers that we are dust. He flourishes like a flower of the field; the wind blows over it, and it is gone, and its place remembers it no more.

As Malachi read, for whatever reason, he took one little step back, not instantly, but incrementally. The slick mud lost its firm foundation, and Malachi's shoes began to slip. His Bible flew through the air, followed by his two feet. A loud thud was heard as his body hit the bottom of the freshly dug grave. He had slipped backwards into the open, muddy, unoccupied grave. All eyes were directed to the grave. There was a collective hush and then almost a groan of consolation.

"Who really knows why anything actually happens?" Momma said. "Maybe it was the rain, and he was having a dickens of a time managing the elements. Perhaps it was his Bible getting ruined and causing a distraction. It's possible that he was overly concerned for the people standing out in the rain like drowned rats and wishing they were anywhere except watching R. C. getting mud thrown on him. Perhaps it was providential, though, mercy me, how it could be something so profound." She did her best to console Malachi after the funeral.

When something takes place right before your eyes, and you have a hard time believing you witnessed it, it's hilarious. Although you desperately want to laugh loudly, you know it wouldn't be appropriate. It seems as if your funny bone, from way deep inside, begins to gnaw at your innards, grasps at your craw, and makes you feel odd because you evidently are suppressing something natural and necessary for godly health. I was dying to let it rip!

"Dear God! Deliver me from this pit!" A loud, almost strange-sounding voice called out. Malachi's voice was heard clearly.

Muffled giggles and guffaws sounded. Malachi managed to get up on his feet, and he placed his hands upon the top of the grave pit. He had a look of bewilderment and blotches of mud on his face.

The very stoic-looking funeral attendant, standing nearby, looked down upon Malachi. With a voice as clear as an angel's announcing the presence of God approaching in heaven, he said, "Preacher, we bury only one man at a time in a grave."

This completely broke up the funeral service. No one could hold back the laughter. The scene and the drama went from tense to celebratory.

Malachi was given a hand, and he was hauled out of the

grave pit. Someone handed him his Bible, and he finished reading his scripture. He said a wonderful closing prayer.

"Dear Father, I beseech you to hear the words of your servant Malachi and comfort the hearts of the loved ones of our dearly departed, Mr. Harker. I humbly beg you to forgive my untidiness." The people began to giggle. "But I offer up a thank-you of praise for the deliverance from the pit. Regardless of how Mr. Harker was buried, we can praise you, dear Jesus, and shout with joy because whether he was buried in six feet of dirt or miry muck, he is in paradise this very hour and awaiting your return, as we all are. May we all be so blessed to have kin and folk from all walks of life come to honor us when the Lord calls each of us home," he said. "There's no doubt that Jesus will greet R. C. with a hug and say, 'Well done, my good and faithful servant.' May it be so to all of us. We ask all of this in your holy name and in your only Son, the savior of the world's name, Jesus Christ, amen."

In the midst of that awful experience, Malachi proved his mettle, and he won the hearts of his congregation. He also caught the eye of a certain lovely lassie, Elizabeth Flynn.

Momma and Martha Flynn soon put out their fowler's net. "We know that in all things God works for the good of those who love him," Momma said as she told us about her and Martha's plan to play cupid with Malachi and Elizabeth.

"We can just throw a few more beans in the pot," Momma would say when we would invite Malachi to have Sunday dinner.

Martha agreed to furnish the chickens, and it was agreed that it would be best to have Malachi get a chance to get better acquainted with Elizabeth in our home. "Less threatening," the woman said. "How romantic can it get when nearly a dozen kids are gawking?" And she looked at us with a knowing look. We were too much of a group of busybodies to suit her.

"Momma, do you think it's possible for people to fall in love over a drumstick?" I asked. I was thinking about the shy, smoky glances Malachi and Elizabeth were giving each other when he was passing the plate of chicken to her. She took a drumstick and thanked him for his help.

"Jessie, I guess Cupid can be cross-eyed and he can still hit his target." Momma winked at me.

"Did he ever hit you?" I asked.

Momma stopped what she was doing and put her hands on her hips and she looked right at me. "With all these kids running around, it would seem impossible he missed, right?" She allowed herself a sigh. "But he did," she said in a whisper.

I felt so awful at that moment. I wished I could take back my question, for I could see the pain in Momma's eyes. I came near her and gave her a hug. I didn't say a word; I left the room.

"Long courtships are for those folks who don't really want to get married, or they are trolling until something better comes along," Momma said in defense of Malachi and Elizabeth's very short engagement. "I suppose there are a few times that rule doesn't apply, but very few."

Malachi and Elizabeth were married in four months. Just over a year later, little Jeremiah was born. Our church was contented with this young preacher and fell madly in love with his spiritual helpmeet.

Momma always held a soft spot in her heart for Malachi. He was the one person on earth who helped my brother Napoleon with his stuttering problem. Once the Lord had won a great victory for Nap, Momma loved to tell the story of how Malachi helped Nap conquer his stuttering.

"Jessie, honey, my hernias are acting up something awful. Come and go with me. You can drive. That clutch puts too much strain on me," Momma said one morning.

"Where do you want me to drive you?"

"We have an important meeting with Malachi."

"What kind of mischief are you two cooking up now?" I teased her.

She nodded and gave me a slight grin. "I do believe it is something providential."

RANNY GRADY

"I'll just sit in the car and wait for you," I said when we arrived at the church.

"If something providential is going to happen, I want you to be there." She smiled, winked, and reached out to touch her hand to my chin.

Malachi had been our preacher for just a few months when he inquired about the speech problem Nap had.

"Mrs. Crandal, how long has your son stuttered?" he asked Momma once we were settled in our chairs in his office.

"He has had a problem with stuttering all his life. It didn't help when kids made fun of him in school."

"Have you had him tested?"

"I didn't know there was a test for something like that."

"When I was in graduate school, I ran into some research concerning stuttering. I guess it's safe to say that not many people know much about it. One thing seems certain: embarrassment and lack of acceptance by others harms any progress to overcome this speech problem."

"That may explain some of Nap's stuttering problems. His stuttering seems to get worse the more he finds himself in a potentially embarrassing situation," Momma said.

"I've been praying about this stuttering problem, and I think God has shown me how we can help Napoleon overcome, well, lessen his problem. Now, I don't want you to jump in and tell me this is a silly or wrongheaded idea until you've heard my reasons." Malachi prearranged his environment to influence.

"At least you've got some ideas." Momma sighed.

"I want to make Napoleon superintendent of our Sunday school program. That means he will be responsible for handling the duties and officiating our congregational service prior to dismissing to our individual classes each Sunday."

That's about the dumbest thing I've ever heard, I thought before Momma echoed my sentiments.

"That sounds like a surefire way to increase his stuttering problem," Momma said.

"At first blush, I must agree with you," he replied nervously. "Our fellow Christians are asked to pray for him, not just on

Sunday, but every day of the week. When we give him encouragement and acceptance, regardless of how he may struggle at first, I'm trusting God to deliver Napoleon from his speech problem." When he announced his divine plan, he was so convincing that Momma sat there and shed some tears.

This is the providential event Momma alluded to? My brother is going to crawl under a rock when he hears Malachi's brilliant idea they have cooked up, I thought.

"How can we convince him to even try?" Momma asked.

"Jesus said, 'Where two or three are gathered in my name, there am I also.' Therefore, I suggest we turn it over to the Lord," he said. "Perhaps I can ask Napoleon to come by my office, and you can arrange to be there. At that time we can ask him to take on this ministry for our church."

Oh great! What a plan! Nap will be submarined, and he will be only too happy to volunteer to publicly embarrass himself. Talk about a lamebrain idea that is sure to fail, I thought.

I wasn't privy to the meeting that took place with Nap, Momma, and Malachi; yet she did fill me in with all the details as soon as she returned from the meeting, after some arm-twisting on my part.

When Nap reluctantly agreed to come to Malachi's office to discuss a ministry he wanted him to accept, when he arrived for the meeting, he felt he had been ambushed because Momma was sitting in the preacher's office. "W-w-what's she d-d-doing here?" he stuttered. "Napoleon, I asked your momma to be here for this meeting because I wanted her moral support." Malachi motioned for him to take a seat. Nap looked at Momma with apprehension his eyes, and then he took a seat. "Napoleon, I noticed you have a speech problem." He looked him dead in the eye and said, "I think I may be able to help you greatly reduce the stuttering or possibly eliminate it altogether." He watched for Nap's reaction to his bold statement.

"I-I-I … d-d-doubt it-t-t," he was finally able to say, and he became flushed and agitated.

"When I was in graduate school, I did some research on the subject," Malachi calmly replied. "Do you know why people stutter?" he asked a rhetorical question. "I don't either." He smiled. "What I do know, though, is that public embarrassment makes it worse." He studied Nap to see how he would reply.

"That's c-c-crazy." He looked frightened and turned his gaze toward Momma.

Momma later told me, "Jessie, I saw him as my little boy. The look on his face made me cry inside. He needed me to rescue him, to kiss his boo-boo."

"If God could help you stop stuttering, would you do your part?" He looked into Nap's eyes, wanting to see some conviction of fire and courage. Even if it meant doing some very difficult things?"

Nap looked at the preacher and then at Momma. "Y-y-yes." He gave a teary, throaty reply.

Malachi looked over at Momma, and their eyes met, and they were filled with emotion.

"Good! I want you to become our church's superintendent of our Sunday school program."

Nap sat in silence for a few minutes. He looked at Momma with puzzlement in his eyes, his eyes watering up. "I c-c-can d-d-do all thing-g-gs through C-C-Christ who strengthens m-m-me," he struggled to say.

"I just wanted to cry a bucket of tears, honest to God, Jessie," Momma told me later. "Malachi and your brother weren't far behind."

Several times before the first Sunday Nap was scheduled to officially become our church's superintendent, he wanted to back out of his commitment. Each time, Momma prayed with him and encouraged him to trust God.

Come Sunday, when Nap marched up and stood behind the podium, we were all emotional basket cases. I'm sure our whole family was almost as nervous as Nap.

"T-t-trust G-G-God and d-d-do not-t-t l-l -ean on y-y-your own understanding-g-g," Nap said as he read a bit from God's Word. "P-P-Preacher has-s-s asked-d-d m-m-me t-t-to b-b-be the superintendant-t-t 'c-c-cause I-I-I speak-k-k so g-g-good," he said, and he looked up at us and smiled warmly. The congregation laughed with him.

"Miracles don't often happen in an instant. I think God wants his children to learn how to appreciate the full measure of his blessings," Momma said when Nap didn't seem to be able to overcome his speech problem right away.

Even though Nap's stuttering problem didn't seem to be better, we all noticed that he was more willing to get up before our congregation each Sunday.

"Have you noticed how many of the people sent a note of encouragement to Napoleon?" Momma asked each of us kids. "Some of them go out of their way to tell him he is doing a good job. One of these Sundays—look out—God is going to shock the world!" She beamed with pride.

"Our Lord rolled away the stone on Resurrection Day, and he gave us everything mankind needed," Momma often said.

The first Easter Sunday after Nap took on the ministry of being our church's superintendent of our Sunday school program, he was behind the podium, and he was preparing to read scripture. Even though he had a devil of a time reading scripture, he had chosen a passage from John's gospel, chapter twenty, verses one through ten. Perhaps it was a portent of a blessing, as Nap stood tall behind the pulpit, Bible in hand. The bright sun's rays glancing off the stained glass windows rising above the pulpit area sent a unique type of colored prism flashing across Nap's chiseled face, making it glow. Slowly he began to read.

"Eear-r-rly on the f-f-first d-d-day of the w-w-week, w-w-while it-t-t was st-st-still d-d-dark, M-m-mary of M-m-magdala went-t-t to the tomb and saw that the stone had been removed from the entrance," Nap read.

The sudden fluidity as he read scripture shocked him. He paused, and the congregation recognized what had just happened. Everyone looked around at each other; Momma was looking at each of us, tears flowing down her cheeks.

Emotions swamped Nap as he stood before us. Now it was as if he was almost afraid to continue reading the scripture because he thought it had been a fluke, a once-in-a-lifetime event. He struggled to clear his throat.

"So she—" Nap paused again. He tested his voice. He couldn't believe what he was hearing. Very slowly, he continued

RANNY GRADY

to read. "So she came running to Simon Peter and the other disciple, the one Jesus loved, and said, 'They have taken the Lord out of the tomb, and we don't know where they have put him!'"

It was easy to see that tears were causing Nap a little trouble as he struggled to continue to read. He brushed them away as best he could.

He read, "So Peter and the other disciple started for the tomb. Both were running, but the other disciple outran Peter and reached the tomb first. He bent over and looked in at the strips of linen lying there but did not go in. Then Simon Peter, who was behind him, arrived and went into the tomb. He saw the strips of cloth that had been around Jesus' head. The cloth was folded up by itself, separate from the linen. Finally, the other disciple, who had reached the tomb first, also went inside. He saw and believed."

Nap lifted up his head and looked directly at us. "Why look for the living among the dead? He is not here; he has risen." As Nap read his voice grew strong and his confidence surged. He shouted in a loud, clear, strong voice as he finished reading the passage from John's gospel. He stood there like a rock, beaming from ear to ear, and his hands shook as he gripped both sides of the podium.

"You can take your dinky miracles like parting of the Red Sea or David slaying Goliath," Momma said as her eyes filled up with tears anytime she told this story. "What God did for Napoleon that Sunday was beyond a miracle, just for me," she whispered.

There wasn't a dry eye in our church before Nap finished reading that passage from John's gospel. Malachi had a hard time preaching his sermon because his heart was as filled with joy as was our families' and Momma's.

God and Malachi helped Nap get a new lease on life. He didn't completely stop stuttering, but from that day forward, he never stuttered when he read the scriptures. He was able to manage his speech problem, and he became a successful businessman. More importantly, he became a godly man who was willing to do anything, even hard things, to please his Lord.

Independence Celebration

"Give beer to those who are perishing, wine to those who are in anguish; let them drink and forget their poverty and remember their misery no more" (Proverbs 31:6).

When the initial shock of the financial disaster known in our history as the Great Depression hit our nation, the resilient attitude of our Tampa community was one of guarded optimism. At the time, it was nearly impossible to discern how the financial misfortunes of people who lived in faraway places on the East Coast of our country could impact a farm town of less than three hundred people. In just a few fortnights, we all learned that it could.

Even in the midst of hard times, maybe even more so because of hard times, our traditional Fourth of July celebration was an event that the people of Tampa longed to celebrate. Our small community park, with its gazebo decked out in an array of decorations reflecting the colors of our nation's flag—red, white, and blue—was waiting to provide a platform for the band to entertain the crowds that would gather. They came to drink in all of the pomp and pageantry a Fourth of July celebration could possibly afford. For those special few hours, the celebration melted away some of the fear, frustrations, and anguish that resided, almost imperceptibly, beneath the surface in every family that was trying to scratch out a living in the midst of economic hard times in Tampa. Businesses proudly flew Old Glory. Barbershop quartets, including mostly men who wore some form of mustache, including the handlebar mustache, would sing favorite songs to entertain the crowds. They would compete for the trophy given to the best quartet. It was an important part of the evening's festivities before the blackness of the night was lit up in a bombastic shower of lights from the fireworks show, which always ended our celebration of Independence Day.

Several farmers would bring in horse-watering tanks and fill them with ice and sodas that they sold for a nickel. I measured the success of how wonderful the day's celebration had been by how successful I had been in finding a way to quench my parched palette by downing one or two of those sodas. On that special day, whenever I would walk by an iced-down tank, it was as if those cold sodas sent out a silent signal to me, saying, "Jessie Crandal, girl, where are you?" They haunted me until I felt that nearly too-cold liquid flowing languidly down my throat. I even worked on a ritual for drinking sodas, which I'm positive enhanced greatly my enjoyment of each soda. I would hold the bottle at the very end and stretch my neck by pulling my head back as far as possible. I wanted to make my throat elongated as much as possible. I would tip the soda bottle and lift it up so that I could control the amount of liquid allowed to enter my mouth. Thus, it would slowly drain down my throat and into my tummy. I soon discovered that the only problem with my ritual was if I allowed too much ice-cold liquid to drain down too fast, I got an awful pain in my forehead. I also discovered that when a body is dying of thirst, it is doubly hard to keep that from happening.

Angela would watch me drink a soda. She would laugh at me and say, "You look like a big old giraffe."

When I could get her to try my ritual, she usually spilled it on her dress.

On that special day, Angela and I arranged to meet early in the morning. We wanted enough time to map out our plan to devise a way for us to win a contest, maybe two. We would practice the two-legged sack race. I was faster than Angela, and I wanted to go faster than she did, so we worked on our coordination. It also helped toughen us up some because even the winners fell a few times.

I also practiced carrying an egg on a spoon. It was always one of the contests. Like Momma always said, "Don't put all your eggs in one basket," so I wanted to give myself more than one chance to drink one of those ice-cold sodas.

"I just don't have any spare nickels," Momma said when we asked her for money for that celebration day. "Well, wait," she teased. She called out our names. "Naomi, Howard, little Deannie, honey, why don't you run out in the backyard and see if our money tree has grown some nickels." She gave us a smirk, followed by her laughter, which we didn't appreciate.

I learned that when you're poor, it's better to laugh than to cry.

"But I hear that the city fathers are holding contests and that the winners win a nickel or two," she added slyly, and her eyes lit up to show us she was rooting us on. "Do you think the Crandals might win a race or two? I can see my Jessie crossing the finish line right now."

On the Fourth of July the men of our community started arriving at the park a little after midmorning. Homemade tables and various other types of presentation furniture were set up to hold all of the food that would be available to eat. Special places were prepared for the baked goods to be judged. Nearly every woman desired to have her specialty recipe awarded a blue ribbon for excellence. Momma had entered the pie contest several times but never won a blue ribbon.

By noontime the people began to arrive with their picnic food. Each one brought enough to feed their family and enough to share some with others. Since it was a really important civic celebration, most of the people dressed in their Sunday-go-to-meeting clothes or as if they were going to a fancy party. The ladies took extra pains to select bright and decorative-looking dresses. It wasn't unusual to see an array of colorful, pretty bows for dresses and hair, along with complementary jewelry. All of the eligible girls did their best to dazzle the would-be suitors. It wasn't unheard of to hear comments that compared this showing of our community's belles at our Independence Day celebration to that of the debutantes of the South. It wasn't a rule, yet it was an unwritten rule that the girl had to be sixteen to be eligible to "sport." I guess that meant old enough to flirt in public. At least my older sisters, Rose, Pauline, and Naomi, took it to mean that because they acted up and did their best to sport all day, even up into the time of the evening's fireworks display.

The men, not to be outdone by the women, wore coats and ties; many of them wore some type of bow tie. Many wore straw hats, which were round with a short wide brim and a flat top. They were much different than the hats they wore for everyday wear. It wasn't unusual to smell the big cigars or pipes that some chose to smoke during the day.

The celebration started slowly. Like a great symphony that plays beautiful music and highly entertains the audience and has the people on it feet, applauding and handing out "bravos" just before the great crescendo comes, it culminated in a great fireworks display that left us breathless and yearning for the next year's celebration. The people discovered that their greatest joy was in the excitement of the day and the special moments of fellowship that the atmosphere uniquely provided. With families gathered together, sitting and lying upon blankets on the grassy hillside that surrounded the park, all would "ooohhh and aaahhh" over the splendid beauty of the fireworks' lights bursting into an art form, like a shower of dazzling, celestial meteorites. Every time a new firework was shot into the air, squeals of delight and a thunderous appreciation for the experience could be heard.

As she often did, as our family were lying on our backs so we could maximize the beauty of the show, Momma said, "Children, take a moment and look past those bursting fireworks. Breathe in God's glorious nighttime show."

She never missed an opportunity to direct our attention to who really knew how to put on a nighttime show of lights. Often she would shush us and say, "Just look at that moon and those stars. Children, we're making memories, the kind you can tell your grandchildren about one day."

Since none of us were married, and most of us were way too young to identify with her wisdom, we would laugh at her respectfully.

"Mark my words, one day you'll see that your old momma was right."

That Fourth of July Momma had a surprise for our family when the Independence Day celebration ended. When all was said and done, I marked it as one of our red-letter days.

RANNY GRADY

My brother Howard accompanied our town bugler, who always ended our celebration by playing "Taps" as he stood upon the small hillside by our community park. Howard used the megaphone and told the Civil War story that inspired the playing of "Taps."

As the bugler softly blew the song on his bugle, Howard told the wonderful story.

"In 1862, Captain Robert Ellicombe of the Union Army was near Harrison's Landing in Virginia. After the day's fierce battle, he heard the moans of a soldier lying somewhere on the darkened battlefield. He went out and rescued him, not knowing whether he was a comrade in arms or a Confederate soldier. By the time he dragged him back to camp, he was dead. When he turned him over, he was shocked and heartbroken; it was his son. He had enlisted without telling his father. The captain requested that he be allowed to have a group of army band members play a funeral dirge for his son. His request was denied because his dead son was a Confederate. But he was allowed to have one musician. His son had been a student of music, and when his belongings were searched, his father found a crumpled up sheet of paper with words of a song written on it. Those words soon became the song 'Taps.'"

Chill bumps had long since given me a tingling feeling, and the lump in my throat made it hard for me to swallow. I kept reflecting how awful that would have been for that father.

Howard cleared his throat, and it was easy to tell that he was fighting becoming too emotional to finish the story he had practiced over and over to relate to all of us.

Day is gone. Gone the sun,

From the lakes, from the hills, from the sky.

All is well.

Safely rest.

God is nigh. Fading light

Dims the sight.

And a star, gems the sky.

Gleaming bright,

From afar.

Drawing nigh,

Fails the night.

Thanks and praise

For our days.

Neath the sun,

Neath the stars,

Neath the sky,

As we go.

This we know,

God is nigh.

Howard remained silent. The bugler once again played "Taps." He was a silhouette-like figure framed against the illuminating moon. He played the haunting music to bid adieu to all who came to celebrate and call our attention to why we celebrated Independence Day. To this very day, I can close my eyes and see that silhouetted bugler, and the familiar, haunting refrain of "Taps" stirs my soul and waters my eyes.

Though Angela and I had a plan, nothing worked. We didn't win one blasted contest or any nickels, but we did enjoy a cold soda. The man who worked the horse tank filled with bottles of liquid gold evidently felt sorry for us. Maybe he just grew tired of us hanging around, looking like waifs.

He said, "Pssst." He motioned for Angela and me to come closer. "My! Don't you young ladies have on such pretty dresses!" He was telling the truth when it came to Angela's dress. I figured he needed glasses because I was wearing another feed sack dress, compliments of Momma. "Since it is Fourth of July, I'm going to let you have two sodas for the price of one," he announced in a near whisper.

"Oh, sir, that is so kind of you," Angela replied. "But we don't even have a nickel between us," she added, using body language that indicated we felt like we were being deprived, even unfairly punished. I had never seen Angela demonstrate that she knew how to be a drama star publicly, like in the silent screen shows.

He looked down and gave us a wink and a nod. "If you promise not to tell a soul, I'll give you one on the house." He quickly pulled two sodas from the tank, opened them, and handed the sodas to us. He said, "Enjoy now. Go on, I need 'paying' customers." He laughed; we thanked him and giggled as we hurried out of sight. Angela and I enjoyed those sodas using my ritual. I seldom can ever remember enjoying something more.

The Entertainers

When a widowed woman with nearly a dozen kids under her roof is left to figure out a way to feed and clothe all of them, it takes a lot of scratching and picking every chance you get to find a way to earn a little money. One just happenstance came Momma's way soon after she had divested herself of the cobbler shop.

Howard had recently found a job with the *Tampa News,* and he had been enamored with the information he had become privy to concerning the movie projection machine. New advancements were being made every day. The silent movies were soon to be passé; talking movies were on the horizon. While doing a little research on this new technology, he spent time learning how the projection machine operated. He learned to operate it and, if need be, to fix most of the problems that could go wrong when it was in use.

"The mystical potion of happenstance is a mix of timing, being in the right place at the right time, and being wise enough to act upon the opportunity," was Momma's explanation of good fortune.

"One of life's great pleasures when a person walks with the Lord," Momma would often exclaim, "is that he opens a door to an opportunity when one is least expecting it to happen."

In more of her teaching moments, she told me, "In my humble opinion, most people live their lives in a state of depression because they didn't recognize that God had opened a door and they missed the opportunity to *carpe diem, carpe diem* (seize the day)."

I think she liked to throw around that Latin term to impress us.

My brother Howard received an unexpected opportunity to

better his life and our family's by just going to a movie. Momma was in the kitchen finishing up a few, last-minute details for the next day when Howard came home.

When he returned from the picture show, he was very excited. "Momma, you'll never guess in a million years what happened to me," he said as he rushed in the door. He just couldn't wait to tell Momma his good fortune.

"Lillian Gish sent you her autographed picture," she said. She couldn't pass up a chance to tease him about Miss Lillian Gish, the beautiful movie star who starred in the great movie *The Birth of a Nation.* She was Howard's favorite screen starlet.

Momma's offbeat answer caused him to stop, look at her, and put his hands on his hips.

"Will you get serious for a minute?" he nearly scolded her. "But what a great idea! I got a new job working at the movie theater!" he shouted with glee. "Yes, and it won't interfere with my newspaper job. They really like me."

"Whoa, slow down," Momma insisted. "Back up and tell me from the beginning."

"Okay, okay," Howard said. "Well, you know that Miss Gish—"

"Yes, we know that Miss Gish is your favorite actress," I said, interrupting him. I had emerged from my bedroom when I heard the door slam and the familiar voice of my brother. "And that you are madly in love with her—"

"That's not true and you know it! Can't a feller admire great talent without you trying to make it out to be something mushy?"

"So what's the racket?" I asked.

"Jessie, just sit down and be quiet. Your brother was just about to tell me how he got a new job at the movie theater," Momma said.

"I went to the movie and was ready to enjoy the show. The movie had just started, and there was a problem with the film projector. The theater manager turned up the house lights. After fifteen or twenty minutes passed, he announced that the movie had to be cancelled for the evening. There was a problem with the projection machine. This greatly disappointed the crowd, especially me. I inquired why. The theater manager motioned for me to come up on the stage.

"'We don't care to announce it publicly, but the projectionist fell ill and is unable to continue his work,' the man said as he leaned close to me. 'I'm embarrassed to say it, but he is the only one who knows how to operate the machine.'

"'If someone could operate the machine, would you still show the movie?'

"'Do you know of someone?'

"'Me,' I told him.

"'You! Where have you worked before?'

"I told him, 'I haven't, but I still know how to operate the machine.' I guess my voice and mannerism convinced him that I knew what I was talking about.

"'Hold on, everybody!' the manager yelled. 'We've decided that it isn't necessary to cancel the movie after all.'

"The large crowd stopped in their tracks and broke into a round of applause while moving back to take their seats.

"'Son, you'd better not just be whistling Dixie, you know what I mean?' he said as he showed me the way to the projection room.

"The projection machine was just like the one I had seen pictures of in the magazines I had researched. I don't mind telling you that I was sweating bullets each step I took to reach that projection room.' Howard laughed, and we joined him. 'Because the last thing I wanted was to come off looking like a big loud mouth who didn't know anything about running a projection machine.

"All I had to do was fix a small glitch and rethread the film, and it was up and running. Right after the show ended, the manager called me into his office and offered me a job. I told him I wouldn't feel right about taking another man's job," Howard said.

"Don't worry about that. You're a boy, not a man!" I said as I chimed in to rag him and get my needle in his hide.

"Despite rude and unwarranted interruptions from your children," he said as he addressed his remark directly to Momma.

"It's times like these that I really do believe that Poppa was right. 'We found her under a cabbage head,'" Momma said

"'He's not too reliable,' the manager said, and he used his hands and body to draw a physical picture that the man was too fond of alcohol. 'Glug, glug,' he said. 'You know what I mean?' he asked me. 'But since he was all that I had, I had to keep him.'

"I told him I would accept the job with two conditions: my newspaper job came first, and my family would be able to attend the movies free." A big grin spread across his face.

When I heard the good news, I couldn't contain myself. I ran and jumped on his lap.

"Free!" I yelled. "Brother, you did a good thing." I reached up to give him a hug.

He laughed. "Now, don't go getting crazy on me." He dumped me off his lap onto the floor.

"Son, I see something providential in all this," Momma said.

I looked at Momma, and I could tell her head was "full of busy bees," as she would say. She was deep in thought regarding Howard's new job.

A few days later, Momma was humming a hymn. It was a sure sign that she was in the midst of developing a plan. What that might be, I couldn't fathom a guess. Knowing Momma as I did, I knew it wouldn't be long before she "spilled the beans." It was a phrase she used when she was conducting an interrogation connected with her children. She looked for the good and begrudgingly accepted the bad. "Jessie, how'd you like to take a little trip with me to Hope?" she asked as she sprang the question on me. "I asked Charlie if he wanted to go with me, but he had more important things to do."

"What you're telling me is that I'm second choice," I teased her.

She looked at me and gave me that I-don't-need-a-smart-mouth-tagging-along look. I had learned that it wasn't best to rile Momma when she was on one of her quests. "I would love to go with you."

"Get your coat and hat; you can drive."

As much as Momma borrowed Nap's or Howard's cars, it's a wonder they could ever use them. Howard's car was a Chevrolet coupe with a rumble seat for storage. When I got to the car and was ready to get in, I looked inside the rumble seat area. To my surprise, it was loaded down with all types of canned goods: beans, corn, Momma's dill pickles, two cherry pies that were still warm, plus some fried chicken.

"Wow, are we going to eat good today!" I said.

Momma was bringing up the rear. "You aren't going to be eating any of that." She corrected my thinking.

"If we aren't, who is?"

Momma climbed in on the passenger side and shut the door. She motioned for me to get going.

"Ingénue I'm not, but ingenuity I've got," she said as I put the Chevy in gear and drove. "Put the pedal to the metal, girl. I want to pay a visit to that junk dealer just outside the town of Hope."

By this time, I was beginning to think, *Momma is losing it.* "Are we going there to look for anything in particular?" I asked.

"Nothing in particular. Just thought we might mosey around. You never know when you might find something you need real cheap."

She's got something in mind, I thought.

Joe the junk dealer wasn't your ordinary, run-of-the-mill dealer. Ordinarily, one might expect to find a junk dealer kind of slovenly dressed and the place a dirty mess. Joe's place was the exact opposite. He wore tailor-made overalls, which had shiny brass buttons, a starched, white shirt, short sleeves, and a bright red polka dot bow tie. His work shoes were spit shined. A handlebar mustache framed his nearly bald head. He had sky blue eyes and a smile that seemed to light up any room he was in.

When we entered the premises, we heard, "Howdy, what can I do for you pretty ladies?" A man walked over to us. "In a few seconds, he was face-to-face with us. "Lou? Lou Crandal, is that you?"

"In the flesh," Momma said as she laughed.

"It has been a quite a spell since the last time you were in my place." He scratched his head with his left hand. "It must have been just before Ranti up and moved away. Mighty sorry to hear about his passing." He offered Momma his condolences.

Momma turned to me. "Jessie, I want you to meet a dear friend of your poppa's and mine, Mr. Joseph Carter."

"Everyone calls me Joe the junk dealer." He smiled at me.

"Jessie will address you as Mr. Carter," Momma said, making sure Joe knew she didn't believe the good Lord wanted children to treat any adult as some type of an equal. "R.H.I.P." ("Rank has its privileges") was a frequent phrase Momma taught in our home. She drilled us kids about the importance of treating all adults with proper respect.

"And just why did you come to pay me a visit?" Mr. Carter asked.

"You're not going to believe this, but I'm looking for a used popcorn machine." Momma let me know the real purpose of our trip.

Joe rubbed his chin with the fingers of his right hand. "Don't rightly recall what something like that even looks like. Are you sure they even make such a contraption?"

"I saw one advertised in a magazine recently, so I know they aren't a figment of my imagination. You know, every county fair, dog-and-pony show has one."

Joe turned away and walked to the back of his building. He took a few steps, stopped, turned back, and motioned for Momma and me to follow him. We wound around a lot of junk, and then we entered into a much smaller room. He pointed to a rusted piece of junk on large wheels.

"Is this what you are looking for?" he asked with a wily look on his face.

"Right, there it is! Now, how in the world do you suppose that of all the junk dealers in Kansas, I'd find just what I need in Hope, Kansas?" She gave him a mischievous wink. She smiled at him, and she bent down to inspect the merchandise.

Joe helped her pull the machine upright onto its wheels.

"Can't rightly say much for the rest of her, but the wheels are in good shape." He snorted and laughed at that pitiful-looking piece of junk.

"This is a joke, right?" *She has lost her mind*, I thought.

"I see that one glass pane is broken, but I can get that replaced with no trouble." Momma was basically talking to herself. She was ruminating about how she was going to fix up the popcorn machine so it could be used again. "Isn't it a beauty, Jess?"

"Momma, you've taught me never to talk disrespectfully to my elders, but I have to tell you, not meaning any disrespect, I think you have gone plumb loco."

"Oh, Jessie, my darling girl, you've got to have vision! If I could have one blessed gift for you, it would be that you have 'possibility vision,'" she said as if she were afraid that I would miss that blessing.

"Joe, tell this girl how much she needs 'possibility vision,'" she implored him.

"Lou, I reckon the good Lord has given you this type of blessing. Frankly, it evidently missed me and Jessie." He smiled and winked at me as we all had a good laugh.

"A ball-ping hammer can knock out a few of those dings, and some bright red lead paint will make her look about brand new." She did her best to convince us that her pet project would turn out great. "You two dullards who haven't any imagination, I challenge you, close your eyes and think about that fresh, hot, buttered popcorn just waiting to let loose your taste buds; that warm, buttery corn, just about melting in your mouth, and its crunchy sensation. Why, I just smell a movie show." She laughed.

"Lou, I think you missed your calling," Joe said as he teased

Momma. "You should have been a star in one of those silent movies I keep hearing people talk about."

"You have never seen a movie?" I asked him. I was dumbfounded to meet someone who was that backwards about the world we lived in.

"Not yet," Mr. Carter said.

"How much for the heap of junk?" Momma asked.

"Now that you want to buy it, suddenly it's a piece of junk?" He toyed with Momma.

Joe stood looking at Momma, and he pulled out a small scratch pad and used his yellow pencil to do some calculating. "Three dollars and you can take it home."

Momma threw up her hands as if she were being robbed. "Jessie James rode a horse when he robbed a bank." She reacted with a mock sense of outrage in her voice.

Joe laughed a little. "You're not the first person who has accused me of that."

"Now, Joe, you know that I don't have three dollars to give you. I'm just a poor old widow with so many kids I'd give Old Mother Hubbard a run for her money. So could you see your way clear to do a little bartering with me?" She gave him her sweetest smile.

He looked at me. "Why do I think I ever have the upper hand when it comes to dickering with a woman?" He sighed.

I laughed with him. "If it's a bartering contest with my momma, you don't have a chance," I assured him.

He shrugged his shoulders. "What have you got to bargain with?" He motioned for Momma to lead the way to what she had to offer him.

Momma and I led him to the Chevy's rumble seat.

"Jessie, climb up in there and hand me down just what the doctor ordered," Momma said. I took out all the canned goods, and Momma placed them on the ground in front of Joe.

"Lou, I've got to tell you, from what I've seen so far, you don't have much to bargain with."

"Jess, honey, hand me down those pies."

Momma had taken them right out of the oven, and even

though a lot of time had passed since we left home, the pies were still a mite warm. When she placed one of the cherry pies in his hands, his eyes lit up like a kid's in a candy shop. The smell of the baked piecrust, light and golden, and the intoxicating aroma from the cherries made his mouth water.

"Now you're talking! Finally getting round to something that can stick to a man's ribs," Joe said.

"And when I get this machine all dolled up and filled with hot popcorn outside the theater, you'll be my guest at the picture show." She grinned and laughed because she knew she had closed the deal.

"It will be worth it just to see you hawking your popcorn," Joe said, and he gave out a belly laugh when he saw Momma acting like she was pushing the machine.

I'm not saying that I have ever possessed "possibility vision" like Momma's, but I can say that ever since that day at the junk dealer's business, I have been willing to look for the pixie dust more often when it comes to making allowances for making a silk purse out of a sow's ear, as Momma might call it.

Momma hummed many a gospel song those twelve miles home. I rarely talked because I could tell her thinking cap was in overdrive, and she really didn't want to be disturbed.

It took her about a week before she started to implement her restoration plan. She enlisted the aid of Earl, and she gained the allegiance of Howard when she told him what her plan was. When Momma explained to Charlie that his job was going require him to use his cheer megaphone, he became nearly obnoxious and antsy until he could fulfill his new job description in Momma's business venture.

"Don't you worry," Charlie said to Momma. "I'll knock them dead," he bragged. "We'll fill up that auditorium so it will need more chairs."

"Let's not knock 'em dead," she teased as she did her best to punch a tiny pinhole in his too-fat head. "We need them to eat our popcorn." She cut him with her dry sense of humor.

"We'll call ourselves the Entertainers," Charlie said in a voice demonstrating that he hadn't paid any attention to what

Momma had said. He took his hands and framed them in such a way that one would guess he was putting up some sort of movie marquee.

Momma couldn't help herself. "That boy is daft." She laughed as she threw up her hands.

With Earl's help, she soon had her popcorn machine looking nearly new.

"The red paint covers a multitude of sins." She showed off her refurbished project to our family, who didn't share her enthusiasm for the popcorn machine becoming a hit with moviegoers.

Momma had ordered some propane for her Bunsen burner, and Mr. Tetson sold her large candy sacks to use for the popcorn she would sell.

"Tomorrow, I'm going to pay a business call on ole Doc Jones." She announced her plans to find a way to get the theater's owner to allow her to set up a popcorn business outside his auditorium.

After supper the next day, when the family was in the throes of settling down for the night, Momma called us into the main room because she had something interesting to tell us.

With her hands thrust up under her two armpits, she put an impish smile on her face and looked around the room at each of her children.

"You are looking at the new 'Popcorn Queen' of Doctor Jones's movie theater," she gleefully bragged.

"He let you have the concession?" Howard asked. "Did you sign an agreement?" I asked.

"Well, nothing has been finalized," Momma confessed. "But he agreed to let me set up my popcorn machine; he especially liked my idea of having Charlie use his megaphone to announce the movie that was playing, the time it is starting, and how long it will be running. When he sees how that popcorn is going to please his patrons,"—her eyes opened very wide and she started to giggle—"he will agree to whatever terms I choose," she said with a sense of cocksureness.

"So you are risking all for another chance at some hare-brained idea?" Rose asked as she found a way to stick the needle in Momma's celebration.

"At least I haven't risked my entire future for forbidden fruit," Momma retorted in a sarcastic manner. "Young lady," Momma directed her comment to Rose, "Why don't you come to the theater tomorrow night, before the movie begins, and judge for yourself. The Lord has already given me his blessing. Charlie and I will be like seasoned pros at the carnival, hawking our popcorn and promoting the picture show." Thus, Momma challenged Rose to "put up or shut up." The rest of the family broke out in a loud applause.

I'm not sure how my momma knew that people just couldn't seem to enjoy a movie unless they were munching on hot, buttered popcorn, but whether she did or didn't know was really immaterial. It is a fact that those two things go together, like a horse and carriage. Momma's grand business venture was a smash hit.

Most of our family chose to be close by the action but remained as discreet as possible. When Doc arrived at his theater that night, there was a line about ten people deep waiting to buy popcorn before they bought a ticket to see the movie. He chose to step into the back of the line as unobtrusively as he could. By the time he was first in line, there were another eight or ten people waiting to buy Momma's popcorn.

"I'll have the largest bag you sell," Doc said.

Momma was so busy filling the bags of popcorn and taking nickels, she did not notice that Doctor Jones was suddenly in front of her.

"I only sell one size," she said, and then she looked up and saw who it was. She stood as straight as she could, wiped her brow with her apron, and smiled at him nervously.

About that time Charlie walked by her and the doctor.

"Hurry, hurry," he yelled through his megaphone. "Just ten minutes to show time," he announced. "Tickets are just a dime! Don't miss James Cagney starring in the movie *Public Enemy Number One*."

"How many bags do you want for the movie?" she coyly asked him.

. His eyes danced with joy.

"I'll never underestimate Lou Crandal again." He puckered his lips and let out a whistle of admiration for her promised prediction of how much his movie patrons would love her popcorn.

He turned and pointed in the direction of Charlie, who was busy charming the people in front of the theater. When the time drew nigh for the movie to start, in less than five minutes, he increased the intensity of his announcements.

"Nice touch," Doc said as he gave his tacit approval of the business being conducted in front of his theater. "Come by tomorrow, late afternoon, and we can draw up a contract."

Momma stuck out her hand. "All I need is a handshake. If you went back on our agreement, I couldn't work with you anyway."

He quickly reached out and shook her hand.

The next morning, before Momma left the house, she handed me the penny postcard she was ready to send to Joe the junk dealer.

Dear Joe,

I sure hope you didn't get too fat eating those pies! When you can get away from your shop, the Lou Crandal family would like to invite you to pay us a visit. We will have a ticket to the movie and a large bag of buttery popcorn ready for you. Thanks for all your help.

Your friend,

Lou

Momma sold her popcorn outside the theater; Charlie announced the movie and helped to hustle tickets and popcorn; and Howard was the projectionist for a number of years. In a short time, Momma was well known in our town as "Tampa's Popcorn Lady," even by the children.

The Kansas Flyer

My momma once remarked, "Your poppa was a man that had ants in his pants (she was referring to his inability to settle down in one place); your brother Charlie was a mite tetched in the head, as if he had been struck dumb with a Blarney Stone. Charlie could make angels weep and drunks reform when he turned on his charismatic charms; your brother Howard was born with fire in his belly."

Howard's future fame came from his desire to avoid a physical confrontation with some bullies in town.

In early spring of Howard's eighth grade of school, when we still lived in Humansville, Missouri, Momma and I were in the kitchen. She was busy making dough so she could let it rise and bake it later. I was perched upon a corner of the kitchen counter, munching on an oatmeal cookie.

"Momma," I started to ask her a question, "do you—" Howard burst into the room. He was sweaty and out of breath. It was unusual for my brother to allow other people to see him in an unkempt condition; he was so fastidious.

"Hurry! I need a cold drink."

"Well, what in the world?" Momma quickly moved to get him the dipper we used to get a cool drink from a bucket we kept in the kitchen. She filled the dipper with water and carefully handed it to him.

He hurriedly grabbed it and gulped it down. He handed the empty dipper to her and motioned that he wanted more water to drink. He took his time drinking the second batch of water. His breathing settled down, and he drew up a chair from the kitchen table and sat down. Momma drew out some of the water and poured it on a kitchen rag. She walked over to him and placed it upon his forehead.

"There, this ought to soothe the heat coming out of your body," she said, applying her mothering to my brother. "Where have you been? Something has got you all tuckered out."

Howard took the wet rag from Momma's hand and rubbed the rest of the sweat off his face.

"Give me a minute, and I will tell you."

"Did you rob a bank or something?" I teased him. "Are you in training to fight John L. Sullivan?"

Howard motioned for Momma and me to sit down with him at the kitchen table.

"I was hurrying to get the errand done you sent me on when suddenly I was facing three bullies who were much older than me," he started to tell us his story. "I tried to ignore them and just ease on by, but they wouldn't let me. The three of them surrounded me and began to mess with me. I was very frightened, and I kept telling myself that I had to do my best to show no fear, though I was quaking in my boots." He smiled.

"'Well, who do we have here?' the biggest one said. 'Oh yeah, he's one of those new kids, isn't he?' He talked so sarcastically.

"'Have you paid your initiation fee?' the smallest of the three asked, and he let out a loud laugh; the other two joined in.

"'He's a little pissant, ain't he,' the middle-sized one said. 'Looks like a four-eyed bookworm to me.' They laughed at me.

"'Look, guys,' I said, 'I don't want any trouble. I'm just trying to finish an errand for my mother.' I tried to reason with them.

"'He has to finish a little bitty errand for his 'precious' mommy. Did you hear that?' the largest one said.

"'Let's turn him upside down and take his pants off and see if he has any money,' the smallest of the three suggested.

"The middle one of them turned to the other two. 'Sounds good to me.' He looked at me with an evil grin. 'How's it sound to you, hayseed?'

"Momma, a fury just built up in me, and I struck like lightning. I kicked the middle one in his privates and threw my shoulder into the one on the right, which knocked him down. Then I hightailed it for home. Promising unimaginable pain and suffering, my attackers chased me. Though they were much older and stronger, they couldn't muster the speed or energy to catch me. They tracked me for over three miles; they finally gave out and gave up."

Howard had a strange look on his face, which indicated he was surprised, yet proud of what he had done.

"Momma," he said, "I'm fast, and I'm a strong runner."

Momma looked quizzically at Howard.

"So, you are fast?" She paused and smiled at him. She reached over and patted his knee. "You as fast as a locomotive? Fast as a horse? Fast as—"

"I ... I don't know, but faster than most high school kids," Howard interrupted Momma.

"And just how did you discover this little gem?" she asked.

"That's why I'm out of breath. Those bullies tried to rough me up, and I made an escape and they chased me. I outran them. I never grew weary running."

"Maybe they were all slow as turtles." I attempted to tease him.

"You don't know anything!" Howard said in an indignant tone. "That one boy wins most of the races during lunchtime." He glared at me, and for the first time in my life, my brother's temperament frightened me a little. "I've decided that next year, when I enter high school, I'm going to run the mile for the track team."

I put my hands together and pretended to have a megaphone.

"Now hear this, now hear this, my brother Howard Crandal is going to be Humansville High's next track star," I said, trying to mess with his mind.

He stood up suddenly and shot me a menacing stare before breaking into a wide grin.

"That's right, smarty pants. I'm going to break the record for the mile run before I'm through running for our school's track team," he announced. "In fact, I'm going out to run some more." He turned and looked at us and said, "Got to start training."

"Don't walk, run!" I hollered. "If you run, someday people will call you the Missouri Flyer." I mocked him. I returned to the kitchen where Momma was once again busy preparing the bread.

"Don't push too hard," Momma advised me. "That boy is going to surprise you." Her voice trailed off. "The Ozark Flyer," she softly mumbled. "Now doesn't that just sound grand? I just wish I could find a way to make sure that the fire in his belly gets stoked."

The very next day, Momma arose extra early. She fixed herself up and put on an attractive-looking dress, but it wasn't Sunday.

"Where are you going all gussied up?" I asked.

"I'm going to visit the editor of the *Humansville Reporter* newspaper," she whispered. "I'm going to see if he can help me to get Howard's belly on fire."

"Belly on fire? Oh, I get it," I said.

"He may have some connections, you know. He may know someone who can give us some tips about how a boy can become a runner." She gave me a small wink. "'Commit unto the Lord all that you do, and he will see that it prospers,'" Momma quoted from Proverbs 16:3 again.

After I returned from school that day and the supper dishes were put away, our large brood had pretty well settled down for the evening. Momma was busy writing at the table, pen in hand, seemingly deep in thought, preparing to write a letter.

I tiptoed out of our bedroom and approached her.

"What are you doing?" I asked.

"Jessie, honey, I'm writing to a very important man up in Topeka." She paused and smiled at me. She turned her face sideways just a bit to invite my good night kiss.

"Why?" I inquired.

"He is the editor of the *Topeka Journal* newspaper. I think he might be able to provide me with some useful information." She put her hand up by her face, and in a whisper, she said, "He could possibly help me find a book that Howard could read to help him become a great mile runner." Her eyes beamed with a glow of excitement. She put her finger to her mouth and made the hush sign. "If I can provide Howard with some knowledge

RANNY GRADY

about how he can reach his goal, who knows, he may start his training right away. Your poppa said, on more than one occasion, 'Talk is cheap, but it takes money to buy whiskey.'" She allowed herself a little laugh. "Time will soon tell if your brother is serious or just a big bag of wind."

I recall remembering my last, fleeting thought as I dozed off to sleep that night. *Sure hope Howard's fire in the belly burns as hot as Momma's.*

True to his word, Howard arose extra early each day to commence his training.

"Now, son, start out easy. You're not running a marathon." Momma did her best to offer her motherly advice, which Howard didn't want.

"He seems to be nothing but skin and bones now. Why does he want to do something that'll make him look like a war refugee?" Pauline offered her assessment of her brother's rigid training program.

"Because it's something he wants," Momma replied in a very challenging tone of voice. "Haven't you ever wanted something so badly you ached for it?"

"Yeah, to have my own bedroom," Pauline replied dryly. This broke the building tension in the room, and we all laughed.

I have to admit that it was a mite difficult watching my own flesh and blood endure immense pain, knowing that it was chosen rather than inflicted. Howard would come home dragging and suffering searing pain in his right side and often smelling like puke because he had forced his body to go past the limit of endurance. He had become nauseated and had forced his stomach to regurgitate. His legs would suddenly cramp up when he was sitting down or, worse, while he was sleeping at night. They often left large, unsightly bulges on the edges of his muscles, which required him to rub down the muscles in order for him to walk.

Momma used some brown paper, which she got from the mercantile, and made a sign that she placed over his bedroom doorway: "You don't have to be great to start, you just have to start to be great," it said.

One day after school, Howard and I came home to find Momma waiting at the front door.

"Howard, something wonderful has happened," she said with a twinkle in her eyes, and she gave us both a hug.

"What is it?" he asked.

Momma handed him a package and told him to open it. "I've already read the letter in it."

Howard gave Momma a puzzled look.

"Is it from the editor?" I asked.

"I'm not going to ruin the surprise." Momma's eyes danced with glee.

Howard took the book out of the package. "Look, Momma, a book on how to train for track!" He showed her the book.

"Open up the book," she said.

Howard opened the book and saw the letter. He unfolded it, and he looked up at Momma.

"What's the letter say?" I asked.

Momma motioned for him to read it.

Dear Mrs. Crandal,

It was a joy to receive your letter, and no, I'm not so busy that I can't find the time to help out a fellow Kansan, even if you are living in Missouri.

Your son is a lucky boy to have a mother who is so interested in helping him achieve an admirable goal, to set a record in the mile run for his high school. I am sending Howard a book that many runners have benefited from. Mr. Alonzo Stagg is recognized as one of America's finest coaches.

If you can find the time and have the opportunity to do a little traveling, I can recommend a short field trip, which may be very worthwhile. As I am writing this letter, an amazing event is unfolding. Over twenty-five hundred runners are running a transcontinental race! They are in the midst of running from California to Chicago. The winner gets the prize of twenty-five thousand dollars! A couple of promoters, Cyrus Avery of Tulsa, Oklahoma, and John Woodruff of Springfield, Missouri,

RANNY GRADY

are the brains behind this race. The local, state, and federal politicians and other government officials are backing this race. All are interested in having the interstate race run so that it will garner some publicity. In the near future, they want that route to become an interstate road for transportation of goods and people.

According to the route and the timetable the runners are keeping, they should be arriving in Springfield in about seven days.

Perhaps if Howard were to witness these runners running that great distance in order to possibly earn fame and fortune, they might inspire him to do great things. Who knows, he might one day be an Olympian.

"Can I go, Momma?" Howard asked as his eyes nearly bugged out of his head with excitement.

Momma looked at him, and she didn't say a word for a few seconds. "Springfield is the largest city in Southwestern Missouri; perhaps it will be an educational trip."

"I couldn't sleep a wink last night. I was just too excited about our trip," Howard said. It didn't take long before he was asleep.

"That boy can sleep anywhere," Momma said as she looked back and saw that he had fallen asleep. She looked at me. "If I should have a short catnap, you're not going to fall asleep and get us all killed, are you?"

"I'm wide awake," I said.

The entire city of Springfield was decked out in a festive manner. Huge banners were strung across the street where the runners were to pass by. The main street, Route 66, was crowded with people. Vendors were busy selling all types of food and just about anything else they thought someone might possibly buy. Flyers and souvenirs were available for a price. The sides of the streets were lined up with automobiles; some were fancy, and some even had chauffeurs standing by them to await their owners' beck and call.

It was the most incredible atmosphere I had ever been in. It was like the Fourth of July and Christmas all rolled into one big celebration. Women were in fancy, fashionable dresses, and dapperly dressed gentlemen escorted them as they walked along the street. They went in and out of the stores that lined Route 66, shopping and spending money like it was going out of style.

"Momma, Momma, I just heard that the runners are going to stop in Springfield for the night," Howard said.

"Well, it will be a fitting place for them to stay. As soon as we see them run, we must get home," Momma said.

"Oh, Momma, can't we stay overnight?" I pleaded.

"Poppa barely allowed us to come, and you want to stay overnight?"

About midafternoon, the excitement level started to rise. Word started to spread that the runners were approaching Springfield. Route 66 had been too crowded with cars, so we had to find parking in another locale. Momma treated us to a hamburger and a Coke. We spent the time looking at all of the marvelous things those stores were selling. Since we were already spending a fortune on the trip, as Momma saw it, all we could do was look.

Shortly after the buzz spread about the runners approaching the city, people started honking their car horns. The band, who wore fancy red, white, and blue, the color of our nation's flag, began to play.

When several hundred runners, not the several thousand who started running in California, approached the city, it sounded like a cattle stampede. A cloud of dust from their running shoes filtered into the air, and the wind carried it up and ahead of them.

"Look, Momma!" I shouted. "I can see the dust coming from all their feet."

In a couple of minutes, we could see what we came for: a large group of very tanned men, who also looked haggard and filled with all manner of hard-edged toughness, came running at a slow pace into and through the city of Springfield. When

RANNY GRADY

they had finished running through the city, they stopped. Even though it was early, they were finished for the day.

While the runners were pacing themselves as they ran through the city, several times I heard people call out, "There's that Banks boy, the one from Oklahoma."

"Those are some fine warrior runners," Momma said, "but my, they do look tired."

"If you had run nearly two thousand miles, you'd be tuckered out too," Howard said. "It's amazing! Just think, twenty-five thousand dollars goes to the winner!"

"Aren't you lucky," Momma said as she looked at Howard. "You only have to run a mile." She punched him in the ribs and smiled at him. "Well, kids, the show is over, and we had better be heading back."

"Oh, Momma, can't we at least wait until we can see the runners interviewed by the reporters and watch them have their pictures taken?" Howard pleaded.

Before Momma could say no, I was off and running to where the runners and reporters were standing. Some of the runners had gathered and were being interviewed while photographers were taking pictures.

I had an important errand to do. Tucked tightly in my hand was the book Howard had received in the mail. He had brought it along to read while we were traveling. I had taken it from the car after we returned from eating our lunch. I wanted to see if I could get an autograph from one of the runners. Momma said that Howard needed motivation to keep the fire in his belly; I figured that might help.

A crowd had gathered, more in a circle, around some of the runners. A light banter was taking place between the runners and the newspapermen. I knew Momma was going to be mighty unhappy with me. I needed to get my task done quickly. I scrunched down and slowly edged my way inside the group. I was suddenly face-to-face with the runners. I was the only girl in the crowd; I guess I stuck out like a sore thumb.

"Get that girl out of here," I heard a man say.

It scared me, and I felt the need to run.

"What's your name, pretty girl?" a smooth baritone voice asked.

I looked up, and I was staring into the eyes of a very handsome young man. He had rather long black hair that he swept back with his hand. His large dark eyes stood out. When he looked at me, I felt like he was peering into my soul. His high cheekbones framed his rugged face. His nose, like most Indians, was long and pointed. He smiled at me, and his dark tan accentuated his very white, straight teeth. His smile could melt hearts.

"I … uh … I'm Jessie Crandal." I blushed.

He noticed I had a book in my hand. "What's the book for?"

"It's for my brother." I looked into his eyes, then I quickly averted mine. "I mean, I want to get an autograph for his book from a runner," I added nervously.

He reached out his hand and motioned for me to give it to him. I quickly handed it to him.

"Mr. Stagg's book. I know it well." He smiled at me. "What is your brother's name?"

"Howard, and he's going to be a great runner someday, just like you," I bragged. "He's going to break his school's running record for the mile."

He gave me a look of approval. "Do any of you guys have a pen?" Someone handed him a pen, and he quickly wrote in the front of the book. Then he doodled something and handed it back to me. "Tell him for me that I hope he becomes a great runner." As I left, I looked back, and he gave me a little wave and a beautiful smile.

"Jessie, you'd better get going," Howard said. He had come to retrieve me because he had seen me take off across the street. "Momma's going to skin you alive."

I quickly tucked Howard's book under my arm, and I hoped he never noticed that I had it. I guess he was too distracted with all that was happening to notice. I was thankful.

Momma was going on and on about the sights we had seen in the big city of Springfield as I was driving. I had managed to tuck the book under the driver's seat without anyone seeing it. Once we were on the road home, I retrieved the book and handed it to Howard.

"I wondered where my book went. Did you have it?" he asked.

"Open it," I said.

"Oh, Jessie, how did you manage that?" He grinned.

Momma's curiosity piqued, and she turned and looked at Howard holding his book.

"What did you do?" She looked at me while I was driving.

Howard pushed his book up so Momma could see it.

"Look what it says!"

"To Howard, a fellow runner. Hope you break your school record. Banks, The Claremore, Okla., Runner."

"Look! Look! At the doodle," Howard said.

The runner, Banks, had drawn an Indian headdress with a couple of feathers.

"Jessie, that was so sweet of you." Momma let out a sigh. "You do beat all sometimes." She reached over and patted my knee.

Howard reached up and put his arms around my neck from the backseat. "Thanks, sis," he whispered.

"Momma said you needed motivation!" We all laughed, and I grinned from ear to ear.

After Momma gave the book to Howard, he devoured every word of it. He committed to memory most of the instructions. Then he drew up a plan written on his Big Chief tablet that detailed how he was going to transform himself from a novice into his high school's record holder for the mile run. He made several signs: 4:31.3, which indicated the time he had to run the mile in, in order to break Humansville High School's record. He put them up in the bedroom he shared with my brothers. Momma allowed him to put one up in the kitchen above the pantry door.

Howard put up with a lot of ribbing from his family, but not from Momma. Except for Momma, none of us kids really thought that our brother would ever become a track star.

Howard's quest to become a champion runner started in Humansville, Missouri, thanks to Momma's little nudge to think big; however, its real fruit would come to harvest after we moved back to Tampa.

It didn't happen the next year, but Howard did make the track team as a freshman. By the end of his sophomore year, his athletic ability had become so apparent that the basketball coach convinced him that he could be the starting guard. By the end of his sophomore year, Howard was the school's leading scorer. He won his varsity letter and was one of the big men on campus, so to speak. He was very good at basketball; it was his avocation; track was his passion. By the time his junior year rolled round, he had run a mile just five seconds slower than the record for Tampa High School. He had the honor of being named one Kansas's up-and-coming track stars by the *Topeka Journal.*

When he wasn't working at the newspaper, Howard's varsity coach spent time helping him hone and train during the summer.

Howard's junior year was a time of great joy because our basketball team had a winning record for the first time in a decade. The townsfolk attributed the team's great record directly to Howard's basketball leadership and scoring ability.

Our nation was still in chaos financially because the Depression was lingering, and there didn't seem to be any end in sight.

Though gloom and doom were daily headlines on the front pages of our newspapers and the airwaves of our radios, nothing dimmed the bright light of anticipation one could find in our household regarding Howard's junior-year track season.

Ever since Momma had written that letter to the editor of the Topeka *Journal* in Topeka, imploring him to provide assistance to her son and his big track dream, he had taken a fancy to her.

"He said that I had a way with words," Momma told me when I quizzed her about the periodic letters she received from that editor. "Maybe I can be a stringer."

"A stringer? What in the world is a stringer?" I asked.

That amused Momma, stirring up a chuckle inside her. "It is someone who writes different types of interesting tidbits that other papers will pay the author a pittance to publish in their newspapers."

"With all the corny stuff you are always saying—well, I have to admit, some it is funny. I can see that you could write for a newspaper."

"Dear child, you are too kind," she replied, making sure I didn't miss the poignant point of her dismissive comment.

Momma cut out the story from the *Tampa News*. It had run a feature on the Tampa track team, spotlighting Howard and the team's pending season. Howard's picture graced the front page of the sports section, and it extolled the story of how he had set a goal when he was a freshman of breaking the school's record in the mile. It detailed how close he had come to breaking that record last year. He was almost certain to set a new record before the track season was finished.

"Maybe the *Journal* will do a story on your brother," Momma said as she finished slipping the newspaper clippings in the envelope. "Keep an eye out for my boy. He just may break the record at Emporia." She wrote on the outside of the envelope, stating the fact that the state track meet was being held at the Emporia State Teachers' College track stadium that year.

"When it rains, it pours," Momma lamented as Howard's track season got off to less than a rousing start. In late February he developed a deep chest cold, which worried Momma because she was concerned it would turn into pneumonia; thankfully it didn't. This pushed back his training until he could regain his strength and stamina. During his first meet, he ran slower than he did the previous year.

"There isn't any need for panic," Howard stated. "The season is young, and my inner self is at peace." He did his best to assure all of us that his goal was still reachable. "You'll see; the next meet is my time to shine." He quickly stepped out of the room where the family had gathered after supper.

At the meet with Lost Springs, we really got our dandruff up from the snide, often crude remarks from the enemy's camp. Every nasty comment was designed to shake Howard's confidence and the team's morale.

"'Kansas Flyer' is more like a turkey than an eagle," the Lost Springs student body cheered and laughed, mocking his racing ability. Howard remained silent, but he spent some solitary moments staring intently at them. It seemed as if the heat of his anger caused smoke to come out of his eyes.

"Look, Momma, his stance just says 'fire in the belly,'" I said, pointing my finger at him and pulling at Momma's coat sleeve to get her attention.

"Ohh, are they in trouble today!" Momma gushed. "Fire in the belly. I sure do like this. Yes, sir, it does a heart proud to see it."

Soon after the starter's gun went off, Howard started in an easy gait and settled into a comfortable pace. Halfway through the race, it was apparent that only a couple of runners would challenge him. Even though he hadn't been pushed, he missed breaking the school record by just one second, amidst a lot of congratulations and tomfoolery. "Unless the wind blows fiercely, that record is mine at Durham," he said, naming the place where he was going to set a new record for the mile run for our high school.

The track meet was contested in the midst of a gale-force wind and a mix of sleet and rain.

"Man plans and God determines," Momma said in a tone of voice that showed we had resigned ourselves to accept that Howard wouldn't be breaking the mile record at the meet in Durham. The day was miserable. The only bright spot was that our team managed to win the meet and qualify for a place in the state track meet. It was the first time Tampa had ever qualified for that big event.

"God is in his universe, and all is right with the world," Momma rejoiced, for the weather was warm and sunny for the trip to Emporia for the state track meet. As fortune would have it, Nap was able to loan us the use of his Ford touring car. Momma was able to get someone to watch baby Arthur and the twins. Earl couldn't miss work, but the rest of the Crandal clan loaded up the Ford. We headed to Emporia to root Howard and the team on with fried chicken, potato salad, deviled eggs, and a jar of Momma's pickles in tow.

Howard was antsy all week. The spring weather had been especially harsh, and he hadn't been able to really have a fair chance to break the high school record in the mile. Twice he had come within one second, but he just couldn't finish the job. He might have spent a little too much time pondering the "what-ifs" and thinking he had missed his best opportunity to break the record when he had been running on his home turf. He had been quick to snap back at all of us for the least implied infringement upon his perceived territorial rights in our house.

"He's like a fine thoroughbred." Momma offered up various excuses for his bad behavior. "His spirit is high, and it needs to get higher if he is to win the race." She did her best to get us to cut him some slack. More precisely, she allowed him to be a brat.

"I've been on my knees so long, they've got scabs on them." Momma told on herself as we all laughed *with* her as much as *at* her. "Praying for that boy has turned into another full-time job," she joked.

The *Tampa News* ran several stories on the track team, especially on Howard and his quest to set the mile record. The stories alluded to the fact that when Howard traveled to Emporia and competed against all those great athletes from the big schools, he would find that he was just a small fish in a large pond.

In my wildest dream I never thought Howard would become famous; nevertheless, I knew that my brother would make history for Tampa High School that day.

He worked himself into a trancelike fury hours before the race. He had an incredible ability to focus and zone out anything that might interfere with his hallowed sanctum.

"When a runner is able to have the event come to him in

slow motion, though everything is moving in a rapid pace and the entire field seems settled and orderly, that's when the zone takes over," Howard said, doing his best to explain what happened to him when he was running the race. "About the middle of the race, something almost mystical happens." He paused to look into my eyes to see if I was following his explanation. "It's as if some inner power, some inner source of reserved energy, takes over my body. It's like someone somehow refigures the way my body needs to work in order to run at my best. My head clears up, and I no longer need to spend energy on strategy for running the race. It's as if some beautiful, symphonic music plays in my heart, my vision gets better, and everything around me gains a sense of dimension and beauty never seen before. After that new gear kicks in, it's as if a cool breeze, maybe more like a zephyr, blows gently against my face, and I am able to run effortlessly. I have the sense that I am gliding rather than placing one foot down after another. I call it the runner's high, though it has been given many other names." He developed his story in such a manner that I was lost in the beauty and splendor of how he strung his words together.

"Magic isn't always in the outcome but always in the doing," Momma once told me.

Howard was standing on the starting line, waiting for the starter's gun to sound. He was wearing his gold and black track uniform. The bright April sun glistened off the sheen from the mix of those two colors. His lithe frame, rock hard from training, and his red hair with natural blond highlights contrasted with his school colors. The scenic beauty of the green grass surrounded the track. I couldn't help but think of my brother as some heroic knight preparing to joust to the death to win the prize and the fair damsel who waited to be rescued.

My reflective reverie was shattered by the loud blast of the starter's gun.

"When a guy runs the mile, it isn't necessary for him to get a fast start," Howard once said. "In nearly every race, there are only a few runners who really have the ability to win. Sometimes coaches will use lesser runners to try and get their opponents to be foolish enough to spend their energy in the wrong parts of the race."

"Oh, I get it," I said. "If a lesser runner starts off really fast and keeps that pace up for half a mile, and other runners decide to match that effort, they'll poop out at the end. But their too-fast pace will have set up their school's best runner to close and win the race."

Howard patted me on the back. "Way to go, Jess! I can see that Rose isn't the only girl to have brains in this family," he teased.

As the race commenced, it was apparent that a very fast pace was being set. Howard had told us that his best competition would come from the runners from Topeka, Manhattan, Marion, and Emporia; each one of those runners had broken their school records that season.

The pace was fast, and all of the runners, except the runners from Topeka, Manhattan, Marion, Emporia, and Howard, did their best to jockey for position with the frontrunners. Howard and his main competition were satisfied to settle back in the middle of the pack.

As the runners approached the halfway mark, they started to show signs of labored breathing; they demonstrated that their bodies were under great duress. The pace slowed a bit by the time they approached the three-quarter mark. The runners who had gone out to set a fast pace were now breaking down. Their fatigued bodies caused them to dig deeper for oxygen, affecting their ability to maintain their rhythmic gait, and they faltered badly.

And then it happened! Although it is more difficult to spot subtle changes in runners' performances with an untrained eye, I attempted to do so. Howard got his runner's high. He had been laboring and running with all of his might, and he had been able to keep pace with the other schools' star runners. When his runner's high kicked in, it was as if the other runners were standing still. He behaved as if a new starter's gun had just gone off. Howard made a move, and his stride lengthened and his legs acted as if they had springs. Although he was using up every ounce of energy left in his body, he lifted up his head, and I could almost hear the music he talked about when he got that blessing of the runner's high.

With Momma and us kids going nuts, screaming our heads off, we watched Howard come down the home stretch. His main competitors made a run at him, and they closed the gap he had created at the start of the last quarter mile. But he crossed the finish line a couple of paces ahead of the best competitor. The official stopwatch read 4:23.1. Howard had done it. He had set a new record for the mile run, not just for Tampa High, but also for the state of Kansas.

Howard's teammates mobbed him, and soon he was up on their shoulders. They paraded him around, shouting his nickname, "The Tampa Flash." Others hollered, "The Kansas Flyer!"

Tears rolled down our faces.

"Who would have believed it?" Pauline muttered through her tears.

Howard was the only member of the Tampa track team to win a medal. It was difficult to remain crestfallen when their team had a state champion who had set a new record for the mile.

As soon as he could arrange it, Howard broke away from his adoring public and raced to give Momma a big hug.

"Momma," he whispered in her ear, but it was loud enough for all of us to hear, "I want you to have my ribbon." He handed her his blue ribbon, which signified to the world that her son was the champion of the State of Kansas for the mile run. She crushed it to her breast. Her eyes were dancing. With the mix of light from the sun, her tears made her face seem angelic. Momma lifted up her head, and through her tears and wide grin, she rejoiced.

"Lord, you can come and get me now," Momma said.

In the background, chants from the Tampa faithful could be heard: repeat—repeat—repeat for the Kansas Flyer!"

It took all of us some time to get used to living with a famous person. The newspapers from the surrounding areas, especially those towns that were in our high school's track conference, all did stories on my brother. They indicated that Momma was his main source of inspiration and motivational support. Some played up that Momma was a widow with a dozen kids to raise.

And the girls took notice of him. For the most part, he ignored them. He stuck to his regime of training four times a week, regardless of the weather.

"Maybe I won't be able to pull off a second win in the state meet," he said to me as he and I were sipping a glass of lemonade after he had cooled down from one his workouts. "But it won't be from a lack of dedication on my part."

"Katherine Ballinger thinks you are the cat's meow," I said.

Katherine was from Hope, Kansas. She was the same age as Howard. She and her family came to the dances that were held in our town's civic hall. When the big bands from Salina came to play, the surrounding townsfolk would show up in droves. With her coal-black hair and ebony eyes to match, an hourglass figure, and creamy complexion, she turned heads everywhere she went. She was a very good dancer. She was such a down-to-earth girl and so friendly. She treated people in such a fashion that one was led to believe she really didn't have a clue how beautiful she was.

A big grin crossed my brother's face. "How do you know that? Are you making that up?"

"God's honest truth," I replied. "At the last dance, she told me she thought you were handsome."

That bit of news jazzed him up. His face flushed.

"Jess, look at me." He demanded my attention. "You're serious and you're not just funning with me?"

"Cross my heart and hope to die; if I'm lying you can stick a thousand needles in my eye," I replied, repeating a timeworn method we kids used to help us determine if someone was a liar.

"Look at me and say 'pork and beans' ten times," he said. It was Poppa's and Momma's tried-and-tested method of helping her sort out the truth from a lie. She said it worked on all of her kids, except for Rose and Charlie.

"Don't be such a nilly-willy. Katherine is sweet on you! At the next dance, if her family is there, ask her to dance."

Howard took up my challenge. They were soon an item, and it seemed to please the townsfolk. I suppose it was proper and fitting: the town's most famous boy and most beautiful girl, cooing like two lovebirds.

"The most wonderful attribute about that Ballinger girl," Momma often said, "isn't her beauty; it's her heart." All of our family was smitten with Kate, which is what Howard often called her.

"Sometimes people find out they were given a cross-eyed Cupid," Momma said as she struggled through tears. Howard and Kate had been going together for three years, and our family expected them to get married; it never happened.

Howard was a teacher by then, and he had to go away on business for a few days. When he got back, he found out that Kate had gone out with another boy. He broke off the engagement that very same day. None of us dared talk about it.

"Some prayers aren't answered in the manner we'd like," Momma said as we quizzed her about this tragic ending.

Momma really enjoyed basking in the limelight of her son's athletic prowess. She'd been able to stop working at the restaurant and was on full-time as a midwife and providing nursing care for the sick and elderly, enabling her to have better control of her work schedule. More importantly, she was able to travel to watch her kids play basketball and attend all of Howard's track meets.

The year 1932 proved to be very difficult for our nation. Despite the catastrophic results of the impact of the Depression, Tampa High School's basketball and track teams gave our citizens much to cheer about. Led by Howard's playmaking and scoring, and most assuredly because of Charlie's fanatical cheerleading, to hear him tell it, our team won the conference title for the first time in nearly two decades. We lost in the first game of the regional tournament at Marion. While it was disheartening to lose to an opponent we had beaten twice before during the regular season, in some ways it was apparent that Howard wasn't too upset because it allowed him to focus single-mindedly on the looming track season.

"It just does something to a momma," she explained, telling how wonderful it made her feel as Howard's track team was announced to the crowd before the competition commenced. "When you hear something like, 'Running for Tampa in the mile run today will be Howard Crandal, the record holder for the high school State of Kansas mile run,' it gives you a sense of pride that melts your body and soul. All that's left is a warm, fuzzy feeling that no one can ever take away." Ralph, the barber, once tapped on his shopwindow and motioned for Momma and me to come in as we passed by. He congratulated Momma on Howard's success.

Howard and the track team were even stronger than they had been in his junior year. They easily qualified for the Kansas State Regional Tournament and then for the state meet. As defending champion of the mile run, Howard was automatically qualified for the state meet. He had increased his training methods to help him get stronger and obtain more stamina. He pushed his body so much that Momma feared he was in danger of causing himself harm.

"The good Lord fit horses and mules to do an astonishing amount of hard labor. I'm not sure he meant for man to nigh on kill himself in the same manner," Momma said to Howard more than once when he would return from one of his grueling runs.

Howard had managed to shave one second off his record run from last year. He felt very good about himself. He had won the regional, but he ran two seconds slower than he had run at the conference meet. The day had been blustery and difficult on the runners, so he wasn't too concerned about his time.

The state meet was held in Manhattan that year at the State Teachers College. Like Emporia, it had a very nice cinder track and could accommodate a large crowd. Usually, track meets didn't draw large crowds; only the athletes' families attended most track meets. But when the best track athletes in the state were competing, and many schools throughout the state were there to root for their teams, it took a large stadium to hold the crowd.

While Howard certainly received his share of the limelight, and he was given his just due as the returning defending state champion for the mile run, he had to share what little newspaper attention editors chose to give the state meet with a much younger mile runner. He was from Elkhart, in western Kansas. He was touted as the "Osage Flash" and even as the "Kansas Flash." While much attention was paid to his talent, even though he was just a sophomore, it was his story of overcoming personal adversity that attracted the people's interest.

Glen Cunningham and his older brother, Floyd (Floyd was ten and Glen was eight), had taken on the job of going to the school early on cold mornings to make a fire so the schoolhouse would be warm for the students. The man who regularly delivered coal oil to the school came down with a sickness. His supplier had to find a new man to deliver coal oil. The new man delivered gasoline instead of coal oil. Floyd didn't know the switch had been made, and when he put the gasoline in the stove, it blew up. Floyd was burned to death, and Glen was so badly burned that the doctors told his parents they didn't think he would live. When he proved them wrong, they told his parents he would never walk again. His legs were badly scarred. Despite all odds, and despite an incredible amount of pain, Glen refused to accept his plight.

One day, when he was twelve, Glen discovered that he had

speed. He entered a race during recess and won. He also found out that the pain he had to endure was less severe when he ran than when he walked in a normal fashion. Glen told the reporter conducting the interview, "From that day on, I ran everywhere because I had less pain from my scars," which added luster to his compelling Horatio Alger tale.

"Howard's got that fire-in-his-belly look," Charlie announced as our family was seated, waiting for the mile competition to start.

"Do you think so?" Momma asked, as she was nervous, maybe more nervous than I had ever seen her before one of Howard's races. "It's stupid of me; the race hasn't even started, and for some reason I feel melancholy. Don't you think I should be higher than a kite in anticipation of celebrating another win for Howard?"

"Now, Thomas, we'll not have any of his doubts on this day," Pauline chimed in.

Momma looked directly at her and said, "Thanks, I needed that."

"That skinny, little, ugly-legged boy shouldn't have won," Rose said, expressing her feelings about the race as our family drove back home. We were all in a somber mood. Frustration and sadness permeated the entire automobile.

"It just wasn't meant to be," I said and then felt sheepish for saying it. Before anyone could attack me verbally, I added, "Howard ran a beautiful race, didn't he?"

The family mumbled and nodded their heads in agreement.

"Remember last night when he told us the strategy he was going to use for the race? He pulled it off to perfection," I continued. "Let's concentrate on how great the race was, not on its ending."

"Jessie's right," Momma said. "Jess, honey, tell us how you remember the race," she urged, I could liven up our attitudes to be more gracious losers.

"All right, Momma, I'll do my best.

"Remember how happy we were as we arrived at the meet? The sun was bright, and the wind was just a soft whisper upon the face. The warmth made the picnic lunch Momma fixed taste better than any fancy dinner rich folk could eat dining out in one those ritzy places in Kansas City or Chicago. Randy Foster won third place in the discus throw, and that was the first ribbon any Tampa High School trackster had ever won, except, of course, Howard's state champion medal, so we have a lot to celebrate.

"When the race began, Howard and those few gifted runners didn't move out too fast, even though some of the runners established a fast pace from the git-go, just like they did last year when Howard won. He allowed the fast-pacing runners to wear out. Just before they hit the three-quarter mark, I'm positive that he got that mystical surge of energy—he calls it his 'runner's high'—because he just kicked it into another gear. At that point in the race, didn't we all just know in our hearts that he was gong to win again?"

"God has his own appointments," Momma interrupted. "Your brother Howard is a very good runner, but that Cunningham boy, hmm, hmm, hmm," she said, demonstrating how she recognized that his talents were superior to our brother's. "Howard's type of talent comes along once a decade. I have a hunch that before that boy is through, the world will say once or twice in a lifetime."

"Why, oh why couldn't God let it be just one more year?" Naomi asked in a woeful tone of voice.

"If you love track, and if you love the mile run, then how could it get any better than what we were able to see this afternoon?" I asked.

"At the three-quarter mark, Howard made his move and roared into the lead. Try as they might, none could keep up with him. Do you remember the roar from the crowd and how our family whooped and hollered and started hugging each other? None, except that skinny kid with those terribly scarred legs, could keep up. I'm not sure what he calls it, maybe a runner's high like Howard. All I know is that in those final one hundred yards, he pulled out on the outside so as not to have to take a chance on getting caught up in the stack of slower runners, and he roared up to where Howard was. He passed him like a freight train does a tramp. All I know for sure is that the crowd was louder than any crowd I have ever heard at a track meet. Cunningham broke Howard's record and set a new state record and a high school national track record for the mile run."

"Don't remind us," Rose said. "Now I'm more depressed than ever since Jess told her little story."

Our family rode the rest of the way home in stony silence.

A couple of weeks had passed since the track meet, and Howard and the family had come to terms with the loss. Howard seemed very relieved not to have to devote so much of his time to punishing his body. He looked forward to graduation. His fame had opened some doors for him, and he was already promised a position as a teacher in the county, even before he graduated from high school.

In early June, after Charlie and Howard's graduation, I was sitting with Howard and admiring the June moon. We were carrying on small talk about nothing, yet about everything important, when I asked him if he would mind telling me his own impressions about that race.

"Oh, its smarts some," he said, "but in hindsight, Glen did me a big favor." He surprised me with his statement.

"So getting your rear kicked is a favor?" I teased.

"I'm not referring to that, you ninny." He laughed. "A favor in the sense that it knocked some sense into my head. Until Glen drubbed me, I had illusions that I might be able to find a way to attend college and run track, you know, with the very best runners in our country. But when he shattered my best efforts, I realized that he had a gift that I just wasn't given by the good Lord. I hate to admit it, but Jess, when I met him and saw how horribly scarred his legs were and how difficult it must have been to overcome the pain associated with that injury, I'm not sure that deep down inside of me I wasn't rooting for him to win," he confessed. "My, what a warrior he is!"

"Did he intimidate you?"

"No! He didn't intimidate me. Momma always told me I needed a fire in the belly to win. I could tell that he had that, as well as the eye of a tiger." It's possible, one day, I will be rooting for him at the Olympics."

We couldn't know it then, but it was a record that would stand the test of time for a long time, until another Kansas boy, Jim Ryun, came along and shattered Glen's mark. Howard proved to be a prophet; Glen did run and win at the Olympic games. He shook the track world for decades. His monikers "The Kansas Flash," "The Iron Horse of the Osage," and "The Elkhart Flash" became well known throughout the world.

The Newspaper Woman

"Taking advantage of life's opportunities is often more than blind luck. It's keeping your intuitive antenna free enough from life's stopped-up clogs, not in the drain, but in your brain, so you are given some necessary possibility vision," Momma said.

It was the answer she gave me when I asked her why she was taking the time to submit some pithy article to the *Tampa News* editor. The paper had issued a plea for a part-time news reporter. It wanted someone who could write interesting stories about the social and civic events of Tampa and the immediate surrounding area.

"Jess, come here a minute," Momma beckoned. "I want your opinion on something I have written. *The Tampa News* needs to hire a part-time news reporter. I'm submitting a story to the editor." She looked up at me as she thrust the paper at me. "The good Lord knows that I love to tell a good story. She gave me a sly wink, and said, "I don't need any unnecessary commentary from you," she smiled. "As I sat reading the paper's employment offer, I realized I was as qualified as most people, so I started working on an article to submit to the paper. The editor said the reporter needed to be able to write using humor and in a style that the reader would consider more storytelling than reporting."

"Well, Momma, if anyone can tell a whopper, it's you!" I gave her a hint of a smirky smile.

"You watch your mouth," she warned in a good-natured manner. "Some of the other kids have already looked at this; come and read it and give me your opinion." She moved out a chair from under the kitchen table with her left foot. She motioned for me to sit down. "Here, take a load off."

I sat down, and she handed me the paper she had been writing on.

Who is it that earns the cash

To run the home and buy the hash?

My dad.

Who is it that stands straight and

Strong

And carries his burden with a song?

My dad.

Who will be missed when shadows

And skies are gray?

With folded hands he is laid away,

My dad.

Father's Day is coming soon, and don't forget to remember him as you did your mother on her day. He will appreciate little kindnesses shown him. He loves you too.

Too many families think Dad is a necessary evil, and everything is Dad's fault. I once heard a schoolteacher make this remark: "Every family should have a father and mother; the mother to love them, and the father to whale the stuffin' out of them when they don't mind." A child that is reared without discipline never respects its parents.

Friday night about ten thirty, one of the worst storms in years struck Tampa. The storm started gathering about six o'clock and looked bad from the start. High wind did a lot of damage to property, and the rain beat the tall wheat to the ground.

Electricity and phone service were put out of commission by a windmill blowing down on the wires on the Fred J. Mier property, cutting them in two. The town was still without phone services Saturday evening. The light men came up early from Hillsboro and repaired the lines. Many of the property owners had extensive damage.

I went uptown Saturday night to hear a few remarks about the storm from some of our citizens.

Mrs. Belton said Leonard started singing "There's a Great Day Coming, By and By" when he saw the henhouse fly by and the door of the house twist off and take after it.

Lawrence Dieker said it was the first time in his life that he was scared enough to take his family to the cellar. Then he got to thinking that the house might blow down on it, so he took them back to the house.

Someone said that Pat Patterson has not been able to wear a hat yet as his hair still stands straight up on his head.

Mr. Baustain got out of bed and put on his shirt and tie and combed his hair. He then called family and helped them dress and hurried them to the cellar. After the storm was over and they were all safe again in their homes, he started to undress for bed. He took off his tie and shirt and started to remove his trousers only to discover that he had never put them on. That's what one calls an "absentminded professor."

I couldn't help myself. I laughed out loud when I read that last bit of Momma's story. I looked up at her and then handed her back the paper. "Momma, that is very good."

"I just feel it in my bones; the good Lord's going to see to it that Lou Crandal is the new news reporter for *The Tampa News*." She acted a bit uppity and then completely changed her demeanor. "Who am I kidding? Probably fifty others will be better than mine."

"Not so," I assured her.

She took her hands and cupped my face. "That's what the

others said. It's real comforting to know that your own flesh and blood is willing to lie just to make a momma feel good." She kissed me on the forehead.

"It's a good thing Howard still doesn't work for the paper; I can just see him lining up a whole host of reasons why this isn't going to work," I said.

Momma looked at me with a sense of relief on her face. Then she allowed herself to crack a big smile. "Me too." She winked.

The weekly paper came out on Wednesday. On Thursday, the preacher called early to talk to Momma.

"I'm sorry. Momma already left to take care of her elderly patient, Mr. Jackson. She'll be home later, around noon."

No sooner had I hung up the phone than Mary Meier called. This was one of Momma's dearest friends.

"Jessie, honey, when your momma gets home from work, have her call me, you hear?" She had urgency in her voice.

After the third or fourth call, I started to quiz the callers.

"Something is going on"—I allowed myself to express my puzzlement over the phone—"because you are the fourth caller this morning," I said to our town's barber.

He started laughing. "Evidently you haven't read the paper." He chuckled. "That Lou sure has a way with words."

"Is Momma in the paper?" Then it dawned on me; Momma had submitted her article to the editor to see if she could get the reporter's job.

"After reading most of the blabber the paper usually prints, Lou is as refreshing as rain on a hot August day," he said. "Get the paper and see for yourself."

Ever since Howard stopped working for the paper, our family didn't get *The Tampa News*. Oh, we were able to read it, but it was usually not until the next week. Momma would bring them home from the places where she worked taking care of the elderly, sick people. I often reflected upon the unceasing vagaries of what it meant to be poor. Just a tiny little thing, such as not being able to afford the weekly paper, abated my soul's hunger not one whit. According to Momma, when I contemplated the truth of its reality, which often sucked the very life from me, it was because I wanted too much.

Later that day, Momma came home just whistling up a storm. A few of us kids were home at the time; I was busy fixing flour and egg noodles.

"I know, I know, somehow folks found out where I was working and people have been calling—calling so much it's a wonder I didn't get fired." She came in the door and took a drink of cool water. She pulled out a chair from the kitchen table and sat down. All of that rushing made her face flushed. She was holding a newspaper in her hand.

"Can you believe it?" She smiled. "They printed my article, word for word."

"Let me see, let me see." I reached out to grasp the paper.

"I guess I got the job."

Ring … ring … ring. Two longs and a short was our party line extension for Ma Bell, and when I heard it, I answered the phone.

"Hello, the Crandal residence," I said. "Yes." I paused and looked at Momma. "She's sitting right here. No, it wouldn't be any problem; it would be my pleasure." I put the receiver on the hook and turned to Momma. "Someone wants to speak to you," I said in a very nonchalant manner.

"Well, Jess, who is it?"

"He mentioned something about being the editor of the newspaper," I drawled slowly, as if the call possessed little interest to anyone in our family.

When Momma realized who was on the phone and how I was deliberately trying to mislead her about its importance, she rushed to take the phone off the hook. She gave me one of her looks that clearly told me I had chosen the wrong time to tease her or to act coyly.

"This is Lou Crandal speaking." She did her best to contain her excitement and maintain complete control over her voice.

"Yes, a number of citizens have expressed their appreciation." She moved closer to the phone's receiver. "Well, I wouldn't go as far as that. Yes, it's comforting to hear such kind words."

Momma turned her head away from the receiver and looked directly into the faces of our family, who had gathered around after I ran to tell them who was on the phone with Momma. She used her right index finger and pointed to herself. She mouthed the words, "He wants me to be his reporter." Her eyes were filled with light and just a hint of tears. "I'm sure that I can meet that deadline."

Momma hung up the phone. She did a little jig and sashayed around the room. For no good reason, or maybe for a million good reasons, all of us kids soon fell in behind her and joined in her celebration.

Momma's column quickly became a must-read for the citizens of Tampa and surrounding areas. Momma had a unique knack for shining a light upon some event—social or civic—that brought out the humor or folly of people's behavior or decisions. It didn't take any time at all before one could hear others make a comment on a regular basis if they said or did something that could become useful fodder for her column. "You'd better watch your P's and Q's, or you'll end up in Lou's column."

Everyone in town took it for granted that Momma sucked the information that finally ended up in her weekly column out of her thumb. Our family knew better, as we watched her sit at the kitchen table, often late at night while everyone was in bed, slaving over her next column.

After Momma had been writing for quite a spell, one day she said, "I've learned, late in life, that there are two types of being tired. The first type I've known all my life: working all hours of the day and night and spending yourself so weak from hard labor you can't even sleep. The second type, Jess, has to do with your brain being worn out. Take it from an old warhorse; having a taxed brain is much worse." She gave me a weary grin. "When one uses her brain to grow weary from, there's something invigorating deep down inside; that's what writing does for me."

When a girl gets a momma like mine, one of the best blessings the Lord Almighty gives is that she is allowed to vicariously peek in on the other side. There is an awesome wonderment that a girl surely gets when her pride in her momma never seems to cease or grow dim, no matter how long she lives.

I knew the editor of *The Tampa News* was a smart man and a very good businessman. He offered Momma her own column within a few weeks of her being hired. Her pay was miniscule, but every dollar was like fresh manna from heaven.

People were soon calling Momma "The Newspaper Woman." She said it was both a blessing and a curse.

"People just don't act normal around me any more," she said, expressing her feelings. "I guess they think I'm going to find a way to use their human foibles against them, and they will find themselves in my column. I suppose the preacher and I have a lot more in common than I ever thought possible. He has always said, 'Everyone loves my sermons because they are convinced that my message goes right over their heads and hits their neighbors. They are of a mind that their neighbors are sore in need of its message.'" She chuckled.

A few months later, just after supper, we were busy doing the dishes and cleaning up the kitchen when the phone rang. Deannie answered.

"Hello, this is the Crandal residence," she said, pausing briefly to listen to the caller. "It's some man," she whispered. She handed the phone to Momma.

"Just call me Lou; everyone does," Momma interrupted the caller. "Yes, I'm proud of her too. It's nice to know your kids mind you once in a while." Momma turned to us and motioned with her hand and fingers. Her hand was cupped into a C formation, and she moved her fingers and hand open and shut to indicate that the caller was blabbering about nothing that was worth listening to.

Suddenly, her body stiffened, and her head moved as close to the phone receiver as it could get. "Certainly, I would be interested ... You ran an old article, and it was well received? ..." Momma's feet twitched, and she was swaying a bit. "You're sending me a copy of what you printed? ... Oh, he did? ... No, I never knew he sent that to you." Momma's conversation was direct and to the point. "A stringer? I can't say that I do," she said. "That much for each paper?" She mumbled a bit. "Sure, absolutely, you have my permission." She coughed nervously. "I'll keep in touch, silly me. You'll keep in touch." She laughed. "Thank you! Oh, yes, thank you again." She hung up the phone.

Momma turned and looked at us kids, a glazed look on her face. When she did speak, it was slower than her usual manner. In a dreamy voice she said, "You'll never guess in a million years who I was just talking to."

"Who was that man?" Pauline asked.

"That man"—Momma purposely inflected the pitch and sound of her voice—"was none other than the high muckety-muck editor of the *Topeka Journal*." Before any of us could say a word, she said, "And he wants me to be a stringer for his paper." She started giggling and then let out a roaring, "*Whoopee!*"

"Why does that man want you to string a ball?" Gracie, who was five, asked.

Momma reached down and kissed her on the cheek. "It has nothing to do with stringing a ball. A newspaper stringer is someone who is paid for their writing by other newspapers when they choose to publish that person's writing."

"So the *Topeka Journal* and other newspapers will pay you if they print your column that runs in *The Tampa News?*" I asked.

"Right you are, my girl. They will pay a dollar a column."

"How many newspapers are there?" I asked as my little math brain was busy trying to calculate how much Momma might earn each week.

"Oh, for heaven's sake. It doesn't matter." Momma looked at us and smiled. "He mentioned five or six, I think."

"Five or six dollars a week." I emitted a low whistle. "That's not just chicken feed." We all laughed.

In the case of her being a stringer for the *Topeka Journal*, "Nothing seems as good as it looks, and nothing seems a bad as one thinks," Momma often said. She was right on both accounts. She did become a stringer, and her columns were published in other newspapers. Unfortunately, the frequency averaged about once a month, not weekly.

RANNY GRADY

Still, Momma's importance in the community continued to rise. I guess it was the potential of her rapier wit.

"The pen's mightier than any sword," she often quoted. "I think it was Ben Franklin who wrote that." It caused the civic leaders to often take Momma into their confidences, lest she find a way to spill the beans and they end up with political egg all over their faces because of some boneheaded decisions or personal behavior choices. I will give my Momma credit for one thing: she never deliberately went out of her way to harm anyone, unless boorish behavior warranted it.

A few months after Momma took up residence as the newspapers' celebrity, she came home beaming that she had another new job. She told our family that she was at the paper submitting her latest column. Mr. Jackson, the editor, was musing over a stack of papers. He was mumbling.

"'If I could just collect from these deadbeats, maybe the paper could operate in the black.'

"'Did you say something to me?' I asked as I was passing by his desk on my way out the door.

"'No, I'm just commiserating with myself about all of these uncollectible bills for the newspaper,' he said in an off-handed way, not wanting to complain too loudly to anyone.

"I had one of those epiphany moments, you know, where a brilliant idea pops into your head.

"'If a person could collect that money, how much do you reckon they could keep?' I asked.

"He looked up at me and asked, 'Do you have anyone in particular in mind?'

"I stepped up closer to his desk, leaned forward, and then I whispered, 'Me.'
.

"'Now, how in the world do you suppose you can get people to pay their overdue paper bills? Everyone I have hired has quit in a week.'

"'So what have you got to lose hiring me?'

"He put a rubber band around the stack of papers and looked

me in the eyes. He gave me a casual smile, and then he handed them to me.

"'I'll give you twenty percent of anything you can collect.'

"I took the bills from his hand. 'Thirty percent,' I said as I walked out the door.

"Now, Jessie, you can drive, and you can go with me to collect these past-due bills." Momma held up the stack of overdue newspaper bills, held together by a red rubber band.

"Momma, I don't think—"

"That's right, leave all the thinking to me," she interrupted. "Saturday is the only day I have free to do any collecting."

Friday night, our house was filled with the wonderful smells of oatmeal raisin cookies, and our family was allowed to barely taste the crumbs. The air was also filled with the refrains of Momma's favorite gospel hymns.

"There's just something special about singing the sweet words praising our Lord and the smell of fresh-baked cookies that makes a body want to fall down on his knees and offer up thanks to our great God." She laughed; she was enjoying her fixing and doing in the kitchen. "Now don't go getting your hearts set on eating these cookies." She used her spatula and pointed to them nicely stacked in our large glass jar sitting on the kitchen cabinet. "Those babies are going to help us collect those past-due bills."

Momma certainly wasn't some big-shot businessman, but she taught me a valuable lesson about people and money that first Saturday we were on the job. As we were driving in Howard's Chevy, her cookies were safely tucked in the rumble seat. We were trying to find the proper addresses when she asked me, "Have you given much thought as to why these people haven't paid their newspaper bills?"

"Most of them just don't have the money, I suppose."

"You may be right. Most folks don't have any spare dimes. I have a hunch there is a lot more to do with it than just money."

"How so?"

Momma lightly patted my knee as I was driving. "First, let's see if my hunch is right."

RANNY GRADY

The black mailbox had a name printed on it: M. Parker. I wheeled the Chevy up beside it. We got out, and Momma fetched a dozen of her cookies and put them in a brown paper bag. We made our way up the steps of the front porch, and I knocked on the door in a timid fashion. When no one immediately answered, Momma said, "Give it a good whack."

This time I rapped my knuckles hard on the door.

"Old people can't hear very well." Momma pointed to her ears as I was pounding on the door.

In a few seconds, an elderly man wearing overalls opened the door a crack.

"Don't want anything you're selling," he grumbled and halfway growled. He started to shut the door.

"Mr. Parker, I'm Lou Crandal from *The Tampa Newspaper*." Momma smiled at him.

"Sure you are, and I'm Balaam's ass," he curtly replied and stared at us. "Lou Crandal is a famous writer; she wouldn't be out at my house on a Saturday, nearly before breakfast."

"No, really, I'm Lou Crandal," she replied with a grin. "Mr. Parker, I have these freshly baked oatmeal raisin cookies with me. Do you suppose my daughter and I could come inside and speak with you for a few minutes?" She held up the brown paper bag.

"Fresh-baked cookies?" His eyes opened wide.

"Just about still warm from the oven." Momma shook the bag a little. He opened his door and motioned for Momma and me to come in. "I could even be persuaded to have some of that fine-smelling coffee." I was taken aback by her almost brazen manner.

"Do you take sugar with it?"

"My dearly departed husband taught me to drink my coffee black. Ranti, that was his name, used to beller, 'If you are going to put anything in the coffee, might just as well drink mud.'" Momma did her best to mimic Poppa, and they both shared a laugh.

"My Bessie's been gone nearly a decade now." It was easy to hear the tinge of emotion come into his voice.

Momma opened her sack of cookies and handed a couple to him. He took them and spent a few seconds admiring them. He lifted one up close to his nose.

"My, do they smell good!"

"They taste even better than they smell," I said.

He turned and smiled at me. He had one tooth missing, right in front. He had just a few strands of white hair circling on the top of his head, as if they didn't really know where they should be. He had droopy eyes, and his ears were rather large. He had enormous hands and long, gnarled fingers. He wore an undershirt under his overalls. He was still barefoot.

He took a bite out of a cookie. "My, my, my, just a little piece of heaven melting in your mouth." He held up the cookie he had just taken a bite out of. He smiled.

Momma took a sip of her coffee, which he had fixed for her. "Mmm, that tastes so good. Funny how a steaming cup of coffee just seems to taste better on some cool, crisp mornings than others, isn't it?"

He nodded his head in agreement.

"No kidding, you are Lou Crandal." He took another bite of cookie, and his eyes took on a shine. He continued to nibble as he eyed Momma. "Why would a woman of your importance come a'calling on behalf of that rag?" he asked, referencing *The Tampa News*.

"I don't want you to think I come under false pretenses," Momma said. "I'll not beat around the bush, Mr. Parker. The newspaper has hired me to collect their overdue bills." She took a long sip of coffee.

"Well, if those other guys had brought me cookies…" He smiled and his missing front tooth was very noticeable. "It's not that I haven't wanted to pay." He looked directly at Momma. "Some days, I just don't have the will to do anything, especially pay bills. Bessie always handled that." His eyes became watery, and he didn't finish his sentence. In a few minutes, he got up and went over to the kitchen counter and opened a canister jar. He reached in and pulled out some money. "What's it say I owe?"

In a hushed voice, Momma said, "A dollar and thirty cents."

He slowly counted out four quarters, two dimes, and two nickels. "Tell that newspaper man that I will be glad to pay my bill any time Lou Crandal comes a'calling." He looked at me and winked.

We said our good-byes and traveled to the next house to collect an overdue bill.

"My hunch was right," Momma said. "The man was just lonely." She sighed in a soulful way. She reached over and patted my knee.

Most of the people Momma visited to collect from weren't nearly as nice or as accommodating as Mr. Parker was. Still, Momma was able to collect a lot of the money the newspaper hadn't collected and probably wouldn't have ever been able to collect.

The lesson I learned about the newspaper business was that it takes a lot more than an editor to operate a successful newspaper. More importantly, cookies go a lot farther than any huffing and puffing with words when it comes to collecting the bill.

The Suitor

In late May of my thirteenth year on God's planet, Momma and I were out in the hinterlands, once again seeking deadbeats to pay their overdue newspaper bills. We were not having much luck. We were in Howard's Chevy coup.

The late spring day was filled with sunshine. Mayflowers could be seen along the road; when we passed the houses along the way, each one had flowers growing, and they added beauty to our idyllic drive. The sun was warm against our skin; I glanced at Momma, glowing in its rays, from time to time while I drove.

"We might as well drive on into Durham," Momma said as I was doing my best to maneuver the ruts in the road so we wouldn't find our insides completely turned wrong side out.

"Perhaps we could go to Martha's." I turned and looked at her with a bit of begging in my voice.

Martha's Restaurant was considered the best place to eat in Durham. A majority of the farmers and businessmen frequented her place any time they could find an excuse to do so. Her lunch specials were worth driving miles for. They consisted of country-fried steak that nearly covered the plate, a huge mountain of mashed potatoes and rich gravy, beans, and cornbread (she was a Southern girl and would never think of serving a lunch without cornbread), vegetables, and a choice of pies. Her pies were at least four to six inches high (her trademark) and sold for a reasonable price. It was a meal that melted in your mouth and made your stomach grin. She had customers waiting to get tables come lunchtime.

Momma and I had gone to her restaurant a couple of times before. What a treat!

"Maybe Martha's is just what we girls need."

I pushed the gas pedal down.

"I'd surely like to get there in one piece," Momma said, and I looked at her and we laughed.

"Jesus said to watch and keep ready. Neither the hour nor the day is known when he will return," Momma told me often. "Life is much like his story, Jess. A body can get up in the morning and think all is well in heaven and earth; by nightfall, that same person may think the whole world's gone to hell in a handbasket."

Before that day was over, Momma proved herself to be a seer.

As bright as the sun was, in just a few minutes, the heavens filled with clouds. We stopped to put up the top on the car. By the time we arrived in Durham, it was pouring down rain.

"Goodness me," Momma said. "I forgot to bring an umbrella."

"We're not sugar," I teased.

"We may not melt, but we'll end up looking like drowned rats." She laughed.

We were fortunate because we found a parking spot very close to Martha's place.

"Let's sit here and see if it lets up some," Momma said.

"I don't care how wet I get, just so I get some of her pie."

"Oh, for the joy of only having to worry about how big a piece of pie one can get." She poked me in the ribs lightly.

After a few minutes the rain let up some.

"We'd better make a run for it," I said.

We stepped out of the car and felt the mud and wetness fill up our shoes.

"Squishy yuck!" I hollered disgustedly and looked down at my feet.

"Don't stop now, Matilda," Momma said as she pushed me to get moving. I never really knew why Momma used that name, "Matilda," when anything had to do with moving on, but I know she used it on me a lot.

We managed to quickly make the trek out of the rain and into Martha's place. The weather evidently scared off the normal lunch crowd; we had our choice of seating.

We were seated and recovering as best we could. Martha spotted Momma and came to our table. The first time Momma and I went to her place, she let Momma know that she was a welcomed guest at her restaurant. She admired Momma and really enjoyed her writing.

"Your words show that you've got spunk," Martha said. "I get to laughing and carrying on sometimes when I read your stories. It shows you've got sass too. I like a woman with spunk and a lot of sass."

Martha was a bit of a legend. She had come to Durham many years ago. Gossip had it that she had been a mail-order bride. She came all the way from Virginia. Vince Gordon was a man up in his years. He was well to do, even though people never could put their fingers on what he did to earn a living. He made trips back east about twice a year for a couple of weeks. Then he kept a low profile and stayed to himself as much as he could.

The story goes that one day he told some business acquaintances that he was tired of living alone, and he aimed to do something about it. The next thing anyone knew, Martha arrived in town on the train. When she opened her mouth, "honey seemed to just drip out" is what the locals said. She was an attractive woman, cut a fine figure, and Vince was one happy man. They were married; a year later she had a baby. Old Vince was quite the talk of the town. Six months later, he fell dead on the street.

While Vince wasn't as wealthy as people thought, he did leave Martha a nice nest egg. She used the money to open up her restaurant. Their daughter was given the finest upbringing money could buy. But she chose to live in the east and had never returned to Durham. Martha had to visit her if she wanted to see her daughter.

After Martha befriended Momma, Martha verified that story's veracity.

"Lou, Eloise (her daughter's name) used her father's money and my sweat to rise above her raisin'." With a little tear in her eye, Martha said, "She just plum forgot who brung her to the dance."

When Martha spotted Momma and me, she came to our table.

"Lou Crandal and Jessie, what brings you to my little Southern mansion?" She and Momma exchanged hugs and warm smiles.

"Good fortune and the good Lord's providence." Momma laughed. "What else? Your pies!" She looked directly at me. "This girl has been talking about nothing but your fruit pie with a big scoop of vanilla ice cream on it for the last half hour." She looked at me; I was blushing but smiling, embarrassed.

"I don't blame you." Martha winked at me. "I have a hard time keeping away from them blame critters myself," she teased. She took her left hand and put it on her tummy and then her hips. "Since it is plain as day, I'm fighting a battle and losing the war." She laughed; we joined her.

"Martha, most any woman would trade yours for theirs, including me," Momma said.

"That's so kind of you, Lou. That's what I like about your momma, Jessie. She's a journalist who knows how to write good fiction." She gave us a sly smile, and we all shared a good laugh.

Momma and I ordered lunch, and I ended my delicious meal with a big piece of warm cherry pie with ice cream; the ice cream was with Martha's compliments. My, how we enjoyed ourselves!

The rain stayed steady all the while we were in the restaurant.

"I'm getting to the stage in my life where I'm about ready for a keeper," Momma said. "Forgetting to bring an umbrella." She used her hands to mimic that she was opening an umbrella.

"We'll just wait it out," I said.

"The first chance it lets up a bit, we need to make a dash for the car," Momma said.

In a few more minutes, the rain slowed down to a light drizzle. "Let's go." We left a dime tip on the table, and we made a run for it. As we hurriedly made our way to the car, a man's voice came from behind us.

"If you ladies will slow down a second, I'll rescue you."

Momma turned around to glance at the man. Suddenly, he was beside us, and he had a very large umbrella. He put it up over us to shield us from the rain.

"Here, hold this," he said.

Momma took hold of the umbrella, and he walked us out to the parked car. He surveyed it, and he shook his head. The rain made the area around it mucky, and it held a lot of water all around it.

"Let's get this started, and I'll see if I can move it closer and in a better spot," he said.

Momma and I looked at each other curiously.

Why is this complete stranger volunteering to be so gallant and so kind? I thought.

He cranked the car and got it started. He backed it up, and he helped Momma and me into the car. He made sure we were in the car and out of the inclement weather. I was driving and Momma was in the passenger seat. He stood on my side of the car, holding his umbrella to protect himself from the rain, which suddenly increased its intensity.

"Do you hang around Martha's place so you can rescue all damsels in distress?" Momma asked him in a teasing manner. "Or are we just special?"

"Hiram P. Dumphy at your service, ma'am," he said. "And if the woman is as comforting to the eyes as you"—he looked past me and directly at Momma—"I'd be here all day long."

"And here I thought chivalry was dead." Momma smiled at him, and I detected a bit of a blush in her face.

It hit me right in the face. No denying it; for the first time in my life I saw my momma flirting with a man. She had never flirted with Poppa that I could recall.

Evidently, she knew what I was thinking. "I'm just being polite," she said in a low voice out of the side of her mouth.

Mr. Dumphy was a middle-aged man of medium girth. His white starched shirt contrasted sharply under the busy design of his reddish brown tie, which complemented a medium brown three-piece suit. A gold chain stretched from a watch fob to his watch pocket, where I suspected I would find a gold pocket watch. On his head was a tan derby hat, and his round face was bespectacled with wire frames, drawing attention to kind, crystal blue eyes. When he smiled, his teeth, white and straight, only added to his appearance.

"Since I did rescue you, I think it is only fair that I know the pretty ladies' names," he said, and he bent down so that he could better look directly at Momma.

"This here is Jessie, my daughter, and I'm Lou Crandal." *What are you doing? Momma, how could you? On Main Street! In broad daylight, flirting with a man you just met,* I thought, as I was shocked at her behavior. "Momma, we'd better be getting home. Your dozen kids will be wondering where we have been," I said in a direct, loud voice.

From the look on Momma's face, I could tell she wasn't happy with me.

"Lou Crandal, are you the lady that writes those funny stories in the newspaper?"

Momma put up her right hand and said, giggling, "Guilty as sin." Mr. Dumphy chuckled.

This is so embarrassing! A grown woman, with more kids than anyone can imagine, and she is flirting with a complete stranger, I thought. It made me very uncomfortable and mad.

"And what does Mr. Dumphy do in Durham, besides rescue poor, helpless women and then flirt with them?" Momma said, and I was taken aback by her boldness.

He turned a bit and pointed up the street. "The mercantile store, I'm the owner," he said with a sense of pride in his voice.

"Be still my heart. A knight in white shining armor, and he has money too," she teased.

Momma! I wanted to scream. I wanted to take my two hands and give her a good shaking. I thought, *If you don't get a hold of yourself, he's going to think you are some hussy.*

"Where are you and Jessie headed?"

If my momma can't control herself in front of the rotund man, it is up to me to keep her from making any more a fool of herself than she has already done, I thought. "We're headed home to Tampa. It's about twenty miles from Durham," I said loudly, and I looked at Momma to impress upon her my urgency to leave.

"Tampa, huh. I get up that way every now and then." He lowered his head and took off his hat so he could move his face into the open window. He looked past me as if I didn't even exist. "The next time I get down your way, do you suppose a fella like me might be able to take you out to dinner and some light conversation?" He smiled slowly at Momma.

Momma passed me, as if I didn't exist, and directly at him.

"A fella like you, no," she said. "You, yes." She slowly added and fluttered her eyelashes twice.

He blushed a bit and smiled big at Momma.

It's sickening, I thought. *Two grown adults, past middle age, mooning all over the place in broad daylight.*

I put my foot on the gas pedal and raced the motor. *This poor woman needs rescuing now!* I thought.

Momma reached over and patted my hand, which was on the gearshift knob. I took my foot off the gas pedal.

"Of course, a fella has to get to Tampa first." She motioned for me to drive off.

As we left, Momma shifted in her seat so she could look back at him. She put her hand out the window and gave him a little wave then turned back around, looking straight ahead as if nothing had happened.

As I drove, I glanced over at her from time to time. After my third glance, she said, "What?" I eyed her coolly.

"It doesn't mean a thing. Can't a woman have a little fun?"

I shook my head a couple of times. "Mmm," I said as I shrugged my shoulders. "Maybe I do understand *fun*..." I quickly glanced her way.

"Jessie, I may look like it, but I'm not dead. Besides, that'll be the last I'll ever see of Mr. Hiram P. Dumphy." She emitted a little sigh. "Especially since you so conveniently let him know that I have a dozen kids."

"Poppa was your man," I said.

"Your poppa is dead ... I'm not," she added in almost a whisper, more to herself than to me.

As we drove home, Momma started humming an old song. She hummed, and the tune was quite catchy. It had a lovely sound.

"That's lovely," I said, and I peeked at her flushed face. "What's the name of that song?"

"*I can't give you anything but love, baby,*" she said as she gazed straight ahead.

"*I can't give you anything but love, baby. That's the only thing I've plenty of, baby ... *"

And she started humming again, and then she broke out singing; I joined in.

"*Gee, I'd like to see you looking swell, baby. Diamond bracelets Woolworth doesn't sell, baby. Till that lucky day; you know darned well, baby. I can't give you anything but love.*"

We finished the song on key, and we laughed at ourselves. It made me feel warm and toasty inside. Momma continued to hum as I drove. She seemed to be lost in a world of her own.

A sense of panic struck my tailbone; actually, it was my heart, because it was the first time in my life I was forced to come to terms with the fact that my momma was more than just "Momma." She was a woman, and she was lonely. At my age, at that time, I was unable to understand how it was possible to be lonely when you have a dozen kids to love you.

For about a week after Momma had met Mr. Dumphy, I was a nervous twit, thinking that he was gong to arrive and take my momma away from us kids and put us all in some godforsaken place where they torture children.

Two weeks passed and still no Mr. Dumphy. Momma never mentioned his name. I was singing praises to the Lord for delivering my momma from the fringe of being a woman who wanted to be a hussy.

Just about a month to the day after Momma and I had met Mr. Dumphy in Durham, Momma was away taking care of her sick elderly people. Pauline and I were home with the younger children, and a special delivery boy came to our door.

"I have a special delivery for a Mrs. Lou Crandal. Is this the right address?" he asked.

When I saw the gifts, my heart sank into my shoes. I was certain it had something to do with my infamous Mr. Dumphy.

"You have the wrong address," I lied.

Pauline looked at me as if I had gone crazy. She stepped out on the porch where the delivery boy was turning to leave.

"Don't pay any attention to her; that's our momma."

He looked at me in a strange way, and I could tell that he was upset with me.

"I don't have time to play," he said. He took a step into our house as we parted ourselves out of the way. He sat the delivery down. "I need someone to sign for this."

"I'll sign for it," I said, as I wanted to control the situation.

"Oh, aren't the roses beautiful!" Pauline said gleefully. "Who in the world is sending flowers to Momma? It must be some secret admirer."

If only it were some secret admirer, I thought.

Deannie picked up the large box of candy and held it up. "Look, candy. Mmm."

"Who's it from?" Pauline asked. She picked up the card. "Yup, it's addressed to Momma." She pushed the card out in front of her for all of us to see to whom it was addressed. "Hiram P. Dumphy," she said. "The card says it is from some man I have never heard of. Jessie, do you know who this man is?"

He's some dumpy-looking old man Momma mooned over and made a fool of herself, like she was some teenager suffering from her first puppy love, in public. She embarrassed all of our future grandchildren and me, I wanted to tell them. But I said, "He's a man Momma and I met while in Durham. He helped Momma and me out of the rain and was a real gentleman."

"You mean Momma's got a beau?" Pauline asked, and she smiled at me as though she had just shared something secret but wonderful.

"No!" I screamed. "Momma doesn't have a beau! Don't ever say she has a beau." I gave her a menacing look.

My words and behavior scared little Arthur, and he scurried behind Pauline.

"Now look what you've done, scared him to death."

In a few seconds, I regained my composure.

"Mr. Dumphy is just a man Momma met for a few minutes, that's all," I said in a soft tone of voice.

"Sure," Pauline said. She picked up the roses and held them close so she could smell them. "They smell even better than they look." She laid them down on the table and picked up the box of candy; she fingered the card lying on the table with his return address on it. "Flowers, candy, a romantic card. Looks like a man courting a woman to me."

I quickly grabbed the flowers and threw them onto the floor.

"Momma doesn't have a boyfriend!" I yelled. "Do you hear me?" I bent over to pick them up but instead kicked them against the wall.

"What in the world," Pauline said as she pushed past me and retrieved the flowers, though now they were in pretty bad shape. "Have you lost your mind? When Momma finds out, I wouldn't want to be in your shoes."

My younger siblings huddled together because they were afraid of how I was acting. "Me neither," they said almost in unison.

I grabbed the flowers and ran out the back door. *I can't have a crazy woman who can't control herself with this…this man,* I thought. *Therefore, if she doesn't have enough decency to know that her only job in this life is to be our momma, I'll protect her from her weak self.*

I was going to tear up the flowers one by one and enjoy the moment of knowing I was saving Momma by putting Mr. Dumphy out of our lives for good; then, I thought of a better, devilish scheme.

I could hear Momma's voice: *"Fresh flowers up on the podium area by the preacher just adds a touch of beauty to any worship service."*

Ranny Grady

I'll take them to the church. At least some good can come from this, I thought.

I did my best to fix them up after mistreating them. I ran to the church and found it closed, so I took them next door to the preacher's manse. The preacher's wife, Elizabeth, opened the door when I knocked.

"Jessie, what a pleasant surprise." She had an apron on, and there was just a hint of flour on her right cheek. "I'm busy making some cookies for the bazaar." She motioned for me to come in.

"I can't stay," I said. "Momma wanted you to have these." I thrust Mr. Dumphy's roses into her hands.

"My goodness gracious, they are so lovely," she said as she gave me a puzzling look.

"Some delivery boy left them at our house by mistake," I lied through my teeth. *Please, God, don't send me to hell for this little white lie,* I thought. I'm sure I showed that I was nervous lying because all I could hear was Momma scolding me. "You can go to hell for lying, just as much as you can for stealing," she told us kids many times.

"Are you sure about this?" Elizabeth asked as she held up the roses, which were still wrapped in the paper they came in. She looked at me as if she were trying to see if I was being untruthful. I was uncomfortable under her gaze.

Let me hear you say pork and beans ten times. I recalled my poppa's voice, as he used that trick to discern whether we kids were lying or telling the truth. It seemed to work on all of us, except Rose and Charlie. "Natural-born liars," he often said in reference to them.

"Yes, ma'am," I said. "Momma insisted on it."

"Well, you tell Lou, much obliged. They will certainly add a spark to Malachi's service."

"Momma said those flowers would be in better hands; we can't seem to find a green thumb anywhere in our house." I waved good-bye and raced home. I gave her a big smile.

As I ran back home, because my plan had just finished its first part, there was no way I could avoid being in absolute conflict with my conscience. "Liar, liar, pants on fire" was the phrase that kept running in my head.

As I walked in the back door, minus the flowers, Pauline asked, "Where did you go? What did you do with Momma's flowers?"

"I took them over to the preacher, and he is going to use them this Sunday."

"You gave away Momma's flowers?" Pauline's voice was filled with impending doom—for me.

I reached out and picked up the box of candy chocolates, and I opened them. I took off the lid and offered them to my brother and sisters. At first they backed up and acted like they were afraid of them and me.

"Here, eat some of them," I said as I picked out one and put it in my mouth. "Mmm, they are so good. Have one."

They looked up at my sister as if they needed her permission. They thought I was a lunatic. Pauline gave them a pensive look. She put her hands up in a manner to indicate that they might as well enjoy some chocolates, and they came close and grabbed two each.

We sat around and gorged ourselves on the candy.

"I wouldn't want to be you," Pauline said to me. "When Momma finds out—whew, you may never see daylight the rest of your life."

"What if she never finds out?" I looked over at the younger kids and then at Pauline. "If we share an oath, Momma may never find out. I may have been the one who started this, but you all ate the candy too."

"I don't want a whuppin'," Arthur said.

"We'll all get one if we don't stick together," I said.

After a bit of coaxing, we all agreed to make an oath not to say a word about what we had done with Momma's gifts from Mr. Dumphy. To ensure that we were sworn to silence, we carried out our oath ceremony. Ever since Momma had introduced us kids to Tom Sawyer and Huck Finn when she read to us at night, we did what they did: we had a blood oath to swear allegiance to any type of secret quest. We used a tiny sewing needle and put the head in some soap. We pricked our fingers and then shared our blood. It became a sacred blood oath that we agreed would never be broken, even if it were built on a foundation of lies.

I took the card, which I really wanted to tear up, but I couldn't do it, so I hid it under my side of the mattress of Momma's and my bed.

When you are just barely a teenager, you can't appreciate just how smart mommas are and how difficult it is to keep a lie from breaking out all over and vexing all who are a part of the lie.

When Momma came home from her nursing job, she immediately had her momma antenna up.

"Is there something going on I need to know about?" she asked a couple of times.

I'm sure we didn't fool her one bit because when we answered her, our replies were too perfect, too rehearsed, even down to little Arthur's assurance that nothing was going on.

Even though she knew we were acting a bit strange, she didn't press us for an answer. We were ready to eat and get ourselves ready for bed. Regardless of how tired Momma might be, if at all possible, Momma liked to spend some time with Arthur, the baby of our family. She always got him ready for bed; it was her quiet time with him so she could wash him up and love on him.

"And how's my baby boy today?" she cooed. "Momma missed her boy." She fawned over him. She was washing his hands and kissing them as she teased and tickled him. She picked up his finger, the one he had chosen to be pricked for our blood oath. She saw the slight wound. "Did my boy get a little boo-boo?" She bent down and kissed it.

Arthur, not wanting to break our sacred blood oath or have Momma find out what had really happened to his finger, reacted defensively, and he pulled his finger away from Momma's lips.

"Did that hurt?" She was surprised by his actions.

"No," he replied too quickly.

Momma looked at him. "Good." She gave him a hug.

"I promised him I'd read him a story," Pauline said as she did her best to rescue him from spilling the beans.

There was a loud, unexpected knock on our door.

"Jess, get the door," Momma said. "Who in the world would be calling tonight?"

The summer sun was going down; it seemed to be so big and orange that one could start walking down the road and soon touch it. It allowed the sun to outline, silhouettelike, the large frame of the man standing at the door. I could tell that it was Hiram P. Dumphy.

As I reached for the doorknob, I wanted to be magically whisked away on a magical carpet, away to a neverland, never to return. I'd like to see if it were true that a person could start digging a hole, and if he dug deep enough and far enough, he'd find himself in China, which, at that moment, was a place I'd rather have been.

I opened the door and looked at Mr. Dumphy's smiling face.

"Good evening, Jessie—"

I slammed the door and turned around. I was trapped and didn't know what to do or where to go. I was numb.

"Jessie, who was at the door?" Momma asked.

I couldn't bring myself to lie to her face, but I didn't want her to know who was at the door. I said nothing.

"What is wrong with you?" Momma asked in a voice filled with exasperation.

Pauline passed me by and opened the door. She, too, was surprised. "Come in," she said, and she took a step back.

Hiram P. Dumphy stepped into our living room. He was wearing another white, starched shirt and dark tan slacks, which had a knifelike crease so sharp it looked like a man could shave with them. He also wore a camel-colored sport jacket and a yellow and brown tie with what looked like a diamond stick tiepin. His shoes were spit polished. He had a dark derby hat with a short brim on it. In his hand he had one red rose, and under his right arm he had a box of chocolates.

His eyes surveyed our home and all of us kids. He saw

Momma and Arthur in the finishing stages of prepping for bed. The jovial smile on his face faded, taking on a look of puzzlement.

"Mr. Dumphy!" Momma was in absolute shock and frustration. "What are—"

"I...I don't understand," he mumbled. He stood dumbfounded. "The flowers, the candy..." His voice trailed off as he recognized his romantic plan had all come undone for reasons he couldn't fathom.

"What are you mumbling about?" Momma asked, growing more flustered by the second. "What flowers? What candy?"

"The card," he said. "I had a special delivery sent so we..." His voice trembled as his sense of embarrassment grew. "Dinner and conversation. I can see this isn't going to work out." He turned to leave.

"Hiram, don't you move!"

Momma came over to where I was sitting, and she looked into my eyes. Without diverting hers from mine, she hollered, "Arthur, front and center!"

He came running as fast as he could. As he was running to her, all I could think was, *The jig is up. He's going to be a little traitor.*

Momma reached out and took hold of his finger.

"Let me see that finger." He obliged her. "How'd you get that wound?" She looked back at me. "Is that a blood oath?" It was clear that she knew I was the culprit in this mess.

"Jessie made me do it," he cried.

I could just picture my funeral: no one there, not even Momma. On my headstone: *Liar, liar, pants on fire.*

"Young lady," Momma said in a controlled tone of anger, "you get to your bedroom."

Momma turned her death-ray look from me and smiled sweetly at Mr. Dumphy.

"If you can give a gal twenty minutes to catch her breath and throw herself together some, I'll be honored to have dinner with you."

The tension he felt faded; he gave her a grin of relief. He pointed to the outside.

"Sure, that'll be just dandy. I'll wait in the car."

I went into the bedroom and sat on my side of the bed, away from the door. Momma opened the door, and she stood very still. Her eyes penetrated my soul, and I felt miserable, all alone. I felt a chill run up and down my spine.

Momma put hands on her hips then tears sprang into her eyes.

"Jessie Crandal, how could you do this to me?"

My grand plan didn't seem so grand. All I had done was in the best interest of our family, especially me, but I didn't want to see Momma hurting in the heart.

"If I was a little younger, and you were a little younger ... I swear I'd get out your poppa's razor strop and skin the hide off you within an inch of your life." She held out her hand. "Where is it?"

I looked up at her sheepishly.

"Give it to me," she demanded.

I reluctantly lifted up the mattress and retrieved the card and handed it to her.

"Sorry," I mumbled.

She snatched it from my hand as if she only had one chance to get it. She sat down slowly on the edge of her bed and opened it. Some of her tears soaked the card, and then she held up the card and said, "This is the first card any man has ever given me."

I had deliberately hurt her, and I didn't know how to fix it. My problem was that I didn't want to fix it. I didn't think Momma was thinking clearly about the whole situation.

"Momma, I'm sorry I hurt you, but I am not sorry for trying to keep you from making a fool of yourself," I said.

Momma's demeanor changed.

"You're not my keeper. I'm free, white, and way over twenty-one. I don't need your permission to live my life any way I choose with any man I choose."

"But you're a momma with a dozen kids!"

Momma's steely eyes looked at me. "And just how do you suppose I got those dozen kids?"

RANNY GRADY

"That's the problem. Evidently, I'm the only one watching out that you don't go using Naomi's favorite word." I regretted saying that as soon as it left my mouth.

Momma got up off the bed and stood very close to me. Suddenly, she slapped my face. I recoiled and put my hand up to my stinging cheek. I started to cry; she had never slapped me before.

She pushed past me and went out the door.

I slowly made my way to the front door, and I looked out as Hiram was helping Momma into his car. I kept rubbing my face where Momma had slapped me. That slap changed Momma and me. Looking back, I believe it was our watershed moment—the moment she recognized that I was becoming more a woman than a girl; I recognized that she was more than just Momma.

"Jeepers, he must be as rich as God," Gracie said as Pauline and the other kids came back into the house.

"I'm surprised to see you're still alive," Pauline said. "You should have seen his car! It's a Packard. It has, honest to God, wood paneling in it."

I didn't reply to her banal conversation, and I went out on the porch. I was irritated at my siblings for going all wide-eyed over his car. I felt like they were traitors to my cause.

Mr. Dumphy caused a breach in Momma's and my relationship. I considered him a worthy adversary. At that time, I blamed him for the breach.

Momma and Mr. Dumphy's relationship matured into one that was more than platonic but not romantic.

She kept saying that they were more than friends, but she denied that they were seriously considering matrimony. She told me the decision was hers, not his. He made the trip to Tampa about once a month. He always sent flowers, candy, and a card in advance of their dates. He wanted to shower Momma with expensive gifts, but she wouldn't allow it. She did accept some lovely lady's hankies.

"He'd marry me tomorrow if I'd consent," Momma said more than once. Even after he had Thanksgiving dinner with all of us, he never wavered from his goal of getting Momma to marry him.

"The man must have a few marbles loose," Momma often said when Hiram's name was brought up. "Why he loves me, I'll never know."

I kept my gills up for a long time, wanting to be sure he didn't find a way to spirit Momma away from our family. After a few years passed, and I grew up, I came to realize what a wonderful man he was to accept Momma's terms about their relationship and to keep on loving her just the same. I changed my opinion about Momma's being married to him.

Mr. Dumphy had to take a trip to Kansas City on business. He was attending some type of exhibition for mercantile shop-keepers. He invited Momma to go with him; Momma agreed to go.

"Now, don't go worrying your pretty little head off about me going," Momma said. "It has all been arranged. We have separate rooms." She gave me a look that told me she was way ahead of me.

"Oh, Momma, I wasn't—"

"Tut, tut, tut, you can go to hell—"

"For lying just as easily as for stealing." I finished her statement, and we both laughed.

"I'm just a little concerned about your health," I said.

"Fiddlesticks." She waved her hand to indicate that she was fine. "This old warhorse,"—she chuckled a bit—"there's nothing to fret about."

Momma had been showing signs of fatigue. She was more inclined to plop down in the easy chair and rest when she came home from nursing.

"Your momma just needs a little more rest," she would tell us when she seemed to be more tired than usual.

I noticed a time or two that her side of the bed's sheet had a few blood spots on it.

"When a woman's had twelve kids, everything inside has been so stretched and rearranged; everything wants to fall out." She used humor to try and cover up her ailments.

Hiram came to pick her up in his brand-new Packard; he had just bought a new and fancier one. Momma was in our room packing a few things.

"I wonder what color this one will be?" I asked.

"I hope it's not black, any color but black," Momma said.

"Momma, why don't you marry Hiram?"

Momma came over to me, and she used her hand to feel my forehead.

"Just wanted to make sure I don't need to call the doctor," she teased me in light of my past behavior and words. "Funny you should say that." She slyly smiled. "I told Hiram last week that when we return from Kansas City, we're going to get married."

"That would be so wonderful," I said. I pulled her close to me and started to cry. "Momma, can you ever forgive me?" I asked as tears ran down my face onto her dress.

"*Shh.*" She patted my back and did her best to comfort me.

"I've been such a fool," I moaned. "He was the right man for you, and I did my best to destroy your happiness."

"Yes, on both accounts," Momma said subtly. The irony of her answer made us laugh.

"I . . . I was so selfish and so stupid. What was I thinking? The kids could have had advantages only money can buy—education, travel!"

"I could have been a lady of leisure and a social bee in Durham," Momma interrupted and laughed.

She used her two hands and cupped my face. "It's all working out for the best. Besides, I'm not sure a sophisticated place like Durham could have survived the Crandal clan." We laughed.

"So when's the big date?" I asked nosily when Momma came bursting through the door upon returning from her trip.

"Hiram and I had a long time to be together, and we had a serious talk about our future. We decided to keep things just as they are." She gave me a light kiss and a warm hug.

"You're kidding, right?" She didn't answer right away. "Momma, let me go to him, and I'll convince him that this is the right thing to do," I said, as I wasn't content to see Momma's happiness thwarted again.

"No!" she said. "This decision has been settled by Hiram and me. No amount of discussion will change it. Some things were just never meant to be.

"'Why do you say, O Jacob, and complain, O Israel, my way is hidden from the Lord; my cause is disregarded by my God? Do you not know? Have you not heard? The Lord is the ever-lasting God, the Creator of the ends of the earth, and he will not grow tired or weary, and his understanding no one can fathom. He gives strength to the weary. And increases the power of the weak. Evens youths grow tired and weary, and young men stumble and fall; but those who hope in the Lord will renew their strength. They will soar on wings of eagles; they will run and not grow weary, they will walk and not be faint.'"

How odd, I thought. Momma was quoting one of her favorite passages in the Bible, Isaiah 40:27. I couldn't understand why she, out of the clear blue sky, would quote that particular passage. Later, when I knew why she had gone to Kansas City, it made perfectly good sense. She was starting to come to terms with what lay ahead of her.

"Just like Isaiah, we all grow weary," she said. "And some of us just run out of daylight." She left me standing there.

Momma's dead and gone many, many years now, and as I have the privilege of looking back across the landscape of my life, the singular regret I have is Momma's missed opportunity.

How grand it would be to be able to pull out the family album and spend precious moments reminiscing over the pictures of Momma and Hiram's wedding, to recall that special day and receive warm fuzzies from their loving relationship, to see Hiram bounce grandbabies on his knees, my children. But none of that came to pass.

Momma didn't go to Kansas City with Hiram to a business meeting. Hiram took Momma to see a specialist for cancer. I didn't find out about the ruse they had pulled off for some time. Finally, Momma could no longer hide her disease from us. Momma was diagnosed with rectal cancer.

Momma didn't die right away. She lingered and suffered for nearly four years.

My Pedagogic Momma

Next to living by God's biblical principles, education was the most important thing to Momma. While she didn't possess more than a sixth-grade education, I was constantly amazed by the breadth and scope of her knowledge. I could tell that she took pride in being able to provide us children with information from all walks of life, enabling us to possibly sound smarter than we looked.

When our school was out, her school began. If she weren't able to be there at our home because of her job, Rose became our headmaster in her stead.

"You may be sharecropper kids, but you are going to be smart ones." Momma used to drill us with her high expectations. "If you remain ignorant, how are you going to be president of these United States?" she would admonish my brothers. She sought ways to motivate her boys to be inspired to greatness. Just because some of us were girls, it didn't mean she cut us any slack. "Women have the right to vote. One day they will have equal rights to own property, and, who knows, a woman may one day be in Congress." She would constantly encourage us girls to strike the fire for learning.

My older brothers were expected to learn how to read, write, and cipher numbers, even if they didn't have the opportunity to attend school. They often grumbled when Momma applied pressure for them to achieve excellence in their studies from a nurturing aspect. She would openly challenge them with performance questions. She was relentless!

Momma made up crude-looking cards that had the same multiplication numbers we used in our arithmetic lessons in school. She did the same thing for phonics, and she always found a way to have money to buy the Big Chief writing tablets for our writing and penmanship exercises.

"Rote memory is what it takes," Momma declared as we would repeat over and over the material she taught us. We Crandal students often balked at her methodology to run through our learning paces one more time. "Most adults don't have the concentration powers of a gnat, and only the good Lord himself knows how far down that learning tree children fall," she'd chide when we complained.

When we would continue to fuss about the onerous demands of our momma, who had morphed, once again, into a tyrant of a teacher, she would seek to prick the conscience of the angel side of our natures.

"Just think how much you are helping your little sisters and the baby of our family learn how to be prepared to start their schooling. When they get old enough to go to school, won't they be some smart whippersnappers?"

She would usually pull out one of the cue cards and direct a simple question to one of us kids. If we could answer it correctly, she would get excited and plant a big kiss on both of our cheeks. If we couldn't provide the answer, Momma would turn to us with dramatic flair, as only Momma could pull off, and say, "There, does that make you proud? You're all sitting there moaning and fussing about having to be better educated. Will you all allow your lazy, sorry examples of not learning all you can when your poor ole momma only wants the best for her children to doom your young brother and sisters to a life of being ignorant dunces?" She really knew how to lay it on thick. Even though we felt used, we learned that it just didn't pay to try and persuade her differently once she had her mind set.

"Momma played dirty pool!" Charlie and Howard often said as we kids dealt with the repercussions of having a mother who, by hook or crook, became well acquainted with the teachers of our school. How did she find the time to keep two or three jobs and still be a very active parent in all of the school's functions? Only the Creator could be in all the places at the same time, as Momma seemed capable of being. I often thought, *Momma taught us that God is omnipresent, which means that he is every-*

where at the same time—maybe he took lessons from Momma. All twelve of us kids knew she had eyes in the back of her head.

Personally, I loved school. I loved the competition of testing myself. I loved the joy of discovering new things, which provided me with new insights, causing me to ponder and reflect, whether it was something scary, funny, incredibly clever, or, in some cases, profound. I was a very good student. The only sibling who was better than me was Rose. Try as we might, none of us kids could hold a candle to her scholastic ability.

"The good Lord puts all of his children on the earthly train," Momma said as she did her best to answer my question as to why Rose was able to get the best grades. It seemed that she put out the least effort. "He has his own reasons for putting some on an engine that can travel faster than most, and he gives them a bigger and brighter headlight." She did her best to assuage my discontent of knowing that Rose had a faster engine and a much brighter headlight than I had. "But Jessie, lots of people possess those advantages, and they still can't find a way to arrive at the right town on time." She patted me on the fanny. "Are you getting my drift?"

I can look back upon my school years, and there were only two times that I wished my life could come to a crashing halt, not counting the zillions of times Momma made an unannounced visit to my teacher in our classroom. It actually wasn't to officially check up on her brood, but it felt like it. With only a rare exception here and there, it was to handle some school-related function that was in the planning.

Until my senior year in high school, our town had a large, redbrick building where all twelve grades were taught. The elementary grades were in the first floor of the building, and the high school had the top floor of the building.

"When a child approaches pre-pubescence," Momma lamented, "it seems as if all their wires get short-circuited, and their brains just take a vacation. Puppy love! It's going to be the death of me," she would say and give off a phony type of wailing as she clutched her breast and pretended to swoon. Every time she caught a whiff of secretive conversations that pertained to the opposite sex, she would play the part of house detective. She did her best to wheedle information out of one of us, even if we had sworn an oath of fealty, upon penalty of having our tongues cut out. None of us would ever fess up to breaking our promise to appease Momma's curiosity.

"You are nothing but a lowlife rat," Charlie said to any of us who didn't keep our promise not to tell Momma; nevertheless, Momma seldom was kept in the dark about the romantic escapades of that often cross-eyed cupid.

My most embarrassing moment during my school years took place soon after my seventh year of school commenced. Momma was right; puppy love was the culprit that was my undoing.

Eddy Slaughter was a boy in my class. Not just a boy; I had a terrible crush on him. He was one of the tallest boys in my class, and I was one of the tallest girls; therefore, I guess we sort of had a natural attraction. He was gangly and a tad awkward; his clothes hung on him rather than fit his body. His curly dark brown hair was coarse to the touch; I had touched it one day when he yanked my hair and I yanked his back. His cheeks had strong bone structure, and he had a square jaw. His lips were full, and his deep blue eyes flashed easily whether smiling or in anger. He had a deep voice for a boy so young. He was a recess warrior. I realize now that I was not much more than a tomboy, and I wanted to compete with the boys in all of the games we played during recess. I was a decent athlete, not afraid to get dirty, much to Momma's chagrin. I often caught him giving me more than a casual glance, even during study time.

It has been well documented that first crushes and puppy love are often marked by halted communication. Often the boy will act out with some form of physical treatment, even an ill-advised use of open ridicule or other types of mistreatment. Since the boy or the girl isn't mature enough to conduct a normalized relationship, which is filled with mutual respect and affection, this becomes the method used to endear him to the girl. Anyway, this was my psychologist Momma's explanation while trying to help me handle the aftermath of my most embarrassing moment in school.

It happened one day at school a few minutes before lunch.

I ran home as fast as I could. I burst into the house, panting for breath.

"Momma!" I screamed. I didn't know if Momma was at home or at work, but if she was at home, I wanted her front and center. Momma was there, and she ran to the front door to see why I was yelling. She had her white apron on because she had been busy fixing our school lunch. When I saw her, I came apart emotionally.

"Momma, Momma!" I cried as I made a mad dash rush to run into her arms. I grabbed her around the hips and allowed the tears to flood my soul. I buried my face into her body, and the softness of her against my face filled me with comfort. I sobbed haltingly. I squeezed her tight and muffled a scream. My emotions spewed out, and I struggled to stifle my inner rage.

"Jess," Momma said as she did her best to comfort me, even though she didn't have the foggiest idea why I had fallen to pieces. She held me as tight as I held her. When I squeezed her tighter, she did the same to me. She began to rock us gently. "Jessie, baby," she cooed. "It's all right. Nothing can be this bad," she calmly said as she lovingly brushed my hair, which had become wet from all my tears. "It's okay; it's okay," she whispered. She slowly and gently pushed me away from her body and looked at my distraught face and red, tear-swollen eyes. "You aren't dead, and you surely haven't killed anyone." She tried to change the somber atmosphere.

"I want to die!" I sobbed as I returned to her arms and warm body for comfort.

By this time my brothers and sisters had arrived for lunch. Momma sent me to our bedroom. She told me to wait in the bedroom until she could get the family their lunch.

Begrudgingly, I went to the bedroom. I must have fallen asleep from all of my spent emotions since I had continued to bawl my eyes out as I waited for Momma to come and love me some more.

I felt Momma's soft hand gently nudge me on my left shoulder. "Jessie," she softly said.

I was startled, for I couldn't believe that I had fallen asleep. When I recognized that it was her, I reached up as fast as I could and hugged her neck. The tears started again.

"Shh, honey. What in the world has happened to you?"

"I'm never going to school again!" I said in a loud voice.

"What do you mean you're not going to school?"

"I can't." I started to blubber and my front lips quivered. "I can't ever show my face"—my tears began to flow more freely—"again."

Momma sat down on the edge of the bed and picked me up and pulled me close to her.

"Jess, just tell me what happened."

"You're going to whip me," I said. "Oh, Momma."

This type of confession changed my momma's demeanor. "Why don't you let me be the judge of that."

"You know Eddy Slaughter?" I looked up at her as I started my story, explaining how I had just seen my life come to an end from my perception of pain and embarrassment.

"The boy you are sweet on." Momma smiled with a hint of a smirk on her face as she let me know that she had discovered my romantic interest.

I must have looked startled, for she laughed softly.

"Used to be," I said in a huff. "Well, anyway, Eddy was at the water fountain, and I was standing behind him. The bell was about to ring to end our recess time, and I was very thirsty. I pushed him on his back to hurry up so I could get a drink and get to my seat so I wouldn't be tardy for class. He deliberately kept on drinking. Then he suddenly turned around, looked into my eyes, and spit the water out of his mouth into my face."

Momma allowed herself the acknowledgment of the event that I was detailing. I could tell that she was fighting to keep from laughing; she had a crease of a smile on her face. Her eyes signaled that she wasn't too concerned that Eddy had done such a horrible thing to me.

"Momma, he made me so mad. I took a big drink, then I filled my mouth with water, and when I entered into the class-room, I ran over to him and spit my water right at him," I said with a tone of voice that indicated I was sure it was a just thing to do.

"Jessie Almeta Crandal, you didn't!" Momma showed her shock.

I put on the best "Miss Innocent" look I could muster.

"Momma, the problem was, I missed Eddy, and the water went all over Miss Babcock's new hat!"

I didn't appreciate how Momma handled my confession until I had children of my own. She managed to hide her desire to laugh out loud, for it was very funny. She was not laughing because she knew it would not sit well with me, considering my delicate, emotional condition. She managed to keep a straight face and allowed me to tell all of the story. She would later find glee in retelling the story at my expense.

"Did you get a whipping?"

"I wish I had," I cried loudly. "Mrs. Babcock came to the back of the room and glared at me. If a teacher's stare could kill a student, I swear, Momma, I wouldn't be here talking to you. She was as mad as Poppa when the bull put the hole in his car's fender."

"What did she do?" she asked, but I could tell she was having a hard time keeping a straight face as I continued to pour out my heart to her.

"Mrs. Babcock brushed the water off her hat and placed it back on a clothes hook closer to the window so the sun could dry it. She looked at me, then at Eddy. She then marched back to her desk and sat down."

"Jess, I can't see why you have allowed this to make you a big bawl baby?"

"Momma, remember, you are always saying that God is always watching over you," I said.

She nodded.

"And, if it takes a lifetime, how he will punish the wicked?" Without waiting to receive her answer, I said, "It was a few minutes before the bell, and all of a sudden I had to use the restroom something awful. I quietly approached Mrs. Babcock's desk. She looked up at me, and her eyes glared like daggers. I whispered very politely, 'Please, Miss Babcock, may I be excused to go to the bathroom?'

"In a soft whisper she said, 'Young lady, you cannot go! The bell will ring in a few moments.'

"A few moments! The urgency of my dilemma caused me to wriggle and churn on the soles of my shoes. I was positive that the yellow color of urine would soon be visible from the upper edges of my hazel-green eyes, I thought as I obeyed her, Momma."

"'Young lady,' Mrs. Babcock openly addressed me before the class, 'you have done all you could to disrupt my class this morning. I have had about all of your shenanigans and tomfoolery I'm going to stand.'

"Momma, her voice grew loud and mean. She pointed to the blackboard next to her desk.

"'Now, you stand right there; don't you move until the bell rings!' Mrs. Babcock said.

"Momma, remember how you are always saying you can't understand why God gave women smaller bladders than men? Well, my bladder was about to burst. I mean, I did all I could to hold it. Remember how you told us kids to think about other things, something you really enjoy, when we were all clamoring to use the necessary place in inconvenient times? Well, Momma I did what you said—nothing worked. I even tried to stand on one leg, which did nothing but make my classmates laugh. I finally turned and nearly jumped up and down to keep from peeing my pants."

"'Miss Babcock, I have to go to the bathroom,' I said through my gritted teeth and loud enough that everyone in the class could hear.

"She just shook her head no and pointed to the clock. 'The bell will ring in less than five minutes.'

"Five minutes isn't very long, unless you can't hold your bladder any longer." I was once again sobbing. I continued my tale of woe. "I did everything in my power to not allow the pee to come out, but it did. A warm, sticky liquid began to flow down my legs, and soon there was a puddle under my feet. There was a collective gasp from the room full of students. The bell rang; I ran as fast as I could." I finished my tale of horror. "So you see, Momma, I can't ever go back to school." I sobbed, and my voice was filled with anguish. "And I'm never going back!"

"Oh, yes you are," Momma said in a firm, no-back-talk tone of voice. I started to cry again. "Jess, right now all of this seems to be about the worst thing that could ever happen to you. But it's high time that you learn life is seldom fair; sometimes it's downright cruel. When you become a woman, the measure of what type of woman you become is not going to be measured by how well you handle success, but how you handle your per-ceived failures, which most assuredly include your most embar-rassing moments."

"I don't care about my successes or failures; I'm never going back!" I screamed. "Please don't make me go back."

Momma grabbed me by the shoulders and looked me right in the eyes. "Jessie, right now you may think I am a meanie, but you're going back," she said as she gave me no wiggle room.

I pulled away from her and flung myself across the bed, sob-bing. I buried my face in the coverlet. "I thought you loved me!" I moaned through my huge sobs.

There was an eerie silence in the room for a few seconds. Momma's voice dropped an octave as she said, "If I have to drag you all the way by your heels, you are going back to school."

Silence filled the room. I was so hurt and angry at Momma because I felt she had failed to protect me when I was at my most vulnerable. It was at the time in my life when I was the neediest.

"Go change your dress and wash your face," she softy said as the silence was broken.

I reluctantly got up off the bed and went to freshen up.

"If I end up with some kind of mental disease where I have to be put in a crazy house from which I will never be normal again, and I am doomed to walk around like I'm tetched in the head, it will be all your fault." I gave her a hard, long stare of disgust.

Momma looked at me, and I could tell that she was struggling not to laugh.

I remember that dreaded walk back to my school. On that day, no one could ever have convinced me that even a condemned man on his way to being hanged could have felt worse. I guess there are some things that happen to people that are considered so awful that even fellow classmates can't bring themselves to use as fodder for the gristmill of humiliation. When I did make my entrance back into the classroom and took my seat, praying and hoping I had somehow become invisible, none of them teased me about the puddle I had made. Eddy even wrote me a scribbled note, apologizing as well as any boy could apologize to a girl.

The Educator

Ever since I can remember, Momma always had two very large, ominous-looking books sitting in a prominent place in our home: the family Bible passed down from generation to generation through her side of the family and Webster's Dictionary, given to her by her mother's sister the first Christmas she lived with her, along with a set of McGuffey Reader and Spelling books from which Momma schooled us.

"If you are going to be president of these United States, you have to be educated." I can recall Momma telling this to Howard when he and the rest of us kids were rebelling concerning her constant schooling, especially in the summertime.

"If you aren't smart enough to outfox the hen, how can you get elected?" Momma asked when repressing our attempted mutiny on her "Lou's Good School for Fools Ship." "A bit of learning from Mr. Webster's book will help you become smart; a little bit of learning from God's book will help you gain wisdom," Momma said. "Remember, being smart isn't the same thing as having wisdom." She worked out of both books nearly every day of our lives.

Momma's school was unique to say the least. As I have the benefit of hindsight, I can recognize that she was progressive and a woman of uncommon valor in a world not ready to embrace the phony façade of the adult society in the life of children. Her school was an open-ended place designed for intelligent inquiry and for vigorous academic pursuit. And for children, it was a safe place to explore the beauty and wisdom of God's greatest achievement, the creation of the male and female species.

Momma didn't trek with much foolishness. Once in a while she allowed her school to become a home school where all questions could be asked and answered. Sex education, unlike today, was something seldom discussed in polite company, and only a little more frequently in our homes. There was an open acknowledgment that men and women had different plumbing (outdoor verses indoor); however, when it came to the explanation of how the plumbing worked outside of the natural uses to take care of a body's waste, we children were left in a labyrinth filled with thick fog.

Like a good soldier, she stood in the muck and mire of the trenches and fielded all manner of questions about life that we shot at her. With a deft manner and an extremely alert mind, she weaved the wisdom and truth of God's Bible into every answer she could. Now, as an old woman myself, who also faced Momma's task, with the right of a more expected enlightenment to help children understand life and all of its marvelous mysteries, I really appreciate the way she handled that daunting task.

I can recall two instances when Momma used God's wisdom and her street smarts to educate our family.

Our school year had recently ended, and we children were once again on Lou's School for Fools Ship. Momma used some butcher paper and concocted a crude, rather large paper ship that she placed on our table when school was in session. She also made a sign out of the same type of paper and hand printed, in large letters, the name of her school. She announced that we would have a free day, and we could ask any question.

My brother Charlie, who did his best to skip Momma's school, sat next to our younger brother Arthur. One day, he whispered something into Arthur's ear. Arthur adored his big brother, and Charlie did his best to spoil him with treats.

"Since this is free day, who has a question?" Momma asked, showing she was in a perky mood.

We older kids usually monopolized any free day; therefore, when Arthur put up his hand, we all looked directly at him and even gave him some encouragement.

"Look, little Arthur has a question," I said, and we laughed at him.

Momma was pleased by his willingness to enter into the fray.

"And just what question does Momma's baby boy have?" Her voice filled with love.

"What does 'fart' mean?" he asked in a bold tone of voice.

Silence engulfed the room. Shock was on all of our faces, except my brother Charlie's. He was busting a gut not to laugh. Momma took a few seconds to recover from the initial shock of having his question fully register with her brain, and she gave a very stern look to Charlie because she was positive he had put his brother up to asking this type of question. Arthur was too young to know he had been set up by his brother.

"Arthur, I'm not sure you will be able to use Mr. Webster's dictionary and read the answer. Perhaps your *brother*"—she put a strong emphasis upon "brother"—"will help you," she said.

Charlie had a sheepish smirk on his face. He looked at us kids, and we wanted to burst out in laughter, but we didn't want to rile Momma, so we held it in. He took hold of Arthur's hand, and together they walked over to where the dictionary lay.

Wanting to be a smart-aleck clown and irritate Momma while entertaining us kids, Charlie opened the dictionary and said, "Arthur, how do you spell 'fart'?" His question caused us kids to let loose with a few muffled giggles.

Arthur looked up at him and said, "I don't know." He quickly turned to look at Momma. "Momma, how do you spell 'fart'?" This brought about some more muffled giggles.

"I'm sure your brilliant brother knows how to spell the word."

Charlie flipped the pages, and when he came to the section for *F,* he began to loudly and slowly say, "F-A-R-T." We kids could hardly contain ourselves, and we let loose with peals of laugher.

"He is so entertaining, isn't he?" Momma said in a derisive manner. "We don't have all day; will you please read the definition so Arthur can have the answer to his question?"

"A fart is when a person passes gas from the intestines— that's your belly—through the anus—that's your rear end,"

Charlie said, and we all broke up laughing. "A fart is also an old person who is regarded as a fool," he added, and we looked up at Momma with shock on our faces; he cleared his throat loudly. "A fart is a small explosion between the legs." He struggled to get it out; he turned around and looked at us.

We could not hold it back any longer. The entire room broke out in howls of laughter. For a few seconds, Momma stood before us with a stoic face; suddenly she broke out in laughter and joined all of us. "A cheerful heart is good medicine," she said, quoting Proverbs 17:22.

Not to be outdone by one of her children, especially Charlie, Momma said, "Mr. Smarty Pants, while you are entertaining our family so well, why don't you look up the word 'flatulence;'" Charlie's face flushed, and he turned and worked to find the word in the dictionary. "Flat—" He turned and looked at Momma. "How do you spell it?"

"What? An expert on farts doesn't know how to spell a word in that family?" Momma stuck him like an ox being gored.

She walked up behind him and helped him find the word. She put her finger upon the word in the dictionary. "Right there it is. Read what it says."

"Of or having gas in the stomach or intestines. Windy or empty in speech, pompous, or pretentious," he read.

Momma motioned for the boys to take their seats.

"So Charlie and Arthur, if you get tired of using the word fart, you can substitute it with flatulence." She looked at Charlie and smiled. "Which one do you think will work best for you?"

Our family lost it, and we broke out in sustained howls of laughter. Momma had skewered Charlie and made him completely undone before all of us.

Once some semblance of order was restored, and we were seated at the table, Momma looked at Charlie.

"A fool finds pleasure in evil conduct, but a man of understanding delights in wisdom," she said, quoting Proverbs 10:23.

Momma's school was a wonderful place to visit on a regular basis. She gave us some insight into the world we lived in. I'm quite certain that most children were never exposed to that type of education at a young age as we were.

While Charlie and Arthur provided the best fun our family ever experienced learning new words and their meanings, my sister Naomi provided us with the greatest shock.

One time, when Momma's school for fools was in session, Naomi said, "I just saw a word that I have never seen before."

"Where did you see it?" Momma asked.

"I saw it written on a freight car in red letters."

Mother's 'momma antenna' went up. "Do you think it's a good or a bad word?"

"I don't know, probably a bad one."

"Why don't you whisper it in my ear," momma motioned for her to come close.

Naomi drew close and whispered in Momma's ear.

Even though she whispered, everyone could hear. The older kids had shocked looks, and I was embarrassed, for a girl at school had told me about that word a few days ago.

Momma looked in her eyes. "That is a tricky word. I'd call it very vulgar."

"Why is it so bad?"

While the word "fart" had set our school abuzz, Naomi's question caused a different reaction to fall upon us. Those of us who already knew the meaning of the word felt very uncomfortable. I'm not sure just how many of us kids knew the meaning. Momma looked at all of us as if she were searching for some way of discerning if that word had been egged on like Charlie's word. It hadn't. Evidently she recognized that truth.

"Why don't we just move on," Howard said.

"No, I think this is a good time to explore the meaning of this word," Momma said.

Though I knew about its meaning, I must admit it was a mite confusing to me.

"Naomi, honey, that word is a vulgar word, and I don't want you to use it or repeat it. It's bad only because people have taken something beautiful and found a way to make it dirty," Momma said. "You won't even find it in a dictionary."

"If it's not even in the dictionary, how's it a word?" Naomi asked.

Momma allowed herself to enjoy a smile. "That is a tricky question, isn't it?" She chuckled. "Honey, that word is an ungodly word people use to describe sexual relations between a man and a woman." Momma started on her odyssey to try and give her the meaning of that word.

"You mean when they get a baby? When the girl gets pregnant?"

"I'm treading on thin ice here," Momma mumbled to herself. "Let me see. It certainly can lead to that."

Momma put up her hands and made a time-out sign. "Perhaps it would be best that the smallest children wait for another day to learn this definition."

I could tell she was growing more uncomfortable by the minute, as all of us who knew the meaning of that word were.

"All of you who wish to know more about this word, follow me," Momma said as she moved toward her bedroom. Only Momma and Naomi moved from the table. "Jessie, why don't you keep your sister company?"

"I already know," I said, protesting, then I reluctantly did as I was told.

When it was all over, I was glad I had gone because Momma filled in a lot of the blanks for me. In a few minutes, Naomi and I were both shell-shocked. I just couldn't keep from conjuring up the vision of Poppa and Momma. After all, they had us twelve kids! I can remember making a solemn vow to myself after Momma's sex education course: it would be a cold day in hell before I let some boy get near me. I also had to laugh at myself. More than once I had secretly sneaked into Momma and Poppa's bedroom to see if his overalls were hanging on the bedpost. Momma had told me that was all Poppa had to do to get her pregnant. I realized then that my efforts to try and help Momma would have been too little, too late.

When Naomi and I returned to the school's table, Momma got out her Bible.

"That vulgar word has many synonyms, and they all have to

do with sexual relations between a man and a woman. In the first book of the Bible, Genesis 4:1, it says Adam lay with Eve. Lay means having sexual relations. Other places words such as 'knew,' 'sleep with,' and 'begat' all mean that a man had sex with a woman. So the word is very confusing for children to understand. Do you understand what I'm saying?" She smiled at us.

The children of our family who had been privy to Momma's information or already understood the meaning of that word nodded their heads.

"Good," she said. "Then I'll close this little lesson on life with this: the apostle Paul tells all boys and girls to flee from sexual immorality. That means you don't have sex until you are married! Our wise and loving God gave this special relationship to a man and a woman as an indescribable gift of pleasure and beauty; mankind has found many ways to misuse it and take away much of its godly purpose."

The emotional pressure and embarrassment for us kids had been building, and when we were pretty sure our school was done, we fled the way Paul told the Christians to flee from fornication. We made a mad dash out of the house.

"And I don't want to ever hear that word used again," Momma yelled at our departing backsides.

Momma ran her school like a captain of a ship. She didn't truck with much nonsense, and she expected results.

"Let's just say it's my maternal need to pique my children's interest in furthering their education. So in the future they don't have a brain drain and, predictably and assuredly, an astronomical amount of stupidity breaks out," was one of Momma's slight-of-hand exercises she ran us through.

"I never had the opportunity to get any really formal learning. My father didn't believe a girl had any business spending time with such foolishness—the old fool," Momma said more than once when she found herself surrounded with a passel of children who didn't want to spend the time learning about the three R's. "I swore that one day, if I ever had children of my own, I would see to it that they got a good education, if not at school, then in my home.

"I can just hear my daddy bellowing," Momma said.

"'Just a waste of time sending a girl to school. All she needs to know is how to cook, clean, and keep house,' he said. 'Keep her barefoot in the summer and pregnant in the winter; that's God's plan,' he told me when I begged him to let me go to school.

"He was nothing but a poor sharecropper. When he died, he died broke and ignorant," Momma said.

"After my folks were killed in that horse and buggy accident, I came to live with my mother's sister. At fourteen I was too old to go to school; therefore, all of my learning was self-taught." Momma did her best to weave a tale of woe bad enough to make us kids see the wisdom of her demanding that all of us achieve new levels of learning each week of our lives.

Momma must have burned the midnight oil many days because each week she had a new list of words ready for us to learn the meaning of, use in a sentence, and know how to spell. Not even the little ones were given any slack. As soon as a child turned five, he or she was given homework.

Momma knew how to make learning fun. She would pass out rewards—mostly her praises—and we all sought to obtain her stamp of approval: kisses, hugs, and specially baked goodies to keep us motivated. The older children became mentors to assigned younger ones. "English Warriors," she called us as we grappled with learning all there was to know about phonics so we could know how to read and spell Mr. Webster's dizzying array of words. She would also read from God's Bible and ask us questions about the meaning of the words found in his book.

"Why don't you go visit old Mr. Webster" was her standard answer when any of us kids would ask her the meaning of a word.

It took us kids a while, but we soon came to realize that one of the best things Momma ever did for us was force-feed us through her "Lou's School for Fools Ship" school. When we started our formal schooling, we quickly found out that we were way ahead of most of our classmates.

"Your heads have been filled with something more than

mush," Momma was wont to say. We discovered that learning was empowering. When a body fights its way past the drudgery of learning the basics and begins to dig deeper into any subject, everything just comes alive; it takes on a life of its own. You become a passenger on a wonderful voyage to places you never knew existed.

Charlie thought learning to read was a stupid waste of time until he heard Momma read the story of David and Goliath.

"Gee, if I'd known it was this much fun, I'd have learned faster," Charlie gushed when Momma was busy reading the story of David and his battle with Goliath. Momma read our most favorite book, *Shepherd of the Hills,* more than once, and I can still hear Charlie begging Momma, "Please, Momma, read just a few more pages," when she was ready to stop for the night.

My sister Rose was so competitive, especially when it came to Momma, I'm convinced that she became our school's valedictorian mainly because she did her best to show Momma up by finding words she could intelligently use in a sentence. One of Momma's ironclad rules was that it didn't count if you couldn't find a logical way to use the word in everyday conversation. Rose did her best to stump Momma.

"The apostle Paul said, 'I would rather speak five intelligible words to instruct others than ten thousand words in a tongue.' And if it is good enough for the Lord's servants, it surely is good enough for the Crandal clan," Momma said as we all fumbled and stumbled about seeking a way to use our "School for Fools" words in sentences. We had some raucous times laughing at and with each other's use of the week's words, which Momma insisted we all learn.

Momma would say, "All together now: 'Listen my son, to your father's instruction and do not forsake your Mother's teaching. They will be a garland to grace your head and a chain to adorn your neck.'" She would have us put a heavy emphasis upon the word "mother's" when we recited Proverbs 1:8–9. This seemed trite, but later it became a source of endearment.

"I can't say I ever really came to know much about the

famous philosopher Socrates; I do know that he was considered a great teacher. He was into critical thinking.

"I'm more into finding a way to teach my children to stop their stinking thinking," Momma would say and then break into howls of laughter.

My momma used to embarrass all of us kids because she often—where she found the time I'll never know—would show up at our school and sit at the back of our classroom.

"I just want to make sure your teacher is as dull as you claim and see if she really does wear a dunce cap when she teaches." She teased us and taunted us when we would ask her why she came to school unannounced.

Even though Momma worked too many hours of the day, somehow she managed to be a friend and a loyal supporter of all of our teachers in the community. She held just about every office the Parents' Association had to offer. She would be the first parent to volunteer to take kids on a field trip or to a sporting event. Most of my teachers treated her more like she was one of them than a regular parent. Her friendship with our teachers didn't sit very well with us kids. While her teacher friends honored her sometimes with little tokens of appreciation, we wanted to send Momma bouquets of skunk cabbage. It seemed as if something was almost unholy with her close ties with the teachers.

"Why can't Momma be like the normal parents and show up only for the Christmas program and graduation?" Charlie asked. "She's just snooping on us."

One day Momma overheard Charlie complaining about her visits.

"Charlie, have you ever had to get an old cow out of the muck?" Unaware that Momma had heard his ranting, with a sheepish look he replied, "No."

"Well, do you think it would be an easy or difficult job to do?"

"I imagine it would be very hard."

"So if you were given a choice, would you rather keep the

cow from getting in the muck or let the cow get into the muck and then have to find a way to get the cow out?"

"Okay, okay, I get it."

We all laughed at his expense.

Momma had a well-deserved reputation in our town for being a parent who provided an enthusiastic support for our educational system. Since she was also well respected as a newspaper columnist, some of the people referred to her as the "Education Lady."

One of the town's leading businessmen, Karl Peavy, who owned the blacksmith shop, held Momma in such high regard (we kids used to tease Momma that he had a crush on her) because every time one of us kids graduated from high school, he sent Momma a lovely note of congratulation and included a gift of a beautiful lady's hanky.

A different type of an example of my pedagogic momma using her wiles and smarts to influence possible outcomes happened at the end of my junior year.

"There's book learning, good-old-horse-sense learning, and then righteous indignation, which forces a person to stand in the trenches and give an account of himself with a good ol'-fashioned knockdown, drag-'em-by-the-hair fight," Momma said when she learned our school board decided to do away with girls' basketball.

I came home from school, near the end of my junior year of high school, bawling my eyes out.

"Momma, Momma!" I screamed as I came through the front door like a cyclone. When I saw her in the kitchen, I ran to her and threw my arms around her. My tears made her cheeks wet.

I took her by surprise.

"What? What on earth?" She hugged me and then pushed me away about a foot. "Jess, slow down; take your time." Her eyes showed concern for me. "Catch your breath. Why don't we sit down, and you can tell all about it." She motioned for us to take a seat at the table.

"Oh, Momma...I...I'll just die." I moaned. "Truly, my life

won't be worth living." I looked into her face, and she was doing her best to console me.

"Honey, if you won't tell me what it is that you are willing to throw your life away for, I can't very well help you stop it from happening."

I wiped some tears away from my eyes with the sleeve of my dress.

"They aren't going to let us girls have a basketball team any more," I said in a meek voice that evolved into rage.

I looked at Momma, and she stared back. I could see the wheels of her brain churning, as mine were. Then, in almost perfect harmony, we said, "Erma Babcock."

Erma Babcock was the wife of just about the most influential man in our area. He and our dentist ran neck and neck on any opinion poll one might care to take concerning their importance to Tampa. Alan Babcock owned and operated the elevator and the mill. Nearly every person in our town was beholden to him because of the wheat harvest every year; it was easy to understand the family's power. He was a very likeable man and highly respected.

"She is a busybody up to no good," Momma often said, referring to his wife, Erma. "He must be a real saint living with that woman."

The past couple of years she had become a staunch supporter of the suffragettes, and she idolized Carrie Nation. Momma admired much of what the group of women was doing, seeking the right for women to vote and equal rights for women in the eyes of the law. She parted company when women wanted to define every aspect of what a woman could and should be allowed to do. Erma Babcock considered all women's athletics vulgar and unladylike. Momma didn't agree! They had shared some polite but heated exchanges from time to time while both served on various school functions.

"I can't help it. Every time I'm with that woman, she just gets my cockles up. When is there going to be a meeting to discuss this decision?" Momma asked.

RANNY GRADY

"There isn't going to be one; it's already been decided," I said with a whimper.

"We'll see about that! I may be a poor old widow woman, but just maybe the pen can be mightier than ... a mill," Momma said.

In the next few days, Momma marshaled her troops, especially the parents of the girls' basketball team. She nearly accosted some of the leading merchants with her vision of what girls should be allowed to do. She wrote a column, leaving out all names, addressing the unfairness of the school board's decision. She ended her article with a call to arms whereby the citizens' reaction to her column should be to demand a meeting to readdress the hastily made decision.

Our phone rang off the hook for several days, and in the end Momma won. The meeting was set for the following Monday evening at the dance hall.

"The pen, for all of its ballyhooed power, wasn't mightier than the dollar," Momma said when we were walking home from the meeting.

Our family had arrived early at the meeting, anticipating a great victory; after all, our cause was just. We didn't see any people milling around when we arrived because we were very early. It didn't arouse our suspicions that things wouldn't go well for our side.

Just before seven o'clock, the school board, the principal, and some of the leading citizens of Tampa arrived and sat with Erma Babcock. As the meeting commenced, two of the parents of the girls' basketball team slid quietly into the back of the room. Momma's boss, the editor of the paper, arrived a few minutes late.

Momma looked at me with a worried look on her brow.

"I feel like David against the Philistines, and I don't have any stones."

I'll give Momma a lot of credit; she did her best to offer a defense for having the decision to cancel the girls' basketball season reversed. She used her newspaper column as the background to provide an intelligent apologetic, but her main problem was the fact that her own daughter was used as exhibit A against her.

During our last year's basketball season, I had been involved with an on-court incident that caused a lot of consternation for our team, for our school, for our community, and especially for the Crandal home.

We were playing our archenemy, Durham, and it was a hotly contested game. Girls' basketball was much different than the game played today. Each team had six players on a team playing at any given time. There were two forwards, a center, and three guards. The game was played in half-court measures. Guards only played on defense, and the forwards and center played offense. There was a jump ball after each basket. I was a forward and only played on offense. I could handle the ball well, was quick, and could shoot well.

Durham had a big, burly, built blonde, a German girl, Ruth Schmidt, who played guard. She liked to mix it up, especially under the basket. She was as strong as an ox. Although she was bigger and stronger than anyone on our team, she was still very pretty. More than once, she bodied me and knocked me to the floor. When my body smacked into hers, it was like having my bones crushed. Earlier in the game, she hit me with her elbow, and my nose started to swell. In spite of all this, we managed to eek out a lead. We were ahead by four points with only a few seconds left. I had the ball, and I drove for the basket. When she came to defend my drive, I passed off to our center. She jumped into me and literally crushed me. It felt like a freight train had run over me. She then jumped back and blocked our center's shot. No foul was called. We were playing in Durham, and my temper got the best of me. I ran after her. I certainly couldn't hurt her physically, though I wanted to. I did the only thing that could hurt her; I reached out and pulled her bloomer uniform pants down to her knees.

I was ejected from the game. Her team was awarded two extra foul shots. We still won the game by one point, and she threatened to do me bodily harm. I was suspended from playing the next game. I admit I felt bad about my conduct, but in a strange way, I noticed the other team's players began to show me more respect, and their reaction to my unladylike conduct lessened my guilty conscience a lot.

Erma Babcock was at that game. I guess it was that incident that gave her the impetus to save all of us girls from ourselves when it came to being involved in activities she considered unladylike.

In minute detail, she gave an account of my improper behavior on the basketball court. She neglected to point out how Ruth had been turning our team into a black and blue team with her roughhouse play. She was very eloquent conjuring up some future, would-be evils girls' sports could bring to our school, our town, and the world. She pointed out that it was the woman's duty to become a helpmeet who would provide a haven where girls would be trained in music, poetry, homemaking, and giving a mother's care to her husband and children. A woman should not run around in bloomers and get into physical fisticuffs because things didn't go her way.

Momma only had one person openly support our side. To our surprise, it was our town's barber, Ralph Stanton.

"Personally, I think this is all a bunch of poppycock," Mr. Stanton said when he came forward and spoke on our behalf. "Girls' basketball has been good for our daughters, and it has been good for our school. Who among you can honestly tell me you haven't enjoyed watching our girls play basketball? If that isn't so, then why did I see most of you at all of the games?" His remarks made those in Erma's camp very uncomfortable, as they squirmed in their seats sitting in front of the room. "You are blowing the harm done by Jessie Crandal's improper behavior on a basketball court way out of proportion." Mr. Stanton turned to look at me. "It was improper behavior, young lady. He stared, for nearly a minute in silence, at the board members, "Isn't this much like burning down the barn to get rid of the rats? What do you say to those girls who have been training and practicing to get ready for their senior season? It just isn't right," he said emphatically. "Go on, take your cue from the side your bread is buttered on." Mr. Stanton sat back down.

In order to keep up appearances that the decision had not already been made prior to the meeting, the principal said, "The board will take a few minutes to make a final decision concerning this matter." They left the stage area and huddled for a meeting. In a few minutes, they returned from their meeting and took their seats at the table.

The president of the school board, Mr. Asa Slaughter, a German-Polish farmer who was well respected, was the spokesman. He spoke in broken English.

"After a lot of deliberation, by golly, and for sure shooting not just this evening, but how is best to say, stretches more than few days, and spending a lot of time thinking on this, it's decided. No more girls' team." He adjourned the meeting.

Momma said our town grew a little smaller in God's eyes after the school board made the decision to do away with a girls' basketball team. The board members lost a lot of the community's respect, including the newspaper editor's. He wrote a story to show his contempt of the decision. He may have suffered financially for the story. Those who carried out this grave injustice were diminished in stature. Everyone knew that Erma had used her pocketbook to wield an unhealthy amount of influence in our town to get her way. Most resented her behavior, though few would openly admit it. Even Momma's friendships were affected because her friends suffered with self-inflicted shame for being a toady who was bought.

More than once I heard Momma remark, "It is amazing what you can get for thirty pieces of silver these days."

We girls were left to wonder for the rest of our lives, *What if?*

When it came to receiving rewards and plaudits for being recognized as a great educator, the good Lord gave Momma one of her red-letter days one year while the Kansas State Teachers meeting took place. It was my first and only year to be a teacher, and Momma almost invited herself to accompany our family's group of teachers, Rose, Howard, Pauline, Naomi, Charlie, and me, to the Kansas City meeting.

We stayed at the famous, and infamous, Blackstone Hotel. It was recognized as one of the finest hotels in the Midwest. Everything about the hotel was first class. It also had a seedier reputation.

"It is a treat to just sit in the lobby and watch the people walk by you and to eat in the dining room and have their staff pamper you. Even if you are as poor as the proverbial church mouse, it makes you think you are rich," Momma said when we first experienced that treat while attending the meeting.

I had already made my decision to quit teaching but hadn't shared that decision with anyone, so I had mixed feelings all during the conference.

On the second day of the meeting, Momma was to meet us for lunch, though she did attend some of the conference's sessions.

"I'm just going to sit in the lobby and enjoy myself. I'll be a people watcher; perhaps I can find some interesting story to write about." She shooed us off to our meetings without her.

True to her word, Momma was waiting for us when lunchtime came. She was seated at one of the largest tables. She left our family name with the maitre d' so it would be easy to find her in that large room. When we arrived at our table, we were surprised to find her sitting with a stranger. We kids all looked at one another with a puzzled look, and we quickly took a seat.

"Joseph, these are the teachers I have been telling you about," Momma said. "Children, this distinguished gentleman sitting beside me is none other than Joseph Childress, the editor of the *Kansas City Star* newspaper." She introduced each of us to him in a very formal manner.

"So this is the famous Crandal family of teachers, which it seems is almost singlehandedly supplying the state of Kansas with all of its educational needs." He did his best to provide hubris, filling heads with excessive sense of pride for accomplishments, real or imagined, to our deeds as teachers for the state and to add a little teasing humor into the conversation.

"If you've been listening to our momma, by now she has probably convinced you we are the state's only teachers," Howard said, and we all enjoyed a good laugh.

"And is it so bad for a poor, old mother to be proud of her children?" She smiled.

"Mr. Childress has some exciting news," Momma said.

"He wants you to join his newspaper and have your own column," Pauline said.

"No," Momma said, then she turned to face Mr. Childress. "On second thought..." She paused. "Seriously, Mr. Childress has been working all morning, well, ever since we met in the lobby, to set up a special recognition for you all during the closing ceremonies of the conference."

"What in heaven's name for?" Charlie asked. "We haven't done anything to deserve special recognition."

"I've already done some investigating, and I've discovered that the Crandal family has the most teachers from one family in the history of the state of Kansas," Mr. Childress informed us. "I'm positive this achievement deserves some award. Besides, I know it will make a great story for my newspaper. The people of Kansas will be interested in learning about the Crandal family's teachers."

"It might have some interest to your readers; I'm not sure we should agree to being singled out as teachers who are put up above the rest of the fine teachers here at the conference," Rose said.

"How many widowed women have reared a dozen kids during the Depression and lived to see half of them become teachers?" He looked at each of us.

We all looked at Momma, and she had a smile from ear to ear. "He's good," she said, and we all laughed.

"I have met with the president of the Teachers' Association and some of his committee; they are in agreement. This honor will be good for the Teachers' Association. Teachers are seldom given a public platform that enables the average citizen to show appreciation for their profession," Mr. Childress added. "Unless I miss my guess, this will be a defining moment for all of the teachers at this conference. I am of the opinion, as an old-timer in this newspaper business, that this award will help teachers leave the conference with a lighter step, a bit more vigor in their constitutions, and their buttons bursting off their breasts. The award is more about the honor for the profession than about any one individual."

"He's even better than I thought he was," Momma said, and we laughed. Mr. Childress blushed, then he joined in our laughter.

"When will this take place?" Howard asked.

"Tomorrow night during the closing program. I will be up on the stage, and just before the conference ends the president will introduce me. I will then ask you six teachers, and your mother, to come up to accept the award and special recognition. After the program ends, we will want to take some pictures of you. If I have my way, this story will be front page in our Sunday paper."

For the rest of Momma's life, the picture of us six kids, all teachers for the state of Kansas and Momma in the middle, smiling like Cheshire cats, hung directly above her bed. The ride home in Nap's touring car was some ride. We filled it with a detailed retelling of the event and then more retelling of the event. Through Momma's eyes, and then through various ones of our family, the story, each time it was told, was embellished to deliberately enhance Momma's importance and how she was able to pull off such a scheme. Charlie's was the best tale.

"Knowing Momma the way we do,"—Charlie paused, and we all laughed and nodded in agreement—"I'm sure she tipped some bellboy to find out if any of the newspapers' big shots were staying in the hotel. She probably tipped the bellboy to help her spot him when he came into the lobby. She probably made sure she accidentally/on purpose bumped into him. I can hear her now, 'Oh, excuse me, and I hope I didn't hurt you. I'm just an old woman, sitting around the lobby, waiting for my children to come back from their teachers' sessions.'

"Not suspecting Momma had already culled him out and was ready to rope and tie him in record time, and him being a gentleman, he probably said, 'Don't think a thing about it. I manage to do that from time to time myself. So you are here with one of your children who is a teacher? How nice. It must give you a real sense of pride to have a teaching professional in your family. What is her name?'

"Can't you just picture Momma's fowler's net closing?" Charlie said, envisioning Momma capturing her prey. "'One of her names is Rose, but another is Pauline; another is Naomi; another is Jessie,' I can hear her say.

"Can't you just see the man's face change as he becomes more curious, he being a big newspaper man?" Charlie asked.

"He would be just about ready to make a comment about Momma having so many teachers in the family, but she would interrupt him. 'One of the names is also Howard, and another is Charlie.' Now this newspaperman's brain is on overdrive, and he is thinking, *This is a great story in the making! Stop the presses; I've got this week's feature story.* Of course, our Momma was way ahead of him!"

We were so amused, we couldn't keep from laughing at the story he was weaving while we were driving home.

"Charles, you make me sound so—"

"Conniving," we all said in unison, and we giggled at Momma's discomfort.

"This is probably truer than you know," Naomi said, and we hooted and hollered in glee.

Charlie continued, "'So you are the mother of six children who are teachers for our state?' he asked. 'That must be some kind of a record, don't you think?'

"Momma says, 'It might be.'

"'Allow me to introduce myself. I'm Joseph Childress, the editor of the *Kansas City Star*,' he told her. 'I'd like to hear more about your teachers because I think it would make a great story for my newspaper.'

"Can't you just hear Momma? 'Now why anybody would be interested in a story about a poor old woman who was widowed at the beginning of the Depression and who has six of her children teaching for the state of Kansas?'"

"Is that how you managed to hog-tie him, Momma?" I

asked as I teased her "That wasn't how it happened! You make me sound like a shameless hussy hustler," she said in a fake whimper.

"Well, tell us the real story," Howard said.

Momma pointed to Charlie. "Mr. Smarty Pants seems to be doing a good job of entertaining you all; he can just continue making a fool of himself."

"I can just hear Momma now," Charlie said.

"'Mr. Childress—'

"'Call me Joseph.'

"'Joseph, do you really think people would be interested in hearing about my six teachers?'

"'We can arrange to tell the story and put a picture in the paper,' he told her. 'Of course, I would want you to be in the picture.'

"Can't you just see Momma?" Charlie asked.

"'Oh no! I wouldn't think of being in the picture. Goodness sakes, why would you want me in the picture with them? I'm just the mother,' I can just hear Momma say."

"Yup, that's our Momma," Pauline added.

"Chuck, you do go on something awful!" Momma said with a fake frown. "It was something real special, wasn't it?" She let out a long sigh, and our car became silent; we all had tears in our eyes.

When we finally returned home and were ready for bed, I watched Momma take off the double truss she wore most of her life to help her live with her hernias, and as we were lying in bed, I took her hand and squeezed it a little.

"Socrates, Plato, Aristotle, and Lou Crandal, the greatest educators of all time," I whispered, and Momma gave my hand a slight squeeze back.

The Dueling Outhouses

In October of my sophomore year, an event took place that ranks as about the funniest thing I ever had the privilege to witness.

Bessie Cunningham was our neighbor, just out our back door and across a garden. I've known some religious people in my day, but she beat them all. She wore dresses that covered her from the top of her neck to the tips of her shoes, provided she chose to wear shoes; she often was barefoot in the summer. She wore a big bonnet that covered her head, and she tied it under her chin. I will say one thing: she usually chose very colorful feed sacks from which she fashioned her dresses and bonnets. She was just a little nip of a thing, and it looked like a good wind would blow her away. I recall seeing her sometimes with her bonnet off, especially if she and I were sitting under the large maple tree in her back yard sipping lemonade. *She really is a pretty woman,* I thought. Her husband of nearly forty-five years had passed a couple of years ago. She spent her days working in her garden and reading her Bible.

"If there was ever a saint on this earth, she's one." I remember Momma saying how she respected her so much.

One day in the third week of October, there was a slight knock on our door just after supper. We weren't expecting any company; it was pitch dark, so it wasn't likely someone paying us a visit unless they arrived by an automobile.

Deannie ran and opened the door. When she saw the person standing there, she must have become frightened because she slammed the door and ran to find Momma.

"There's some weird-looking person at the door," she said.

Momma briskly took off her apron and laid it on a chair in the kitchen where she had been finishing up from supper. She rushed to the door.

"Deannie, why did you shut the door on our guest?" she asked as she opened the door to discover Bessie. "Why, I never...Come in, Bessie." Momma invited her in. "Kids! A body does all it can to teach them manners." Momma smiled at her. "What brings you out at night at this hour? Hope it isn't anything bad. Did my kids do something to make you mad?" Momma was offering up an apology, not even knowing that an apology might be due, just to head off any possible trouble with her fine neighbor.

"I'm much obliged to you for letting me barge in on you, Lou," Bessie said. "And heavens no, your children are always so polite and kind to me." Her reply allowed Momma to calm down and lose her apprehension concerning Bessie's visit.

"I was about to have a hot cup of tea; won't you join me?" Momma caught herself in midsentence. "Oh, I forgot, you don't drink any coffee or tea."

"Stirs a body's workings too much; it seems to make the brain race too fast," she added.

"You don't mind if I have one, do you?" Momma asked.

"I'm not one to go around telling people how to live. Now, the Good Book will, but not Bessie." The two women giggled.

"Bessie, there must be something powerful on your mind for you to get out at night." Momma started the conversation that soon became so fascinating that none in our household could hardly believed what we were hearing.

"Halloween has been a real sore spot with me for the past few years," Bessie confided.

In Tampa, Halloween was a high time for foolish high jinks, particularly with the high school boys. The younger children were out paying visits to the neighborhood houses to trick-or-treat them so they could gather a bagful of wonderful treats to get spoiled on. The high-school-aged boys were being mischievous and, in many cases, cruel and hurtful. Their favorite Halloween trick was to turn over the outhouses and allow the stench to rise from the refuse and permeate the air. In too many cases the outhouse structures were heavily damaged, which required the owner to build a new one.

"I realize that it isn't a problem so big you'd want to have the town constable pay a visit," Bessie said. "But it can be a big problem when Mother Nature comes a'calling." She gave us all a wink. "Sometimes the old slop jar just won't do the trick." She laughed with us. "If you have to go for a spell without a proper outhouse..." She made a face that indicated she was suffering some pain. It made us all laugh loudly. "If I get a choice, I'd rather not."

While her outhouse had been attacked nearly every year, ours had remained unharmed, probably because Howard and Charlie were well known and well liked by most of the older boys, roughies, as they were called in our school.

"I've been doing some thinking," Bessie said. "And for an eighty-year-old brain, that takes some doing." She laughed, and we laughed with her. "I suspect that I am going to get hit again this year. It rankles my gizzard." She leaned forward in her chair. "What if"—she allowed herself a little, soft laugh—"there was to be a new hole dug just before they come a'calling on Halloween night?" Her countenance changed as a sly grin crossed her face.

Momma and our family sat there for a few seconds, allowing the full impact of her plan to penetrate our brains. Momma suddenly slapped her knee.

"Bessie, that is the most ingenious thing I believe I have ever heard." She giggled loudly.

Pauline was home from her job at the restaurant that night.

"If it works, that will be the smelliest Halloween trick ever pulled off in our town," she said as she joined in with our laughter.

The plan was concocted that night in our kitchen. The aftershocks live on in Tampa's folklore.

The success of our little group depended on our ability to find a way to secretly dig a new outhouse hole to be ready for use the day after Halloween night. Momma and Bessie acted as ramrods of the plan. Our family became the gravediggers, as Charlie told it. We did some of the work by oil light at night so we lessened the chances that anyone would discover what was happening at Bessie's place. With the work completed just before Halloween, we moved the outhouse off its standing foundation and placed it just a few inches in front of the old hole filled with dung and urine.

"That is exactly where we need to place it." Bessie instructed. "Each year I wasn't able to stop them; hopefully now I will." She laughed, almost cackled. "I noticed they come in from the back so they are provided the best protection from being noticed and caught."

"What if there's a full moon?" I asked.

"Jessie has a point," Momma said as we all gathered around the new hole with an oil lamp to light our path.

"I've been contemplating on that for a spell," Bessie said. "If we put some hay down and found some type of cloth covering, maybe some old worthless feed sacks..." She opened our eyes to the possibilities of how easy it was going to be to camouflage our work. "I can measure the exact size we will need to properly cover the old hole, and I will sew together as many feed sacks as we need to do the job."

"What a great idea!" Momma said as she gave her a little hug. We got busy and put the finishing touches on our plan to ensure its success.

"Lou, I sure do appreciate you letting me use your facility for a day while mine is out of commission."

The younger kids were torn between going trick-or-treating or staying home to see if our plan caught some boys doing mischievous things on Halloween night. After a lot of soul searching, the allure of receiving candy, apples, and baked goodies from our neighbors and friends won out.

It was a good thing we did a very good job of camouflaging our project because the October moon was magnificent, bright and illuminating. The worst part about that type of moon was the high school boys were able to have good night vision to sneak about as they chose their victims. The better part about that type of moon was we were able to see clearly see everything that unfolded that night.

After we had finished our supper, our family members who were a part of the ruse made a quick trip over to Bessie's. We went one at a time over a period of an hour so we didn't call attention to ourselves, just in case those boys had been watching Bessie's house to make sure their target was ready for the picking.

We had a prearranged place where we could gather and wait to see if the roughies came to take the bait. We had several oil lamps ready to be lit.

For a while we thought maybe we had done all the planning and work for naught because it was after nine thirty, and they still hadn't come.

"I guess I should have done this a year ago," Bessie lamented. "I'd have for sure gotten them then," she added. "It's getting past my bedtime, has been for an hour or so."

"It's getting to be pretty late," Momma added. "Well, if they don't come in the next few minutes, I'm afraid I need to get home. I'm sure the little ones are back from trick-or-treating by now."

"No matter what, I'm much obliged to you, Lou," Bessie said.

"*Shh!* I think I hear something," Howard said in a loud whisper.

We all grew silent, and we acted as if we were afraid to breathe. In a few seconds, Howard's admonishment proved correct. We could see four silhouetted forms of boys in the background of the bright moon. They did their best to sneak up with very little noise so they could turn over Bessie's outhouse and leave without anyone being the wiser.

"The old lady who lives here is one strange person," we heard one of them say as they slowly made their way to the outhouse.

"Did you ever see her uptown? The funny way she dresses?" another one said.

"Just a few more steps, then we will see who looks funny," I said under my breath.

After they came within ten feet of the outhouse, they huddled, as if they needed to form some type of plan to get the job done.

"Let's just form a line, shoulder to shoulder, and we can rush the outhouse. We will get it on the ground in nothing flat," one of the boys said. He evidently was the ringleader.

It took only a few more seconds for Randy Hoff, Marvin Slaughter, Fred Heitzman, and Buddy Clarkson to become a part of Tampa's folklore.

When they rushed the outhouse, which was sitting in front of the old hole, three of the four ended up hip deep into the old hole.

One of them screamed, "Holy crap ... *Momma!*"

Bessie, Momma, and our family members rushed to the outhouse with our lit oil lamps to witness the most entertaining, stinky, comic scene anyone ever dreamed about. We shined our lamps upon those helplessly confused and disgusted Halloween would-be tricksters. Howard took pictures of them in the mire and muck of that puke-smelling hole.

"Smile," I hollered at them as the newspaper camera, which Howard had borrowed for the special event, made a few flashes, capturing them in all of their devilish glory.

Howard had told his boss about the possibility of Bessie's outhouse caper being successful, and his boss offered the use of a camera. He guaranteed Howard the pictures would be front-page news; in addition, he would give Howard a photographer's credit.

It's a wonder our laughter didn't wake the dead, I remember thinking as I laughed myself silly.

It became even more fun when the one boy, Fred Heitzman, who had escaped the other three's fate, joined in our laughter. Finally, one of the boys reached out and pulled Fred in with them. Howard got that picture too. It was as if they were trapped in the hole and would never find a way to crawl out; it only took them a few seconds to extricate themselves. With feces all over the lower halves of their bodies and their hands and arms, they ran like scared rabbits. We laughed until our sides hurt; we expended so much energy, we had to sit down to keep from falling down.

Bessie, Momma, and Howard were celebrities for quite a spell, especially with the folks who had had their outhouses turned over and destroyed. The culprits were punished. I guess the law just followed their noses to arrest them. For months after the caper, Bessie would trek over to our house and show Momma some of the gifts people left on her porch anonymously. Some left candy; some left flowers; some left thank-you notes.

"It feels kind of nice to be appreciated," she told Momma and our family on several occasions.

The story was received so well that some other papers sought permission to use the pictures and ran the story. Those four boys never lived down the Halloween prank that backfired.

Momma eloquently described that Halloween's shining moment: "It's a Halloween tale that oozes with its own frightening ending."

The Valedictorian

The summer after I finished my seventh grade, Momma hired us girls out to help some of the farmers' wives to prepare meals for the hands during the wheat harvest. The harvest was meager by our usual standards because a drought continued to plague the farmlands. The farmers ran out of options, with one exception: to pray for rain. Every Tampa church—Lutheran, Catholic, Evangelical Community, which was our family's church—held prayer vigils asking the almighty Creator to send rain.

"The good Lord hears our prayers. His timing isn't ours. Nevertheless, he never fails to answer prayer," Momma said as she defended him in the face of people showing an open disgust for not having rain. "Sometimes he says yes, sometimes no, and sometimes wait."

Sometimes the people would grow weary with her biblical perspective.

"And sometimes too late," they would counter.

My excitement about working to feed the harvest hands knew no bounds because I was going to be able to earn some money of my own. Momma would allow me to keep a small portion of my earnings for my own wants and needs. It took but a couple of days of work to realize just how hard I had to labor to earn that money; my weary bones educated me.

"Those farm hands," Momma said, "could eat the back end out of a bear…twice a day." She laughed at how tired we were at the end of each day.

"Two weeks of slinging hash was like an eternity in hell," Pauline said.

Pauline and I were busy doing our best to earn our keep. Even though I was quite young, I wasn't blind to how muscular and good-looking some of the young hands were. Rose had just finished her sophomore year; Naomi, her freshman year. The farm hands noticed how well built my sisters were. It didn't take long for the workers to warm up to them, especially when they were being served at the table.

Momma faced a thorny challenge trying to manage her older girls, particularly Rose. "Lordy, Lordy, she is sixteen going on thirty-something," Momma lamented. "You are hell-bent to find your life in a one-hole outhouse." She warned and scolded Rose about her take-no-prisoners type of living. "Mark my words! If you don't change the direction you're going, one day, much sooner than you can imagine, you'll have two or three snotty-nosed kids, a pile of dirty laundry, and a husband who tips the bottle too much and chases other women. You'll come running home." She paused and wagged her finger at Rose's nose. "I'll send you back, and then you'll discover that life passed you by."

"Just because you are a used-up old woman who wasn't smart enough to stop having more kids than the old lady in the shoe …" Rose roared right back at Momma as she moved right into Momma's face. In a hateful manner, she said, "It won't happen to me; I'm smarter than you."

Rose's set of values just ran contrary to those Momma had done her best to instill in our family. If something was black, she called it white. If something was declared black and white, she considered it gray, particularly if it was something she wanted.

Robert Hudson was his name, and he was something she wanted. He was the most handsome and winsome of all the hired harvest hands. The second he spotted Rose, and she saw him, sparks flew from across the room.

It was a wonder some people didn't suffer harmful burns by the force of the electricity zooming around that mess hall, I often thought.

It was my first experience watching a male and a female shot with Cupid's arrow. Rose played the part of the coy, innocent damsel during their first encounters.

"He's mine," Rose warned my sisters as she put a claim on him, whether he knew it or not. Rose was the only one who served his end of the long mess hall table, regardless of where he ended up sitting.

While she was serving the hands their meals, Pauline scolded her. "You are acting like a hussy! It's possible to serve a man his dinner without rubbing yourself all over him."

When we saw her sashay around him, all of us sisters were aghast with embarrassment. Rose possessed a rough edge, and she could banter with men better than most men. While she wasn't vulgar in public, she would give as well as she got, mixing in a man's world. Since she constantly crossed the lines of familiarity, I'm sure they saw her as a worthy conquest.

Naomi warned, "Momma would skin you alive if she saw the way you're behaving with the men. No decent girl would do that."

"You are just jealous that all the men like me." Rose gave her a mean stare and used her body to brush her aside.

My sister Naomi was a willowy, dishwater blonde, who was actually much prettier than Rose. She too had an hourglass figure and brought lightning into the mess hall; Naomi was gentle, quiet, and very ladylike in manner and speech. Her smile came with baby-blue eyes and very long, seductive eyelashes that fluttered when in conversation with men.

"Back off, little sister," Rose warned Naomi. When she would notice Robert sending a glance or two Naomi's way while the meals were served to the harvest hands, she acted defensively. "I'll scratch your eyes out," Rose threatened.

In the company of my other sisters, and even from a distance, Rose scared me to death, and I urged Naomi to steer clear of her and Robert.

The harvest ended, such as it was. It was so meager that Elsie Schmidt, Homer's wife, the man we all were working for, spent time crying when she thought no one was watching. It would happen nearly every day in between preparation for meals but usually after the noon meal.

During one of those times, I approached her.

"Mrs. Schmidt, the harvest will be better than you expect."

I did my best to give her some hope about their impending financial doom.

Mrs. Schmidt looked up, and she reached out for me. I stepped into her open arms, and her head fit into my breast area. Her tears increased, and her sobbing grew constant.

"Homer told me this morning"—she sobbed, coughed, and dabbed at her swollen eyes—"that we are going to lose the farm," she mumbled through her tears. She pulled her arms away from around me. She sat up quite straight and began to wring her hands over and over. She had a strange look come into her eyes. She rocked back and forth as if she had been cast into some odd trance that compelled her to behave in that manner.

"Jess, honey, poor old Elsie was showing signs she was about to crack up mentally," Momma said.

"Do you think it's true? Are they going to lose their home?"

"Lots of folks are." Her voice sounded very sad.

"Momma, are we going to lose ours?"

"Just don't you lose one wink of sleep about that." She reached out and touched my face. "Your poppa, God rest his soul, saw to it that we don't have to worry about losing our home. It is paid for, and no bank can come and take it from us." Her words comforted me.

Our work on the Schmidt farm finally ended. I was thankful to get back into a routine that didn't include slaving away for more than ten hours a day. My older sisters were back into the regular grind of backbiting and put-downs; most of it was good-natured. Even Rose was in a decent mood most of time. She remained that way until about three weeks after the harvest hands had moved on. Momma caught her coming home very late one night, and she had the smell of whiskey on her; she was drunk.

Rose did her best to enter the house and find her way to the bedroom where Pauline and Naomi also slept. She was under the influence of alcohol, and she wasn't as steady on her feet as she thought she was or as quiet as she needed to be. When Momma pulled the light on, Rose was halfway to her room.

RANNY GRADY

Rose had a disheveled appearance. Her hair was a mess, and she was holding onto her shoes with one hand as if she was tippy-toeing through some hip-deep water when the light startled her. When her eyes became accustomed to the light, she saw Momma's face; it was filled with fury.

"Rose Alice Crandal!" She confronted her with gritted teeth as she did her best to control her emotions and the pitch of her voice. "How long has this been going on?" Not really wanting an answer because she already knew the answer: way too long. I was startled by the voice in the middle of the night, and I immediately got out of bed and opened my bedroom door. The scene unfolding before me was one of high drama.

The possibility of watching Rose "get hers" from Momma was something that I would have gladly paid to watch. Evidently, Pauline and Naomi felt the same way, as I saw them peeking out of their bedroom door.

Rose was too potted to really appreciate the depth of Momma's wrath, which she was trying to coyly inflict upon her.

"Momma,"—she grinned—"you-us didn'tsh needs to waits up for little ole, ol Rrh-ooR-osy." She slurred her words.

"Is this Robert's doing? Does he know how old you are?"

Rose put her left index finger up to her mouth.

"Shh, don'tsh tells any-nos-bod-one." She laughed a silly laugh, as if she had let out a secret. "Olds enoughus, Momma girl, olds enough." She burped. "'Scuse me." She showed she had manners, even when she was drunk.

Momma's voice cracked with emotion, and it was easy to tell she was having a hard time keeping the tears from coming.

"You're in no shape to even waste my breath on. You get yourself to bed! We'll deal with this in the morning." She reached out her hand and gave Rose a slight push in the direction of her room.

"Don'tssh pushss, don'ssht pushssh me. I'ms goooing," she mumbled. Pauline and Naomi had been peeking out of the door, and they rapidly slammed it when they saw her approach.

Momma looked around the room and saw the other witnesses.

"The show is over," she said in a disgusted-sounding voice. "Let's all get back to bed." She pulled the light switch, and our home went dark.

Momma and Rose had quite a set-to the next day. Momma set ground-rules; Rose ignored them.

"Like a bitch in heat," Momma said was how Rose was acting around that Robert. Momma kept a vigil and did her best to put up fences between them. Things were pretty tense for a short time. Then Robert went away. Rose was brokenhearted. Momma was relieved. Life settled down, and we were soon back to scratching for a living.

In October of Rose's junior year in high school, I had cramps. My "friend" was unhappy with me, and I was a mess; so, the teacher allowed me to leave school and go home.

"Embarrassment is good for the soul." Momma often touted her homey-type wisdom, which was seldom appreciated by her children. I am of the mind that even Momma wouldn't have classified my particular type of embarrassment as good for the soul.

I sneaked into the house and took care of myself. I did my best not to make any noise because I really didn't want to explain my predicament. As I was gingerly making my way to my bedroom, I quietly started to open the door. I saw Momma on her knees beside the bed. My brother Earl was sitting on the bed, and he was bending down and doing his best to comfort Momma. She was an emotional wreck and was crying loudly. I silently closed the door before they noticed I was there.

"It's not polite to eavesdrop on private conversations," Momma had instructed me time and again when she caught me trying to be nosey, but I was drawn to my momma's obvious discomfort.

I situated myself so that I could look through the keyhole. Lovingly, Earl was patting Momma softly on her shoulders and then would gently stroke her hair while she sobbed and cried her heart out.

"Don't worry, Momma. We'll get through this," he said a

number of times, doing his best to give her some assurance that whatever had triggered this crying fit would soon pass.

Momma pulled her head up and looked at him. She used the large red bandana handkerchief Earl had given her to help her mop up her tears and running nose.

"Get through this! How do we get through this? It will never be done! Not in my lifetime." She sobbed more. "And certainly not in Rose's. Oh! I could just kill that girl." She looked up at him, and she smiled as they both recognized how harsh her comment had been. "I've been on my knees so long over that girl; I've got a case of arthritis," she lamented. "I swear, it's just like the apostle Paul asking the good Lord to take his thorn from his side, which he never did. That girl has been my thorn in the side, and for certain he hasn't taken it from me either." Her voice dripped with exasperation and frustration.

Earl's face was sweaty, and his emotions were on the raw edge.

"Perhaps Eddy could help us out of this dilemma." He was referring to the Boschs' in Humansville, Missouri.

Momma got off her knees and sat upon the bed beside him. It was like my brother had offered a life ring to a drowning woman. A hint of a smile crossed her face.

"That's a brilliant idea!" She reached over and gave him an embrace. "We will send her away before anyone knows. That fool girl just found out, so she can stay at home for a couple of months, then we can concoct a story that most people will believe. Then we can send her away to have the baby and arrange for her to give it up for adoption.

Rose! My sister is pregnant! She didn't learn a thing from Naomi's word, I thought.

"She can come back to school, and we'll pray that no one will be the wiser."

"What about the father?" Earl asked. "Doesn't he have any say in this?"

"She told him about the baby; he just laughed at her. He accused her of trying to trap him; he even accused her of sleeping with other men."

"Is there a chance that is true?" Earl asked.

"Knowing that girl"—Momma paused—"I…I guess anything is possible. But Rose assured me he was the only man she had messed with."

"I don't want that S-O-B in our family anyway," Earl said.

Momma reached out and patted his right hand. "There's no need for profanity." She allowed herself a big sly grin, and then she added, "But I couldn't have described my feelings better." She gave him a wink. This caused both of them to enjoy a much-needed laugh.

"Son, as much as it did my old heart good to see that wayward girl get knocked down a peg or two, it broke my heart to see a child of mine suffer so," Momma confessed. "She demanded to be treated like a grown woman, but when the chickens came home to roost, she didn't have any way to use her wiles to best a bad situation. She couldn't avoid the consequences of her sins; she had to come and confess to me what a pickle she was in. At that moment, she realized she wasn't so growed-up." Momma deliberately used the wrong verb.

"A haughty spirit goes before destruction" is the last part of the verse from the book of Proverbs that warns people not to get too full of themselves, most assuredly like Rose had done. It must be something like wanting to see an evil murderer get executed for some terrible crime. Then, when it comes to pass, you can't stand to watch it happen. That was how I felt when Rose was forced to sit at the family table, and Momma told our family Rose was going to have a baby.

Once in a while I let my imagination run wild. I conjured up a situation in which I was forced to endure the worst type of humiliation possible—the type when you just wanted your life to end right that instant; *poof!* and you were gone. And you would count it a blessing. Well, I'm positive my sister Rose lived that nightmare, in the flesh and blood, because Momma made her sit at the table, though she tried to leave several times, while Momma told our family about Rose's predicament. She also told about the plan she and Earl devised to provide the child-to-be with the best chance at a decent, Christian life. Momma thought it was the best opportunity for Rose to have a life. She made each of our family take an oath upon the Bible not to share this information with another living soul.

Howard's only comment sent Rose into fits of crying, but Momma didn't cut her any slack; she made her remain at the table.

"This is going to make Alice very happy," he said disgustedly.

He was referring to Alice Brown, Rose's only real competition for earning top honors for academics in high school. They had been heated adversaries since grade school. With Rose out of the picture, Alice would become the valedictorian of their class. It was a prize that Momma coveted for Rose as much as Rose did. Momma didn't like Alice's mother, Hazel's pompous airs. If given a couple of minutes of idle conversation, Hazel could find a way to make sure everyone knew they had money to spend for more than just the necessities of life "Maybe not," Momma said. "I've been doing some investigating, and it is possible for Rose's grades to be documented and transferred from another school for the semester she will have to be away. There is one exception allowed—a medical condition." She moved her eyebrows up, and her eyes took on a sly, wise look, and she allowed herself a little sneaky smile. Our family recognized the full hidden meaning of her comment, and we all began to laugh. "It didn't specify what qualified as a medical condition, so we will assume it covers pregnancy." Momma chuckled.

Momma wrote to Eddy Bosch and explained her situation, and she sought her help and her counsel. She and Horace readily agreed to do all they could to help Momma's plan work.

Eddy wrote a letter in care of Momma, detailing her need for assistance. Her letter stated she had come down with a debilitating disease. She would recover from it; unfortunately, it would require a great amount of personal care. Horace, her husband, couldn't handle the nursing duties because he was having some problems with his heart and a hip joint. She was seeking a favor from Momma; her letter asked if Rose might be sent, just for a few months, to help them get past this difficult situation.

Since the Boschs' were known by townfolk from a previous visit to Tampa, little suspicion was raised when Momma took Eddy's letter to the school superintendent to request that Rose be allowed to help them in their time of need. He readily agreed, but he needed the approval of the school board to grant the request. The Browns protested vehemently, but the request was granted. Rose could rescue the Boschs', and her grades were transferable if accredited by the State of Missouri.

For the next few months, I learned how difficult it is to keep a secret; it's nigh impossible to do. I wanted to share our family's secret with Angela, but I had to keep my mouth shut. In order to keep a secret, one must learn to lie. When conducting a conversation, if its turns toward the information contained in the secret, you must learn how to remain calm while your brain and heart are busy building up pressure, an attack against your conscience, unceasingly shouting its message: release the pressure, share the secret. After a while, you discover your mind and speech get twisted, confused, and your mouth wants to go one way while your conscience another. In a while, you clam up. This produces a sinister effect: the other person becomes suspicious of your motives. The friend gains the perception that you don't trust them, which is true, and it eventually harms the relationship. That happened to Angela and me. She felt I didn't trust her with my most intimate thoughts, and she chose to cool our relationship. It caused a rift; it was never the same! That exercise in keeping a secret taught me a valuable lesson about life's choices: sin's consequences force other people to suffer, the innocent and the guilty. Nap drove Momma to Missouri in late January of the New Year.

Momma arranged to arrive in Humansville a couple of days before Rose gave birth to a baby boy. With Momma's approval, the Boschs' had arranged an adoption for Rose's baby by a fine Christian couple who had been unable to have any children, try as they might, for nearly a decade. It was a closed adoption. Once Momma signed the papers, the records were sealed, and the baby's birth mother would never be known to the child unless the adoptive parents revealed it. The birth mother would never know who adopted the child. Since Rose chose never to discuss the child she gave birth to and then gave it up for a closed adoption, I never really knew how much that changed my sister, if it did.

It is strange how God works. He gives one man a quiver full of arrows and another just a quiver. As a young girl just becoming a seeker of worldly knowledge, it was one of the many perplexing questions I was adding to the list I was going to ask the good Lord about when I saw him face-to-face.

Momma used biblical references every chance she got when trying to teach us about the world we lived in.

"Of course, if every man's quiver was filled with arrows, who would be there to extend Christian love and charity to all those who run afoul of the misfortunes of this world? Where would the children come from who soothe the broken hearts of the barren women? If it weren't for girls who make poor decisions or other women who die untimely deaths at a young age, how would their lives find a sense of fulfillment and contentment, which only God can give to a mother? It doesn't have to be natural born." She did her best to defend her choice for not allowing Rose to bring the baby home and into our family.

Try as I might, and I considered myself a fair detective— Momma called it being a snoop—I was never able to find out how the Boschs' pulled off that incredibly complicated scheme with nary a hitch. When I was much older, she allowed me to read the correspondence Eddy sent her. Her letter detailed the ingenuous plan.

Prior to Rose's arrival, Eddy paid a visit to the high school principal and weaved a sad tale about this very troubled girl and a destitute family. I concurred on both points. She played upon his sympathies and his Christian duty to extend a helping hand. She used a different name for Rose and our family. She had some documents made up that indicated that Rose was Clare Hawkins, and Momma's name was Ethel. If a girl was pregnant, even if she had the gall to try and do so, at that time in history, she wasn't allowed to attend school when she was pregnant. The majority of the girls' parents didn't put much stock in a girl's formal education. Our momma was an exception. Therefore, if the girl's parents insisted on the girl still finishing her education, a private tutor was hired, paid for by the school system, and was arranged to visit the home every day to make sure she kept up with the studies. The tutor possessed the power to certify the course work had been completed, the grade earned, and it was documented it in a letter. The school system provided the necessary personalized stationary.

Eddy persuaded, perhaps paid the tutor, the tutor to help her prepare a second letter of documentation, which was for Rose Crandal, that she could use to show the school board in Tampa Rose had completed her academic classes while serving as a nurse for Eddy Bosch. It just required an extra sheet of stationary. Eddy had assured the principal a fine Christian couple was preparing adoption papers. They were just waiting on the birth of the baby to complete all the legal documents required to take the baby into their home and hearts.

Eddy gave Rose's academic record glowing praise, and this enabled her to get the principal to help her secure a documented record of Rose's grades that she earned while in Missouri. As usual, Rose made straight A's in all her subjects.

Rose's tutor, while deeply troubled by her delicate condition and obvious stupidity concerning intimacy with a bum, recognized how bright and intelligent she was. Soon after she started to tutor her, she urged Rose to become a schoolteacher. When I heard that, I nearly died laughing. My sister, a schoolteacher! The idea of Rose putting her students first and herself second, knowing the sister I knew, was not going to happen. Of that I was positive. Little did I suspect that not only would she be a teacher for many years, but she would become one of Kansas's first women superintendents.

When it came time for Rose to have her baby, Momma said, "Jessie, I want you to accompany me to Missouri. You can drive, and that way I won't be so tired when I get there."

Ever since Momma taught me how to drive, I had become her chauffeur.

"Will it be okay for me to miss school?"

"I've already spoken to your teacher, and she gave me your schoolwork for a couple of days." She glanced at me. "I hate to disappoint you."

"How soon are we going to leave?"

"As soon as I can arrange to get Nap's car. He said he would bring it in another day or two."

We left on Friday morning so we could be there over the weekend. The doctor said Rose's baby should be delivered either Saturday or Sunday.

"I want to be there on Friday night so I can make sure that nothing goes awry with the adoption," Momma said.

Driving a car is fun. It is exhilarating, and it makes a girl feel important and all grown-up, unless you have to drive hours and hours and hours. Then, you'd like to just crawl in the back of the car and snooze while someone else does the driving.

When I tried to get her to drive awhile, Momma said, "That's why I brought you along. Besides, I've just got too much on my mind for me to be a safe driver."

I convinced her to stop for me to get a cup of coffee, against her better judgment because she didn't like for me to have coffee at my age. After a long drive, we arrived in Humansville just before dark.

Eddy Bosch greeted us warmly and gave us hugs.

"I'm so glad you made it safe and sound." She smiled at me.

I yawned; I just couldn't help myself.

"Sleepyhead, huh? It's tough on a girl when she has her sleep disturbed, right?"

I looked at her with a blank look. "Sleeping…"

"Oh, Jessie wasn't sleeping; she was my driver," Momma said.

"Well, a young girl like you already driving. Jessie, you continue to surprise me." We both laughed.

"How's my girl?" Momma asked as she motioned with her hand to another part of the house where she supposed Rose was.

Eddy was nervous and hesitant and in her speech. "I ... I'm afraid, Lou ..."

"What's wrong?"

"Oh no, Rose is fine. It's just ..."

"Eddy, for goodness sakes, just say what it is you're trying tell me but are having a dickens of a time doing."

"Rose told me this morning that when her baby is born, she has decided she is going to keep it. She has changed her mind about the adoption. She doesn't care if you like it or anyone likes it." Tears came to her eyes.

Momma recognized Eddy was upset because she was blaming herself. Momma grabbed her and gave her a big hug.

"Eddy, it's not your fault. Where is she?" She pushed Eddy away from her breast. "You haven't said anything to the adoption couple, have you?"

Eddy started to cry softly. "I ... I just didn't know what to do, Lou. But I probably messed this all up. In all good conscience, I just couldn't let them come to get the baby and then have to leave empty-handed."

"So you told them that Rose has changed her mind?"

"I ... I only told them Rose was having second thoughts."

"Can you contact them tonight?"

"Possibly, but for sure in the morning."

"Good! You contact them and tell them to be ready to come and get that baby as soon as it is delivered."

"But what about—"

"Rose has no say in this decision! She is just a girl, and I'm responsible for her. I'll do what is best for her, even if she doesn't like it or agree with it. Where is she?" Momma asked.

Eddy took us to a back bedroom and gently opened the door.

"Look who has come all the way from Tampa to see you," Eddy said to Rose.

It is funny how a person has perceptions she believes couldn't possibly be changed, then she sees it in a different light and everything suddenly changes; that happened to me with my sister Rose.

She was lying on the bed on her back, and her belly was so swollen up she couldn't see her feet. Her brash, bawdy countenance, which made me quake in my boots, was gone. All that was left was a high school girl, alone and frightened about life.

When she saw Momma, she started to cry. "Oh, Momma, I missed you." She opened up her arms.

Momma easily slipped into them. "Hi, Rose, honey, how's my girl?" She held her close and did her best to rock her gently.

It was the only time I ever recall that Rose and Momma exchanged any intimate moments, especially hugging each other and kissing one another. I stood in the background, and I shed a few tears, enjoying their touching moment.

"What's she doing here?" Rose asked as she opened her eyes and looked past Momma and saw me.

"Jessie came along so she could be my driver."

"I didn't want her here; get her out of my room."

The old Rose didn't take long to lose her lovey-dovey way, I thought. I started to leave.

"Jess, stay! For heaven's sake, she's your sister."

Momma gently dried Rose's eyes with her hanky, and it seemed like just a few seconds until she changed her demeanor.

"Eddy told me some very disturbing news," Momma said.

"That I wasn't going to give my baby up for adoption?" Rose said. "If this is going to be one of your lectures, tell her to leave." She pointed to me.

"Jessie isn't leaving. Stay!" Momma said, and her voice was strong and commanding. "It will do you good to hear what Rose has to say. More importantly, what your momma's final words on this matter will be."

"I don't care what you say," Rose snarled. "It's my baby; it's coming out of my body!"

"You are a guest in this house, so please keep a civil tongue in your mouth." Momma glared at Rose. "Now you can rant and rave all you want; you can make a complete you-know-what out of yourself, but when you are all through being ugly"—she moved over close to Rose's bed and pointed to her huge belly—

"that baby is going to a fine Christian home, and you are coming home to Tampa to finish high school."

"Fine! Then we aren't coming home; we will stay in Humansville," she screamed at Momma. "You just don't want your pure, lily-white reputation soiled. Lou Crandal would be the laughingstock of Tampa." Rose spit out her words.

"That's an unfair and a very un-Christian thing to say and to think."

"Do you think I shamed God?" Rose laughed. "Want to give me one of your lectures on fornication, huh, Momma?" She started bawling.

Momma walked over to her, looked her in the eyes, and then she raised her left hand and slapped her hard across the right side of her face. She stood above her and did not move or say a thing for a few minutes.

Rose stopped bawling and pressed herself down on her bed. She turned her head away from Momma's glare.

"You're about to have a baby. We are all tired. Perhaps we should leave it till morning," Eddy said, as the ruckus had caught her attention and she had come to the bedroom.

Momma looked over to Eddy. "Perhaps you are right. Rose has a big day ahead of her tomorrow." The tension subsided in the room.

"Come, Jessie and Lou; I'll show you your room," Eddy said.

Momma stopped at the bedroom's entrance. "Rose, honey, you don't have a choice in this matter." She walked away.

Later that night, I'm not sure what the hour was, I felt Momma's body absent from the bed. I quickly got up to see if she was all right. I saw a little light coming from Rose's room. I tiptoed quietly to the door; I heard muffled crying, and I recognized Momma's voice. I strained to hear what was said.

"Shh, let it all out." She was comforting Rose. "Oh, Rose, baby. I wish things were different too. And I agree that I have never had to lose a baby of my own, thank the Lord. But you're just a girl, and there will be time enough for you to be a woman and a momma."

I could hear Rose sobbing softly as Momma talked.

"That couple will give your baby a home and a real chance at life. Can you?"

Rose did not answer.

"You're right! I don't want to live with all the pointed comments and gossip about you as it affects our family. And I admit, maybe I take too much pride in our family's honor; what else does a poor family have to hang its hat on?"

"But I ... I'd get a job," Rose said.

"Who'd take care of the baby while you are working?"

"You could."

"Your momma's worn out! And I am telling you that I will not do it. Rose, you can still be valedictorian of your class. The world's changing, and a woman is going to be able to do things your momma never had the chance to do. Do you really want to throw all of that away only to discover, in a few years, that you are an unhappy woman with at least one child to rear?"

"But I could do it somehow, if you helped."

"Do you want your child to go through life being called a bastard?"

Rose broke out in soft sobs. "No."

"Then it's settled."

I hurried back to the bed and pulled the covers up. I pretended I was asleep. Momma climbed into the bed and rolled over on her left side.

"How'd your momma do?" she whispered.

I just couldn't believe Momma was aware I had been out of the bed and listening to their conversation. I didn't say a word. In a few minutes, I heard Momma crying quietly. I wanted to comfort her. I didn't want her to know she had been right.

Rose gave birth to a fine baby boy. Momma saw it; neither Rose nor I ever did see the baby. He was given up for adoption. Momma signed the papers. We stayed in Humansville for a few days, and then we bundled Rose up and drove home.

She arrived home just as school was out for the summer. Rose resumed her studies for her senior year without a hitch. When Rose returned from Missouri with all A's documented on Humansville school's stationery, which Momma took to the principal, it kept my sister in the hotly contested competition for being named senior class valedictorian.

Alice's mother told everyone she didn't believe the story Momma and Eddy had concocted. While she wasn't able to prove anything was a mite misconstrued regarding Rose's medical exception, she gave it a Herculean effort to try and find out if it was true or not. Momma told us there was gossip around town that she had been doing her best to discover just where in Missouri Rose had gone to school the previous semester. She knew if she could prove that Rose had lied about the reason she went to Missouri for a semester, Rose would automatically be disqualified. Rose would have been forced to quit school, and Alice would be handed the valedictorian award.

"Now, children, you watch your P's and Q's when you are out and about. Some of the townsfolk aren't too happy about Rose being granted that medical exception." Momma warned us to keep our mouths shut. "Just act natural—play like you're dumb." She would tease us and give us a big smile that indicated that she was just "funnin'."

"I remember," Charlie chimed in, "that Mr. Wilson says loose lips sink ships." Charlie used that slogan from the history of World War I; he had read it somewhere and evidently thought it was funny or profound since he used it whenever he could.

"Loose lips will not only sink ships; they will cook our goose," Momma said, and we all laughed.

She was right! Momma had enough on her plate to worry about, so I never told her about my troublesome encounter with Alice and her mother before Rose came home from Missouri.

It happened one day while I was on an errand for Momma.

Momma sent me to fetch some supplies from Mr. Tetson's Mercantile and General Store, where we kept a charge account. As I was coming out with the supplies in my arms, Alice and her mother were coming into the store.

Alice Brown and her mother, Elsie, were some pair. "Plain Jane" was the description that fit them. Some of the boys teased that Alice was a chip off the old block, which was a quaint saying for boys but was seldom used in connection with girls. The boys were nasty and they said Alice was ugly and was missing too many chips. Momma cautioned me about allowing myself to get too uppity when I was in the company of girls who weren't nearly as "well crafted." It was Momma's polite way of contrasting attractive versus less attractive women. Unfortunately for Alice and her mother, anybody but a blind man couldn't help but noticed both were not only poorly crafted but mightily flawed in the comely department. The most amazing thing about the family was that the townsfolk ladies considered Alice's father very handsome. One didn't need to lower oneself to being a snoop to hear a whispered refrain: "When you see Mr. and Mrs. Brown out in public, it can't ever be denied that love is blind and beauty is in the eye of the beholder," the townsfolk would say.

They may not have been too pleasing to the eye, but they sure knew how to dress. All of their clothes were store-bought, certainly not from feed sacks, like all of mine, and they looked so prim and proper. It took a lot of makeup to cover the "Plain Jane" they carried everywhere "skin deep."

"Jessie, how are you?" Alice's mother asked. Even as a young child, if one is paying close attention, it is easy to discern phoniness that seems to seep out of a person's mouth. She couldn't have given a whit about my welfare. "Alice and I were just talking about your sister Rose."

That may be one of the most honest statements that lady has uttered in a month of Sundays, my mind flashed. *And how many needles did you all put into that pin-cushion voodoo doll,* I thought as I flashed my brightest smile.

"Yes, Jess, I was telling Mother that I thought it was so noble of Rose to interrupt her junior year in high school and her studies just so she could go and rescue some poor creature." Alice's voice dripped with mettlesome honey. "Why, it's stuff fit for a romantic novel, her being so benevolent and all, sacrificing her interests for those of others."

As I said before, keeping a secret means a body must not only learn how to lie convincingly out of necessity, but one must continue to become more experienced in how to lie so that one doesn't get caught. Each lie ensures that the communication will become thornier because the web of deceit grows exponentially every time a lie is told about that particular secret. It also gets very confusing!

"Momma received a letter just the other day." *It was from Eddy Bosch and not from Rose,* I thought. "Rose just sent a glowing report about how happy she is taking care of our dead poppa's good friend," I said as I squirmed inside with great anxiety but did my best to smile and allow my hazel-green eyes to confuse them.

"Well, praise the Lord!" Alice's mother remarked. "Alice was just mentioning to me the other day that she thought Rose's gesture of Christian charity should be honored. Alice has longed for the opportunity to one day emulate your sister's example." She continued to heap compliment upon compliment.

I know it was sinful of me, but all the time she was talking, all I could hear was my poppa's voice, direct, profane, but true: *When the crapper is full, it's time to move to a new hole.* Since she didn't stop talking, I was thinking, *I am going to need waders to make it home.*

"We thought we might be able to get Rose's address so Alice could send her a letter, just to keep in touch and to wish her well," she said. Her subtle, oh-so-sweet voice would have fooled everyone, except our family, about the real intention of her inquiry.

"I am sure Rose would really appreciate such a thoughtful gesture," I replied as I did my best to put a blank look on my face. "The only thing I recall is that she is somewhere in Missouri; Momma tries to shelter her children from worrying our little, pea-picking brains too much about trivial things that really don't concern us." I was doing my best to deflect any more inquiries by acting dumb as a box of rocks.

"Surely you jest," Alice's mother said.

At that point in our fencing contest, I decided to up the ante and make myself out to be even more of a dunce. "No, ma'am, best I can recall, it's somewhere in Missouri that ends with"—I paused to hopefully allow my hayseed act to influence the moment—"-tion or something close to that." I smiled meekly.

When Alice and her mother became cognizant of the fact I was willing to come off as a brainless twit to foil their attempt to squeeze pertinent information out of me in order to harm Rose's chances for the award, they made a hasty retreat.

Alice's plain face was flushed to the gills. Her mother, always the overly polite one, said, "Well, you give our best to your momma. I don't know how she is able to manage a dozen kids." She made a hand gesture toward her daughter. "It's all I can do to keep this one on the straight and narrow." She snickered. As they were leaving, I heard her mother utter, "Lordy, that one is dumb as an ox."

I watched them cross the street and enter a store, and then I lit out for home. I didn't tell Momma about my meeting with the Browns because I didn't want her to worry; I did enough for the both of us.

That secret nearly did all of us in. It was as if someone had inserted a big balloon into the middle of our lives, and it found a comfy place in our house. Every day we were tested with some challenge of our wits against our consciences. It seemed as if part of our punishment was that each time we kept the secret, we had to blow more air into that balloon. In no time at all, it looked as if it had reached its capacity and couldn't possibly hold one more breath of air without exploding and ruining all the secret had been designed to deliver: a valedictorian award for Rose, for Momma, and for our family. Each new insertion of air caused all of our family to shudder in the potential wake of its consequences.

Once in a while, we would discuss our encounters where we nearly spilled the beans, and we encouraged each other to keep the faith and remain diligent and armed so that we didn't let our loose lips sink the ship.

As I look back upon that secret and how Momma chose to handle it—enlisting our family to aid and abet her efforts—I can see it was a sinful thing to run that ruse on the board of education, the principal of the high school, and even Alice

Brown. The most honorable thing would have been to fess up about Rose's indiscretion and allow her to be disqualified academically for the award. In hindsight, I'm sure Momma felt that way because she never sought counsel with our preacher.

When I asked her if she was going to pay a visit to the preacher to help her with the decision about what she should do about Rose, she said, "God knows my sins, and I don't need anybody else to point them out to me."

I guess it was much like my math teacher who cautioned us students when we were ciphering numbers. He said, "When calculating formulas or dealing with money and investments, or any number of various and asunder areas of one's life, a decimal point put in the wrong place can make a great deal of difference with outcomes." When all of the grades and points of all the seniors were added up, my sister nosed Alice out by just a few hundredths of a point. It was a bitter pill for Alice to swallow; it was a once-in-a-lifetime celebration for the Ranti Crandal clan.

On graduation day, Momma was up extra early, and she was in high spirits, humming to entertain herself and, in her own unique way, worshipping the Lord.

"Even though it isn't Sunday, it's a great day in the Lord. Let us rejoice and be glad in it." Momma challenged our family to join her rejoicing for the imminent celebration.

The commencement day celebration, which signaled the official end of Rose's high school studies, allowed our family the opportunity to listen to the valedictorian's speech. The valedictorian speech was presented to her fellow classmates, their families, and all of the distinguished guests. The valedictorian was Rose Crandal!

"Momma, if someone didn't know any better, they would think you had won the award and you would be giving the valedictorian speech," Pauline teased Momma.

"Pauline, dear, I didn't have nearly the pain when giving birth to a dozen kids that I did getting your sister ready for this world."

By noon the sun had burst forth and the blue sky, filled with white cumulus clouds, provided just the right environment our bustling community needed to make its way to the community center for the august occasion. The commencement exercise where the graduating class seniors would receive their diplomas was held at the Hubert P. Jones Community Center. Mr. Jones was the town dentist, and he owned the community center, the theater where silent movies were shown each week, as well as other businesses. He had arrived in our town many years ago and hung out a crude-looking sign that said "Dentist." In a few years, he had become rich and influential in our town and throughout the state of Kansas.

Mr. Jones had a philanthropic spirit, and he allowed the city fathers to use the Jones Community Center for school functions and sports programs. At different times of the year, swing bands, particularly from Salina, would come to perform so that all of the townsfolk could dance and enjoy life.

The center was decked out in an array of our school colors, black and gold. The school banners, with different artistic flairs, depicting our school's athletic prowess, particularly for basketball and track, were proudly flown. The Tampa Haymakers, the well-oiled, fighting, dueling pitchforks, signifying our school's logo, were festooned upon the many banners. The students hated that name and the logo. We played against the Durham Devils, the Lost Springs Hornets, the Cottonwoods Titans, and any number of schools that had city fathers smart enough to give their school a name that helped define them in such a manner that their opponents didn't laugh at just the sound of the name. The fact that the Haymaker was a signification of the rich tradition of our farming community did not impress us students. Tampa had the reputation for producing the best wheat harvest, bar none, just about every year. The other teams made up cheers to try and humiliate us by using our school's name.

I wasn't the only Crandal kid to complain about our school's logo name. All of my brothers and sisters who came before me and after me had the same complaint. Every time a small cadre of students tried to get the school officials to accept a petition to the school's board of governors to change the school's name, it was shot down. They would wax eloquently about Tampa's historic tradition. "When you kids get older and have families of your own, you'll come to appreciate that name" was the boring refrain they handed out as they refused to even consider the petition. I can attest to one thing for sure: all of us students learned to elevate the English language to empower the word "haymaker." The good Lord gave us one saving grace; our farm kids were good athletes, and we were fairly consistent winners. Our school's basketball team won district two years in a row. Even if you have a sissified-sounding name, when you drub the other team, they are obliged to give you respect.

Our beloved basketball court had been turned into a civic auditorium fit to hold important events such as the high school graduation commencement program. The dais was feted with a number of chairs and a podium. Everything was ready to send the class of 1931 into the scary world to fulfill their dreams and goals.

The Crandal clan took up one entire row of seats. All twelve of us were spit-shined and polished.

"Every one of you will be wearing your finest." Momma handed down her edict when the first question arose concerning the apparel we kids would be wearing to the commencement program.

"We're going to shine like a nigger's heel," Charlie shouted, and some of us laughed.

"Charles Crandal," Momma said in a curt, indignant manner. "I'll not have any of that kind of dirty talk in my house." Her ire was raised, and her body language backed it up. "I should forbid you to ever darken that pool hall's door. It's the devil's den." She moved toward him to help put the fear of God in him. "That crude remark is something you're bound to hear down there, mixing with the likes of them." Charlie just stood there with a look of embarrassment flushing his countenance. He didn't want to cause a big ruckus and spoil the day, so he meekly said, "I'm ... uh ... I'm sorry, Momma." The tension melted away, and we all resumed our preparations.

"Even though it isn't Saturday, I expect everyone to take a bath, and I want all of us smelling good. I'll be much obliged if we don't have Lou's Dirty Dozen fouling up the place." Her instructions elicited groans from some and happy refrains from others.

Momma said, "Our family's bath time is a logistic event that takes the patience of Job, the strength of Samson, the servant's attitude of Mary, and the wisdom of Solomon to get all of Lou's Dirty Dozen clean enough to be seen in public."

I can still recall the day that Nap came driving up to our house with an honest-to-goodness bathtub awkwardly balanced, half in and half out, of his car. It had claw feet. It didn't matter that we didn't have water in our house; to Momma it was a thing of beauty. It was beat up, and it looked like it had suffered in the halls of hell. It was badly chipped and wore several shades of rust, but it held water. She just stood there looking at the ugly thing and saucer-sized tears ran down her cheeks. She reached out and gave Nap a big hug and kissed him on the cheek. "You done good, boy." She praised him for his gift.

Momma put up her hand, indicating that Nap didn't need to keep on struggling to tell his story. "My treasure, his trash. Thank you, Jesus," Momma murmured softly as our family gathered around Momma's new bathtub.

"You'll not get me in that thing," Rose said. "It's not fit for a pig, let alone a human."

"You've got to have vision," Momma said. "When we get it fixed up and cleaned up, I'll have to serve as a referee at a boxing match to see who gets to use it first." She laughed.

We didn't have water in our house, but now we had a bathtub to put the water in. To take a bath in hot water seemed impossible to me. The thought of relaxing for a few minutes in the tub made me feel as though I had become a princess. If it were as wonderful as my mind experienced, it would magically transport me into an ethereal place of rest and beauty—unless you have to share it with ten other brothers and sisters! It may not seem to be much of a luxury to some folks, but when it was filled with hot, at least lukewarm water heated on the coal and wood-burning stove, it provided one's body with a sense of relaxation that drains all the cares of this old life into an ethereal place of rest and beauty, unless one has to share the bath.

In my old age, now that every family in America has hot and cold running water in a house—in fact, it wouldn't pass inspection if it didn't—I know it seems unsanitary to have more than one child take a bath at the same time. It also seems unsanitary to have more than one child use the same bath water to take a bath once a week, as we did. Not just poor people in farm communities lived under these primitive conditions; no houses in our community had indoor plumbing. Therefore, any time a minute blessing, like a bathtub that could be filled with water for a bath unexpectedly arrived at our doorstep, gratitude was the mission for the day.

Modesty was the hallmark for bath day.

"Now, you kids mind your manners," Momma would warn us. "We must all respect each other's privacy as much as possible." She would do her best to protect her girls. "I don't want any nudist colony springing up."

We did give respect to each other; yet, I saw more bare bodies than I ever wanted to see. When you are trying to bathe nearly a dozen children, and over a fourth of them are nearly adults and three of them are too young for school, "It's nothing but a three-ring circus in here!" as Momma would yell. Often, she was forced to rush in and take control of the bathhouse environment because water was being used for more than bathing.

The ritual took several hours each Saturday.

"Sunday-go-to-meeting may have delivered a tiny piece of heaven on earth, but Saturday produced too much hell on earth," Momma often lamented when the aftermath of a bath hurricane had passed over our house.

So for six days everyone did a hit-and-miss job of cleaning the filth off the body; some of my family only gave it a lick and a promise. One time, on a lazy summer afternoon, I was sipping lemonade and resting easy in the swing; I overheard a conversation that made me laugh.

A lady friend of Momma's paid her a visit. She had her sister with her who lived back east. She was visiting for a spell. The lady told Momma, "My grandmother always told me, 'Wash up as far as possible; wash down as far as possible…Don't ever touch possible.'" I guess we followed that lady's grandmother's formula.

With just the right amount of pomp and splendor, the commencement program came off without a hitch. Rose's speech became the focal point of conversation when the parents, dignitaries, and school officials mixed in polite intercourse. My sister had written her own speech, and no member of our family had privy to it prior to her standing before her peers.

Rose's name was called last to receive her diploma. When it was called, the principal, Mr. Howard, announced that she had been awarded the Valedictorian award. She had a perfect four-point average. Alice had been awarded the Salutatorian award for finishing second. With diploma in hand, Rose quickly took her place behind the podium.

"Without further ado, I give you the Valedictorian award winner, Rose Crandal. She will now honor us with the traditional valedictorian award speech," the principal said.

Rose was dressed in a very fashionable-looking navy blue dress that had a sailor's collar and puffed sleeves. She wore a green scarf that set off her reddish blonde hair. She quickly moved to the podium and, for a few seconds, allowed her eyes to survey the audience. The silence seemed to bring some unease into the room.

"My fellow classmates, teachers, mentors, and coaches, and to our dignitaries, civic leaders, parents, and family members, as the valedictorian award winner of the class of 1931, it is my privilege and high honor to speak from my heart for a few minutes.

"I am not going to stand up here before this august body and spew forth the usual poppycock one hears at this time of the year during graduation day commencement exercises all across this great land called America. Oh sure, I want to challenge each of my classmates to dig deep within themselves and to allow the fresh air of visionary dreams to become white hot with desire, like lovers in heated passion."

When Rose made that reference, it was as if the entire audience had been hit with a hot prodding iron. I looked at Momma, and I worried she was going into a fit of apoplexy. She was shaking her head, and she lowered it a bit, as if she could possibly make herself invisible. Her big eyes rolled in the back of her head, and I could tell that she was flushed and embarrassed.

Earl, who was sitting next to me, mumbled, "I'm going to kill her."

"As I have done my best to become a student of letters and learning, I have come to the conclusion that my generation's most fervent, demanding job isn't going to be how to become rich and famous, though that is an admirable goal. No, our job is to become the fulcrum for change," she said as she looked intently in all directions of the audience, and she smiled. "My academic background has proven that I am capable of meeting life's intellectual challenges, as is Alice Brown"—Rose turned and looked at Alice—"and a number of others in my class. Despite this record, my choices are very limited. Why? You need not answer. We all know it's because I am a girl."

If Rose's first statement about heated passion caused a stir, it was a silent note compared to the nervous body language that followed that declaration. When I looked at Momma, this time she had a wide grin on her face.

"Has not my academic record earned me the right to be a doctor or maybe a lawyer? Why should any girl be denied the right to follow her dream? I will be fortunate to be allowed to be a schoolteacher, not that there is anything wrong with being a teacher. It's a noble profession; I may one day choose that path. But should I have limits put upon me because I have indoor rather than outdoor plumbing?"

A bunch of coughing followed that little ditty about plumbing. One could tell that the self-incrimination quotient was rising the longer Rose spoke. It was very interesting to watch the difference between how the men and the women were receiving her speech. The men began to sit up straighter, and their motions became stoic. The women began nodding their heads in agreement; their bodies became more active.

"The great Creator may have made the female to be the

male's helpmeet, but he uniquely created us so that we might have fellowship with him and to honor him with the firstfruits of his blessings. My momma, bless her soul, has proven that there isn't any greater calling than to be a wife and a mother." She looked directly at Momma and grinned. This statement brought a round of spontaneous applause, and it sustained itself for too long. It happened because Rose's speech had been producing a division between the genders; then her statement about mothers, God, and no higher calling, gave everyone the opportunity to give a show of unity.

"And I am looking forward to that role someday." She smiled and paused before she continued her speech. I could tell that her voice was suddenly filled with pain and emotion. Most of our family looked down the aisle, and we could tell that Momma was choking back tears.

"But no one can convince me that the Almighty wants a girl who has brains and talents to just sit on them," Rose said. This emitted a little laughter from the people.

"The world that I visualize for the future for me and my classmates will include women in the highest offices of our nation. The unfair property laws of today will give way to equality in the eyes of the laws of our land." She gave a description of a different world than women existed in.

"Some of my classmates call me a warrior, mostly behind my back and possibly to try and harm me emotionally. But when they do, they honor me." She turned and gazed at them, and some of them laughed. "It's possible I will go through life sorting it out—like my momma has often scolded me—like a bull in a china closet; nevertheless, my challenge to my classmates is that they take a page out of my momma's book of education. Every chance you get, take a bite out of life. Leave no stone unturned. Trust always in God, and *carpe diem, carpe diem, carpe diem!* Seize the day because no one is promised tomorrow."

When she finished her speech, my sister's classmates and the audience offered Rose polite applause. The atmosphere was thick with a sense of consternation because her speech had been filled with truths that only a few in the audience cared to be faced with because to do so called for action, which would demand a cultural change in society as it was known in that day.

With a sense of manly indignation, her speech riled up my brothers and stirred up my sisters because she forced us to do some soul searching. Momma fielded some very pointed remarks from some of our classmates' parents. Momma mostly just smiled and did her best to ignore the subtle innuendos cast her way in the midst of the conversations she conducted during the celebration of the graduation exercises.

"Sixteen graduating seniors seemed to have a hundred and sixteen parents who all wished to comment upon the speech Rose gave," Momma moaned when we finally returned home. "That girl has been a pain in my backside more than I care to admit it." She took off her shoes and allowed her feet to get a breath of air, and she plopped down in a chair.

"But everything she said wasn't all wrong," I said.

"Yes." Momma sighed. "I must give the devil her due. Rose just flat peeled the scab off the wound and exposed it to the world. But why didn't she wait until she had that teaching contract signed?" Momma said in a tone of exasperation. "If she can still keep her teaching job, she'll be mighty fortunate."

"If those mealy-mouthed hypocrites take their job offer away because of my speech, then they can all just go to hell," Rose said as she came into the room, having overheard the last of Momma's conversation.

"Child! You and Carrie Nation may want to be president of our country; however, you aren't given the luxury of living in a fantasy world of your own making. You must navigate the world that you exist in now."

Rose stormed out of the room, muttering, "I'd like to put my foot on every man's neck."

"Rose, honey, one day you will find that when it comes to men, you can't live with them, and you can't live without them!" Momma hollered after her. I looked at her, and we shared a laugh.

The school principal was a man of integrity. He told Rose that he had some grave misgivings about how she might possibly provide an improper influence upon the children with her suffragette thinking; nevertheless, he had offered her a teaching position prior to her valedictorian address, and he was going to honor his offer. Rose listened to Momma's advice, kept her mouth shut, and demurely thanked him for the opportunity.

She became the first of six teachers that would come from our clan.

That night, after all of the graduation celebration had died down, I found a quiet place and watched a shooting star race across God's celestial canvas. I reflected upon the events of the previous day. While my relationship with Rose would always be more like a prickly porcupine than a cuddly teddy bear, it was the first time in my life that I was genuinely proud of her. I suspect that my sister is the only valedictorian in Kansas's history that was a momma before she was a valedictorian.

The Gambler

Momma told all of our family that she was expecting my brother Charlie to one day be a famous preacher.

"That boy can charm snakes," Momma often remarked when he had found a way to escape her wrath and leave her laughing even though she should have been hopping mad.

Charles Crandal was an enigma. "He had been blessed with the gall to steal the leprechaun's Blarney stone and then charge him a fee to kiss it," Momma said when she was asked to describe her next-to-youngest son.

He had personality to burn, and he knew how to turn it on when he wanted something. The ladies found him oh so charming, though not handsome. His winsome ways found him constantly surrounded by girls and all manner of women waiting to comfort him and all of his needs; he had lots of needs. He wasn't athletic like Howard, who was a star athlete in school; still, he was as popular because he was the head cheerleader. It didn't bother him that he wasn't on the court shooting the winning basket as long as he was in the limelight entertaining or being entertained. "Good Time Charlie" is what most people called him.

When he took that megaphone in his hand, dressed in black slacks and a gold cheer sweater with a huge black T on it, there probably wasn't a soul on earth better suited for that shining moment. He came out on that basketball court floor and began to get the crowd riled up and raring to cheer our Haymakers on to victory, week in and week out. During the basketball season, he was given what he needed most: center stage with a great deal of focused attention.

My brother Howard, the star of the basketball team, was directly responsible for our team winning nearly every game we played, but he often received fewer accolades than Charlie. When the game was over, "Charlie really got the crowd going in the fourth quarter" was an often-heard comment. It wasn't unusual for some ditzy, empty-headed girl to come to me and gush, "Your brother is *so* cute. I just don't think we could win all those games if he didn't lead our cheers when we really needed the team to play better, do you?" These were comments that came my way on a regular basis. I never quite knew what the proper reply to those remarks should be; I often just smiled and nodded my head, showing that I agreed with their opinions.

Unlike his other brothers, as far as I can recall, Charlie never held a real job, at least one where you clocked in and did a specific job for a predetermined amount of pay, but he always had a pocketful of money. He had a type of cockiness about him that the girls loved and most of the boys detested. He wasn't very big, yet he wasn't afraid to strap it on with anyone. He possessed a quick wit and a very clever mind, so he seldom used his fists; he just outwitted them.

"Most people are a few bricks shy of a full load," he used to remark, as he would laugh in his overly cocky manner. "More than a few of them think that they are smarter than they really are; those are the easy-picking ones," he would declare when he got around to explaining how he always had money to spare.

One late spring evening when the new moon was rising—which all those who love their gardens swear is the best time to plant—Charlie was home for a change. He and I were just drinking in God's beautiful nightly canvas. I asked him some personal questions.

"Charles, how did you get so good at checkers and pool? Did you read a book?" *Fat chance of that,* my mind reflected.

"Oh, look! Did you see that shooting star?" he whispered. "I'm not sure that what I was taught can be found in a book," he said. "Besides, when was the last time you knew your brother to read a book, and Momma's reading *Shepherd of the Hills* to us kids don't count?"

"Never!" I exclaimed.

"If you really want to know, then I'll tell you an interesting story. After Poppa died and we moved back to Tampa, and Momma was a bit of an emotional wreck for a spell, I just had to find a way to help her take care of all of us. I was a little over twelve years old. I was nothing but a nip of a thing, as scrawny as the scarecrow Momma put in her garden to scare away the birds. I was not like the strapping 140-something guy I am now." He paused and looked at me. We both recognized that he had changed, but he certainly could never be accused of being strong and muscular; he had deliberately denigrated himself for my entertainment; we both laughed.

"I was out about town looking for any kind of a job that would help Momma feed our family. Some of the businesses that I was told were in need of help never hired me when they saw how little I was. I was feeling low and a bit useless when I passed by Joe Houseman's pool hall. I went in the door and took a few minutes to survey the place. Some men were playing pool, and others were playing checkers.

"'Does your momma know you're here?' a man with a large beer belly asked. He had a cigar hanging out of his mouth. He was sweating profusely; he had on an underwear tee shirt and a green apron. He had large arms, and on his right arm was a very visible tattoo, a picture of an anchor. I found out later he had served in the U.S. Navy during the war. He wore glasses, and they were riding off the edge of his nose more than in a position for him to see properly.

"His looming presence scared me.

"'Oh, no sir,' I quickly replied. 'If she knew I was in here, she'd skin me alive.' I regretted that I had made that remark.

"'Your momma isn't another Carrie Nation, is she?' he asked with a sly kind of smile on his face.

"I didn't know who Carrie Nation was, so I just remained mute. I could hear Momma's voice: *If you don't know anything about a particular subject, keep your mouth shut; that way they will give you the benefit of the doubt; if you open your mouth and spill the beans, you'll remove all doubt.* So I just looked up at him in embarrassment.

"'So, you're a shy one, huh? Are you looking for a game?' he teased me. 'Are you looking for a job?'

"I nodded my head.

"'This is your lucky day because I'm looking for a rack boy and someone who will help me keep this place up, at least keep it looking presentable, if not clean.' He looked down at me and made me feel that he was staring right through me.

"Well, Jess, you know how much Momma was against my taking that job—"

"I remember you sweet-talking Momma into allowing you to take it," I interrupted.

He enjoyed a big smile. "Yeah, that was one of my better performances, wasn't it? As I look back, it wasn't my great sales ability as much as the fact that we needed every penny we could earn for the family." He took back some of his bragging rights for once again besting Momma in a contest of wills.

"After I had been working there for a few weeks, and Joe was more than pleased with my job performance, he noticed I had spent every moment I could observing the pool players. I watched how they held the cue and made their precise bridge and how they surveyed the table and the positions of the balls. The best players played a game that indicated they were planning shots three and four balls down the line, versus the poor players concentrating on the shot at hand.

"One afternoon, business was slow, and Joe offered to teach me how to play pool. 'Would you like to become a really fine pool player?'

"'Mr. Houseman, I want to be the best pool player that ever lived!'

"He looked at me and snorted and chuckled. 'Well, why not just shoot for Tampa first,' he teased me. 'Let's get started with your lessons.'

"I immediately ran to one of the many pool tables in his place to get a pool stick to break the rack. 'Not so fast,' he hollered at the backside of my fleeing body. 'Come with me.'

"He took me back into a private room, and the sign on the door read 'Private.' I had never gone in there before. As I

RANNY GRADY

stepped into the room, I was surprised to find a different type of pool table.

"Joe pointed to the table. 'This separates the men from the boys.' He chuckled.

"It didn't have any pockets for pool balls to fall into. On the table were two red balls and a white cue ball. I was shocked and fascinated by what I saw. On the wall beside the table were two long, leather containers. Joe unzipped them and took out two pieces of a cue stick. 'This is private stock,' he said as he quickly screwed them together. They made the most beautiful cue sticks I had ever seen. The handles were pearl inlaid, and the pool sticks felt different from any I have ever held.

"Joe pointed to the table. 'Charlie, my boy, this is how you become a great pool player. This is a real billiard table, not a pool table. If you want to become a shark, you must learn how to work the balls on this table. You should learn how to groove your stroke and how to use English with your cue stick. You must learn how to use geometry, the math of angles. The angles give you the knowledge of how the cue ball is going to react coming off the cushion rails; if you can't master the angles, you will be a good, but probably never a great player,' he said as he began his schooling.

"He picked up his cue and walked over to the billiard table. 'Charlie, the object of this game is to use your cue ball and at least two cushions to make contact with both red balls.' He took a shot and demonstrated the proper way to play the game. It was a much larger table than a pool table. It didn't have any pockets. 'When you are able to master this game, then you will be ready to become a pool shark.' He motioned for me to come and take his cue and make a shot.

"Who knew that geometry could be fun? If Mr. Jones had used a billiard table to teach our class, I probably would have learned something." He laughed. "Jess, I hate to say this, but Mr. Houseman became the father I never had. Oh, Poppa had his moments," he quickly added, "but I was his favorite whipping boy too many times for me to learn to care very much about him."

"I can't really blame you. He was too prickly, though I did love him."

"Sis, Mr. Houseman let me practice in his private domain any time I had a spare minute to burn. I would come in early and sometimes stay late, which made Momma mad. He would teach me to see the angles and the finer points of gamesmanship, which allowed me to learn how to present myself in different hues, shades, and fashions in order to look like I wasn't a very good player. When the right amount of money was at stake, I would play very well to clip the pigeons (opponents).

"'Charlie, my boy, you have a gift,' he told me. 'Some guys play all their lives, and they never are able to really be great. Others, like you, are like a fish in water. If you handle yourself well, son, the sky's the limit.' He would emit a low whistle to emphasize his belief in my playing ability. Usually he would quickly add, "Don't forget for a moment that there is some guy out there who is a lot better than you are, than you will probably ever be. It's just the way things are."'

"If you spent all your time learning how to be a shark at pool, how did you get so good at checkers?" I was fascinated by his story, and I wanted to know more.

"I had a different tutor. Pops—I don't know his real name, not sure if anyone does. Word is that he came from back east to tend to a sick relative and fell in love with the wheat fields of Kansas and never left. Some of the old guys allow a rumor to float around that has him as one of Teddy's Rough Riders. They say that he fought in the Spanish American War. Don't know if any of that is true. What I know is he is the best checkers player in Tampa," Charlie replied.

"Each day Pops holds court down at the pool hall. Folks gather around to watch him take on all comers. He is a gangly, thin, balding man with a bit of a hooknose. He said it was broken in a fight many years ago. He wears a white, starched, short-sleeved shirt, navy blue pants, and a big silver belt buckle with an eagle on it as he presides over his checkers kingdom. He smokes a corncob pipe, mostly chews on it. He has a low, guttural tone of voice, which makes it difficult to understand him sometimes. He has bright blue eyes that are able to penetrate a man's mind when he is playing with his opponent before he kills him with kings," Charlie elaborated.

"One day, as I was busy sweeping the floor and doing my best to eavesdrop on the conversation taking place between him and his pigeon, he hollered at me. 'Hey, boy.'

"That's what he called me," Charlie said. "I don't know if he knew my name, still don't. He called me over and asked me a specific question about which move he should make in the game. I could see that his opponent had left him an opening for his checker to jump and be kinged, so I told him the move.

"'Hey, boy, you're purdy smart,' he complimented me. I realized he was putting me on a bit, but it felt good nevertheless.

"From that day forward, he took me under his wing and started to pelt me with questions concerning the game of checkers. His questions dealt with strategy to some extent but were mostly about studying the human condition."

"'Hey, boy, to be a real checkers player you have to be able to get into the other man's mind.' Pops would challenge me to think differently. 'If you learn about the human condition, you'll win a lot more than you lose,' he promised.

"At the time, Jess, I didn't have the foggiest idea what Pops was talking about. Later, I discovered that it is really the success of every gambler. Pops's human condition entailed the ability to read the opponent's minute movements.

"'Boy, the body has its own language, and your ability to read it and produce a symphony from it will be the deciding factor of whether you are a gambler who wins or just a lousy gambler.' I was trancelike in my attention to Pops's schooling. 'If you are perceptive enough under the bright gaze of pressure during any type of competition, you will be able to obtain a lot of useful information that your opponent would rather you not know. Unless the man has been trained, he will allow his emotions and nervous energy to sneak out and betray him.'

"'How could a right-thinking man allow his body to betray him?' I interrupted.

"'Hey, boy, if you will, just hold your horses for a minute.' He good-naturedly admonished my impatience. 'Suppose you were in a game, and there was a considerable amount of money riding on the game. Wouldn't you like to have an edge on that guy? If you pay close attention, he will provide you with a multitude of clues, such as a slight movement of a lip. The ole eyes are a window to your soul, and when your soul is stirred up, it causes your eyes to do some funny things, possibly a slight twitch of an eye. When your nervous system starts acting up, it sends signals to your mouth, and for some strange reason, many people find that their lips tremble.'

"'That's the God's truth,' I blurted out.

"'It's refreshing to know that you believe me to be a man of integrity,' Pops teased, laughing.

"'Now, the scratching of one's nose…I'm aware of the old saying. "If someone scratches his nose, he is going to get some money or kiss a fool." Pops chuckled. 'But if a checkers player scratches his nose too much, you're looking at a loser. My mentor taught me that when your opponent kept rubbing his hair, it was because he was frightened about an impending decision. It seems that when the pressure of decision making is cast upon a man, the hairs of his head start tingling, and he begins rubbing his hair to make the sensation go away; rubbing one's hair usually indicates that he doesn't have a winning situation.'

"Jess, I just couldn't help myself. I shouted, 'You're so right! I find myself doing that very same thing.' I was just dumbfounded that anyone could be that smart about people," Charlie said.

"Pops took a hard chomp on his pipe and grinned at me. 'And here all the time you thought old Pops was just a hayseed, didn't you?' Without expecting or waiting for an answer, he continued. 'Now, you take sound; it is a dead giveaway. If one is coughing or clearing his throat too many times, it's a sure bet that he is on the horns of a dilemma. The body desires for him to emit sounds to provide some relief from the pent-up emotion the dilemma has caused. It's a clear sign of great nervousness. The same applies to movement; if your opponent moves his body, his seat, his legs, his arms, or his body's position, even changing the inflection of his voice or the speed of his speech, he is providing unintended signals. It could even be because he becomes too quiet or stoic,' Pops stated. He spent time delineating all of the ways an opponent could greatly increase the chances that he would lose the contest.

"Jess, he captivated me with his thinking. I marveled at the depth of his knowledge about the human condition," Charlie told me. "Pops said that I was a natural-born learner."

"That certainly would have fooled your teachers, right?" I laughed at his expense.

Though I certainly had never darkened the pool hall door, though it wasn't from not wanting to, I had heard talk that my brother had a reputation around town as one of the best sticks in the area; next to Pops, he was considered just about the best checkers player. He was young and looked even younger, which allowed him to gain an advantage in just about every gambling competition.

"Everyone is always searching high and low for a patsy." He laughed in a derisive manner.

"What's a patsy?" I asked.

"A patsy is someone who the other person is absolutely certain is inferior to him, regardless of what might be at stake in any type of a contest two people might compete in, especially for money. That's why I am always winning money." He gave a big, cocky grin. "I make sure the other guy is very confident that I can't be anything but a patsy. I do anything I believe is necessary to create this false impression so he will challenge me in some money game, nine ball in pool or checkers, where I have few equals. When he takes the bait, he then becomes a pigeon ready to be dressed for the skillet." He would chuckle and jiggle his pants pockets, which held all those nickels he had won. "As long as I can be the patsy, then the pigeons will come home to roost, and I will own them, lock, stock, and barrel."

Charlie's attitude about life often rubbed Momma the wrong way. Those two regularly found themselves in a battle of the wills. Momma often tooted her horn how she could get the best of him if she wanted to, but she seldom did.

One evening Momma was preparing supper and was waiting on Charlie to arrive with a few grocery items she expected him to bring when he came home from his job at the pool hall. He was late, as usual. Her patience was growing thin.

More than once I can recall sitting around our kitchen table while Momma was putting last-minute touches on our dinner, and she would be waiting on Charlie to arrive with something she needed; it really didn't matter what it was, but earlier that day she had given my brother a job or an errand, and once again he was not handling the responsibility on Momma's time line. Her patience grew thin when he constantly disappointed her.

"If I ever get my hands on that boy,"—she fussed about his cavalier attitude—"I'm going to wring his neck." She walked to the back door and peered out. She sat down in Poppa's chair and slowly tapped her foot. "That boy is going to be the death of me, making me wait. He's not too big to get a whipping." She asked Deannie to get Poppa's strop; she did her best to convince the family she was going to use it on him when he got home.

Whenever Momma had to wait until Charlie decided to come home, she got mad; we kids thought it was fun. When he finally chose to show up, never on time, it was like watching a drama unfold. It was Momma and her "mad on" versus my brother's charm and wit. Momma knew that we kids really enjoyed seeing her try to stay mad at Charlie when he would arrive, often without either bringing what Momma asked him to bring or forgetting to accomplish the task. that he was asked to do.

"This time that boy has gone too far. This time, this time he is going to get punished," she declared.

We had gathered around waiting for the show to begin. Momma glanced at us. We knew what she was thinking, and she knew what we were thinking. "You don't think I can win, do you?" The room remained silent. "Just because he wins most of the time—" She stopped talking because most of us kids were looking at her and shaking our heads.

"Well, you're a bunch of smarty pants! Just hide and watch," Momma challenged us.

My brother Charlie was one slick, snake-oil salesman. If he

was late, and he knew he was in Momma's doghouse, he always came prepared to disarm her anger. He would come in the door whistling one of Momma's favorite hymns. She loved to hear him whistle because he was such a wonderful whistler. When we kids would hear him coming to the door whistling, we got excited. We would wear big smiles and sometimes enjoy a few guarded laughs; we knew Momma was about to lose another confrontation with our brother.

Charlie wore a brown derby hat everywhere. he went. It had become a signifying fixture of his persona. When he knew he was in big trouble with Momma, he would throw his hat into the room and stand behind the side of the door. When we would see this, we would all giggle.

Charlie would gingerly step into the room and stand directly in front of Momma. She would have a stern look on her face and a mean glare in her eyes. She wanted him to know that she wasn't anybody to fool with. He often was carrying flowers and candy. He would look at her with his charming blue eyes and slowly raise his arms and offer up his pleasing gifts to her. If Momma stood her ground and was determined not to give in to his wily ways, he would move close to her and play the repentant son. In a very humble manner he would say, "Don't be mad at me. I'm sorry I messed up." He would wait for Momma to make the first move.

If I had been Momma, on many occasions, I would have whipped the tar out of him. Momma couldn't keep her "mad on" when it came to Charlie. She would do her best to fume and fuss, but try as she might, she usually became a victim to his charms. When he realized that he was really in trouble, he would deftly rush her and give her a big hug, squeeze her tight, and kiss her on her cheeks.

"I love you so much, Momma, I could just squeeze the packing out of you," he'd say.

By that time, she had lost another contest with him, and she would often reply, "I wish you could squeeze the packing out of me." Then they would both laugh. Charlie would soon have

Momma waltzing around the room, and he would be whistling some of her hymns.

More times than not, after he romanced her, he would jump back a step or two, put a huge grin on his face, and announce, "Watch out! Charlie's coming on strong!"

We kids would act like a roaring audience, and we would egg him on and laugh at his antics, especially Deannie, Gracie, little Arthur, and me.

He would spin around three hundred and sixty degrees.

"Lou's favorite son has found the pot of gold," he'd brag on himself, and he would reach into his pockets and pull out some nickels and place them in her hand. It was his peace offering, and to a family that never had enough money to make ends meet, it was very welcome. Sometimes he would walk over to the kitchen table and pull out two fists full of nickels. He would hold them above his head and allow them to slowly fall onto the table. The nickels would bounce around and find a place on the floor. How he loved to show off in front of Momma and our family! He would exclaim, "Pigeons, pigeons, they are everywhere!"

Momma did her best to warn Charlie that he was just too full of himself and that one day he was going to get taken to the cleaners. He never paid her any mind!

Once Charlie finished school, he quickly graduated to a different level of gambling.

"I just have a gift for it," he told me, and he would unravel an exciting story about how he won a lot of money playing poker.

Cards, women, and booze seemed to work for him. It certainly didn't work for Momma! "One of these times, your brother is going to mess with the wrong crowd, and he's going to get hurt." It was easy to detect that she worried about his sinful life.

I could never understand why he would choose that kind of life. One month, or even one day, he would be riding in some fancy auto, and it seemed he could buy the world; unfortunately, the next day, he would be walking and using his charms to get someone to give him a "grub stake," as he called it.

RANNY GRADY

While his choices for his life never brought Momma a moment's peace, he did bring our family Fanny Adams. She was a little, wisp of a blonde thing who had ebony eyes, a smile that made every light in our house green with envy, a sun-kissed complexion that seemed to glow, and a disposition that could melt stone hearts. In addition to all those superb qualities, she could play the piano.

She played "like God's celestial angels must be able to play to entertain the Almighty himself," Momma said. Momma was simply enthralled by her son's young wife's ability to play our piano. It took only a minute or so for Momma to forgive Charlie for bringing her to our door unannounced one Christmas Eve.

There really isn't a nice way to say that Charlie was a scoundrel through and through. He was a moody, sometimes almost cruel man, especially when he was drinking. If he were winning, he was a delight to be around; if he were losing, he was a mean-spirited man.

More than once, Fanny walked around with bruises. She tried to camouflage them with her makeup, but she never failed to protect the love of her life. She would lie to save him any public humiliation or Momma's wrath.

"That girl isn't fooling anyone, especially this man's momma," she remarked after Fanny left our home on a number of occasions, suffering from being boxed around by Charlie.

"He's my son, and the good Lord knows how much I love him, but what he needs is to have his teeth kicked down his throat," Momma told me once after she had spent some time with Fanny.

Back then, a woman's relationship with her husband sometimes included physical pain and sorrow. More than once, I made a pact with myself that I was never going to get married. Of course, it was silly of me, and I couldn't keep the oath.

While my brother was a great encourager for my life, on many occasions he also made me ashamed of being his sister. I could never truly understand what made him tick. He would breeze into our house with Fanny in tow, after he had boxed her around to keep her in line, and she would present herself as a dutiful wife whose life was nearly perfect. Charlie said a man had to kick tail sometimes to make sure she knew who was boss. He would find a way to insult her publicly if he didn't think it was sufficient to keep her in her place.

He would embarrass her and the rest of our family by running his hands up the back of her skirt and feeling her up.

"Oh, what this woman can do to a man," he'd brag and laugh and dare anyone to take an offense to his choice of words or behavior. This usually would happen when he was on a losing streak. If he were winning, she would be wearing something new, expensive, fashionable, and he'd want to show her off.

Regardless of what heated situations Charlie and Fanny may have found themselves in, when they paid a visit, she always found time to play our piano. The Ranti Crandal clan would form a choir and entertain themselves singing many of Momma's favorite hymns and other popular songs of the day.

As much as Fanny loved my brother, even though they had two small children, their marriage was over in just four years. Divorce was just about the worst sin a person could commit that didn't carry jail time, and Momma suffered as much as if she had to spend time in the slammer.

"It's all coming true," she remarked one day after their divorce. It was a dank, rainy day, which fit Momma's mood too well. "My wayward son has a floozy on the line before the train whistle blows." She lamented about Fanny and her grandchildren going back to Pittsburg to live with her parents. At that time in our family's life, Momma loved Fanny much more than Charlie. Big ole tears ran down Momma's cheeks and spilled onto the floor at her feet. "He's going to be the death of me," she softly murmured.

It always stumped me how my brother, an uninhibited lothario, managed to find two women who loved him; both were willing to be treated like whores when it suited him just for the privilege of being in his company.

Valerie Golden, a Georgia peach, was a girl from near Atlanta. When she opened her mouth to speak, sweet nectar flowed from it. Her Southern drawl could melt any man's heart, as it did my brother's. Charlie met her on one of his gambling junkets, and he was on a winning streak, just enjoying being Charlie like no one else could. He dropped in to get a bite to eat at an all-night café; Valerie was a waitress in that joint.

As Valerie later related the story after they were married and she became a part of our family, Charlie was quite the "dapper dandy," even though he had been playing cards for more than ten hours. He still had a crisp look about him. His expensive suit, vest, and colorful tie told the world that Charlie was very successful. The fancy roadster he drove up in just added ammunition to that statement. He had a cocky-looking, brown derby hat, that he twirled with ease to help draw attention to him. Just inside the left side of his suit jacket were a shoulder holster and the nickel-plated .38 pistol he always carried. The pistol was for "mad dogs and bad men" he joked with her when she first questioned him about the gun.

"Have you ever used it?" she asked as he was sipping a cup of coffee and carrying on light conversation with her on the night she first met him.

He gave her a big ole grin, and at first she thought he was going to tell her some manly story about how he protected someone's life and ended up a hero.

"One time," he confessed, "and it nearly scared me to death," and they both laughed.

Valerie was nearly as pretty as Fanny but was different in one respect: she was a godly woman.

"She may be a godly woman;"—I offered my assessment of Valerie when he finally got up the nerve to bring her to meet Momma and our family—"however, in my humble opinion, if she remains married to my brother, she won't be godly for long." I made a declaration that no one in our family disagreed with.

He treated Valerie as badly as he had treated Fanny. The difference between them was that Valerie announced that she was praying to Jesus that he would change Charlie's heart. She said that to Charlie over and over, whether he was drunk or sober, winning or losing. He often made fun of her religious fervor.

He must have had some type of magic potion that made women desire his attention because Valerie was as much in love with him as Fanny had been.

Charlie and Valerie moved close to Atlanta, Charlie's major gambling headquarters. They had a passel of kids—six—in a few short years.

"It's for the best," Momma told us.

He continued to gamble, and he lost more than he won; therefore, they had a very rocky financial life. Valerie never allowed their money problems to affect her relationship with Charlie.

When Momma died, Charlie and Valerie returned to Tampa for the funeral. After the wake, Valerie and I visited. She told me a story about redemption that defied all odds.

We found ourselves in the tiny kitchen, alone. She was fixing a cup of tea. She asked me to join her. When we sat down, she told me the story.

Did you know I nearly divorced your brother?"

I looked at her for a few seconds. "I certainly wouldn't have blamed you if you had."

"Yup! Can you believe it?" Valerie said to me. "After we moved to Atlanta, I called up a lawyer. I finally found the gumption to make a stand against his foolishness. As much as I knew it was going to hurt the kids, and I dearly loved Charlie, it got to the point that I just couldn't pretend any longer. I went to see a lawyer, who was a member of our church, about filing for a divorce."

"Jessie, there at the last, I became as unstable as he was."

"Who wouldn't be unstable with what you were forced to put up with ..."

"That wasn't the worst of it," Valerie continued. "Charlie lost our house playing poker again, and since the house was in both our names, he had to have my signature to pay off his gambling debt."

"You lost your house ... twice?"

"I'm ashamed to say it's true, but it is. 'It's just a temporary setback, honey.' Charlie tried to assure me that he still had everything under control. I know he saw the fright in my eyes. 'I'll win it back, honest I will.' He tried to comfort me. 'I'll...I'll win it back by tomorrow tonight.' He put the deed to our house in front of me for me to sign.

"Jessie, I wanted to just run, anywhere, out of my house, out of my life. I'm sure the devil was having a field day. My eyes felt strange; they were full of rage and anger.

"'Charles Crandal, this is the last time I am going to cover your rear. If they want to put you in a cement mixer, I'll let them before I sign over the deed to our house again!' I yelled at him for the first time in our married life.

"'I...I'll win it back by tomorrow tonight! I promise.' He shoved the deed toward me and handed me the pen he had at the ready."

"What did you do?" I asked, as I just couldn't wait to hear the rest of the story.

Valerie started laughing.

"What's so funny?"

"Well, it really wasn't funny. Actually, it was frightening; yet, it just turned out funny."

I smiled at her and almost laughed because of the way she was trying to tell me her story.

"After that terrible evening, and I had reluctantly signed the deed over to Charlie for his gambling debts, Charlie slept in late and left the house about noon," Valerie stated.

"'Your Charlie is off to win back your house,' he said as he tried to give me a kiss, and I only offered up my cheek.

"About an hour after Charlie left, I heard a knock at the door. I looked outside, and I saw a luxury automobile parked out front. I think it was a Cadillac. I opened the door, and there stood two rather large men. They were dressed in dark suits with nice ties; one had a blue tie; the other, a red one. They wore hats. One man was large, and the other much shorter.

"They looked at me, you know, Jessie, that up-and-down-and-all-around look we women always get with men. The larger one said, 'Is Charlie home?'

"'What do you want with my Charles?' I asked, and I gave

them a direct stare. I figured they were some men who had something to do with Charlie's gambling debt. Charlie had persuaded me to sign the deed because he and I both knew that he could be killed for welching on a bet.

"'He left about an hour ago.' I smiled. 'Whom should I say came calling?'

"The smaller man asked, 'Are your children home, all six of them?'"

I immediately recognized what a frightening position Valerie had found herself in. "Oh, Val, how afraid were you?"

"I was quaking in my boots." She made her body quiver and shake, then she laughed. "I decided that the best, maybe the only way to play this situation was to try and take away the initiative from the men. 'Are you the leg breakers?' I asked.

"My comment threw them off balance. Each of them looked at one another. 'Naw, lady, we're not that kind of guys,' the smaller one said as they became uncomfortable under the stress of my unexpected question. 'My buddy here, he sometimes lets his mouth override his ..." he looked at me. "Well, you know," he smiled. I nodded.

"Jess, I figured I had them on the defensive, so I just ran with it.

"'If you do find Charlie, if you'll bring him back home,'"—I started to really look into their eyes—"if you will hold him, I'll beat the stuffing out of him for you.'"

"Val, you didn't!" I gasped.

"The two men looked at each other. I could just see the exchange of their eyes. It was as if they couldn't believe what they had heard. In a few seconds, they both broke into sheepish smiles.

"The smaller man looked up at me as I stood in the doorway. 'That's okay, never mind.' He grinned. 'We're sorry we bothered you, ma'am.' He tipped his hat. He motioned for his buddy to follow his lead to leave.

"As they were about to get in the car, I hollered, 'If you change your mind about my offer, y'all come back, ya hea'ah.'

"I heard the larger one say, 'Can you believe that dame?

She's got brass ones, more than most of us guys,' as he got in the car and drove off."

I started laughing. "I just can't believe you actually did that."

Valerie looked at me; she smiled a bit. "Neither can I." We both laughed.

"I don't know how he managed to do it, but true to Charlie's word, he won the deed to our house back that night.

"We had a verbal, knockdown fight, and I said to him, 'Charlie, I can't stop you from gambling, because if I could, I surely would. But I can make absolutely sure that you won't ever be able to lose my house gambling again.' I made him put the deed to our house in my name only. He reluctantly agreed to my demand. I told him, 'Those cronies or crooks, they are all the same to me, may come and break your legs—God forbid—even take your life. But they are not going to ever take my house away so I don't have a home for my babies.'

"One night, after that deed incident, Charlie returned home very late, as usual, from gambling. He had been drinking and was trying to be a mean drunk. He was 'needy', and he wanted to have sex.

"'If you take one step toward me, I'll get the boys' baseball bat and coldcock you,' I warned.

"Even is his drunken stupor, I could see the look of utter shock come over him. I had never refused any of his advances before that night. It was as if I had just hit him with an axe and split his heart wide open. It stopped him in his tracks. For the first time in our married life, I saw my husband shed tears.

"He dropped to his knees and began to sob.

"'I ... I ...' He tried to speak, but the effect of the booze and his emotions just weakened him. Still on his knees, he began to crawl toward me.

"Jessie, my poor old heart was breaking, and I didn't really know what to do.

"'*Please*—,' he moaned as he drew near to where I was sitting on the edge of our bed. He put his head on my lap and his arms around my legs. I was a bit frightened of finding myself in this position.

"'Oh, Charlie, oh, baby, honey, we just can't go on like this,' I said softly as I stroked his hair.

"I kn-n-ow, I knows," he sobbed, in a soft voice. "I'll ch-ch-change ... I'll r-r-really ch-change," he grew silent. "I-I-I m-m- mean it-t-t-this time," he cried and heaved deeply several times.

"After what seemed like an eternity, he slurred his words less, and he said, 'I'm going to go out and get me a job.'

"I lay back on the bed and pulled him over to me. We slept the night with him close up against my breasts, and for the first time in a long time, I felt warm and safe on the inside.

"It didn't happen the next day, and it didn't happen for about a month, but things slowly changed for Charlie and me. He started treating me more tenderly and with some kindness. He treated me even better than he did when he was courting me. Laughter returned to our home. Cautiously, his children began to trust him once again. They all loved him."

"When did you decide not to seek a divorce?"

"When I saw those tears of remorse that night. When he had his head in my lap, my heart told me that God was answering my prayers."

The retelling of this story played heavily upon Valerie's emotional strength, so she stopped for a few minutes and fixed us a cup of tea.

"A nice cup of tea helps calm my unsettled being." She grinned.

We sipped tea and remained quiet for a few minutes.

"Out of the clear-blue sky, one day, about a month later, Charlie showed up with an old, beat-up looking truck. He had lost our nice new roadster gambling. 'This is going to make us a million,' he announced as he came home full of excitement. None of his kids were excited about his jewel.

"In the back of the truck were brooms and mops. 'I'm going to peddle them all over Atlanta,' he announced with his usual bravado. 'Charlie Crandal, the king peddler of brooms and

RANNY GRADY

mops.' He teased me and insisted on kissing me in front of the kids. They soon rushed us and joined in the lovefest. However, his voice possessed a sense of resolve that I hadn't seen in him since we were married.

"I can remember standing there and thinking, *This crazy man, who is the father of my six children, is going to become rich selling brooms and mops out of the back end of a beat-up old truck. We stood a better chance when all he did was gamble.*

"Jess, the one thing everyone could agree on about your brother is that when he got hold of something he wanted, nothing could stop him." Valerie slapped her knee and let out a laugh that indicated she was proud of her Charlie.

"Oh, he struggled at first and was even a bit discouraged. But Charlie needed his fix; he had stopped gambling. If he could sell something to someone who initially wasn't interested in buying his brooms or mops, he got his fix. In about a year, he had established a regular route with stores, and they continued to buy more and more of his mops and brooms. The fact that the old darkies (Charlie's term for the negroes who made the mops and brooms that he sold) from whom he bought them and made the best mops and brooms one could buy, gave him an edge in his business. He could sell them cheaper because he paid them less to make the brooms, helping him beat the competition. It took a few years, but one day he told me that he was going to start hawking carpet remnants, which he could buy for a song (his way of saying very cheap).

"While all of this was happening, everything about our life grew much sweeter. The only sticking point in our marriage was the emotional distance our family suffered every Sunday morning. The kids and I went to church. Charlie stayed home, read the paper, and worked on his books for the business.

"Jess, I can remember your momma, before she died, telling me, 'God always answers the prayers of his children,' when she was doing her best to comfort me regarding Charlie's and our personal troubles. 'Sometimes he says yes, sometimes he says no; in your case, honey, I've a feeling that he is saying wait.' She did her best to encourage me.

"Our little church was having its spring revival. It was just before the celebration of Easter, and I was leaving Sunday services the weekend before the revival started. Our preacher, Harry Johnson, asked if it would be all right for him to pay a visit and see Charlie. He wanted to invite him to the revival. I knew my husband didn't want the preacher to come and visit him.

"When I intimated that I wanted him to at least entertain the idea of listening to what the preacher might have to say if he were allowed to make a visit to our home, Charlie bellowed, 'And don't go inviting any of your church people to come and try to save my wretched soul.'"

"What did you do?"

"Jessie, I know he was brought up in your momma's house, and when he was young he was very active in a church. Why, he knows more hymns than most Christians at my church; I even catch him whistling some of them from time to time. Why do you think a man who believes in the Creator, and even believes Jesus is God's son, would still turn his back on God?"

"I think he believes he has lived the kind of life, let's be honest, a very sinful life in the past, and he thinks he will just never be good enough for the Lord to be able to forgive him."

"I spent the day in prayer. I prayed that Charlie wouldn't embarrass the preacher, himself, and our home."

"Did he?"

"It was the strangest thing. Charlie was the perfect host. He shared a hot cup of coffee with him and enjoyed some of my freshly baked banana bread. I left them alone, and they spent over a half hour visiting.

"After the preacher left, Charlie said, 'Now, are you satisfied?' He smiled and gave me a hug. As he casually left the kitchen, he remarked, 'He invited me to the revival.' After a long pause, he added, 'I told him I would try and make it one evening.'"

"Could you believe it?" My voice was filled with joy.

"I was stunned, and I didn't say a word as he walked out of the room. Jessie, can you remember as a little girl how excited you could allow yourself to get in the anticipation of being able to have something wonderful take place in your life? Well, that

RANNY GRADY

is just how I was for days. Jess, can you also remember how horrible you felt when you allowed yourself to contemplate how badly you would feel if none of that potential joy came true? That's how I felt!" Valerie said.

"As long as the good Lord lets me live, I'll never forget that night at the revival. I will never forget the message the evangelist preached. He said he had stolen it from a famous preacher. The title of it was "Sinners in the Hands of an Angry God." As the evangelist preached his sermon, I kept glancing over at Charlie, and I swear he looked like he was in some kind of pain. He was struggling with an invisible adversary. In reflection, I am convinced that he was. When the invitation was offered, he moved down to the front, not even looking at me, and when he reached the altar, he started to sob loudly."

"What did you do?" I asked in a somewhat hushed tone.

"I didn't really know what to do at first. The first thing I knew, I was down the aisle and on my knees beside him. I put my left hand on him, and just the touch of my hand on his body caused him to reach out and nearly knock the breath out of me by the strength of his hug. We looked into each other's eyes; they were filled with tears."

"'Thank you for loving me,' he said in a whisper I could barely hear. 'Thank you for praying for me.' He buried his head in my breasts.

"History has recorded that a Yankee gave one of the most profound speeches the world has ever heard. It was at Gettysburg battlefield, a place the South will never forget. President Lincoln saved a nation, they say. It was just a few hundred words, and even critics marvel at its brevity and its lasting influence. Its message knitted and united people. Charlie Crandal's confession, like Lincoln's Gettysburg Address, was amazing in its simplicity and its power," Valerie said.

"'I, Charlie Crandal, believe that Jesus is the Christ, the son of the living God, and I take him as my Lord and Savior' were the twenty-four little words he uttered. It was a simple confession. He chose to be baptized and buried with Christ. When he came up out of the baptismal water, he shouted, 'Thank you,

Jesus! I'm going to live only for you.' The crowd hollered "amen" and broke into sustained applause. If the lights had gone out, Charlie's smile would have lit up the entire go-to-meeting place. The entire group of believers began to softly sing, 'Now I belong to Jesus; Jesus belongs to me; not for the time of years alone, but for eternity.'

"Jess, people tell me today, 'God doesn't do any of his miracles such as he did back when the apostles were building the infant church.' But your brother is living proof that he does." Valerie started laughing for no apparent reason. "It is true what they say: 'There's nothing like a reformed drunk becoming a Christian.'" She giggled. "It took me a while to convince him that we didn't need to start wearing togas and sandals just because he wanted his family to walk the talk like Jesus taught.

"The changes in Charlie were more than I could have ever hoped for." She started laughing. "When old Charlie got to going on his repentance journey, it was a beautiful thing."

"What do you mean his 'repentance journey'?"

"You know, when a sinner comes to accept the Lord and he repents of his sins, if it is possible, he needs to seek forgiveness from people he has sinned against. In addition, he needs to seek reconciliation and even restitution if he has harmed or cheated someone.

"With the type of scoundrel Charlie was before he turned his life over to Jesus, he had a heap of work to do," Valerie said, and we both laughed.

"Jessie, as bad a person as he had been, Charlie became a better man for God. The sweetest thing he did, at least it touched my heart the most, was his willingness to seek forgiveness, reconciliation, and restitution from the one businessman he had sinned the worst against. It was an old Negro man.

"One day, soon after he became a Christian, Charlie said, 'Val, honey, I want you to come with me to visit the family who makes my brooms and mops.'

"I remember telling him, 'I really don't have the time to go running halfway across Atlanta; I have too much to do here at home.'

"He came over to me and gave me a kiss. 'I want you to go on my repentance journey with me.

"'I should have made this part of my journey first, not the last,' he told me as we were driving.

"'Neither Jew nor Greek, slave nor free, male nor female, for you are all one in Christ Jesus,'" Charlie mumbled Galatians 3:28 a few times.

"He turned and looked at me, and he smiled at my surprised look.

"'It's Paul's letter to the Galatians.'

"I nodded my head, and I was fighting back tears.

"We pulled up to a brick building not much bigger than a garage that might hold three cars. 'Smith's Factory,' the sign read. The inscription read, 'Atlanta's finest brooms and mops.'

"'Come with me,' Charlie said. 'I want you to meet one of the finest Christian men I have ever known in my business world.' He helped me out of the car.

"'Mr. Charles Crandal, sho 'nuff. I haven't seen hide nor hair of you in what, a month of Sundays,' a medium-sized black man said as he gave us a big grin. 'Boss, I's been working ever since you left, sho 'nuff, jus' so your big order would be ready whens you gets back.' He put out his hand, and Charlie shook it firmly.

"'And who might this pretty thing on yo arm mights be?' he asked as he sort of drew himself up some and came to a stance like military attention would be.

"'Valerie, this here is none other than Isaiah Washington Smith.'

"'Jus' can't bes your wife.' He smiled at me. 'Her being too young for ol' man likes you.' He flashed a smile at me. He was as black as the ace of spades, and his teeth were a brilliant white.

"Jess, I recall thinking, *He is a delightful man and quite a handsome one.*

"'Hope Isaiah isn't being toos forward?' He chuckled a bit and looked into my eyes. 'Sometimes us ol' coloreds don't seems to knows jus' how fur the line is 'tween joshing and disrespects, if'n you knows whats I means.'

"Jess, his comment possessed ugly submissiveness to me.

""Course, boss man Charlie.' He looked at him. 'He's good ats making sure Isaiah toes the mark.'

"Jess, I had lived in the South nearly all my life, had been around colored people, mostly from our people's expected, safe, and polite distance. As God is my witness, so help me, until my conversational encounter with Isaiah, I never really understood how evil and sinister the white race's relationship with the black race was. Isaiah was playing the role of a slave even though he wasn't tethered. Since he purposefully denigrated himself so he would please Charlie, Isaiah made sure he would be able to continue to make brooms and mops for Charlie to sell.

"Jessie, I felt dirty on the inside because I couldn't deny that I had been an indifferent person all of my life. I had accepted the generational hate-filled message: black people really are inferior to white people. I wanted to reach out and give Isaiah a hug. I wanted to tell him to stop what he was doing, but I did nothing.

"'Is there somewhere we can go and take a load off our feet?' Charlie asked.

"'Sho 'nuff,' he said. 'Perhaps my missus mights fetch us some cold lemonades to cool us down from this morning sun.'

"He took us to a little table with four chairs on the west side of the building. There was a huge oak tree nearby. As we were all sitting down, Isaiah hurried to help me with my seat before Charlie could even do it.

"'Neither Jew nor Greek—' Charlie started saying.

"'Slave nor free, male nor female, for you are all one in Christ Jesus,' Isaiah said as he interrupted Charlie. The men exchanged surprised looks and then tearful smiles.

"'Boss man, you's gone done quoting God's Word, and so earlys in the morning.' Isaiah had a strange look in his eyes. 'What's eating you?'

"'Mr. Smith,' Charlie said.

"I could see the light in Isaiah's eyes start to flicker, and a jolt came into his body. His countenance changed.

"'Boss man, don't gos confusin' Isaiah now.'

"Charlie pulled out his wallet, and he slowly counted out twenty ten-dollar bills, and he put them on the table.

"'Do you suppose this might be close to the amount?'

"Isaiah looked intently at him. He didn't say a word, but his eyes started glistening. He slowly reached out and put his right hand over the stacked bills.

"'Maybe a bit mores than needs,' he whispered.

"'His Word told me that I needed to have a renewed mind,' Charlie said. 'I figured it needed to start where I'm the ugliest.' Charlie slowly reached out and placed both of his hands on top of Isaiah's.

"I guess from ingrained training, Isaiah tried to immediately pull his hands away from Charlie's touch. Maybe it was out of fear or from his teachings about how black men and white men are to conduct themselves.

"'Don't do that! My lily whiteness won't rub off.' Charlie smiled, and his voice broke as tears welled up in his eyes.

"Isaiah broke into a big grin, and tears started streaming down his face. Both men gripped each other's hands.

"Charlie reached in his shirt pocket and took out the card he had crudely made. He handed it to Isaiah, who put it up close to his eyes and read, "Atlanta's finest brooms and mops." He looked up at Charlie and then continued to read. "Hand-crafted by ..." He paused. "Isaiah Washington Smith. Now don't that beat all?" He chuckled and repeated it in a near reverent manner.

"'I don't want our business relationship to be a "boss" man anymore; I just want to be a Christian brother who is a businessman with Isaiah,' he whispered softly.

"Isaiah sat up straighter and he stared at him. "'People gon say you dones fallen in loves with a nigger.' Isaiah gripped Charlie's hand again. 'Putting my name on things you sell, signify for shore.'

"'I'll just tell them they're right!' He started laughing.

"'Maybe yous and Isaiah both bes in poorhouse.' He smiled back.

"'You're the finest and most decent businessman in all of Atlanta. If God is for us, who can be against us?'

"Jessie, I have often wished that I could have somehow captured those entire few precious moments that Charlie and Isaiah spent finding a way to provide each other with forgiveness where it was needed, reconciliation for both, and restitution of more than one type for Charlie. If I could peddle it to the world, my how the world would be changed!"

It is with fond remembrances that I can know that my wayward, rascal of a gambling man brother ended up as a businessman's evangelist for God's kingdom. Back in our high school days, who'd have thought it?

An Ill Wind That Blows

The drought that plagued most of our entire nation continued to cause the farmers of our land to see their agricultural
dreams go up in ashes. Our weekly newspaper where Howard
worked detailed the miserable economic conditions that persis-
tently doomed one farmer after another into bankruptcy. The
banks were forced to foreclose on the debt owed. Those who had
money stashed away were able to capitalize on the misfortunes
of others. Neither side was to blame, but the residue set off
some very hard feelings when the property changed hands. The
family that had sacrificed blood, sweat, and tears ended up the
losers while those who sacrificed nothing ended up the winners.

Mr. Roosevelt took quick action to remedy this sad tale, but
regardless of how much our government tried to help the destitute farmers, for most of them, any aide that finally arrived came
too late. By then, too many of them had packed their belongings
and headed west to California. Momma told me that our Tampa
farmers were some of the more fortunate farmers because we
had received more rain in the past four years than many other
areas of our state or even our section of the United States.

That may have been true, but our area still looked as if it
had been neglected and unloved. It was desolate and very dry.
The incredibly beautiful golden wheat fields once shimmered
and glistened as if they possessed some magical essence as they
swayed against the summer wind. They had always brought
prosperity and rejoicing; they were now just a glimmer of themselves. They barely produced enough to keep the farmers from
being foreclosed by the bank. It could honestly be said that
bleakness lived inside nearly everyone in Tampa.

"Poor ole Job! He was living his life as well as he knew how,
and look what happened to him," Momma said as she was busy

teaching her family about the uncertain vagaries of life. She was trying to explain why God would allow our nation to suffer so much. People were killing themselves; factories were closing; men were losing their jobs; farmers were being forced to move from their homesteads.

"In just a blink of an eye, that man lost everything he loved. His entire family was killed in a terrible storm. His wealth was stripped from him. He was given an affliction of terrible, ugly boils. He was blindsided to no end, and for me, the worst part, the very worst part, was that his so-called friends accused him of having done something so sinful that God had to punish him."

"But God wasn't punishing him, was he, Momma?" Charlie asked.

"You're so right, Charles. God was just testing Job while he was busy rubbing the devil's nose in his own doo-doo." We all laughed at her choice of words. "God knew that Job was a good man, and he just wanted the devil to know that Job loved and worshipped him because he wanted to, not because he had to or because of what he possessed here on earth."

"And when Job remained faithful, God restored Job's life, even though Job had to suffer. In the end, God blessed him with more than he had ever taken." Charlie once again added his own two cents worth of commentary to Momma's story.

"So, what you're telling us is that this devastated country, a nation of people who don't have enough to buy a new out-house, is being tested by God?" Rose asked as she interjected herself into the conversation. "My God isn't capable of being that mean." "Then your god isn't the God of the Bible," Momma said as she quickly took up Rose's challenge.

"Our God has chosen to punish us, I mean, *test* us with ruined crops and ruined lives?" Howard quizzed Momma.

"That's the hard part about being a Christian, coping with the truth that he sometimes allows the innocent to be punished with the guilty. He sends the life-giving rain and sunshine to provide life for the just and the unjust. God loves all of his creatures."

"What you are saying is that you think God's kicking our

butts because we have too many sinners in Tampa and all over these Untied States?" Charlie did his best to insert humor into our conversation.

"We have too many sinners right here in this room," Pauline said in her dry sense of humor. "And Charles Crandal is one I can name," she quickly added, and we all laughed at Charlie's expense.

"It might be the reason, but I'm not God," Momma replied.

"You could have fooled me," Naomi said as she jested with us, and we all broke out laughing. Momma laughed the loudest.

"Seriously, only God can answer that question. I will say that it might be the reason, but it might not be. The Good Book doesn't specifically tell us."

Charlie used his hands like a megaphone, like the one he used to lead the cheers for our school, and said, "Now hear this! The tiny farm town in Tampa, Kansas, is filled with all manner of dreadful sinners. *So,* God has sent a plague, and no rain will fall until every last sinner has come to repentance." He toyed with Momma and greatly entertained us.

Momma studied him and allowed a big grin to come across her face. "Will you stop your tomfoolery, please?"

With a sheepish look that indicated that he was quite proud of himself, Charlie mumbled, "Sorry, Momma, just got out of control."

"Charlie, I could just wring your neck. If you don't mind, I'm trying to teach something important here. The apostle Paul teaches the believer that God won't put something upon us so difficult that we can't bear up under it. In addition, he will provide us the strength, courage, and smarts to handle its consequences." Momma paused. "And here is the most important part to that promise to remember: If we remain faithful, he didn't promise us a rose garden, just the abilities and means to grow one."

"Tell me, Momma, how soon will we be singing all the way to the bank?" Howard had a trace of a smirk in his voice.

"Since you've never been to a bank, because only people

with money need to visit one, it may be a long time coming," Momma said with a chuckle. "I trust God, and he tells us that even if we are experiencing bad times, and we consider them evil, in the long run, they will work out for our good. One day, these trials will be considered historical events that enriched our lives. He has the ability to look past our wants and provide what we need."

Momma's teachings were uplifting and inspired soul searching.

I can remember lying in bed that night next to Momma and believing that our world really wasn't coming apart, at least until the next day.

The early August heat was beginning to rise so that a mistlike effect rose on the horizon. The hot sun was mixing with the heavy dew deposits left from the sultry night, and that caused a fog to engulf our house.

It seemed so peaceful and scenic that morning. I took a glass of blue milk. My poppa's half sister allowed Momma to send me, only me, to fetch two gallons of milk after it had been separated from the cream twice a week. While I dearly enjoyed the milk, I hated fetching it because by the time I walked that half mile carrying the milk, my arms ached so badly they were nearly numb. I took a piece of Momma's freshly baked bread with some oleo on it. I craved butter, but we couldn't afford any. I enjoyed another summer day off from school.

It was our designated wash day; therefore, our household was about to become a busy beehive.

"I need lots of worker bees," Momma declared as she began her organized system of making sure all of our family wore clean clothes each week. She was busy sorting when I poured myself a glass of blue milk.

"Momma, I'll be back to help you in a few moments," I said as I walked out the door onto the porch.

I couldn't help but chuckle as I saw her conducting her ritualistic "see and smell" test. If the garment didn't look dirty and didn't smell offensive, then it wasn't washed that week.

"You get your little fanny back in here. You've just five minutes, you hear?"

Even using Momma's sorting method, we still had a mountain of clothes to wash, wring, and hang on the clothesline to be sun dried before sundown.

I quickly ate my bread and gulped down my milk. *It's going to be too hot a day to have Momma on my back,* I thought as I scurried back inside to help with the laundry.

Momma made each of us girls, well, except the littlest one of our family, do our own wash. We took care of our own 'necessity' rags for our personal hygiene and our other clothes. Momma took care of hers and all the boys' clothes. In no time at all, we were scrubbing on the washboards, and the sweat came a'pouring down our faces. By then we were hoping for any small breath of fresh air to cool us down, but none came. We stopped to fix lunch.

"Jessie, honey, go fetch some meat from the cistern and get some cool water in the water bucket," Momma said.

Since we didn't have refrigeration to keep meat from spoiling, we used the bottom of our cistern, where the temperature was cool, to hang jars of cured meat that we kept on a rope.

I was busy focusing on my assignment and retrieved the meat jar. I pumped some water and was making my way back into the house when I looked out upon the distant horizon. At first what my eyes saw caused me to rub them so I could focus better. *That can't be what it looks like,* I thought.

"Momma!" I screamed a bloodcurdling yell. "Momma, come quick!" The screen door flew open and Momma rushed out. "Will you shut up? You're going to wake the dead! What in tarnation—" Momma never finished her sentence because she lifted her eyes, and she saw what I had seen. She reached out and grabbed me violently, causing me to drop the water pail and the jar of meat.

"Good Lord-a-mighty, get in the house," she instructed, and her tone of voice frightened me.

It would last nearly three days; it left many dead in its wake. History records it as one of the worst dust bowl storms that ever hit this nation. Off on the horizon, there was a monstrous cloud of dust that had been gathering its contents from the desolate farmlands in southwest Missouri. We later found out that this particular part of Missouri was the hardest hit of the farmlands ruined by a lack of rain. When the ferocious winds came out of the Rockies and blew into the Texas and Oklahoma Panhandle, they gathered strength as they swept up, twisted, and churned the black earth and made their way to our town. Their lightning-strike speed gave no warning.

Momma halfway dragged me into the house, and she became General Sherman preparing to take Atlanta. She began to bark orders, and her manner of speech frightened me so much that the hairs on the top of my head felt tingly, and I had chill bumps running down my spine. I just wanted to find a place of my own and have a good cry, but there wasn't time for it.

Earl was away from home, working, and Howard was working at the newspaper. Charlie had moseyed home just before lunchtime. The rest of our family was home. When Momma first spied the storm on the horizon, she became unglued as she escorted me into the house on a dead run; however, once we were inside, she became very calm. She informed us as to what she needed us to do to prepare for the dust storm.

"Charlie, you and the boys get to the well and draw as large a supply of water as you can to fill up containers. Look under the kitchen sink and pull out any container you can find. Get moving, now!"

She turned to us girls. "I want you to shut all of the windows as tight as we can get them. Some of you pull off all the bedding from the beds: any sheets you find, wet or dry, put them up and secure them to the windows. We need to stuff throw rugs or whatever we can find to use under the doors. If we can find a way to keep the dust from seeping inside our house, we will survive this storm."

Just before the storm hit, Howard came running in the door.

"Oh, thank God you're home," Momma said as she gave him a hug. The phone rang a few minutes later, and it was Earl. He was safe inside the farmhouse of the man he worked for. He had called to let Momma know that he was okay and not to worry about his absence.

In my wildest, most frightening nightmare, I never thought it possible for the bright summer sun to just disappear. It was light, and then it was dark. In the twinkling of an eye, night had fallen upon the land. The gale force wind of the storm blasted our house, literally blasted it. The wind was so strong that the tiny dust particles, which were nothing more than BB-sized missiles, hit the wooden frame of our house. It sounded like a million rocks had been shot at our house with a shotgun. The never-before-heard sound caused most of us to scream in terror, and Momma had to yell, "Don't worry, it won't come through the walls!"

It came in waves, one after another, sometimes very rapidly. Sometimes it was a long time in between the hits. Each time it blasted our house, I thought it would penetrate our fortress, and we would all die. I couldn't help but conjure up a horrid picture of what our family's bodies would look like after the full force of that dust storm rolled over us. The individual dust BBs were strong enough to leave a body looking as if it had been skinned alive; I was sure of that.

After a while, we grew accustomed to the blast effect upon our house because we stopped reacting to its impending doom. Our attention turned from being overly afraid of the storm's winds to the more serious problem of finding a way to keep breathing in the midst of an unceasing, increasingly more dangerous atmosphere. There wasn't any way a body could keep the dust from seeping into the house and entering into our bodies. No amount of shoring up could hold back the dust.

Momma had the boys fill a large crock with water, and we placed it in a very small closet. We did all we could possibly do to seal it off from the penetrating dust. It was our safe house. When one of us couldn't handle the puzzle of breathing while still trying to limit the amount of dust we took in by that breathing, we would go to the safe house and stick our heads deep into the big crock and breath some of the freshest air we possessed, near the cleanest water we possessed.

"Now, you get any cloth you can, and you cover your mouths and make sure that you blow your noses every few minutes," Momma instructed us. "Blowing your nose will help you keep your nostrils as clean as possible; your nose will be ready to act as a catch-all each time you blow it, so keep it as clean as possible."

The first time I blew my nose, I couldn't believe what I saw. It was nothing but blacklike soot. It made me shudder with revulsion, which made my stomach churn.

Please, Lord, don't let me throw up, I thought.

I suppose that a body can handle just so much adrenaline flowing through it, especially from being scared to death, before it just shuts down.

I remember Momma telling us the story about the day the Lord made the sun stand still. He made the sky dark for three days, as it was at our house. I suppose it's God's provision and protection when a person is so stressed and traumatized from worry, he really doesn't have much of an appetite. It was a good thing because that dust got into nearly everything that wasn't sealed tight. Even though our bread had a gritty taste, we ate it sparingly to keep up our strength.

There was one light in the middle of our main room. We sparingly used it; each time we did, it flickered. Each time we saw that flickering, "Kids, say a prayer that the good Lord won't let that light to go out," Momma would yell.

I'm not sure where the Almighty was in that harrowing experience, but at least our light stayed on.

"Can you imagine how frightened Noah and his family must have been?" Momma asked as she attempted to calm our nerves. She told us a biblical story that she evidently thought would make our dire situation seem like child's play next to Noah's.

"Six months in a boat and the torrential rains drenching that vessel! We've only been in this storm for a day and a half ... Okay, it's close to two days. It's bound to be over in a very short time, don't you agree?" Momma began softly humming one of her favorite hymns: "Rock of Ages." Then she began to sing, "Rock of ages cleft to me." She paused for a second or two. "Come on now, join me."

Pauline and Naomi started humming, and then they harmonized as they joined in with Momma's song. The beautiful singing signaled a changed attitude in all of us. It's funny how godly music can do that to bone-weary people shot through and through with too much adrenaline in their systems; nevertheless, our entire family spent hours singing, even though there was a lot of coughing going on at the same time.

By the middle of the third day, we were beginning to act like treed coons, and it was evident that the stress of impending doom, the loss of sleep, and growling stomachs were taking a toll on our community. The least personal slight triggered a disagreement, and a near war would break out.

Momma often said, "Nothing stops the living except dying.

When Rose and Naomi began to fight over whose clean 'necessity' rag Rose had (Naomi said it was hers, and Rose claimed she was lying), Momma's profound declaration passed the test of time.

"What would the odds be of two girls having their periods at the same time?" Momma sighed. "What color is it?" She demanded information.

"It's blue," Naomi replied. "That's why I know it's mine; the blue ones are mine," she added.

Momma quickly moved to the bedroom door and yelled, "Rose, you know good and well it isn't yours," she scolded. "I just can't believe you two. In the midst of this god-awful mess, you two nincompoops are having a war over a rag."

"From the midst of a storm God sends his glorious light." As quickly as the storm came, it left. It was nearly dark, and then our house was filled with sunshine. We thought we had done a decent job of shoring up to keep the dust out; we hadn't. Our bed sheets, which we had hung up and doused with water from time to time to lessen the effect of the dust storm, were no longer white. They were black. Every corner of every room had piles of dirt heaped up. Every inch of our house was covered with dust.

"You could write the Gettysburg Address, and even a blind man could read it," Momma said, expressing her shock at what was left after the storm moved on.

Soon we had the freedom to venture outside and breathe clean air once again. The small kids were able to run wild like new colts just let out to pasture. Momma garnered us all back into the house. The house had light, and windows were opened to let in fresh air. The family conference table was dusted off and cleaned with water. It was time to offer prayers of thanks to the Lord for sparing us.

When Momma called one of her impromptu prayer meetings, grumbling could often be heard from her children, but there wasn't any grumbling this time.

The Letter Sweater

"Momma, why can't I have one?" I was in the kitchen with Momma and the little ones, Deannie, Gracie, and baby Arthur. I was doing everything in my power to convince Momma that my life would suddenly disappear in a vapor or, worse yet, that I'd become the laughingstock of my high school because I didn't have a letter sweater to put my varsity letter and gold basketball on.

"Go on and tell me, how many freshmen have ever earned a varsity letter? I mean, in the history of the school, how many? Two! That's how many!"

Momma stopped mixing her pie ingredients for a moment and looked at me.

"I'm proud that my Jessie has done something very special; however, it doesn't change the facts. We don't have money to fulfill your wants, just our needs."

"Freshmen are too stupid to count on to help the team in crunch time; they are only good for fetching water and towels," Coach Lamey was known to say until I came along.

"Way to go, sis!" Howard said to me when Mrs. Helen Stoops, the girls' basketball coach, asked me to come out for the varsity after she saw me shooting hoops with Howard and the boys during the summer.

"Did you know that, Momma?" I asked.

"Jessie, no amount of finagling or massaging my heart can change the fact that I don't have any money to spend on a luxury. If things work out just right, we might see our way clear to get you your sweater by next basketball season."

"Next season!" My voice had a catch in it. "I'll die! Just positively melt away and die!" I whined. "I'll be the laughingstock of our whole school, not wearing my letter sweater, that's what I'll be."

Momma gave me one of her looks indicating that she was fed up with my antics. "Stop this foolishness, and get out of my kitchen."

I stopped long enough to take a sugar cookie out of the cookie jar. I took a bite. "You're going to have one teenager with a case of arrested development," I warned her.

"Arrested development! Where did you come up with that?" She started giggling; howls of laughter followed me as I walked outside.

I loved the game of basketball. I loved the fact that a girl could literally spend hours in solitude and spend her energy challenging herself to reach for new levels of excellence. It was great if she had the opportunity to practice with and against others. But it wasn't necessary to have others to practice with because she could learn the basic skills: body position for defense, rebounding position, handling the ball, dribbling drills, and, of course, putting the ole round ball through the peach basket. She could also do the physical training necessary to get her in shape to play.

"You watch and see," I had bragged to Momma and my family while Howard was busy leading the Tampa Haymakers to a sectional title in his senior year. "I'm going to be a star for the girls' team."

I usually got a lot of good-natured ribbing about my bragging from my sisters in particular. The ribbing from my brothers was in a much kinder fashion.

"You leave Jessie alone," Momma scolded as she stood with me. "The Good Book says, 'A nation without a vision will perish,' and Jessie has a vision. Don't you, honey?" She lent me her undying support. "I can just see me cheering loudly for you as the ball slips through the net, and the announcer will send someone over to the stands. 'Tell that loudmouth lady to pipe down.'"

True to my prediction, I played on the varsity as a freshman, and I was one of our team's best players. I played the forward position, so I was counted on to score points and do my best to encourage my teammates to win. We didn't have a very strong team that year; we were in the process of becoming champions.

If any athlete was good enough to win a letter for the sport he or she played, regardless of what year in high school, it was a crowning achievement. When you won your letter, you were then allowed to wear that letter and the sport symbol in gold on your letter. The letter had to be affixed to the coveted gold and black school letter sweater. The school provided the athlete with the letter and the gold sport symbol; you had to provide the sweater.

I have often reflected upon the absolute worst things a girl had to suffer because she had the misfortune of being born into a dirt-poor family. At that time in my life, not being able to afford that gold and black letter sweater was the most devastating turn of events.

In a few minutes of being outside by myself, I came back in the house. "People can die from a broken heart, you know," I said.

"I've heard that they can die from a broken tail too." Momma gave me her end-of-the-discussion look. "Why don't you write to Mr. Rockefeller and see if he will send you the money?"

"Very funny. Ha ha."

That night I slept the sleep of the damned. I pictured myself on the school campus. Since I was too poor to buy a letter sweater, I kept pinning the letter with the gold basketball on it to whatever dress or blouse I wore that day. When my classmates saw my pathetic, makeshift letter sweater, they pointed their fingers and laughed at me. I told them it was all my momma could afford; I tried to get them to be sympathetic to my plight but nothing helped.

I remember waking up in a sweat, and even after I awoke from the nightmare, the dream was so horrible and so real, I had to jump out of bed to make sure it had only been a dream.

"Old Noah thought he was going to have to exist with cloudy days the rest of his life, and see, it wasn't long before he had a rainbow," Momma said when I moped around a few days after she told me that it would be a year, maybe never, before I could get my letter sweater.

My rainbow came in the form of a letter from my brother Sammy. We were all so excited to receive the letter because until it arrived none of us knew where he was or if he was dead or alive. He had left a few days after Poppa's funeral and just disappeared from our family.

"I'd like to take some time and mourn over the loss of my Sam, but the Lord knows I don't have that luxury," Momma said when we asked if he was dead or alive.

When a child is reared in a large family—and I was near the middle—it's hard to figure out why one brother or sister favors another over some of the others. Sammy favored me. Perhaps it had to do with the fact that Sammy and I accompanied Poppa's coffin home. I witnessed his weird antics. I think he favored me even when he was still living at home before he ran off, or before Poppa ran him off.

Arthur ran to the door to meet the postman. He and Al, the mailman, were buddies. Al fussed over him, and Arthur loved to give him the fudge or taffy Momma made during the Christmas holiday season.

I saw him take the mail from Al and head to the kitchen, where Momma was busy working.

"Art, come here," I said. "Let me see the mail." In his hand was one letter, and he handed it to me. I looked at the letter, and it was addressed to "Lou Crandal and family." I looked at the return address, and I read, "Samuel Ranti Crandal." I couldn't believe my eyes.

"Momma! Momma! Come quick," I hollered. "He's alive! Momma, he's alive!" Momma came running as fast as her legs would allow. "What on earth are you shouting about? Are you trying to wake the dead?"

"Wake the dead! Wake everybody in Tampa. He's alive! Sammy's alive!" I jumped up and down with pure joy.

I handed her the letter with his return address on it. She gasped and brought the letter close against her breast, as close to her heart as she could get it. Tears were in her eyes. She was smiling in the midst of her tears. "Oh, sweet Jesus," she whispered.

"I'd better sit down before I fall." She sought out her easy chair. She held the letter by its end and used it as a fan. "I'd better let my old ticker catch a break."

"Open it, Momma! What's it say?" I asked, and the other children chimed in for her to hurry and read the letter.

Momma opened the envelope, careful not to destroy the return address, and then slowly opened the folded letter. I was struck by how I suddenly saw that letter become much more than a way to communicate. It seemed to transcend communication, and it became symbolic of a momma seeing her dead son come alive, right before her heart's eye. Momma read the letter.

"'Dear Momma and family, don't pay the ransom; I have escaped—just kidding.'"

"He still has that sense of humor." Momma laughed.

"'I know I have been a heel and have been wrong not writing before this, but I made some poor choices I regret; I will probably do so again before my life on earth is through. Momma, I love you! Nothing will ever change my heart's position on that, and you can take that to the bank.'"

"He still loves you." Deannie giggled.

Momma reached out and touched her right cheek. "Yes, he does." She struggled with her tears.

"'I am up here in Chicago and am doing real well working with the Rock Island Railroad. I'm part of a section gang, which lays new rail for the trains. I'm working real hard, having a lot of overtime, and I'm bucking for a foreman's job. When I get that promotion, I'll be able to pay you a visit.'"

"Sammy! Coming here?" I shouted as I tried to move in closer to her while she was reading the letter.

"It says pay a visit." She pushed me away. "He's not in the letter," Momma said as she teased me.

"'Give all my best to everyone in the family. Please give Deannie, Gracie, and little Arthur a hug and a kiss for me.'"

"Did he really say to give me a kiss and a hug?" Arthur asked.

"He sure did," Momma said, and she reached out and gave him a hug and a big kiss.

"Me too, me too!" his sisters yelled. Momma obliged them.

Why didn't he mention my name? I thought I was his favorite in the family, I reflected.

When Momma got to the last page of the letter, she said, "Oh, mercy me." She held out the letter and showed us that Sammy had affixed some money and some type of a ticket to the page.

"What's it for?" I asked.

"'Enclosed you will find some money and a train ticket. If she will come, will you send Jessie to visit me for a while in Chicago?'" Momma read those delicious words. The words I repeated over and over again as I planned and preplanned my trip to see my brother in Chicago.

"Love, your son, Samuel Ranti Crandal.'"

"He wants me to come to Chicago?" I squealed. "Can I go? Momma, can I go?" Momma looked at me with a look in her eyes that told me her mind was racing wildly. "This has been such a shock to my heart. You'll have to give me a little while to make a decision; I'm not sure it's the right thing to do, Jess."

"But the ticket is for Friday; today is Wednesday," I pressed.

That night Momma told me she was going to allow me to go. "Jessie, it's against my better judgment, but I have to face up to the fact that you're a young lady and not a little girl anymore, so you can go visit Sam." She smiled at me. "You always were his favorite." She winked at me.

I'd hardly been out of Tampa, let alone all the way to Chicago. It might as well have been the moon.

As Friday morning approached, I began to have a lot of misgivings and second-guessing about going on the trip. Wednesday, I was a brave woman conqueror, ready to venture into the great unknown for the sake of mankind, at least for the honor of the Crandal clan. By Friday morning, I was a frightened, timid twit who didn't know how she could find the courage to put the first foot on the porter's bench to step up into the train car.

Even if the platform needed a good cleaning, I knew I had to keep myself from flooding the train station with my tears. If I didn't, Momma would figure that I was too young to go to Chicago.

"Prayer makes everything grow a little smaller," Momma said. "When we take our problems to Jesus, he picks them up, and suddenly they grow lighter." I decided to put Momma's theory to a test.

"Dear God, please don't allow my knobby knees to shake so much when I am saying my good-byes. Please don't let my trembling lips betray me and cause my innards to make me gutless. And please, please don't let me cry when Momma and the kids hug and kiss me good-bye. I'm pretty sure Momma is just looking for an excuse not to let me go to Chicago, and, and maybe I am too. Momma says you will pick up this heavy load and handle everything. Sure hope she is right. Respectfully yours, Jessie Crandal, your servant. In Jesus' name."

The big Rock Island engine steamed into our railroad station, and it was loud. I could feel the heat from the engine car, and I could smell the steam's mist.

"Now, Jessie, you mind your manners." Momma was giving me last-second instructions. "And you stay away from strangers on the train. Most people are very nice, but a girl all alone can never be too careful, you hear me?"

Yes, Momma. I know, Momma, I thought. Momma's prayer thing works, because I was doing quite well saying my good-byes.

Then Momma undid all that was working. She reached out and pulled me as close as she could get me, almost cutting off my breathing.

"Oh, Jess, how am I going to live without you?" she whispered in my ear. "You're more than my child; you're my rock." She started bawling.

Momma's bawling caused the little ones to start crying, and

my floodgates couldn't withstand the onslaught. We were soon a mess, all of us.

"All aboard!" the conductor yelled.

"You got to go," Momma said as we broke up our little lovefest. She grabbed me with two hands cupping my face; she showered me with kisses. "You make your momma proud, you hear?" she yelled as I was stepping into the train car.

I was numb from all the emotional good-byes, and I took a seat by a window so I could still see Momma and the kids waving at me as they stood on the platform. We waved until we couldn't see each other any more.

I sat back in the seat and allowed myself a few minutes to relax and dry my tear bank. I almost laughed, but then I nearly started crying again as I recalled Momma's words.

"Honey, don't fret yourself over having tears to shed when you need them, because our wise Father in heaven gave you a supply that never runs out until you die. I figure he does that because he knows all of his humans are going to have to endure all kinds of pain, suffering, but, most importantly, joy. A body needs water to wash out poison, and a body needs water to wash out dirt, slime, and such. So, he gives us the ability to keep our hearts clean and pure. He gave us the Holy Spirit to live inside us, and he gave us a supply of tears to keep our hearts healthy."

I turned my head to sneak a peak around me to see who was sitting where in relation to my seat. The seats behind me on either side were empty. The seat in front of me was empty. There was an elderly lady sitting in the seat directly across from me. I glanced at her and then quickly turned my head back.

"Now, don't talk to strangers," I heard Momma's instructions in my head. *You probably look like a scared little rabbit poking his head out of his hole to check out the danger before venturing out,* I thought.

"Have you been to Chicago before?" I heard a voice ask, and it broke up my reverie.

Two minutes on the train, and I already have a dilemma, I thought. *Momma told me to keep to myself and not to talk to strangers. She also taught me, all of my life, "You respect your elders."*

I decided the latter was straight from the Ten Commandments; therefore, in Momma's book, it can't get better than that. So I answered her question.

"No, heavens no. I've barely been out of Tampa." *Why did you go and tell a perfect stranger that you're nothing but a hayseed?* I thought.

"I'm on my way to see my son in Chicago," she said as she offered personal information.

I looked at her timidly. "I'm on my way to see my big brother. He has some important job with the Rock Island Railroad; I think he said he was a section hand," I told her. Some time later, I thought about how stupid Mrs. Cordelia Goodman must have thought I was. But at the time I didn't know that a section hand on the railroad was the lowest job on the totem pole. "He's going to be a foreman soon."

She laughed a little and gave me a wink. "My late husband once was a section hand on the B & O Railroad."

"I'm Cordelia Goodman," she said with a sweet smile.

"I'm Jessie Crandal," I said, blushing.

"Jessie, that's an unusual name for a girl."

I felt myself blushing a bit. "Yes, ma'am, it has given me—"

"Jessie James and all that?" she interrupted and then nodded.

I smiled back.

"Cordelia!" she said, and she made a face as if she had sucked on a lemon. "Try living with that for over seventy years." She muffled a giggle. She patted the seat beside her. "Why don't you come over here? It will make it much more accommodating for us to visit."

I hesitated a few seconds.

"I won't bite; don't have good enough teeth to do it." She winked, and we laughed.

I had often dreamed about having a grandmother and how wonderful it would be to have an older woman to talk to from time to time, especially when I had done something I shouldn't have and Momma wasn't in the coddling mood for children misbehaving. I could have paid her a visit, and she would have had a sympathetic ear to my plight. She could have dried my tears and spoiled me with fresh-baked cookies and some real milk for a change, not the leavings our family was used to drinking. She could have provided me with just the care I needed to survive Momma's wrath, like a safe haven to a sailor on an angry sea.

I moved over, and we began to visit. Before we knew it, the colored porter came into the car and announced that dinner was being served.

"Would you like to go to the dining car and have a bite to eat?" Cordelia asked.

"Oh, I would love to eat in the diner!" I opened my small purse and pulled out the money Sam had sent. "I have my own money," I whispered.

After I got to Chicago, I wrote Momma that eating a meal with my pretend grandmother, Cordelia Goodman, was one of Momma's "It-can't-get-any-better-than-this-I'm-ready-to-come-home-sweet-Jesus" moments in life.

We were seated in elegant chairs, and our table was covered with a freshly starched and ironed white tablecloth. The silverware had the engraved initials *R. I.* on them to signify Rock Island. The menus were in leather binders. The porters were impeccable in their dress and especially in their manners.

"My momma would be mighty proud of the porters' manners," I whispered.

She smiled at me. "Any momma would be proud."

I had a wonderful rib eye steak, cooked medium, mashed potatoes and gravy, some green beans, two glasses of milk, and chocolate ice cream for dessert. She had a small egg salad sandwich and a cup of vegetable soup.

"My,"—she chuckled a little—"you can put that food away for a skinny girl. Do you eat like that all the time?" she teased me.

"*Carpe diem,*" I said.

She laughed. "Where did you get such a sophisticated word?"

I finished my ice cream. "My momma told me to seize the day every chance I got." I used my napkin with a beautiful *R. I.* embroidered on it to dab the milk off my lips.

I bent my head closer to hers. "It's the first steak I ever ate," I confided in her, and my eyes told her how thrilled I was.

During our meal, Mrs. Goodman told me that her son was a lawyer in downtown Chicago. She hadn't seen him in quite some time. He was an important businessman and was heavily involved in the civic things that took place. He had said that he just didn't have the time to come to Oklahoma City to visit her.

As naïve and as unsophisticated as I was back then, I could spot that Cordelia Goodman was a woman of means. Her dress was different than nearly any woman's I had ever seen in Tampa, except Gloria Jones. I was certain that her broach and wedding rings were expensive diamonds. Even her purse looked as if it had gold trimming. She spoke using precise diction. She carried her frame as if she could walk with a book on her head and it wouldn't fall off. To top it all off, she had beautiful silvery hair, and she was still very attractive, even though she was over seventy. I was floored when she insisted on paying for our lunch. "Jessie, you keep your money. I'm sure an enterprising girl like you can find a way to spend your money on something much more interesting than a meal on a train."

"I'm sure I can, but it won't be with anyone as interesting as you." I smiled at her.

She laughed. "I'd like to meet your mother; I have a feeling we'd be kindred spirits."

She gave me her son's name, Harold Goodman Jr., and the telephone number where she might be reached. "Perhaps, if things work out, we might do this again in Chicago," she suggested as the train approached our destination.

I leaned over and gave her a slight kiss on her right cheek. "I'd think I had died and gone to heaven if we could."

She gave me a hug, and there were tears in her eyes and mine.

I stepped down off the porter's step amidst the steam and the loud noise of the train engine. I spotted a man waving. It was Sammy. He was grinning from ear to ear, and he rushed to me and picked me up and hugged me.

"Dear Jessie, I'm so glad that Momma let you come." He pushed me away, holding me with his two hands by my shoulders. "Let me look at you. My, my, you're becoming a beautiful lass." His eyes suddenly showed disapproval. "You could use some different clothes, but you cut a fine figure of a woman."

Momma had made me wear my brown dress with a white collar. I had put a green ribbon in my hair.

"If you are eating on the train, it can be tricky with unexpected bumps, so wear the brown dress in case you spill something; it won't show so much." Momma did her best to make sure I didn't go out in public making a fool of myself.

Sammy got my luggage, and we made it to his car. He had a car that looked brand new, something like Hiram's, only Sammy's was cream colored. He was very proud of it, and he spent time telling me how it was better than most other cars. His car, from the inside, was a lot like Mr. Dumphy's Packard.

He drove me around Chicago and pointed out the various places of local and national interest, including the Art Institute.

"That place is built upon the site where Mrs. O'Leary's cow supposedly started the fire that burned down the first city of Chicago," he said.

"My history teacher told us about that infamous date in our country's history last year," I said.

"Say, I can see that my sister has a pretty fine vocabulary in her head." He smiled at me.

Sammy lived in a tenement house where several families lived. He lived on the second floor. He had a large apartment that was as big as our house.

"Imagine," I said with a sigh, "having all this room for one person."

He laughed. "It's quite a change from living in a house made for four people that houses a dozen or more."

He led me to a room that had French doors. "This is your room." He pointed down the hall. "My room's down there."

I stepped into the room, and it had a bed like I had only seen in a movie. There was a canopy and white cover with frilly lace ends hanging down. The bed had a white spread and huge pillows, and there was an assortment of smaller, different-colored pillows.

It's so beautiful, yet almost too feminine, I thought. There were actual screens on the windows, and he had them open.

My eyes scanned the room, and I didn't see any washbasin or slop jar sitting in the room. I turned and looked at him.

"Where's the, you know, things to wash with and such?" I asked, a bit embarrassed to have to talk about such things.

He crooked his finger and motioned for me to follow him. He took me to a door adjacent to his and opened it. I couldn't believe my eyes: it was a bathroom with a flush toilet, a sink, and a bathtub.

I let out a whistle. "You must be rich."

He laughed at my reaction and said, "I'm doing okay for myself. Lots of people have bathrooms like this in Chicago."

I stepped into the room and ran my hand over the sink and the bathtub, and I messed with the pull chain for the toilet.

"Go ahead and pull it, if you want. There's lots more water from where that came from." He laughed at me again.

I pulled the chain, and the toilet flushed and filled up the tank. "I'll probably never want to go back to Tampa again." I grinned.

"That would suit me just fine." His comment took me off guard.

"If I ever experience a hot bath all to myself, with clean water and all, I...I'll probably be ruined for life; nothing will ever satisfy me again," I whispered in a dreamy tone of voice.

"You can have a bath every night if you want to," he said as he continued to laugh at my reaction to how wonderful his apartment was.

He took me downstairs and introduced me to Maggie O'Hoolihan, a woman in her midthirties. She had a ready smile, which came from the left side of her mouth. She had smiling, sparkling eyes, a fine and delicate nose, and a complexion that gave her fits from time to time. She had a few pockmarks. Her hair was strawberry blonde. Even though she was fair, I didn't notice any freckles.

"So, this is the lass you've been telling me about," Maggie said in her Irish brogue. "A bit too skinny but a fine-looking one to boot." She shook my hand and gave me a big smile.

I shook her hand with a firm grip.

"When you meet people, shake their hands with a firm grip," Momma told me. "Don't put a limp fish out there; it makes a person think you don't have a backbone."

"The lass has a good handshake," Maggie commented. "Her fine red hair and hazel green eyes say this girl has spunk, by golly." She winked at me.

She stepped past me and went to the front door. She pulled something from her dress's collar, and then I heard a very loud whistle blow. In a few seconds a bunch of children came running up the steps.

"Children, this lovely lass is Jessie Crandal. She's Sammy's sister, and she has come to visit him for a spell, all the way from Kansas."

The O'Hoolihans had five children, three boys and two girls, all several years younger than me. They were all smiles and giggles as they told me their names. I tried to repeat them all after we were introduced but couldn't.

"Don't you worry your pretty little head. Before you know it, you'll know their names"—she looked over to where her children were standing—"probably too well." We all laughed.

Sammy arranged for Maggie to watch over me during the day while he was working on the railroad. The O'Hoolihan children became my playmates. Sometimes it was fun; much of the time I was nothing more than a glorified babysitter.

It was lonely during the day, and I soon got a powerful case of homesickness. I did my best to deny it all the way down into the deep recesses of my bones, but my heart couldn't be fooled. I wrote Momma that I wanted to come home.

"Jessie, darling, I didn't want to see you go, but now that you are away in Chicago, I can see it was good for you to take this trip. It will give us both a little time to grow up some without each other," Momma's letter said. "You need to just tough it out; remember, the Lord has you in the palm of his hand."

I had a good cry that day. *My own momma doesn't want me to come home right away.* The thought was too awful to think about.

My days might have been complex and too lonely, but my nights, and especially my weekends, certainly weren't.

Sammy would come home from his job dirty beyond belief. He would take a bath and put on clean clothes that were very fashionable, often a suit and tie. We would go out to a restaurant and have supper. He always had a glass of wine with his dinner.

"It's what I love about living in Chicago," he said. "All of the neighborhood restaurants—some are little more than a dive, but most are family owned—treat you like family when you come."

For a girl who had eaten at only two fancy places in her entire life, the Emporium Hotel in Humansville, Missouri, and Martha's place in Durham, running with Sammy made me think that I was a princess in some fantasy world.

We'd have dinner at O'Malley's, and the owner would greet us.

"Sammy, my boy, how are you?" he asked. Sammy introduced me, and they all made some remarks about me that made me feel pretty and all gooey inside.

It didn't seem to make any difference where he took me; they all knew Sammy.

"Is there any place in Chicago we can go where people don't know you by your first name?" I asked as I complimented and teased him.

He grinned. "Not if I can help it." We laughed.

I wrote Momma a letter nearly every day. She wrote back less frequently; the one letter she enjoyed the most was when I described how I felt taking my first bath while visiting Sammy.

I wrote the following:

Momma, I turned on the spigot for the hot water, and it ran for what seemed to be forever. I guess it takes that Chinaman a long time to get that boiler up to speed so the hot water can come up two floors. It did show up, and after a while I had to put cold in the tub so I could stand to get in it.

Sammy got me some little pellet-looking things for the bath. He told me to use just a few of them. I put in more than I probably should have because in a minute or so, they created a bunch of bubbles and just about covered me up. They tickled my nose, and it felt strange and so wonderful.

I probably had the water too hot when I first stepped in, and it took me some time to get used to it on my skin. But once I was in the water, it was heavenly. Momma, I thought about you and how I wished that you had the chance to take a bath in Sammy's tub. I'm sure it would do wonders for your aching body, especially your hernias. Honest to God, Momma, the hot water just melts into your bones. It's as if my chest was being massaged while I just lay there and breathed deep breaths, and each one made me feel better. Washing yourself in hot water with a fine-scented soap all over your body is hard to describe. I'm not sure I should ... if I could. Momma, I remember your follow-up teaching regarding Naomi's 'word', where you talked to me about the choices a girl has when it comes to the value she puts on her virginity, and I have to admit it cleared up a few more things ... but it also confused me more. Does that sound foolish? I saw a couple kissing in the hallway yesterday, and I mean kissing like they don't even do in the movies, and it set off a bunch of those 'bees' inside me. One's I didn't even know I had. You told me one day I'd have them. Do you remember telling me? You referred to it as 'birds and bees' stuff. While I'm in this bath, the water warm against my skin, well, it makes a girl's mind play tricks on her; like I'm more of a woman and less a girl. Do you know what I'm trying to say? I guess you were right again! Your Jessie can now be counted among those teenagers who don't know if they are 'fish or fowl'. Is it a sin to have ... ? I'd better save that for another time

I must have sung a hundred songs while I was taking a bath. When you have something that makes you feel that good, well, at least for me, I just couldn't keep from singing. Sammy laughed at me, and he said he enjoyed my singing. Some of the rest of the tenants did too because they told Sammy. Momma, I've made a solemn vow: Someday, I'm going to live in a house that has a bathroom like Sammy's.

Someday, I hope you get to take a bath like this.

While I had a wonderful time with my brother, there were some things he did, and some things he wanted to do for me, that puzzled me and made me feel awkward and somewhat uneasy.

"Jessie," he said, "you need to wear clothes that are more fashionable. They need to show off your figure more. It's time you get more in style. This is Chicago, the place where the flappers are the rage."

I looked at myself in the mirror, and all I could see was Jessie Crandal, a girl who was barely a teenager.

He took me to an expensive women's clothing store, and he asked for the headmistress to show me some fashionable dresses. It was a fancy store, and it had its own models. The décor was set up to meet the needs of the richest people in Chicago. Sammy talked privately to her, and then we took a seat in a couple of cream-colored chairs with soft cushions.

For the next half hour or so, different models came out wearing dresses, and the headmistress would make a descriptive announcement about it; then Sammy would make a critique about her comments.

I was happy that the store was so fancy; it didn't have any flies buzzing around, but if it had, I'm sure my mouth would have caught a few. My mouth was open wide in amazement as I saw the gorgeous women come out and show us the incredibly beautiful dresses.

Sammy never bought a thing in that store. I found out later that one of the important people of the store knew Sammy quite well, and she was always willing to do him a favor.

"Now that we know what is fashionable and in style, we can get you some new clothes," he said as we were leaving the store.

It certainly wasn't as fancy as the first store; however, Marshall Fields was the second nicest clothing store I had ever been in. It too had a dressing area where clothes could be tried on. Sammy and I spent an entire morning looking at clothes. I tried on a lot of their dresses. It wasn't even July, but to me it was Christmas.

"We'll take this and that and those," Sammy told the executive sales representative. That's what her name tag read. We left Marshall Fields with our arms loaded down with shopping bags with the store's name on them.

When we arrived, exhausted from our shopping, Sammy wanted me to show him how everything looked on me.

Not only had he purchased dresses, but he bought me shoes and purses to match. I put on the first dress, which he liked the best. It was Kelly green and had puff shoulders. I had three-inch high heel shoes to go with the ensemble, which made my feet and legs look more attractive. I had never worn such an elegant pair of shoes before, and the neckline of the dress was much lower than any dress Momma would ever allow me to wear. He bought me a medium brown hat that had a brownish orange feather in it.

After I got dressed and looked at myself in the mirror, it stunned me to see the metamorphosis. Looking back at me was a much older-looking girl. I turned around and examined myself in the mirror from every angle. I just didn't realize my figure was so pronounced. The stranger in the mirror who looked back at me frightened me some.

I made a grand entrance and did my best to act like a Hollywood actress.

"Ta-dah," I said as I rushed into the living room where Sammy was sitting.

He used his finger and twirled it, asking me to turn around. I did as he directed. "Jessie, it's incredible." He had a broad smile on his face and let out a soft wolf whistle. "You are stunning, absolutely beautiful!"

I was blushing and embarrassed, but it felt so good getting

compliments from a man, even if it was from my older brother. "Do you really think I look pretty?"

"Trust me. You're a bona fide heartbreaker; you're breaking my heart." He put his hand over his chest, and we laughed at his joshing.

"Go on, put the others on." He wanted to see how I looked in all of the clothes he had bought me.

I did as he asked. Each time I slipped into something else, he continued his lavish praise.

If there were one other fairy princess on earth being more spoiled than I was at that moment, I didn't envy her one whit.

"Don't you think these dresses are a mite risqué for me?" I casually let my fingers drift to my cleavage.

"Oh no!" he assured me. "Pretty baby, that's what sets you apart from most of the other girls. You are beautiful, and you don't even know it." He chuckled.

"They do make me look good, don't they?" I blushed some and smiled at him.

"You will just have to wear them when we go out for dinner," he declared.

"Aren't they a bit fancy for O'Malley's?"

"Oh, we're not going to a neighborhood establishment; we're going to some ritzy place in downtown Chicago. All dressed up like that, you're too fine a woman to waste on anything but the best."

When Sammy called me a "fine woman," something clicked inside of me, and it made me very uncomfortable. *Why is he referring to me as a woman?* I thought.

"Pay attention to your senses that don't have any sense," Momma said when she talked to me about keeping my antenna up in order to keep from getting myself into awkward and even dangerous situations with boys.

I couldn't allow myself to think of my brother as someone who Momma warned me about; yet, some of the things he said and did caused my antenna to become a bit hyper.

The following weekend Sammy told me to get dressed in

the Kelly green outfit with matching shoes and cute hat because he was taking me to Lowry's.

Lowry's was just about the best restaurant in Chicago. It was famous for its prime beef. I didn't know the difference between prime beef and corned beef.

Sammy wore a white starched shirt with his initials on the right cuff and a black silk tie that had little black-and-white-checked designs on the bottom third of the tie. He wore gold cufflinks that had an onyx stone in them and a black-and-white-herringbone sport jacket with a silk kerchief in the front pocket, folded just so. His black slacks had a sharp crease, and his shoes were black and white and pointed at the toes. He looked like a movie star.

When I saw him, I let out a low whistle, and we laughed.

"Boy, do you clean up good," I teased him. The transformation from coming home after working on the railroad, dirty as one could imagine, and then to end up looking like he did, very handsome, made me proud to be his sister.

"Do you have a big club?" I asked.

My question caught him off guard, and he looked at me. "A big club?"

"So you can beat the women off." I acted like I had a big club in my hands and was swinging it around. "Get away from my brother," I warned the imagined storm of women trying to catch him. I put my arm up over my head as if I were protecting myself from their charge.

Sammy looked at me, dressed to the nines, and said, "You are some doll. Let's go; we'll knock 'em dead." I took his arm, and we left his apartment.

Sitting next to him in his big, fancy car and tooling down the road to downtown Chicago, I could just imagine myself having an apartment, an important job, and Sammy's money to live like a queen.

"Someday, these are the only kinds of clothes I'm going to wear," he said. He kept making furtive glances at me as he drove. "Gee, Jessie! I'm so glad you have come to live with me. It's so nice to have a beautiful woman in the house."

I wanted to put up my hands and make a referee's time-out sign because what he was saying made me feel funny inside. As much as I would like it to be, I was not a woman yet. I was Jessie Crandal, a sophomore-to-be. As Momma would say, "still wet behind the ears."

He pulled the car into the valet, and we were whisked into the dinning area. He had made reservations for us, and we were quickly seated. I noticed that the maitre d' knew my brother. Karl, the headwaiter, knew Sammy too. We were helped with our seats, and the staff was extremely attentive, as if Sammy was some very important man.

I sat at the table and became intoxicated by the ambiance. I looked at the exquisitely designed floral arrangement and the dizzy array of silverware. There were three forks of different sizes, three spoons of different sizes, three knives of different sizes, and a beautiful linen napkin with the initial *L* on it. The napkin was sitting in a pearl-colored ring. There were also several plates of different sizes.

My eyes must have been blown wide open, showing how utterly intimidated I felt at that moment, because Sammy cleared his throat to get my attention.

"Just follow my lead," he whispered, and he smiled at me. "Don't worry; you'll do just fine."

I put my hands on my knees so they wouldn't betray me; I'm sure I could have cracked all the walnuts Momma would need to make Christmas goodies this year.

Karl, the waiter, made small talk. We ordered the house special. While we were waiting for our dinner, the maitre d' came by and Sammy introduced me.

"Jason, this—"

"This beautiful creature is a high step up from what you are normally squiring," he said, interrupting Sammy.

"You're absolutely right! Isn't she lovely?" Sammy said. "This is Jessie—"

"She is a little young for you, isn't she? Oh, so sorry, I must see to my duties," he said and left.

Sammy smiled at me, and we both laughed.

The meal was seven courses. Until that night, I never knew people numbered a meal. I followed Sammy's lead. We had soup and bread, which had gobs of real butter, not oleo with red dye in to make it look like butter. We had some emperor's salad, Caesar, and the prime beef melted in my mouth. The meal was topped off with a cheesecake that was beyond description. We had coffee, and I drank it when I got enough cream in it.

Sammy sipped wine. "Here, Jessie," he said, "take a little sip of this." He gave me a sip of his wine. "Now you can say that you have officially tasted champagne." He laughed I took a tiny sip, and it made my nose and throat sting. I didn't think it tasted very good. I made a face to show how I assessed the sip.

Sammy laughed. "It is an acquired taste."

"Let's dance." He reached for my hand. We went out on the floor, and I noticed that the band's name was up front for all to see. "Tommy Dorsey Band," it said.

Sammy was a great dancer, and I wasn't too bad myself, thanks to my brother Howard.

"Jessie, you are a great dancer," Sammy complimented me as he twirled me around. We danced just about every dance, regardless of the music, including the Charleston and the Black Bottom.

Before he was ready to leave, I was getting sleepy. I seldom stayed up late. Who does in Tampa?

As we were driving home, he asked me to move over close to him. I looked at him in a perplexed manner.

"I won't bite, I promise," he teased.

I felt odd doing so, but I did as he asked.

He talked about how he was going to be a rich and important man someday. He said he had a plan. He knew exactly how he was going to accomplish it.

"As my kid sister, would you like to go along on that dream?"

"Maybe not me, but I'm sure a lot of women would."

"You're the only one I would consider taking." He looked at me in a serious manner.

"It's difficult; sometimes it's wrong, if it harms you to rise above your raisin's," Momma said. She was explaining how people get themselves into all kinds of trouble when they strain to be something they aren't comfortable being.

After that night, I had an uneasy feeling that I was "rising above my raisin's," so much so that I started to tell Sammy that I was ready to go home.

"But you've only been here a month." He worked to persuade me to not leave. "I want you to stay all summer."

I agreed, reluctantly, but after another week I wrote Momma a letter and told her all that Sammy and I had done. I told her how he was treating me, more like a grown woman than a teenage girl.

In a couple of days, the phone rang in the apartment. Sammy answered it.

"Momma, what a wonderful surprise!" he said his countenance was cheery.

He held the receiver to his ear. In a minute his countenance had changed. "Yes, that is true ... No! Absolutely not! ... It's a slight possibility, but yes, I would say she looks different ... I'm really not wanting to let her go. I can provide for her better than you can ... Yes, I know I'm not her mother ..." I could only guess what Momma was saying on her end.

Sammy handed me the phone. He had a frustrated look on his face. "Momma wants to speak to you."

"Hi, Momma," I said, and my missing her brought tears to my eyes.

"Jessie, you listen to me. I told Sammy if he didn't put you on the train Saturday morning, I would be there on Sunday." There was bluster in her voice. "And Jessie, you leave all those clothes he bought for you in Chicago; don't bring them home. Do you hear me?"

"I will, Momma," I said. "I love you." I hung up the phone.

Sammy fussed and fumed for two days, but he did what Momma told him to do. He tried to get me to take the clothes, but I didn't dare.

He took me to the train station on Saturday morning.

"Jessie, you have brought sunshine into my life. You will

always be special to me." He hugged me and gave me a kiss on the cheek.

Maggie O'Hoolihan and the kids cried when we said our good-byes.

"For sure, you are one fine lass," she said when she hugged me. "This neighborhood will never be the same."

As I was riding the train home, I did my best to sort out Sammy's and my relationship. There was much that made me feel so great; some of it left me feeling odd.

Momma and the kids greeted me at the station, and Momma's huge dictionary couldn't hold enough words to describe how wonderful it was to be home.

The following Wednesday, I had another red-letter day. The mailman delivered a box addressed to Jessie Crandal. It was from Sammy.

My younger brother and sisters hollered, "Hurry, Jessie, open it!"

I opened it up, expecting it to be one of the dresses he had bought for me; it wasn't. Folded ever so neatly in the box was the most beautiful gold and black letter sweater God ever gave a woman the talent to weave. I remember that the first time Sammy took me to buy fancy clothes, I casually mentioned that all I really wanted was a gold and black letter sweater to wear my basketball on.

Inside the box a note was pinned on the sweater: "To Jessie, my darling sister; you earned your letter with me. Love, Sammy."

That was the last communication with Sammy that Momma ever saw. He disappeared from sight.

Many years later, my brother Charlie, who was very well known around Atlanta, went into a restaurant that he frequented for coffee.

A blonde waitress came to serve him as he sat on a counter stool.

"Mr. Broom and Mop Man,"—she called him that because he was well known for how he made a living selling brooms and mops—"back so soon?" she asked as she poured him a cup of coffee.

"Back so soon? I haven't been here in a month. But I just couldn't stand not seeing your pretty face, so ..." he teased her.

"You're joshing me, right. You're not joshing me, are you? Then your twin is running around Atlanta impersonating you." She laughed as she walked away with his breakfast order.

This piqued my brother's interest, and he started doing some investigating on his own. After a while, he gained enough information to give this twin a call.

"I know that you are probably going to think I am rude and a little crazy," he said when he finally reached the man who looked a lot like him. "I have a brother; his name is Sammy. He has been missing from our family for many years. Sammy Crandal, are you my long-lost brother?"

There wasn't anything but silence.

"Sammy Crandal, Lou Crandal's boy, lived in Tampa, Kansas. Are you that man?"

"I'm sorry; you have the wrong person." He hung up.

A week later, Charlie got a phone call, and the man confessed that he was our brother Sammy. The Crandals had a family reunion, and only Charlie's and Grady family went.

Sammy lived in a gated community. We had to give our names to a watchman, and he checked to see if we had been invited to enter. His home was located off a well-known lake, a house that was at least four times as large as the one Pete and our family had. His wife was diminutive, well coiffed, dressed elegantly, and chain-smoked. She was very pretty. Several times during our visit, I thought she would drown if it rained her nose was so far in the air.

She didn't cook, and their cook wasn't there, so Sammy took us out to an expensive restaurant. Sammy's wife took some of her leftover filet steak home to her three white powder-puff poodles. They didn't have any children.

Within a few minutes after we arrived from Kansas, Sammy did his best to separate me from the rest of the family. His affection for me hadn't waned. His possessiveness bothered me, Pete even more. He wanted to leave that same day!

We had a picnic on his palatial grounds, complete with a gigantic pool, which none of the family used. Later, he took us to his private domain: his beautiful wood-paneled den in his basement. The walls were decorated with animal head trophies: lion, tiger, leopard, elephant, bear, antelope, and deer, which he had bagged with his bow. He then put on a shooting exhibition using his bow, showing us that he was an incredible marksman.

Sammy made me feel uncomfortable, sexually, like he did when I spent time with him in Chicago. He never made any improper physical movement toward me at any time, yet he made me feel as if he were violating me in some odd manner. Pete must have sensed this in some intuitive way, because he wanted to leave or punch his lights out.

After that strange event, I never saw Sammy again, dead or alive. I have no idea what happened to his wealth. None of the Crandals inherited it.

Sammy had carried out the plan he had talked about many years ago when I visited him in Chicago. He had gone to Africa and had become an important man helping that country build its rail system. He had become rich in the process.

The reunion was less than a success.

FANCY

At the start of my junior year at Tampa High, Fancy Chambers moved to our town. Her father was a sharecropper like Poppa had been. They moved to Tampa from some place in Nebraska.

Fancy, next to my sister Rose, was the most pushy, brassy girl I had ever known. The boys liked her because she was openly flirtatious. She was full bosomed, curvaceous, and all the boys panted when she walked by. The girls envied her and kept her at a distance. She wore her hair "tatted," and it was the color of a morning sunrise. She had freckles that stayed hidden during the winter but had a coming-out party in the summer. She wore a lot of lipstick.

In a town as small as Tampa, it was difficult for anyone to live on the wrong side of the tracks, but Fancy did.

"Now, Jessie, God is no respecter of persons," Momma said when I told her about Fancy. "God looks on the inside, not on the outside, and he surely doesn't punish a child for what her parents are. I've heard some gossip about her folks." She gave me a look of disapproval. "Oh well. There isn't any reason why you can't be friendly toward her."

"I know she needs a friend, but I'm not sure she knows it," I said in a pensive manner.

"You're much more perceptive than I have given you credit for. Perhaps you might fix a sack lunch and see if she'd like to share it with you."

The next morning, I fixed a lunch for two and took it to school. I made sure I arrived at school early. I spotted her sitting under a tree near the playground of the school. Usually the area had students milling around, acting up and stuff. That morning, there were only a couple of students there.

"Mind if I sit down?" I asked

"It's a free country."

"Hi, I'm Jessie," I said demurely.

"I know who you are."

She intimidated me, as my sister Rose did.

"I…I was wondering if you'd like to share my lunch?"

She looked past me. "Did someone put you up to this?"

"Put me up to what?"

"Is this some do-gooder thing?" she said, staring up at me.

I gave her a look that told her my feelings had been hurt.

"No." I was a bit embarrassed. "I'll go"—I started to leave—"I just thought you could use a friend."

"Why would you want to be friends with me? All those horny toad, pissant boys want is to touch my breasts, and all those miss-goodie-two-shoes girls want is for me to leave their pissant boyfriends alone."

I looked at her, and I remained silent for a few seconds. I could tell she was getting uncomfortable under my stare.

"Well, because we are the girls with the most freckles in our school," I replied in a nonchalant way.

She didn't respond.

"I just thought you needed a friend and that we may just be kindred spirits." I looked into her eyes.

"No, don't go. Please." I could tell she was flooded with emotion, and her voice was filled with tension. "I can see now I was reading it all wrong." She stuck out her hand. "I'm Fancy Chambers."

I took her hand and shook it firmly.

"Say, you've got quite a grip," she teased me.

"From cranking the car," I said. I looked at her, and I could tell my remark puzzled her. "It's a long story. My momma taught me how to drive a car when I was eleven. I had to"—I made a cranking motion—"to get the car started." We laughed.

Later that day, we shared my lunch. I did get some glances, which told me I was doing something most of the other girls did not approve, including my sisters.

Fancy and I became friends. I can't say we ever became kindred spirits because she was just too crude, brassy, and profane.

When I told Momma about my friend Fancy, she was concerned about my reputation.

"She's too worldly. Jessie, I told you to be nice and Christian-like to her, not start spending a lot of time with her. When I tell you that Fancy's poppa and momma are seen coming in and out of Sadie's at all hours of the day and night, I'm not spreading gossip; it's the unvarnished truth."

"Didn't you tell me that Jesus spent most of his time amongst the drinkers and carousers?"

"That was God, and he could handle the temptation. You're just Jessie Crandal, and the Good Book says, 'Bad company corrupts good morals.'"

"She told me her parents are drunks."

Momma sucked in her wind. "If she can talk to perfect strangers about something so personal, my, my, what that girl must put up with."

"I'm not a stranger," I said. "Momma, you've raised me right. I know when to draw a line." I shifted my eyes to hers.

"Good for you, honey. But sometimes the wrong kinds of friends discover that your line is little more than a chalk line."

"I'm the only friend she has in school. Do you want me to leave her friendless?"

"God love you, no, I don't want you to leave her friendless. But I don't want her friendship to cause you to end up being one who is friendless. Remember, God's Word teaches us, 'Even a child is known by her actions, by whether her conduct is pure and right,' Proverbs 20:11."

Tampa didn't have any colored families, but it had one Mexican family. Joseph Martinez was a sharecropper, but he was also a crackerjack mechanic. When he wasn't busy farming, he was fixing some farmer's machinery. Juan Ricardo Martinez was his oldest son. Everyone at school called him Ricky. He was one of the shortest boys in school and one of the fastest. He was a track star in the one hundred- and two hundred-yard dashes.

He didn't care for basketball, but he probably would have been a star in that sport if he had played it. Ricky talked about football back in his native country. It was soccer. The game was played with a round ball, not an oblong-shaped football. One had to kick the ball into a net to win the game. Fancy used to tease him about such a silly game.

Even if he was a star athlete in our town, most of the people were still prejudiced and found it easy to openly slander his family because they had darker skins.

I had no way of knowing how many students in my school were still virgins. I just knew that Fancy and Ricky weren't. Fancy told me they were having sex. One weekend, we were returning from seeing a movie, and we were walking and talking about nothing in particular.

"Jess, being with a man is the best thing you'll ever get to do," Fancy said.

It was nearly dark, but I was still positive she could see me blush.

"Fancy, quit talking like that. Do you want someone to hear you?"

She laughed.

"It hurts like hell the first time. After that, it's all pleasure."

"My momma says, 'Forbidden fruit tastes great until it rots your innards.'"

Fancy laughed.

"Your momma sure has some funny sayings."

Her laughing about Momma made me think of my sister Rose.

"You ought to try it," Fancy suggested. "It makes a real woman out of you." She sashayed around with her hand on her hip, trying to act sexy and all grown-up.

She pulled out a cigarette and lit it. She took a long drag and blew the smoke out slowly. "What? You've never smoked?"

"Once or twice, but it made me dizzy and sick to my stomach." I made a face to show her how disgusting I thought smoking was.

She laughed at me.

"Jessie, I don't know why you're my best friend. You're the most goodie-two-shoes girl in Tampa," she teased. "No pain, no gain." She handed me her cigarette. "Take a puff. It won't kill you."

"If I go home smelling like smoke, Momma will know. Besides, it stinks. I'm never going to smoke, even if you think I'm a prude."

"If I came home drunk, my old man wouldn't know." Fancy laughed.

I halfheartedly joined in with her laughter, but I knew Fancy's attempt at humor was more of a cover-up for her hurting heart, and I did a poor job of laughing.

At different times I tried to analyze why Fancy was my friend in spite of all her moral lapses. Why was I willing to be in her company and allow myself to be put under the heat of her urging me to join her in behavior that was guaranteed to leave a girl with the kind of reputation respectable boys and their families wouldn't tolerate, especially when it came to picking a wife? I can honestly say I didn't know.

Maybe it's the same reason kids stand too close to the freight train as it rumbles by. It has a mesmerizing effect upon a person's mind. It can be dangerous because it makes a person want to jump into the middle of the tracks.

When one is naïve about the world and really enjoys the innocence it provides, being next to the fire, but not in the fire, gives one a sense of living dangerously yet safely. Fancy was the "bad boy," and it was exciting to be on the edge of living recklessly. Her profanity that shocked, her *carpe diem* attitude about life, her open disrespect for her parents, her willingness to flaunt the moral code of the day by talking about having sex with a boy, and her willingness to take me along for the ride, yet respecting my values and not putting me down for them, piqued my curiosity. I willingly followed her lead. Neither did she demand that I exchange my value system for hers in order to remain friends. It was probably because she allowed me to be singed, not burned.

I was a "big man" on campus in basketball. I had won a

varsity letter my freshman year. I was considered a leader, and because of that position I was able to keep Fancy as a friend and yet have other friends. Save for me, Fancy's other friends were also from the wrong side of the tracks.

If Fancy hadn't been my friend, I might never have known a story that became a legend in Tampa. In an indirect way, our family was a part of it. Fancy said her poppa came home from having a few beers, and he told her momma the story.

Sadie Moon was the owner of a nefarious beer joint called Sadie's Suds House. It was a local watering hole where men, and some women, went for beer and other pleasures, according to gossip. Sadie was an extremely large woman with enormous breasts, which she liked to expose as much as she could without being arrested. She wore suggestive clothing to enhance her breasts.

She was well known in town because she had two tiny dogs that she took for a walk each day, up and down the road in front of her place. They were always on leashes. She gave them beer so their coats would shine. When Sadie walked her dogs, they were a sight to behold. Sadie's dress hemline always dragged on the ground, and she wore them with large pleats. No one, before that famous night, could recall seeing her legs.

Rumor had it that she had been married several times. The last husband she ran off. If any woman in town wore a scarlet letter, it was Sadie.

"She looked like a bell holding two leashes with tiny dogs staggering a bit," Momma said. "If I didn't know better, I'd think they were all drunk."

We all laughed.

It was Saturday night, and around midnight the alcohol had begun to work its magic elixir. One old fella decided he would try to find out just how much Sadie weighed. The word was spread, and the bar patrons took bets to see who would be the closest to being right. Fancy's father said a lot of money changed hands.

When Sadie first found out what all the commotion was about, she was unhappy with their suggestive shenanigans;

however, with some coaxing, and the promise to share the winning bet with her, she soon changed her mind.

In the beginning they were going to take her word for how much she weighed, but those who had placed large bets wouldn't settle for it. For a few minutes they were stumped for a solution. Then a man, who was nearly as fat as Sadie, hollered, "We can take Sadie to the elevator and settle this." The elevator had a scale, the only one large enough to accurately weigh Sadie.

In a few minutes, one of the more sober patrons who still could think creatively, showed up with a railroad baggage cart he had borrowed from the train station. They loaded Sadie up and took her to the elevator. One of the partygoers was the brother-in-law of the elevator's owner, and he got the keys to operate the scale.

The sheriff showed up in the midst of all the carryings-on and evidently didn't want to mess with a bunch of half drunks. He told them to keep it down to a low roar, and then he left.

Sadie was put on the scale and weighed, and despite being full of beer, they all made it back to her Suds House. She weighed four hundred thirty-one and a half pounds. If he even knew, Fancy's dad never told her who won. The people in town who went to church on Sunday morning wondered why the railroad baggage cart was sitting in front of Sadie's place.

A different type of driver's education became a part of my memory bank at the end of my junior year of high school. It was our end-of-the-year school picnic, and every student was in high spirits. We were so glad school was out; we were anxious for summer to get into high gear.

Ricky Martinez's dad helped him fix up a Pontiac convertible. Once black, the convertible was now a pale yellow. Ricky drove it like a madman on the loose. Fancy loved to ride in it.

"Ricky and I are going riding in a while. Do you want to come?"

"I have some things I need to do. I think I will have to pass."

"Come on, live a little," she whined and challenged me a bit. "We can do the Charleston on the running boards." She enticed me.

Fancy and I loved to ride and act silly on the running boards of Ricky's car. Looking back, I realize now just how dangerous it was. When you're young and believe you are bulletproof, you choose to do stupid things.

"Okay, can you come by and pick me up a little later?"

Ricky and Fancy came by about two o'clock. I jumped in the car, and off we went. After we got outside of town, he slowed down, and Fancy and I climbed out on the running boards. We held onto the sides of the car doors, sometimes onto the door-frames where the windows rolled up and down, for support, and did the Charleston with our feet.

We cut quite a rug.

"Jessie, look at me!" Fancy hollered. She was doing the dance and not holding on to the car, which was very dangerous because Ricky often drove zigzag style. He made sharp turns, forcing us to hold on tight. It was great fun to sing songs from the top of our lungs and do the dance steps to the Charleston while flying down the road.

"Hey, Fancy, look at me!" I yelled as I joined her doing the Charleston without holding on to the car. We laughed and sang our heads off.

We were having fun, and all was going well until Fancy started messing with Ricky. She was on his side of the car, and she tried to put her hands between his legs while he was driving. He laughed, slapping her hands away and trying to drive.

"How's Fancy's little spic?" she cooed loudly.

"How can you call Ricky that?" I hollered at her.

She looked at me. "What? You mean my 'little spic'?" She laughed.

I looked at her; I looked at him. He smiled at me and put up his hands as if to say, "What am I going to do with her?"

"He's my Mexican jumping bean too!" Fancy yelled and laughed.

Fancy kept bothering him, and he kept fending her off playfully.

Suddenly, I felt the car make a quick turn to the right. I could tell Ricky was losing control of the convertible, and it was going down into a ravine. I jumped backwards, and when my feet hit the ground, my momentum caused me to somersault. I rolled down into the ravine.

I heard the car's motor race, and then I heard a loud crash. I faintly thought I saw Fancy's body fly up into the air. I was a bit dazed from the fall. I got up on my shaky legs and started to climb out of the ravine. As I reached the top, I saw Ricky climb out of the back of the wrecked car. He saw me and gave me a frightened, sickly smile.

"Where's Fancy?" he hollered.

I was sure she had to be on the side where the car had gone. We ran to the other side of the road, and we soon saw Fancy's body lying in the other side of the ravine. We rushed down to her. Her body was lying on the ground, sprawled out in an embarrassing fashion: her dress was about up to her waist, exposing her thighs and underpants.

"Is she dead?" I asked and began to cry.

"Mother of God, please Mary, Holy Mother, don't let her be dead," Ricky said in a prayerful tone of voice as he bent down to give her aid. He gently pulled her dress down to cover her up. "It looks like she is unconscious," he said.

"Is she still breathing?" I asked.

Ricky took his hands and put them on her ribs, and he put his head upon her left breast to see if he could hear her breathing.

"That feels good. How long can you keep it up?" Fancy said in a groggy-sounding voice.

Fancy's voice startled him, and he pulled his head away from her. Then just as quickly he bent down and tried to hug her; he was so relieved she wasn't dead or hurt badly.

"Not in front of Jessie," Fancy teased.

Ricky and I helped her up and gave her a hug.

"Thank God you're alive." I laughed through my tears.

I'm not sure what came over me, but when I saw that Fancy was okay, I looked at them and said, "I've got to go," and I just took off running. I never knew how far I ran, probably several miles, but I didn't stop until I was safe at home on my own front porch. It took me a long time to stop shaking. It seemed that my bones had a delayed case of fright from that near-death experience because I swear I heard them rattle all that day.

I made myself a solemn vow: I would never do the Charleston on a running board again as long as I lived.

It did little to provide the type of healing balm my heart needed since I discovered that Fancy had up and moved away without so much as a "by your leave," "good-bye," "kiss my foot," nothing. I knew she had a hard life, and because she had brought so much joy into my life, if only for a season, I chose to forgive her, even when my poor heart ached for her.

When I talked to Momma about my problem with forgiveness for Fancy, she said, "Forgiveness is the wellspring of life. Not giving someone your forgiveness means that all that poison stays inside you. It doesn't harm the other person, only you. When you get older, you will discover that God usually gives us friends for a season, not a lifetime."

Any time I ponder Momma's wisdom concerning Fancy, it causes me to reflect. Then again, I've never seen a convertible flying down the road without feeling a quick rush and a warm glow because I once knew a buxom broad named Fancy. In hindsight, she was a kindred spirit.

Chicken Bill

Momma never ceased to amaze me when it came to finding ways to challenge her children. She wanted us to reach for goals that would provide us with the rewards that come from looking fear right in the eye, finding ways to become overcomers. One such lesson she taught my sister Pauline and me took place in the early summer of my sophomore year.

As poor as our family was, we still managed to own a Philco radio. How Momma ever managed that financial miracle, I never did know. Momma and our family loved to listen to the famous radio personalities spin their tales of humor and drama. I suppose it was customary for all radio stations to air local programs that allowed them to sell advertising to businesses and keep the doors open and the stations in the black economically. One such program was "Chicken Bill's Amateur Show." The show's sponsor was a company that sold chicken feed. I guess it was a natural segue for the amateur show to be given the title of "Chicken Bill's Amateur Show." The show was produced in and aired from Salina, a city about thirty-five miles from Tampa.

Bill "Red" Hooten was actually Chicken Bill. He was the emcee of the program. He was the sole decision maker for who was allowed to be on his show. He was a "one-man band," according to Momma.

We loved to gather around the radio each week to listen to the contestants demonstrate their talent, or lack of it. Our family would place small bets (they had to be confined to slave labor from one member to another) on whom Chicken Bill would choose to win and who would be runner-up.

One particular group of poorly talented contestants sang and played their instruments way off-key. None of them were worthy of winning anything, but winners had to be chosen each week regardless of their worth, Momma said.

"Pauline, you and Jessie can do better than that."

"Sure we could," Pauline said. "But you'll never get me to make a fool of myself like some of those people just did."

"But you and Jess can harmonize so beautifully," Momma countered.

"Jessie, tell Momma it's just a pipe dream," she said as she turned to me to help her find a way to stop Momma's scheming in its tracks.

Before I could say a word, Momma said, "Just think of what our family could do with twenty-five dollars."

"Twenty-five dollars wouldn't begin to cover the expenses that could incur if we went up there and laid a big fat egg. Why, I'd have to have some shrink work on me day and night so I wouldn't end up in some funny farm," Pauline said as she became overly dramatic.

"Have you ever been down at the pond and spent time skipping a stone on the water?" Momma asked. The sudden shift in the topic of conversation startled Pauline, the rest of the family, and me.

"Well, sure—"

"Why did you spend time skipping that rock?"

"To see if I could skip it all the way across," I said as I jumped into the conversation.

Momma slapped her knee, and it made a loud noise. "That's right! You did it for the challenge! If you don't take a bite out of life every chance you get, what's the use of living?"

"Now, none of you can tell me that Pauline and Jess can't sing rings around that bunch of caterwauling we heard tonight."

All the children, except Pauline and me, nodded their heads in agreement.

I looked at Pauline; she looked at me. We had fear in our eyes, yet there was excitement in our hearts.

"I'll do it if you'll do it," I kind of whispered to Pauline. With a shrug of her shoulders and a loud breath of frustration, she replied, "Okay."

Momma gave both of us a big hug. She had a broad smile, and her voice was filled with joy. "I'll get busy and see about contacting Chicken Bill right away."

A couple of days passed, and Momma called Pauline and me to the kitchen table and read the letter she had written to Chicken Bill.

"Dear Chicken Bill, my name is Lou Crandal, and my family lives in Tampa. I am a widow with a dozen children (their poppa died just as the Depression hit), and I want you to allow my two girls to be contestants on your amateur show. Pauline and Jessie are a very talented duo. People around our parts say they are the best! Some say they are easy on the eyes, too.

"I am always looking for new ways to provide my children with challenges that will allow them to measure just what kind of stuff they are made of. Naturally, I'm positive that your show would do the trick.

"I am much obliged to you for any kindness you may choose to favor our family with. Sincerely, Lou Crandal."

"That was a nice touch, putting in there about you being a widow with twelve kids," Pauline said.

"Your poppa, rest his ornery soul, said to always keep your powder dry and use all the leverage you possess." Momma looked at us, smiled, and giggled. "It wouldn't hurt me if the post office train was robbed before this letter was delivered," Pauline said as she and I were on our way to mail Momma's letter to Chicken Bill.

"Wouldn't help none. Momma would just write another."

A month passed, and we had heard nary a word from "Chicken Bill's Amateur Show." Then, one day, just after breakfast, our party-line phone rang.

"Hello," Momma said. "Edna Mae, you'll need to get off the line now," she said as she easily detected that one of our nosy party-line phone members was once again eavesdropping.

Click was heard as she hung up her phone.

"Sorry about that," Momma said as she offered an apology for how their conversation was developing. "People are so rude."

"This here is Chicken Bill, and I'm needing to talk to a Lou Crandal. I believe she is the matriarch of a whole passel of young'uns," the voice on the phone said.

Momma motioned for Pauline and me to gather close to the phone so we could hear.

"In the flesh," Momma said. "I was wondering when I was going to hear from you. Took your sweet time, didn't you?" They both laughed a little.

"Normally, I don't do this," he said. "I have me a girl that handles our bookings and such; however, after I read your letter, I just had me a hankering to talk to this woman with a dozen kids."

"You liked that bit of information, did you?" She laughed.

"I'm always interested in knowing to what lengths a mother will go to get her precious children on our show." He cackled with glee.

"Chicken Bill, are you making fun of me?"

"Oh no! I'd never do that." He laughed, and Momma smiled. "Could you see your way clear to find a way up here to Salina in a week so we can have your girls on my show?"

"Just tell us when and where you want us," Momma said; she let the phone drop from her ear and held her hand over the receiver. "Chicken Bill, can you speak up so my girls can hear what you're saying."

He laughed a jolly laugh. I thought he sounded like a fat man might sound.

"This here is the one and only Chicken Bill," we heard him say. "The 'Chicken Bill's Amateur Show' is extending an invitation to Momma Crandal's girls, Pauline and Jessie, to perform on a week from this coming Saturday."

Just hearing the words of that invitation caused me to sweat, and my body's senses heightened. *Nervous-pervous* was the thought that crossed my mind. I suddenly pictured myself on Chicken Bill's show on that big stage. Everything was in perfect order: musicians, radio sound team, announcer, a large audience, Pauline at my side. When the music commenced, Pauline fainted.

"Now I can officially start to worry," Pauline said. "It's two weeks away, and I already want to throw up."

Momma laughed.

"Is there anything wrong on your end?" Chicken Bill asked.

"No…no, everything is just fine," she assured him. "We'll wear our best bib and tucker, and we will look forward to meeting you a week from this coming Saturday."

Momma hung up the phone and turned and looked at us. She wore a big grin. "And you thought we had been forgotten. We're going to have to really crank up that piano." She walked over to it and sat down on its bench. She patted both sides of the bench as she motioned for Pauline and me to sit down. She started to hum the melody of one of her favorite songs: "By the Light of the Silvery Moon." We sat down, and soon we were in harmony. "See, you girls have such beautiful harmony. I can see it now: the *Tampa News* with you two pictured on the front page, announcing to everyone that you won first place on *Chicken Bill's Amateur Show*."

"Yeah, if we don't die of stage fright, and, instead of having a celebration, you are forced to conduct a vigil at our funeral." Pauline offered her assessment of our predicament. Her comment caused all of us to break out laughing.

Momma did her best to get Nap's touring car, but it just wasn't available; therefore, we had to settle for Howard's Chevy with a rumble seat. Only Momma, Pauline, and I made the trip to Salina. The rest of the family had to be content with gathering around the Philco radio and rooting us on from home.

I learned a thing or two about perceptions that day. We arrived in Salina. Since "Chicken Bill's Amateur Show" was so well known in Salina and the immediate surrounding areas, he was a radio personality. I assumed that everything associated with the show would be first class; that was a term Momma liked to use to describe how she preferred everything. It wasn't first class.

The show was held in an old, rundown building.

"Everything was dirty," Momma described it.

The stage floor had rough spots and visible gouges. It had been painted at one time and was in need of another coat. The musicians played well, but they looked like a ragtag bunch of urchins. The building was rather small, and it really only accommodated the contestants and their families.

I did get one perception right: Chicken Bill was a large man with a very big stomach. He had a rather large head with dark-colored hair on both sides. He had a prominent nose and very wide nostrils. His large eyes were framed by big, bushy eyebrows. An unlit cigar was sticking out of the right side of his mouth. He wore a red long-sleeved shirt that had an embroidered emblem of a large rooster in gold. Under the emblem were the words "Chicken Bill's Amateur Show." He wore white slacks that were too short because of his enormous girth. His black shoes and white socks finished off his appearance.

As he approached Momma and us, she said, "God awful, just God awful."

"He looks like a big ole red and white toad," she whispered through her teeth, and Pauline and I struggled to keep from laughing out loud.

When he came to meet us, he said, "So, you're the little lady with so many kids." He stuck out his beefy right hand.

Momma did a half curtsy. "They told me they're cheaper by the dozen," she teased.

He shook each of our hands. He looked down at Pauline and me. "Good luck, kiddies. Say, I really like those dresses," he complimented us. "I've got to go; the show must go on you know."

Even though it was radio and the audience didn't know what we were wearing, Momma had made Pauline and me matching dresses. The dresses were white with puffed sleeves, and small red and navy music notes adorned the hemline. The dresses had a large music note across the heart. Pauline said we looked more like … well, I won't say what she said we looked like.

The show had time for six contestants, and we were last.

"I think we drew the best spot for all of the contestants, don't you?" I asked Pauline. "This way, we will get to see what talent has already been shown." I was sort of rambling, mostly out of nervousness. I was doing my best to keep Pauline from passing out because she was acting more scared than I was.

My mind kept playing tricks on me. There I was, ready to participate in a musical event on the radio, and I should have been single-minded and focused on the nerve-racking job that lay in front of me; yet my mind went blank. Where I was or what I was thinking during this time, I don't have recall. It may have been a blessing from the Lord.

I became aware of Pauline punching me in the ribs on my left side. "That's done," she said.

"Done what?" I asked.

"There's no way we are going to beat him." She pointed to a handsome-looking teenage boy standing front and center on the stage. He was dressed in an authentic-looking cowboy outfit, down to his boots. His red bandana set off his white hat. He could make that guitar sing, and his baritone voice made Hank William's "lonesome cry of a whippoorwill" sound mournful and emotionally needy.

Once Pauline had interrupted my reverie, it seemed as if only seconds passed until Chicken Bill was announcing our names and the song we were going to sing. I felt as if I were almost dragging Pauline with me out to the stage to sing. On reflection, I was probably the one who was being dragged. When I was confronted with a task I didn't want to do or to face, I remember Momma telling me on more than one occasion, *"Embarrassment and failure is good for the soul."*

My soul must really be feeling good, I thought as I felt the trickle of sweat run down my inner thighs; I hoped it was sweat.

When the music commenced, somehow Pauline and I hit our cue on time, and we did a very creditable job. Our harmony really came off well. We knew it was fine by the expressions of the audience, and they nodded their heads and turned to look at people sitting on either side of them.

When we finished singing, we heard the applause. The crowd's stamp of approval thrilled us. We smiled and bowed. We did it in a very ladylike fashion. We turned and nearly ran off the stage.

"Lordy, Lordy! I thought I was going to throw up," Pauline said. She turned to me, and we shared a warm embrace. "If Momma ever gets another harebrained idea like this"—Pauline did her best to find the right words—"I'm going to, oh, I don't know, run away or just brain her." She made us break into fits of laughter.

Chicken Bill soon walked out to the center of the stage. He took his cigar out of his mouth.

"On behalf of our proud sponsor, Purina Chicken Feed, I want to extend our congratulations to all of our very fine contestants.

"While every show can only have but one winner, I'm sure that you all will agree with me that everyone on this show is a winner," he said. The audience clapped their hands. "As you all know by now, but just in case we might have a new listener for our program, as much as we would like it to be different, we only award prizes to the first- and second-place winners.

"Before I award the winners with their prizes, let's have them all come out on stage so we can give them a round of applause."

As we were in Howard's Chevy, driving back home, Momma was humming a hymn: "The Old Rugged Cross." Every now and then she would sneak a peak back into the rumble seat area of the car. The box, which held a twelve-piece setting of blue Currier and Ives dishes, was resting comfortably and safely.

"And in second place, runner-up to our champion, is the girls' duet from Tampa," Chicken Bill had said as he informed us that we hadn't won the contest.

"That boy could play, and my, how he could sing," Momma said as she broke the silence in the car.

"And he was so good looking," Pauline said. "It was worth losing just to have him smile at me and shake my hand."

This brought laughter from all of us. "I thought Rose was man crazy; I'm afraid you're following in her footsteps."

Momma started to sing the song we had sung for the show. We spent the rest of the drive home harmonizing. When Momma joined in, we sounded much better.

Howard coaxed his boss into doing a little story on our escapade to Chicken Bill's show. The notoriety was fun, but it gave some kids the opportunity to use our second-place showing as fodder to inflict spiritual murder, which is what Momma called harmful gossip and slander.

Even though I didn't want to be a contestant on Chicken Bill's show, mainly because I didn't want to be humiliated by doing a poor job, I'm glad that Momma insisted Pauline and I take on the task. I can't say how well my soul really felt, handling all that potential infusion of embarrassment and failure. Momma did her best to tell us that it would be good for us; I know that it better prepared me to face obstacles, which I found distasteful, head-on.

The Debt

"Jessie," Momma yelled at me, "honey, I need for you to run to the store for me."

She notified me that it was necessary for our family to make another dreaded trip to the Tetson Five and Dime Mercantile store.

Being raised in a two-bedroom home, which had to sleep nine kids and a mother, and forced to wear hand-me-downs was a hard pill to swallow. I was often told that my dress looked just fine when it came from Purina feed sacks. We girls were farmed out from time to time to various neighbors so that Momma might manage to work longer hours, and we girls could earn a little money. Sometimes we got paid a dollar or two for working long hours at jobs few people desired. In my judgment, being poor was certainly enough punishment. A body didn't need to add insult to injury by having to run to the store and endure all of the personal slights from the clerks, which were inevitable when you were forced to say, "My momma said to just add this to our bill." Even I knew that our grocery bill was large enough to choke a horse! What was worse, I knew that Momma didn't have a clue as to how she would ever be able to pay that debt.

"Oh, Momma, can't you send someone else?" I begged off having to be put in that humiliating position again in order to get food for the family.

"Jess, the good Lord promises all of his children that he won't force them to endure difficult situations that he won't provide a way out of. They may have to crawl out on their bellies and escape with no clothes on." Momma brought forth one of her teaching moments; I wasn't impressed.

"Well, why don't you send another of your super bright kids?

You can bring them in and give them that precious teaching moment you just laid on me, and—"

"You are going to the store, young lady," she snapped at me. "I don't need you to sass me." Her anger came and then went away. "Now, Jess, you know that nearly every time I have sent someone else, they have come home empty-handed or without the right items. I just don't have the time or the inclination to do a redo today." She handed me the list. "Just be nice, regardless of how you are treated." Her eyes told me she knew the chore was distasteful.

As I slowly made my way the few blocks to the store, I pondered how I had ended up being the step-and-fetch-it kid of the family.

Just maybe it was that piss-and-vinegar thing about me that Poppa said I possessed, I reflected. At that very moment, if it were, I wished I had a lot less piss and vinegar.

Momma had pressed two pennies into my hand as she gave me the grocery list. "Treat yourself." She gave me a loving wink.

My spirits rose as I thought of how I would enjoy some of Mr. Tetson's sweet coconut. My mind raced a bit as I approached the store door. *Hope he has been in the sauce,* I thought.

I just loved to come into the mercantile store when we didn't owe them a huge debt. It was literally filled with the types of supplies and goods any family might ever need. My favorite place in the store was up at the front counter. That is where he kept kegs of different kinds of sweets: pickles, cheeses, fresh fruits that were in season, and, of course, my favorite item: coconut.

Before the hard times hit most of our townsfolk, Angela and I would find a way to get a few pennies, usually from her father, and we would make a beeline to the mercantile. She would urge me to enter the store and see if Mr. Tetson was in. He may not be at the front counter, but if he were in the store, we knew we could usually find a way to coax him to wait on us. It was a well-known fact that Mr. Tetson liked his bourbon and tobacco. He didn't smoke, but he chewed Mail Pouch tobacco. By the

RANNY GRADY

early afternoon of any day, he was known to be staggering, spitting, and telling jokes as he sold his goods and good-naturedly entertained his customers. He didn't have an unkind bone in his body, people would often remark, but he was a drunk.

I am shamed to admit it, but I always hoped that he would be in his normal condition when Angela and I went to the store to buy coconut. He really didn't spend much time at the front counter. His wife, Betty, frowned upon his presence there, but he liked me, and he was always willing to wait on Angela and me. Often he was, as Momma would put it, "three sheets to the wind," and he would stagger a bit. Often, some of his chaw, with a slight mix of saliva and tobacco juice, would run down the side of his mouth, like some form of putrid drool. However, it was during those times that he would give us very generous helpings of coconut in our brown sacks.

"I can stand a little spit and tobacco drool in my coconut, if he fills up my sack," I used to tell Angela when she would nearly gag if she found a smidgeon of his drool in her sack.

On that day, I said a silent prayer before I entered. *Be nice; be nice,* I told myself as I readied my resolve to mind Momma's instructions. I gingerly made my way to the front counter.

"Is Mr. Tetson in?" I figured that I would try and get my sack of coconut filled by him before I ventured into asking for another please-charge-this-to-our-bill plea.

Betty Tetson was Momma's close friend, at least until our family built up a large bill that we couldn't pay. She tartly replied, "He isn't available at the moment." She deftly lifted up her glasses from off the edge of her nose. She and Momma were about the same age. The biggest difference between them was that Mrs. Tetson didn't have any kids. Momma had a dozen. She was a well-coiffured woman, and she wore dresses that came all the way from St. Louis. Her facial features were fine in nature, and she had lovely blue eyes. She often had a hearty laugh.

"Is he not in the store today?"

"I suppose he is out back somewhere." She looked at me with the look adults give to kids when they see them as pests. "Is there something I can help you with?"

"No, no thank you," I replied. "You're so kind to ask. Maybe later." I made my way to the other end of the store.

"Nearer my God to thee…nearer my God…" I heard a man's voice humming and softly mumbling the words of the song.

As I opened the door to the back of the store, there he was, singing, staggering a bit, and stacking boxes.

I wonder just how God would look upon this scene, I reflected. He was potted from bourbon, and he was singing about his love for the Lord. "Mr. Tetson, your wife told me that I would find you out here." I smiled at him.

He put down the box he had in his hands. "Jessie, it's good to see you; what can I do for you?" He winked at me. "As if I didn't know, right?" He chuckled and laughed merrily. "You're my sweet little coconut girl." He almost cooed as he said it.

I quickly retrieved the grocery list I had from my pocket-book, and I handed it to him. "I sure do want some of your great coconut, but Momma sent me with a list of things she needs."

He adjusted his horn-rimmed glasses. He had tied heavy twine to the ends of the parts that fit around his ears. He wore them around his neck so that he wouldn't lose them. He staggered a mite but caught his balance. He looked down at me, a little embarrassed by his behavior.

"Been suffering with a dizzy spell now and then." He offered up his lame excuse to try and hide the fact that he had been drinking again.

"May I help you?" I offered him one of my arms to escort him into the store.

He emitted a little chuckle and accepted my offer. "A fair damsel comes to rescue the old man, huh?"

We slowly made our way from the back of the store to the front counter. I could tell that his wife was none too pleased with either one of us as he let go of my arm and went around to the back of the counter.

"Get out of the way, woman," he addressed his wife in a demanding manner. "Jess and I have some important business to attend to." He turned his attention to me. He winked and then said, "How much do you want? Wait a minute." He laughed at himself. "I'd better rephrase that, hadn't I? How much can you afford to pay for?" He corrected himself, and we both laughed.

He staggered over to the barrel where he kept the coconut and pulled the lid off. He opened a sack. "Well, how many pennies do you have?" I put up two fingers.

"A whole two pennies." He looked down at me and grinned. "Sure you can eat that much coconut?" he teased me because he knew two pennies wouldn't fill up a small candy sack. To my surprise and to my great pleasure, he opened up the largest candy sack he sold. He filled it with coconut to the brim. He gave off a loud belch, which was more like a hiccup. "There, that is just about two pennies worth of that good stuff." He gave me a great big knowing wink.

His wife was less than thrilled that he had been more than generous with their coconut. He rustled around in his shirt pocket and retrieved the grocery list I had given to him earlier. He straightened out the crumpled list and handed it to his wife.

"Jess here needs some things."

She took the list from his hands and read off the list of ten items. She glanced down at me and gave me that dreaded stare. It was a look that poor urchins all over this land had endured; it was disdainful, and it made my heart hurt. Begging does that.

"Mr. Tetson," she addressed her husband formally. I suppose it was like when Momma uses my first, middle, and last name; I know I'm in trouble. "May I see you in the office for just a minute?" she asked in a stern, yet polite-sounding voice.

The look that crossed his face was the kind that we kids often had when we knew we were headed for the woodshed and the strop.

"I'd only be too happy to accompany, Mrs. Tetson," he said, as he wanted her to know that she wasn't fooling him by her phony demeanor. He winked at me as he left.

They stepped back into the office and closed the door. I wasn't privy to most of what was said; indeed, it was very animated. She put her finger in front of his nose and waggled it a few times. I heard him say, "And you call yourself a Christian." Then, in a minute or two, I heard, "I thought she was your best friend." The last thing I heard from behind that closed door was his wife saying, "It will soon be five hundred dollars!"

As the door was opened, I heard him say, "But Betty, she is a widow with a dozen kids." He walked up to the counter. He had the list in his hand. "Glen," he addressed one of the store's clerks, "see to it that Jessie gets everything on this list." He looked down at me and emitted a little sigh. I thought I saw tears well up in his eyes. "Don't never mind." He paused and pointed back to where he and his wife had been arguing. "Just a small disagreement over high finance." He did his best to help me feel better about getting more food for our family without actually paying any money.

"I don't really blame her," I whispered. He reached down and tousled my red hair, and I moved behind the counter and motioned for him to bend down. I reached up and gave him a kiss on his left cheek.

"You'd better get on home now," he said through a mix of tears, his and mine.

After supper that night, I was helping Momma with the dishes. She inquired about my visit to the store. I chose not to tell her the entire story; I left out the parts that hurt my heart. She did get a good laugh about Mr. Tetson filling up my candy sack with coconut.

When you sleep with your momma, it's difficult to find a place to cry. I had a fitful night because I found it burdensome to cry and sob, even mourn a bit for all that Momma had to put up with, yet not shed one tear that was seen.

Even when mommas aren't given all the information, they still seem to be able to sift the chaff from the wheat.

After breakfast the next morning, Momma asked, "Was Betty rude to you?"

I could tell that she had been crying. Her question told

me that it was over her changed friendship with Betty Tetson. "Princes and paupers seldom mix," Momma told us kids when we would openly fantasize about marrying someone rich.

"I wouldn't call it rude," I said, as I didn't want to give Momma any more reason to be hurt about Mrs. Tetson. "It was a bit…" I paused to try and find the right words and proper tenor of my answer. "She was very concerned about our family."

"She didn't want to give you the food until I paid the bill, right?" Momma didn't mince her words, even though saying them hurt her badly.

I just hunched my shoulders, looked at her, and nodded my head.

I swear my little "yes" hit her like a dagger through her heart. She even clutched her breast and let out a little gasp. "I've just got to find a way to pay that bill," she said more to herself than to me. She started rubbing her face and scratching her hair.

I couldn't stand to see her suffer; I slowly got up out my chair and left her alone.

I wished that I could say it was the last time Momma sent me to the store to get food that we couldn't pay for, but it wasn't. It became more difficult each time I went. I recall that there was a period of time when I thought Momma should have been obliged to go to the store, but in hindsight I'm awfully glad she didn't.

After a time, I told my brother Earl what had taken place at the store with Mr. and Mrs. Tetson because he commented that Momma wasn't herself and seemed depressed.

My brother Earl is a mountain of a man in size; when he is riled, I pity his adversary.

"Don't you fret," he told me. "I'll figure out a way to handle this," he promised, and he told me not to say a word about our conversation. "Remember, mum's the word." He left to get home.

In late summer, after most of the plowing had been done in preparation for planting next year's wheat crop, my brother Earl knocked on our door just after supper. The heat of the scorching day's sun still kept most people outside the house, away from the direct path of its rays. The large elm tree out back of our house was our family's gathering spot. If there were any breeze, it usually came out of the southwest at that time of the year. We often would take blankets and spend the evening watching heaven's celestial show.

"Who will you compare me to?" Momma often would recall a bit of scripture as we sat amazed at the orange, sometimes nearly blood red, sun disappearing on the horizon. We would look in the opposite direction and see the first glimpse of the moon rising. When no one answered Earl's knock, he made his way out back.

"I thought I would find you all out here," Earl said as he laughed a little and bent down to where Momma was sitting and gave her a peck on the cheek.

"You gonna have to do better than that," she told him as she opened up her arms.

Dutifully, he lowered himself on his haunches, and he reached out and gave her a big hug and a kiss.

"That's much better," she said, and she patted the place beside her. "Take a load off and sit a spell."

"I really can't stay long. In fact, I came over to tell Jessie something." He looked directly at me and motioned with his head that he wanted to talk to me in private.

"So, how does Jess rate more than me?" Momma asked.

"Now don't go getting your knickers in a twist," Earl said. "It isn't anything important; it will take just a minute."

Momma laughed and pushed him away. "Son, you're too gullible."

I ran over to where he was seated. I motioned for him to grab a hold of my hands so I could help him up.

He ignored my offer. "I'm not old yet." The rest of our family did their best to make him regret his overly defensive comment.

Once we were inside the house, I thought my heart was going to stop forever. I recalled that I had heard a story one day: Some old folks talk about a person's heart racing so fast that it caused it to stop and he died. They mentioned something about a compromising position, but I didn't have a clue about that until later in my life.

Earl took out his wallet slowly. He thrust some folded-up money into my hand.

"Go ahead and count it." He was acting weird, and it made me jumpy inside.

At that very instant, as I started to unfold the money and to count out the hundred dollar bills, I couldn't help but wonder, from a scientific viewpoint, just how big a person's eyes are able to open. Whatever it might be, I'm sure I set a new world record.

"Five hundred dollars!" I yelled.

"Will you shush up?" Earl said in an authoritarian tone of voice, which he seldom used. "You don't want to spoil the surprise, do you?"

When a girl has a million little "screaming meemies" charging up and down and all over her body, each one carrying some sort of party hat or noisemaker, all of them are in a raging war to see which can escape from her body and fly out of her mouth in a celebration of joy. I felt greater joy than the children of Israel must have felt when the walls of Jericho came tumbling down. It was all Earl could do to keep me from tearing out of the back door like some deranged banshee running among civilized people.

He pressed his hand up against my mouth. I rigorously moved my head up and down, doing my best to communicate that I wasn't about to ruin his surprise. I was giggling, jumping up and down, smiling, and crying at the same time. My emotions were so out of whack that I was afraid I was going to wet my pants. He evidently believed me, and he took his hand from my mouth. We looked at each other, and then we embraced. I could feel the wetness of his tears on my cheeks. I quickly grabbed his hand.

"Come on. Let's go tell Momma," I said.

"You tell her," Earl replied.

"Not in a million years!" I smiled through my tears. "She is going to hear it from you."

During the time that Earl and I had left the family sitting under the tree, Howard had returned from working at the newspaper. Evidently, we had been the topic of conversation.

"You spent enough time to plan a good bank robbery," Howard said; he teased us as we came strolling out of the house.

"That wouldn't be a bad idea," Momma quipped. "Maybe then I could pay our grocery bill." Everyone laughed, except for Earl and me.

"So, what are you two so secretive about? Earl's got a girlfriend?" she asked as she continued to tease.

"No," I said. "But Earl has something he wants to give you."

"I hope it's chocolates," Momma said. "Only the Lord knows how long it has been since I have had some good chocolate." She added.

I looked at Earl and motioned for him to get on with it. He was a bundle of nerves, and his voice started shaking. He stuttered a bit as he sat down beside Momma. "Momma, you must close your eyes, real tight, and open your hands," I instructed her.

She gave me her fish-eye look but obeyed.

He didn't say another word. He just placed the money in her hands.

The evening's light was rapidly disappearing, but it was still light enough for Momma to see the money. Her eyes spied the top one-hundred-dollar bill. She ever so gently lifted it up in order for her to see what was beneath the first bill. By the time she had flipped through the first four, her body was beginning to shake. Tears welled up in her eyes, and they started to overflow and run down her face. It seemed to me that it took forever for her to finally reach the bottom of the stacked bills. She couldn't say a word; all she could do was sit there. Her body shook, and she began to cry softly.

"Thank you, Jesus. Thank you for giving me such a son."

"What's Momma crying about?" Charlie asked, and he was already tearing up. Our entire family was, though only Earl and I knew why.

Through my tears I explained, "Momma's crying because Earl just brought Momma five one-hundred-dollar bills."

When that bit of good news hit their tailbones, they all started jumping up and down; the whole group ran to hug Momma. When Arthur saw this, he ran and jumped in the middle of all us kids around Momma. This made us all break out into an uproar of joy.

Momma reached out and pulled Earl over onto her lap. As big and husky as he was, being a man and not a boy, he was reluctant to do her bidding. This just upset her a bit, and she started to cry a little louder. Earl relented and moved into her waiting arms. It was the tenderest moment I had witnessed since Sammy returned for Poppa's funeral back in Humansville, Missouri. Momma rocked Earl against her breasts, and she stroked his hair. We all moved back and allowed the silhouette of their frames against the clear moonlight to wax eloquent amidst the silence of the moment that God blessed us with.

The silence was allowed to remain until we couldn't keep little Arthur from pulling away as he ran to join in with his momma and big brother. Even then, the picture grew sweeter because they allowed him to enter into their lovefest.

"Son, how in the world?" Momma finally began to speak. "Tell me you didn't do something illegal." She continued to fumble with her words. Tears have a way of getting in the way of clear communication, and she was in that struggle.

"No! I didn't do anything illegal," Earl replied in a curt manner.

"Oh, Earl, I didn't mean"—Momma quickly realized what she had implied with her halting questions—"It's just . . . it's so much money."

"Do you really want to know?" he asked in a loud whisper.

We weren't coached, but, almost in perfect harmony, all of us said, "We really want to know." Then we burst out laughing as we realized what we had unintentionally done.

Earl sat up and made himself a little more comfortable. He cleared his throat, and then for the next hour he told us a story that left us limp from the emotions he lived through. We were totally spellbound by its contents.

"Well, it all started when Jessie told me about the incident at Mr. Tetson's Mercantile."

"Son, I'd rather you not go there," Momma interrupted him.

This startled him. "Okay, Momma. It isn't important that you know all of the details about the incident; it is only important that you know that our family has bought our food on credit for too long. Momma manages to pay something on the bill each month, so it isn't as if we aren't paying our debts." He did his best to shore up our family's good name.

"When Jessie told me about the incident, which you don't need to know the details of…"—he stopped and looked at Momma—"this is more difficult than it looks."

"Just skip to the part where you found a way to earn five hundred dollars," Momma said softly.

"Well, it made me mad, and I decided I had to find a way to do something about our grocery bill," he continued his story. "I went to my boss and told him of our dilemma and asked him if he might have some ideas of how I might earn a lot of money in a short period of time. I guess I shouldn't have overreacted to Momma's question 'Did I get it legally?' because his question to me was, 'Are you planning on getting it legally or illegally?'"

This made our family break out laughing.

"He suggested that I look into hiring on for some night plowing. When the harvest is finished, the fields must be dressed for the next spring's planting. By the time the harvest is finished in western Kansas, it's necessary for some of the farmers to plow at night in order to get it all done; besides, it's so much cooler at night. I guess it is true that when you are too close to your problem, you can't see the forest for the trees." Earl allowed himself a little chuckle. "I had experience in plowing but had never plowed at night. I couldn't imagine it would be much different, so I made a few contacts with my boss's help. I was able to be hired to plow at night. I soon discovered that the farmers paid a premium for night plowing, and that really made me excited. I figured that if I could plow for two months, at least five nights a week, I could earn five hundred dollars.

"I soon learned why they pay a bonus for men who will plow at night," he said.

"When you are plowing at night, the light from the tractor blinds you to everything except what is directly in front of you." He began to weave his story. "This type of vision allows you to plow straight rows." He paused for a few seconds; the tension of anticipation was building among his audience.

While Earl was naturally shy, it seemed that he had settled in and was relishing the idea of telling his story.

"But it doesn't allow you to see anything else," he said. "A little farther west of Tampa is a natural habitat for snakes, especially big rattlers," he added creepily, sending chills up and down his listeners' spines.

"Every now and then, as we were busy plowing, we'd come upon a nest of those creatures"—he lowered his voice—"and when the tractor or plow hits them and disturbs their nest, they come a'flying up in the air. You don't have any idea where they are or what direction they may be coming, away from the tractor and plow or right at you," he said in a hushed tone of voice.

"*Oh*, did any of them get you?" Deannie asked.

"No, thank God!" Earl smiled at her. "But one fellow from Cottonwood Falls was hit by three or four of them."

"What happened to him?" Charlie asked sympathetically.

"The poor guy was so filled with their poison that by the time he could get any help ... he never made it."

"Do you mean that he died in the field?" I asked.

"It is sad to say, but yes, he died right there."

"Oh, son, why did you put yourself at such risk?" Momma moaned. "It just tears my heart up thinking you could have been killed."

"We needed the money."

"What did you and the rest of the men do?" Rose asked, showing that she too was enjoying Earl's story.

"We got back on our tractors and continued to plow."

"Did you ever hit any nests of rattlers?" Pauline asked fearfully.

"Once or twice," he said, and Momma let out a moan. The rest of us sucked in our breaths loud enough we could all hear it.

"It was too scary for words. When the nest is hit, you seldom can actually see them, though sometimes you can. Usually, you see silhouettes of them coming up in the air after the nest has been struck. The tractor is so loud you can't hear them. You don't have any way to gauge how close they might be. All you can do is pray that they haven't come up in the air and will come back down landing upon you, the driver."

As Earl was weaving his scary story, Deannie and Gracie joined Arthur on Momma's lap. The scarier it became, the tighter they hugged Momma.

"Perhaps I had better stop," he said as he noticed how the younger children were reacting.

"No, we want to hear all of it!" Deannie cried in a loud voice.

"Is that what happened to that driver from Cottonwood Falls?" I asked.

"I'm afraid so."

"What did you do when that happened? That man died from those snakes?" Pauline asked.

"When it is over, and you know you are safe until the next time"—he continued the story—"your body breaks out in a different type of sweat than you had already been giving off while plowing. The hair on your head feels itchy, and your emotions are set on a raw edge to the point that you want to just break down and cry," he whispered. We could tell that he was not just telling us a story. He was reliving the nightmare. "You allow yourself a few minutes to calm down and to decide if you want to continue working. Then you either continue plowing or quit.

"After that poor guy from Cottonwood Falls was killed, I gave some serious thought about quitting; then I recalled what Momma taught me: 'If God be for us, who can be against us?' and I continued to work."

"They say that God takes care of fools and drunks," Momma said. "Now that it's over, I'm glad that you did what you did; I'm not convinced that it wasn't too foolish."

"It's getting late, and I have to get up real early," Earl said. He stopped talking and readied himself to depart. He helped Momma up, and then they embraced, which caused the tears to flow from all of us once again.

"Jessie, we have an important call to make tomorrow," Momma said, and all of us laughed. Everyone knew that she was referring to paying off the grocery bill. I'm sure that our laughs held more than a hint of prideful smirks.

"I'd pay a nickel to see what happens at the mercantile tomorrow," Rose said. That statement was greeted with all of our family saying, "Amen."

"Now put on your best finery," Momma said to me. "We are going to look our best when we make our call."

"Do you want me to wear my Fourth of July dress? The brown and white one with the puffed sleeves?" I asked.

"Yes, that will do fine," she said. "I will wear one that has puffed sleeves too."

"We're gonna knock 'em dead," I teased, and I came to her so she could help me get my dress zipped and cinched. Momma put on her only Sunday-go-to-meeting dress that had puffed sleeves. If I had to say it myself, we made a couple of good-looking dolls.

Before we walked the few blocks to Mr. Tetson's store, we waited until it was midmorning.

"Momma," I said as we were walking, "I have enjoyed some walks in my lifetime: those special walks that Angela and I had when we spent time down around the creek where the spring flows, walking with Howard when he trained to become the record holder for the mile run, and strolling with a beau or two. But nothing compares to this walk we are making this morning," I squeezed her hand.

We walked along in silence. Momma squeezed my hand back. "I feel the same way, child," she answered after a time. I could tell that her voice was filled with emotion.

As we approached the store door, I ran and opened it and prepared the way for Momma to enter the door in a dramatic fashion. I held it open and curtsied as she walked by.

"Let's not overdo this," Momma said through gritted teeth. I shut the door and quickly caught up with her. In a very graceful manner, we made our way to the middle of the front counter of the store. Momma and I stood quietly before the clerk.

When he looked up and saw us standing before him, he looked at Momma, whom he didn't know well. Then he looked at me, whom he knew very well, and he gave me a frown.

"May I help you, ladies?" he asked with an attitude that was just a bit above disdainful.

"We'd like to have a moment with Mrs. Tetson," Momma said.

The clerk looked down through his glasses and then looked back toward the office where Betty Tetson was sitting at her desk. "Is there something that I may do for you? She is a very busy woman. Perhaps if you tell me what it is that you want to see her about, I can figure out how to solve your little problem."

Buster, if you don't come down off your high horse and accommodate Momma's wish, I'm going to break out all over you with my piss-and-vinegar disposition, I thought.

"I'm quite sure that someone who is so qualified to meet this store's customers' needs, like yourself, ordinarily would suffice for most any situation," Momma said as she returned his intended slight to us with kindness, if not too much of aggrandizement. "However, today, I'm not content to work with any second banana." Her voice grew more pointed and commanding. "Just get your tail back there and tell Betty that Lou Crandal is here to see her." She flashed him a sickly sweet smile.

When he realized that Momma hadn't been building him up, but rather was setting him up for a fall, his countenance changed abruptly. He turned and made his way to the office. He went in and closed the door. I couldn't tell what he was saying, but I could see the flailing of his arms.

In a few minutes, Mrs. Tetson came out of the office.

"Why, Lou Crandal!" she exclaimed. "It is so good to see you. We see a lot of Jessie, but we seldom are graced with your presence." She quickly approached Momma and gave her a peck on the cheek. Momma held her body rigidlike.

"It seems like only yesterday you and Ranti were playing cards at our house." She carried the conversation. "Goodness, how time just flies. How long has it been? A couple of years?"

"Ranti has been dead four years," Momma said.

"My, has it been that long already?" I could tell that her attempt to be phony had trapped her. She was showing that she was embarrassed by her disconnect with Momma since Poppa had died.

"Howard here"—she pointed to the rude clerk—"said you wanted to see me. I don't suppose it is about your bill." She allowed herself a snide little remark, and she emitted a little, coughlike laugh. Her clerk joined in her sad attempt at humiliating humor.

"Matter of fact, it is," Momma said, and her answer caused Mrs. Tetson to nearly choke on her words.

She pointed the way for Momma to follow her to the office.

"Jessie, why don't you stay out here and have some of your favorite coconut while your momma and I step back to the office and conduct our business."

She may have been condescending, or she may have had some real concern for me because she was sure that Momma was going to have to beg for more time to pay the debt. She wanted to spare me their difficult discussion.

"No, I want Jess to hear everything," Momma said, and she extended her hand to me. We marched back to the office together.

She was just about to close the door when Mr. Tetson came around the corner and stuck his head in the doorway. "Is this a private party, or can anyone come?" he asked.

"Lou and Jessie are here about their bill," his wife said. "I can take care of this. It isn't necessary for you to stay."

"Why don't you stay?" Momma said as she countered his wife's directions. "I think it is fitting that you hear it all."

He came in and took a seat at the side of the desk. His wife started to get up out of the seat behind the desk, but he motioned for her to remain seated.

"First, I want to tell you both that my family and I have been so very thankful for the Christian way you have handled our very difficult situation since Jessie's poppa died and we moved back to Tampa." She started her conversation. "I want you to know that I realize that we have been—and there isn't any better way to say it—deadbeats when it came to paying for our food." Momma's voice cracked with emotion.

"We'd never consider your family deadbeats," Mr. Tetson said as he interrupted.

"Well, maybe you wouldn't"—Momma pointed to Betty—"but your wife has." The tension in the room increased greatly with her remark. "And I can't say I can blame her," Momma quickly added, which seemed to diffuse some of that tension.

"Now, Jessie isn't one to tell tales out of school, but I've been really hurt by the way she has been treated by Betty and nearly all of your clerks when she has been forced, by me, to come and get groceries and charge them to our huge bill."

"I told you that your way of conducting business wasn't fooling Lou," Mr. Tetson said as he interrupted. His wife gave him a look that if looks could kill, he'd have been dead in his chair.

"I'm not mad at you"—Momma directed her comment to Betty—"because you were openly concerned about the debt I kept adding to each time Jessie came to the store. Shoot, I'd have been more than a little concerned if a customer like me was doing the same thing. I'm not even mad." Her voice filled with tears. "It's much worse; my heart hurts that you have allowed money to come between what we used to mean to each other before Ranti died.

"Betty, you and your clerks have been rude and hurtful, in a very public way, to Jessie." Momma struggled to keep control of her emotions. "And I can tell you, the last thing on earth Jess wanted to do was come to your store to get food because of the way you made her feel.

"I don't include you, Mr. Tetson." She looked at him with a smile in her eyes. "Jessie has a real sweet spot in her heart for you. She always told me how wonderful you treat her when she comes to the store."

I looked at him; he winked at me. It made me feel embarrassed but awfully good on the inside.

"She's like the girl I never had," he said, and my glow just grew warmer.

"Lou." Mrs. Tetson's voice was now filled with emotion, and her voice cracked with a hint of tears. "I may have unintentionally done what you accused me of"—she did her best to defend her behavior—"it's this darn Depression." Her lips quivered. "We have many customers who can't pay their bills either." She paused to gather herself emotionally. "If we end up losing our store, no one will have food." She took a lady's hanky and dabbed her eyes to catch her tears.

Momma opened her pocketbook and retrieved the folded five one-hundred-dollar bills. "Before we get too emotional and maybe end up saying some things that would be better left unsaid that we will regret all our lives…" She stopped talking and just laid the money down on the desk before Betty.

She looked up at Momma with a shocked look on her face.

She slowly picked up the money and counted the bills. "Five hundred dollars!" she almost shouted in utter disbelief. She turned to her husband and showed him the hundred-dollar bills.

"Yup, they are hundred-dollar bills." He winked at me. "I recall a feller once showed me one of them. Seems like it was a long, long time ago." He smiled.

"You are insufferable sometimes," she said to him.

"And no, I didn't rob a bank, and no one in our family did anything illegal," Momma said, as she wanted to beat them to the punch. It seemed to be the most logical next question.

This caused all of us to break out laughing, which was good, because it took away much of the tension that had been built up in the room.

"Seriously, Lou, how did you come by this money?" Betty asked.

"Earl earned the money plowing at night."

"I hear that is very dangerous work," she said.

"That's not the half of it," I interjected. "If you heard the story he told our family…it still gives me the creeps to think about it, rattlesnakes and all."

Mr. Tetson hurriedly got out of his chair and moved over to the desk. He pulled out a large ledger that the store used to keep its bookkeeping records. He laid it on the desk and opened it to the proper section where the Lou Crandal charges were listed. He scanned it, and his eyes saw a line drawn across. He motioned for me to come near. "Jessie, why don't you come and help me read this small print that tells me what your family owes."

I moved to his side and started to read the figure, 501.75, but he interrupted me. "Doesn't it say 450.15?" He looked at me with his eyes, telling me to agree with what figure he had just quoted.

I hoped he was able to see the smile that burst forth from my heart so that he could see how wonderful I thought he was. "Yes, that is correct," I lied.

"You mean we get something back?" Momma asked. She was greatly surprised. "Let's just leave it so we have credit." She looked directly at Betty. They both enjoyed a smile for a change, and we all laughed.

"Jess, why don't you and Mr. Tetson leave Betty and me alone for a few minutes? It will give us some time to catch up on a few things we have been missing." "Jessie, make sure he gives you some coconut," Mrs. Tetson said as she gave her husband carte blanche to treat me.

I don't know what all was said when I left the room. I do know that Momma and Betty embraced as she left. This time it was genuine and possessed warmth, which made my heart glad.

RANNY GRADY

As walked home, I felt on top of the world. Momma started crying softly.

"Momma, why are you crying? We kept walking, and she didn't answer. "I thought everything went better than expected."

"There's no need to cry over spilled milk." She sighed through her tears. "But once the milk is spoiled, it's never sweet again."

As we continued to walk in silence, I knew she was referring to Betty Tetson's and her friendship. It was a lot better since the events of today, but it would never be like it was.

Foreign Language Lessons

Glorious summer arrived at the end of my junior year. Momma came home from tending her patients, and she called me to the kitchen.

"Jessie, come here. I've got some good news for you."

"I don't have to work for Old Lady Stinson anymore?" I asked as I came in the house.

Momma frowned. "Don't be disrespectful. I think I got you a better job."

"What is it?" *Anything would be better than that old battle-ax,* I thought. *She is such an ingrate, I can't please her. Serve her right if she had to rely on someone not as good as me.*

"None other than Dr. Jones." Her eyes opened wide.

"Really!"

"Really! I happened to meet him on the street, and we were visiting. He mentioned he needed a girl to clean his office. His wife has someone for the home, but it has been a while since the last girl up and left. The office needs the 'touch of a woman' is how he said it." She stared for a second then smiled.

"How much does it pay?"

"He said he was willing to pay twenty cents."

"Twenty cents! Oh, Momma, when can I start?"

Laughingly, Momma said, "Jessie, you don't have the job yet. You go for an interview first."

I didn't sleep well that night. My imagination ran wild.

"Oh, you work for Dr. Jones, lucky you. I'll bet he is a great boss to work for."

"So, you work for Dr. Jones. I'll bet that is interesting work."

My mind was full of silly thoughts. I was caught up in my own self-importance, yet I heard Momma say in the back of my mind, *"Pride goeth before destruction and a haughty spirit before a fall... ' Proverbs* 16:18."

"What should I wear to the interview?"

Momma put her fingers to her chin. "Let's see, hmm Will you be doing any dancing?" She gave me an impish look. "Probably not. Will you be serving tea for important guests and dignitaries? Fat chance!" She giggled. "Since you won't be required to be 'fancied up'"—Momma gave me a dead-pan look—"you might struggle along with one of your old, stylish feed-sack dresses."

"Oh, Momma, you do beat all; can't a girl care about how she looks?"

"I'm concerned you may forget you're going to the doctor's office to be a 'charwoman,' not a debutante or his nurse," she said, raising her eyebrows. "If you don't present yourself in the proper light, the good doctor may decide you need lessons in a foreign language," she added coyly.

"I know a little Latin but not much else."

Momma's eyes showed shock. She clasped her hands and lifted them toward the heavens. "Thank you, sweet Jesus. Not that kind of foreign language lessons, you nilly."

I looked at her in a puzzled way.

"Foreign language," she emphasized. "'Roman' hands and 'Russian' fingers." She danced her fingers up and down her torso.

"Momma!" I said. "He's a married man."

"He's a man," she replied.

"Well, I never..."

"Your old momma's been around the barn a few times, and I'm very familiar with the old adage 'When spring comes a young man's heart turns to love' may be true; however, he often has other things on his mind, like getting to 'know' you in a biblical way."

"If I get the job, I'll only be concentrating on cleaning his office."

"I'm not overly concerned about what you concentrate on...It's his line of concentration I'm a bit concerned over." Momma lowered her eyes. "Forewarned is forearmed."

I wore a plain dress. However, I did put a bright green bow in my hair. Momma said the green gave my eyes and hair a shine.

"Arrive early; it makes a good impression," Momma taught.

My interview was for three p.m. I arrived ten minutes early.

When I entered the office, I presented myself to the lady in his reception room.

"Hi, I'm Jessie Crandal. Dr. Jones is expecting me."

She was busy with paperwork and didn't respond for a few seconds. She wore a white nurse's dress, and her brown hair was in a bun. Her thin, elongated face gave her a cool demeanor. She wore a little pink lipstick. When she stood, she was dainty, nearly doll-like.

"Doctor Jones is busy; you'll have to wait." She slowly looked me up and down; then she motioned for me to take a seat.

Her sizing me up and down made me feel uncomfortable.

The room was empty. While waiting, I dozed off a couple of times, which I didn't want to do.

"The doctor will see you now." She led me down a narrow corridor. We passed a couple of operatories and turned into the last room on the right. The room was large and had beautiful wood paneling. Book cases filled two sides of the room, one directly behind a large desk, where the doctor was sitting. It nearly touched the ceiling. Both cases were filled with books.

Gee, I wonder if he has read all of those books, I thought.

"Yeah, I've read most of them," he said, and he smiled at me.

I was embarrassed, and it showed. *Is he clairvoyant?*

"I get that question all the time," he said and waved his left arm around to the bookcases.

"Dr. Jones, your job interview...ee is here," his nurse said.

"Thank you, Sally; that will be all."

I took a seat in one of the two beautiful deep tan-colored leather chairs that sat in front of his desk. The chairs had bright brass rivets that the upholsterer had used to frame them. His chair was larger and had a high back. It matched the two sitting in front of his desk. I guessed that his desk was mahogany.

Very impressive! Just what a man of substance should have, I thought.

Doctor Hubert D. Jones was a man in his midthirties. Momma told me that he had come to Tampa after graduating from some school back East, Yale, if I recall it right. He was about five feet nine or ten. He had wide shoulders and a dark complexion, and his hair was nearly coal-black and a bit wavy. I had heard the ladies talk about his deep blue eyes and how good looking he was. They were right. He wore a long-sleeved white shirt with a tab collar and a maroon tie, which he had pulled slightly loose, giving him a casual appearance. His shirtsleeves were turned up. His hairy, muscular forearms were exposed.

From yanking all those teeth, I thought.

That thought nearly caused me to laugh as I recalled Charlie saying, *It doesn't make any sense; why does a dentist want to go and pull a person's* wisdom *teeth? If the poor guy is dumber than a box of rocks, why take what little wisdom he has?*

"So, Jessie, Mrs. Stinson tells me you are a hard worker ... and your momma said the same."

I was shocked. I couldn't believe Mrs. Stinson would pay me a compliment.

I smiled at him nervously. "Momma calls it 'charwoman.'"

He laughed. "Your Momma doesn't mince any words, does she?"

"She can skin the hide off a cat like nobody's business," I blurted, and we both laughed.

"I know you haven't had time to look around the office, but it needs a woman's touch." He looked at me and smiled. "In your case ... a girl's touch." I blushed. "It's a pretty straightforward job. I need this office cleaned each week. I take a break on Wednesdays after two; therefore, I'd need you then."

"Since you already asked Mrs. Stinson—"

"Oh, I didn't ask her about you. Sometime back, she and I

were at a social function and your name came up. She sang your praises."

My mouth dropped open.

"Does that surprise you?" He laughed. "Surprised me too, knowing her reputation. If she sang your praises, and Lou Crandal adds her recommendation, I'd be a fool not to hire that person...right?" He glanced at me and smiled.

I sat there blushing and smiling.

"By the way, I like your ribbon." He motioned to my green ribbon. "It makes your eyes sparkle. Sally, will you come here a moment?" Dr. Jones asked.

Sally appeared in just a few seconds. She poked her head in the door and looked at her boss.

"Jessie, we have a uniform you will need to wear when you are working. There might be a time or two when you are here that there may still be a patient in the chair. Do you mind wearing a uniform?"

"No, no, that will be just fine. What does it look like?"

"A charwoman worrying about what she looks like?" he teased.

"I, I didn't mean it—"

"It is just like the one Sally's wearing. It gives the place a professional look," he said, waving his hand toward Sally. "Plus, there may be a time or two when I may need you to clean up in the operatories while a patient is still here. I want my girls to look alike."

She crooked her finger at me, indicating that I follow her. She took me to the supply room and handed me an ironed and starched white uniform.

"You can change in there," she said as she opened the door to a small closet-like room and pulled the light on for me. "Let me know when you are ready."

I quickly removed the drab dress I had worn and slipped into the uniform. It was a little shorter than most of the dresses I wore. The cut flared some, and it had a belt that cinched up the waist. When I put it on, I noticed that it greatly accentuated my bust line. I looked into the mirror, which was conveniently placed on the wall. I gasped. The girl staring back at me startled me, because she looked more like a woman than a teenage girl. The uniform did things to my frame that no other dress had ever done, including the dresses Sammy had me wear when I visited him in Chicago. It made me look much older; it made me feel different inside. It was a wonderful feeling!

I stepped out of the room, and when Sally saw me, I could tell she saw what I had just seen. I detected anger in her eyes. She took a few seconds and sized me up. I felt very uncomfortable under her gaze.

She led me back to the doctor's office. She stopped at its entrance and slightly pushed me forward.

"Here she is," she announced.

Doctor Jones was busy with some paperwork. He only glanced at me for a second or two. "She'll do fine, Sally," he said and quickly returned to his paperwork.

Sally motioned for me to leave the room.

"Twenty cents an hour sound right to you?" he asked without looking up.

I stopped and looked at him. "Yes…twenty cents will do just fine." I hurried to catch up with Sally.

Sally told me I needed to come at three o'clock each Wednesday. It would take three or four hours to do the job. She showed me where the cleaning supplies were stored.

"When you come to work, the first thing you do is change into one of our uniforms."

I nodded.

"One more thing; Dr. Jones doesn't want anyone to know you'll be wearing a nurse's uniform."

"But I—"

"Not even your momma," she added. "People might not understand the doctor's penchant for professionalism."

I put my finger up to my lips. "Mum's the word; not a word to my mum" I said, and we both laughed.

My feet fairly flew home. I was sure I had just found a way to step onto that magical cloud that mystically leads a girl to a kingdom where she is metamorphosed into a beautiful woman, where many suitors came to joust for her hand in marriage.

"So are you a high-priced charwoman?" Momma teased.

I did a slow bow, like a ballerina might do. "Thank you very much. Twenty cents an hour!" I squealed.

Momma gave me a big bear hug. "The lass has done herself proud," she whispered in my ear. "How was Sally?"

I thought it odd she would ask me that question. I looked at her with surprise. "A bit prickly, if you ask me."

"That's what I've been told. How was Dr. Jones?" she asked, using a different tone.

"He was very nice."

"That's just the way I want him to be, nice...but not too nice."

"Momma! You do carry on so. I hope people don't think ugly things about you."

"Jessie, when it comes to men, as the Good Book says, 'There are a lot of wolves running around in sheep's clothing'; and the good Lord meant that to apply to people running around pretending to be Christians; but I'm quite sure the practical application can be made to men and women or, in your case, girls."

"As if a grown married man would have any interest in a little-bit-of-nothing like me."

"Sad to say, girl, but you're more than that now." Momma sighed. "You listen to me, Jessie; when you work in that doctor's office, you keep your distance. You hear me?"

I sighed. "Yes, Momma."

I was vigil about the doctor and myself and soon discovered that Momma was worrying about something silly. Doctor Jones remained very distant emotionally and exceptionally professional in the way he spoke to me. If I had any reason in my mind to sound an alarm, I was soon convinced it was unfounded.

A month after I started working for Dr. Jones, I came to work, slipped into the uniform, grabbed my cleaning supplies, and got busy. After a few minutes, I was busy working and humming a song, "In the Garden," when the room's atmosphere changed. I had felt that same feeling before when I was caught off guard doing something silly and not aware that anyone was watching. I felt the presence of someone behind me.

"Jessie, Sally isn't here today, and I will need you to help me in the back with a patient," Dr. Jones said.

His voice startled me, and I must have shown it.

"Sally had to visit her sick mother over in Marion."

I stood up, straightened my uniform, adjusted the ribbon in my hair, and smiled at him. "Just show me what you want me to do."

The assisting job really consisted of nothing more than handing him some gauze and a few funny-looking instruments. We were done in a few minutes.

"You did a good job," he said. "A regular Florence Nightingale." He smiled at me.

"When a person gives you a compliment, don't slobber all over yourself and try and deflect it or, worse yet, hand them a compliment back; accept it and thank them," I heard Momma's voice in my ear.

"Thank you." *Momma would be proud,* I thought.

Dr. Jones walked over to a large cabinet, about chest high, which had many drawers that were about four inches deep. He pulled out a couple of the drawers.

"Come over here, Jessie."

I stepped over next to him. I was amazed to see all of the funny-looking instruments.

"I want you to spend some time cleaning these," he said, and he reached in and retrieved one of them. He handed it to me, and when he did, I felt the back of his hand rub against my right breast.

I was positive it was an accident when he quickly pulled his hand away. He looked at me, and we both shared a sense of embarrassment.

"Well, you can clean these," he said, and he left the room.

I thought about telling Momma about the incident but decided against it. *It wasn't anything he planned,* I convinced myself.

The week after our big Fourth of July celebration, I went to work. I did my usual routine and was busy cleaning. I looked for Sally when I came in, and she wasn't in the front office. I didn't think a thing about her absence because sometimes she was in the back assisting the doctor.

"Jessie," I heard the doctor call me.

I put down what I was doing and went to his office. He was busy with bookkeeping. As I stepped into the room, he put up his hand with one finger up in the air. "Just give me a minute … Jessie, I have some errands … oh, by the way, Sally's gone to visit her mother again; I want you to spend time cleaning up my office first thing."

I slid my hand over the top of a credenza, and it left a dust mark. I held up my hand. "It sure could use a good cleaning." I smiled.

"That's what Gloria said the last time she was in my office," he said, referencing his wife. "I don't know how long I will be gone, but you can have the office."

"You will be able to eat off the floor," I promised him as he started to leave. "Do we have a stepladder?" I knew it would take one for me to clean the book cases.

"There should be one in the work closet," he replied as he walked out the door.

I went to the work closet and found the ladder. I soon had it up and was busy cleaning. After cleaning much of the lower areas of the office, I took the ladder and adjusted it so I could climb up and find a way to dust and clean the top of the book case. In order to accomplish this task, I had to climb up about halfway on the ladder. I discovered, rather quickly, that when you first start climbing off the ground, your body receives some type of message about potential danger, and you have to adjust your sense of balance. I was busy doing those things so I could concentrate on getting the cleaning finished before my boss came back and needed to use his office.

"Cleaning a house makes a woman feel like she has accomplished

something worthwhile," Momma had told me more than once. *"Taking care of your children and your husband's needs, it gives a gal a warm fuzzy."*

As I was busy cleaning, I was reflective. I felt so good that I started humming some different hymns, and once in a while I would break out into a song, singing the words softly. It may have been my singing that kept me from being vigilant.

Suddenly, I felt the touch of a hand up under the hem of my dress. At first, it felt like a piece of ice had been placed on my inner thigh; then the feeling turned hot. I looked down in shock, and I was filled with fright. It was Dr. Jones. He sneaked his hand up under my dress, and his hand was sliding upward between my thighs. I squeezed his hand tightly between my thighs, so he couldn't move his hand. Suddenly I felt his other hand on my rear, and he was doing his best to pull down my panties.

"Dr. Jones!" I screamed. I decided that I would try to take a step up and force him away from me. When I did, the sudden jerking of my body against the ladder caused it to teeter and lose its support. He was against the ladder with part of his body. The awkward position of his hands and arms forced him to lose balance. The ladder tilted and started falling away from our two falling bodies. He grabbed at me, and I did my best to fight him away from me. Somehow, through all of the pushing and pulling of the ladder, our two bodies were suspended in midair for a second. Because we lost our balance, it made us fall crashing upon the large desk. I fell on top of him.

I was dazed and frightened to the point that I couldn't speak. I recognized that I needed to do my best to escape. I pushed down on his chest and struggled to get free. He reached up and roughly grabbed me by my hair and pulled. I screamed loudly from the pain. I was instantly on the bottom, and he was now on top of me. His brute strength made it easy for him to roll me over.

He pinned me to the desktop while he unbuttoned his shirt collar and pulled off his tie and threw it.

"Jessie, baby, it's time to come to the doctor." He laughed, but it sounded more like a howl to me.

He tore my uniform top open. He tried to kiss me, but I kept shaking my head violently.

As frightened as I was, I kept telling myself to keep calm. "No! Don't do this!" I screamed.

"You little tease. It won't be long before you can have what you've been wanting," he said in a guttural voice.

It seems impossible that the mind can shift focus from a violent sexual assault scene and suddenly be in a car riding with Momma.

Jessie, if some boy gets fresh and is manhandling you, if it's possible, kick him in his privates, and run like Lot fleeing Sodom.

"Please, don't!" I pleaded over and over again.

My pleading seemed to arouse him more, and he started laughing.

"No! Don't! Please…I…I've never…"

My confession inflamed his lust even more.

He leaned back again to gaze at me. When he leaned back, he lessened the force of his hand on me, which he had used to pin me to the top of the desk. I raised my head up and moved closer to the hand he was using to keep me pinned down with.

"I'll bite you!" I screamed as I did my best to bite him so he would lose his grip on me. My threat angered him.

As he leaned back more, I raised up as far as I could. This gave me a bit of leverage, and I lifted up my legs and used my knees to bump him forward. When his body started falling toward me, I sat up as much as I could and then placed my hands upon his chest and pushed as hard as I could to force him backwards. He lost his balance and let go of me as he grabbed the edge of the desk. I knew I had one chance, and I took it; I slammed my fists into his groin area.

His eyes opened wide. His lustful eyes instantly showed pain.

"Ohh," he moaned.

His body became rigid. He raised up, and in that instant I managed to push him off and roll out from under him.

"You animal!" I wanted to attack him and pummel him until he was a bloody mess.

He lay on the top of the desk and rolled over on his side. He had his hands and arms inside his thighs. He moaned from pain.

"Why?" I screamed. "I'm going to tell…and my brother is going to kill you," I shouted.

"Jessie! Stop! Don't go!" he yelled. He tried to get up, and he couldn't. "I'm going to be sick."

"I hope you die!"

I started to run out the door, but I realized that I was half undressed. I ran awkwardly up the narrow hallway. I kept bumping into one side of the wall then the other.

"Come back here!" he shouted. "Jessie, don't go. We can talk about this!"

I opened the supply room door and snatched my dress. I clutched it to me and ran. Just as I was closing the back door, I glanced over my shoulder; Doctor Jones had climbed off his desk and was standing in the hallway; his trousers were down around his shoes, and his underwear was showing.

"You wanted it as much as I did!" he yelled. "No one will believe you!"

I ran as fast as I could. There was a clump of trees a hundred feet behind his office. I ran and ran until I reached the trees then slumped down on the ground and began sobbing uncontrollably. I felt dirty from the inside out. I couldn't stop feeling his warm hands on my body, and it made me want to puke.

I'm not sure how long I lay there crying, but after some time, I took inventory of myself. I saw that my breasts were exposed, and the uniform was torn wide open. I looked around to see if anyone had seen me come into the trees. It was near our park, so other people could have easily seen me. I heaved a huge sigh of relief, as I was pretty certain no one had. I struggled to put my own dress over the torn uniform but managed to do it. I took a few steps toward home—slow ones—then I ran as fast as I could. I never stopped until I reached my front porch.

I stood outside for a few minutes, praying and hoping that none of our family would show up while I allowed my breathing to become more normal. I quietly opened the screen door and quickly went to my bedroom.

RANNY GRADY

Luck would have it, Momma had some clean water in the washbasin she kept by her bed. I slipped out of my clothes and took a washcloth and washed myself. I saw myself in the mirror, and I started to cry. My face was red, rash-like from his whiskers. My breasts had red welts, and my left one had tiny teeth marks. They seemed swollen to me. Just above my navel was a red mark, evidently put there when he ripped the uniform front open. There was a bruise mark just below my panty line, probably given to me when he ripped them off me. I had red marks and bruises on my thighs. I had a welt, red marks, and a large bruise just between my thighs from when I locked his hand between my thighs so he couldn't move his hand around on my body. I took my time and washed each area five times or more; nothing made me feel clean.

"I'll never feel clean again," I moaned as I lay on the bed.

I wanted Momma to come home, but I didn't want Momma to come home. I kept vacillating between what my heart's needs were and what my mind thought I could handle. I crawled up into bed and pulled the sheet over my bruised and beaten body. I fell asleep.

"Where's Jessie?" I heard my Momma's voice.

I heard some sort of communication but was unable to understand what was being said or who was talking.

Suddenly the bedroom door opened. Momma was in the room.

"What's the matter, honey?"

I didn't respond.

"Oh, you got your friend," she added, in reference to my period.

I still didn't respond. *How do I tell her?* I kept thinking as she stood over the bed.

Momma bent down, and she looked at my face. She saw the red rash from the doctor's whiskers. "Jessie, honey, what has happened to you?"

I had taken off my clothes and crawled into the bed naked. I slowly pulled the sheet down and exposed my body.

I heard Momma gasp, and she turned her head away, as

if somehow when she turned back around what she had seen would be have disappeared like a mirage.

"Good God almighty, who did this to you?" She bent down and sat on the edge of the bed and reached out her hand and gently touched my face.

Tears streamed down my face. I reached out and grabbed her hand and held on tightly, as if it were a life ring of some sort. I looked up at her, and I moaned loudly.

"He …" I tried to say his name.

"Dr. Jones! It was him, wasn't it?"

I began sobbing. "It … It was awful," I cried.

"How did it …? Never mind." She drew close to me and began to stroke my hair. She pulled the sheet all the way off my body and looked at it. "He's an animal! Did he … you know …?"

I shook my head. "No. Not because he didn't try," I whimpered.

"Thank you, Jesus," Momma said, and tears came flowing out of her eyes.

"That's what I said." In the midst of horror, humor helped. We both realized what I had said and smiled at each other.

"Good for you," Momma whispered. "Jessie, baby, Momma has to leave for just a minute or so and then I will be right back." She lifted the sheet back up over my naked body.

In a few minutes she came back. She had heated some water, and she had some soap and a fresh, clean washcloth.

"I already tried that, five times!"

"Then this will be the sixth," she whispered.

"Nothing helps; I'll never be clean again." I broke into sobs.

"Shh, shh, Momma will make it better." She pulled the sheet down, and she began to gingerly wash my bruised body. The warmth of the cloth against my skin made me feel better.

Over the course of the next hour, Momma soothed my physical ailments, and she provided a measure of healing balm to my badly confused soul. When she finished bathing a portion of my body, she would kiss two fingers on her right hand and softly place them upon the injured area. Momma winced when she came to the areas that were more injured. When she finished an area, she pulled the sheet down farther; then she repeated this wonderful exercise of a momma loving her daughter under the most trying of times.

After she bathed me, she brought me some hot stew. She sat on the bed and fed me physically and, more importantly, spiritually.

"Jessie, this isn't going to be better in the morning." Her lips pressed together. "In time, with God's help, you will learn to live past this, but it isn't going to be easy."

"I...I know it," I said tearfully.

"It will be hard to get sleep tonight, but do the best you can. We'll wait until the morning to figure out how we are going to handle this." She kissed my forehead and turned out the lamp.

Mercifully, I slept some that night.

Momma didn't go to work the next morning. She took care of our household needs before she came into our bedroom. She arranged for the girls to have the small kids out of the house. No one was there but Momma and me.

"Does anyone know?"

"I have chosen not to say anything. Jessie, I probably haven't slept any more than you have. I've been up half the night praying, reading the Bible, and seeking his counsel."

"Why did God let that happen to me?"

"Honey, it never changes; when bad things happen to good people, it's because of sin," Momma said. "Don't ever get so confused that you buy into that old biblical 'saw' that God causes sin. He hates sin! That's why he sacrificed His only Son." She drew near. "He isn't some god that treats us like we are mechanical beings that he pushes and pulls. He gives each human being free will. Dr. Jones had a choice; he chose to do evil."

"But if he is so powerful and controls the universe, why doesn't he prevent evil things?"

"Boy! If we could only be God for a day, we'd really fix things right," she said and put her hand on my shoulder and gently caressed it. "Malachi tells me some of those questions are part of the deep theological mysteries of God." She softly brushed my hair with her hand.

"Sounds a bit too deep for my pea-sized brain," I said, and Momma smiled.

"Honey, your old momma will give it her best shot to help you make some sense of this evil that has been visited upon you, which our loving God did not cause. Jessie, I think our relationship with our Creator, and our constant battle with his fallen angel, Satan, comes down to our truthful perceptions of the God we are going to serve. If a god claimed to be the only true and living God, and it was said this god was the most powerful one, how could that god prove he was the only god worth worshipping?"

"I don't know."

"Put your spiritual thinking cap on."

"I suppose, if he didn't have to exercise his powers to have people love him, he could prove his power."

"There! I knew my lass was brilliant. Can you think of another way?"

"He could also prove it if he were willing to give up his life for mine."

"Does that remind you of anyone you know?" She smiled and winked at me. "All the other gods that this world worships do not meet those two requirements. It's a lot like the neighborhood bully; if he has to resort to threats, intimidation, and physical harm to prove how powerful is he, and this type of power loses one iota of its ability to control the kids in the neighborhood, the kingdom in place falls to the ground in shambles, right?"

"Quick as a wink."

"What if the power in the neighborhood has this power and control because the kids wish to follow that leader out of love, devotion, and respect? Will this power become weakened?"

"Probably never!"

"Jesus Christ is just this type of God. He shed his blood and gave his life up for you. He is the only God who truly possesses power because his subjects choose to serve him. He grants all of his creatures the gift of a free will. Regardless of who you are or where you are, at any point and time in your lifetime, you can choose to serve or reject him."

"And this then applies to evil and good that coexists in our world? So our God believes that it is more important for mankind to have the gift of free will than for Him to control man's evil choices?"

"If we only served our God because he uses a club on us when we refuse to acknowledge him and to follow his wishes, how weak a God would that make him?"

"And we know that God hates sin; but he loves us and our free will more than controlling the evil that men do?"

"That's right, Jessie. Don't ever confuse the idea that if one has control, it automatically means causation. Well, that's certainly enough of Malachi's deep thinking," she said, and we both laughed. "Are you feeling up to doing some talking about all this? Perhaps maybe we can do some 'tegious' thinking?"

I smiled when Momma used the word "tegious." It was one of her favorite terms to demonstrate that she was doing some heavy thinking. "Not really, but I know it has to be done."

"Now, Jessie, some of the things I need to say will probably upset you; the good Lord knows they have already upset me just having to think about them. Nevertheless, we don't have any choice."

"I just want to run away."

Momma bent down and kissed my forehead. "Me too." She sighed. "We have to be realistic about this; do you agree?"

I nodded.

"If we go to the sheriff and tell him what happened, and we ask him to arrest Dr. Jones for sexual assault, but not rape, since he didn't actually put his—"

"No! Oh no…Momma." I burned with anger and embarrassment.

"After he listens to your story, he is going to ask you a lot of questions, very personal questions. Do you understand?" Her lips pursed and trembled.

Tears welled up in my eyes.

"It stinks!" Momma said. "But like it or not, we must recognize this is a man's world; therefore, in anything like this, Dr. Jones is going to be given the benefit of the doubt."

"But he tried to rape me!"

"Truth is often treated as fiction," Momma said. "Our whole society's mores have been constructed around the 'fallen woman' cliché. If a man is the sexual aggressor, then a scarlet woman, even if she is a high school girl in pigtails, enticed him beyond what he could control."

"So any man can use me or any other woman and get by with it?"

"That uniform...What were you thinking?"

"He wanted me to wear it when I worked in the office!" I yelled.

"Oh, baby, don't get me wrong, I'm not blaming you. I'm just doing the best I can to help you understand the predicament we are in."

"I'm sorry...I know it."

"After the dog has finished chasing his tail, I believe the sheriff will choose to side with the rich and powerful and let the poor and weak suffer. And, in case you missed it, that's us."

I started crying. I pulled my pillow out from under my head and held it in front of me. Then I started striking it, just a soft jab as first. In a few seconds, rage had consumed me, and I was pummeling it with both fists. I was screaming and crying uncontrollably.

Momma just stood there silently as I let the pain and degradation come out in a fury of violence. It was the kind of punishment I wished I had the opportunity to give Dr. Jones.

After a while, I was physically spent, and all I could do was moan and weep. Momma picked up the pillow and tossed it on the floor. She walked over to it and kicked it in the air.

"Now we both feel better."

I looked up at her; she smiled at me. I attempted to laugh between my tears.

"I'm not going to make your decision. If you want to file a complaint, we will."

"No, as bad as I hate to admit it, you're right," I said softly. "Everybody will paint me as the vamp, a little 'tease'; I'd die thinking people would see me like that." I looked at Momma and screamed, "I want revenge … someway … somehow … someday!"

"I have a plan," Momma said. "But it will take a great deal of courage on your part."

"If it makes him pay, I'll do anything,"

"I believe God gave me this plan. I couldn't sleep last night, so I got out my Bible and opened it. I find that it helps me to sleep better than any type of medicine. When I opened it, it opened to the book of Genesis, chapter fourteen. When I started reading it, I was sure the Lord's hand was in this plan."

Leave it to Momma to find a way to weave God's Word into every situation, I thought.

"The scriptures tell a story that is very appropriate to our dilemma. If we do things just so, I'm convinced, Jessie, that we will feel a whole lot better about this terrible incident. Do you want to hear the story and the plan?"

"Oh, if it'll get him good!"

"Okay, it goes like this.

"Jacob's daughter, Dinah, went walking in the fields, and a young man named Shechem sexually assaulted her; the idea of a man sexually forcing himself upon a girl, and especially one mistaken for a slave or field maid, was considered fair game to any man of means and wealth, which Shechem certainly was. After his selfish pleasure, something happened: he fell madly in love with Dinah. Hamor, his father, was a Hivite and the ruler of that area. Shechem pleaded for his father to strike a deal for him to marry Dinah. Hamor wanted to please his son, who was his heir. He went to visit Jacob to see if he could convince Jacob to allow his son to marry Dinah and to seal a marriage arrangement. He offered Jacob anything he wanted as a dowry for his daughter.

"When Jacob told his sons what Shechem had done to their sister, they wanted to punish Shechem. Instead of a marriage arrangement, they wanted to seek 'an eye for an eye, a tooth for a tooth' retribution. They wanted to avenge her honor and to kill all of Hamor's clan. Jacob was more inclined not to seek revenge but to arrange a marriage that God would find pleasing.

"Shechem was a pagan, and Dinah was an Israelite. Jacob agreed to the marriage, with one condition: all of Hamor's men had to be circumcised to fulfill the Jewish law. Hamor thought this demand was onerous but reasonable. He agreed. All of the males, regardless of age, had their foreskins cut off."

"Oh, wouldn't that be great! I'd take a big knife and—" I stopped in midsentence, Momma smiled at me, and we both shared a giggle.

Momma stopped laughing. "Circumcision can be done in a number of ways.

"On the third day, when all of the males were weak and in so much pain they could do nothing but rest, Dinah's brothers carried out a sneak attack and struck down all of Hamor's men. They burned their tents, enslaved their women and children, and looted their wealth.

"When Jacob found out what his sons had done, he was very angry because they had caused him to dishonor the oath he had given to Hamor. Jacob and his clan were few in number, and now he feared retribution. When he asked them why they did it, they asked, 'Should he have treated our sister like a prostitute'?"

"If Earl found out, he'd kill Dr. Jones," I whispered.

Momma nodded. "That's what I'm afraid of. Doctor Jones would be dead. But so would Earl." Momma took her hands to show Earl would be hung.

"Your best type of revenge will be one that forces Dr. Jones to pay you more for cleaning. I'm talking about cleaning at his home, with his lovely wife, not at the office," she coyly said.

"How is that possible? I-I don't have to see him again, do I?"

"That's the part where I asked you to be courageous. If we are going to extract a measure of revenge, you're going to have to face him. Don't worry, he's a coward, and you will frighten him to death.

"I will pay a visit to Dr. Jones and arrange for us to call on them at their home in the early evening."

412

"What if he refuses?"

"That is the least of my worries. We'll show the good doctor we can perform our own circumcision ... on his wallet." Her face shone gleefully.

While I have lived nearly a century, and I have never really found a reason to be overjoyed about having the "curse," I was thankful it could be used as an excuse for not partaking of the normal activities of our family. Momma let everyone know I was having a particularly difficult period. They were willing to baby me and give me much-needed space.

Momma arranged for our visit to take place at the end of the week on Thursday evening. We took pains to dress in our finest and did our best to look our best.

The early July sunset was an incredible orange hue, and it seemed extra close to the ground.

"I'm so nervous; I pray I don't wet my pants," I confided to Momma as we approached the house.

"You're not in Mrs. Babcock's classroom now," she teased me, "but you still have to hold it," and we both laughed.

The Jones Mansion, as it was known, was a huge, three-story home with turrets and a wraparound porch. It had intricate fretwork. It was a pale yellow, and it had white trim and black window shutters. It was summer, and Gloria, his wife, had the window boxes filled with an assortment of flowers. It deserved to be known as the most beautiful house in Tampa.

"Momma! I want to turn around and just run."

Momma reached out and grabbed my hand; she squeezed it and then turned and gave me a hug.

"Thanks, I needed that," I said and smiled at her.

"You let me do all the talking. Don't say a word unless you are directly addressed, okay?"

We stepped up to the door and knocked three times. In a few seconds, Gloria Jones opened the door.

When the good Lord sat down and decided he was going to bless Adam with a wife, if he were in a good mood and wanted to give Adam a woman who would "ring his chimes" and make every other woman he created jealous, Gloria Jones was his model.

She was tall for a woman, slender, lithe in frame, but endowed with breasts, which she couldn't hide even if she had to wear my feed-sack dresses. She had blonde hair, which she wore long below her shoulders, and had a tan from the sun. People said that she had been a beauty queen and had even been a contestant for Miss America. I think it was the second Miss America Pageant held. She had a flawless, fine-featured face and wore bright red lipstick. She even possessed a Southern accent; I believe she was from Virginia.

"Lou and Jessie, come on in." She ushered us into her gorgeous home. Momma had been in her home before for some civic thing, and she told me that the Jones had furniture fashioned after the French Emperor Louis XIV. It was so beautiful and elegant, I was afraid to sit down.

For sure, the Depression hasn't depressed the Jones, I thought.

"I was so surprised when Hubbie …"

I almost laughed out loud when I heard her refer to Dr. Jones as "Hubbie."

"…told me that Lou and Jessie Crandal were going to pay us a visit." She smiled at us. "Oh, don't get me wrong; I was as pleased as punch. Hubbie, darling, our guests are here," she said, and her voice was just a bit louder than normal. "I don't want to forget my manners. May I get you a cup of tea or perhaps a blueberry scone?"

"I think a cup of tea would hit the spot," Momma said.

Gloria left the room, and as she went to the kitchen, she paused in its entrance.

"Our guests are here," she said with just a touch of impatience in her voice.

She came back and fixed tea and handed us each a scone on a china plate, which was gold trimmed. It looked as if it had been hand-painted. The scone was delicious.

She has everything a woman could wish for, and she can cook too, I thought; I could hear Momma's voice in my ear, "*It's a sin to covet; it's one of the Ten Commandments.*"

In a few minutes, Dr. Jones walked into the room. I noticed that he had swelling around the right side of his mouth, and it seemed puffy.

"Darling, please come and join us," Gloria said. "Did you see it?" She pointed to him. "He is so clumsy sometimes; I swear, I don't know if Hubbie's patients are safe with that man."

I must have hit him when I was fighting him off, I thought. I could feel my insides bubbling, churning, and wanting to turn over; my throat got a lump in it as if I might need to throw up. I felt as if my head were getting lighter. "*Breathe deeply,*" I could hear Momma's voice as she was instructing me on how to keep from hyperventilating when I was waiting to sing on "Chicken Bill's Amateur Show."

I reached out and gulped the last of my tea, hoping it would calm me. At first I didn't allow myself to look directly at him. I was positive that if I did, I'd start crying. In a few seconds, I gained my resolve, and I looked directly at him. I could feel the heat from my anger, which was stored up in me. It sent out rays from my eyes, which I hoped would sear his heart and soul. I was sure steam was about to flow out of them, and, possibly, it soon would come from my ears because my brain just couldn't manage all of the heat it had suddenly received.

Momma must have sensed my discomfort, as she reached over and patted my knee.

"I thought it best to have Jessie see just how much she was going to have to take care of," Momma said as she controlled the direction of the conversation.

Gloria looked startled. She looked at Momma; then she looked at her husband.

"What?" she said. "Hubbie, what's Lou saying?"

He sat there diverting his eyes from his wife but looking directly at Momma, because he had already turned away from my stare. I could tell that he was upset.

"Well, I didn't mean to spoil the surprise," Momma said and looked at him.

He cleared his throat and sat up a little straighter. "Why, yes. I, I meant to tell you—"

"He wants to spoil you some more," Momma said. She smiled at Gloria. "If that's possible." Gloria blushed and

Momma laughed. Dr. Jones joined them, but it was a half-hearted effort.

"He told Jessie that he wants her to help you take care of this big house; he will find someone else to clean his office." Momma glanced at him. "Isn't that what you told me the other day?" She looked at him and gave him a look that said, *This is only a tiny part of what you are going to pay.*

He wilted under her gaze.

"That's, that's right," he said. "Actually, I've been thinking about this for some time," he began to weave the lie. "This house just keeps you on the go all the time; when I saw what a great job Jessie did at my office,"—he got up out of his chair and walked over to Gloria and bent down and kissed her cheek—"I thought Jessie would be a big help to you and the kids." He turned and looked at us. "Consider it an early birthday gift." He touched Gloria's face lovingly, and he smiled sheepishly at Momma and me. He sat back down.

Gloria got up and walked over to his chair; she bent forward and kissed his forehead.

"I don't know what to say. I mean, that man has been singing Jessie's praises about what a great job she has been doing at the office." She turned and smiled at me; then she sat back down.

"Yes, Dr. Jones has told me too what a great job Jessie has done," Momma said as she stared at him.

"Then it's all settled. Can you come on Wednesdays? Perhaps you might be able to help a little more if we are entertaining?"

"Whatever pleases you," I said softly.

"And Jessie wants to thank you for her new job. She especially wants to thank Dr. Jones for insisting on paying her twenty-five cents an hour for her work."

Gloria turned and looked at him. "Mr. Moneybags there," she teased. "He is a generous man; he always finds a way to give something away." She chuckled.

I wanted to jump up and charge at him like a raging bull; I wanted to knock him down and stomp him until blood spewed forth from his guts. I wanted to scream "rapist" and tell Gloria how sorry I was for her. But I took Momma's cue to get up and leave.

As we were ushered out the door with inane small talk to cover our pain and his embarrassment, Momma said, "Dr. Jones, Jessie won't need to wear a nurse's uniform to clean for Gloria, will she?"

As the door was shut, we heard a loud voice say, "Uniform! Why would you require her to wear a uniform? Is there something going on that I don't know about? What was the real reason for their visit?" and with each question her voice grew louder.

As we walked home, mostly in silence, Momma put her arm around my waist and squeezed. "Circumcision completed," Momma said, softly.

I couldn't speak; tears filled my eyes. My heart was bursting with joy because Momma loved me so much.

Momma told me that horrible day would take a long time to fade down to a low roar in my reaction memory bank; she was so right. All of my Fourth of July celebrations would be tempered with a tinge of sadness for being forced to lose my naiveté about a woman's place in a man's world.

I worked in the Joneses' house until I graduated. Gloria was cordial, but we kept our distance. I enjoyed working for her.

Leo the Lion

Fresh out of high school, I took a job teaching in the local elementary school. Kansas didn't have any professional teachers' certification requirements. You did, however, have to pass a proficiency test, which the state gave to any applicant. This allowed the local school governors to know who was qualified; therefore, the elected officials were free to hire whomever they chose. Rose, Howard, Charlie, and Naomi had proven themselves to be very capable and competent teachers. Evidently, it was easy for the school board to hire another Crandal. I was eager to get my teaching career started, and I was excited to teach children to love to learn about the world they lived in. But before the year was halfway finished, I knew I wasn't cut out to be a teacher. At the time, I didn't really have a good explanation for my feelings and decision to seek work in a different area. However, after I was married and had children of my own, I realized that I just didn't have the desire to nursemaid children not of my own making.

"Jessie, honey, there's nothing inherently wrong with you for not wanting to teach any more," Momma said, doing her best to console me about my guilty feelings for not wanting to continue being a teacher. Though the pay was pitiful, being a teacher was just about the most prestigious job a woman could hope to have in those days.

"Since our family already has four teachers, I am convinced that it takes a special person to make teaching one's life's work. I figure it is almost like being a preacher, you know, receiving a call from the Father up above. Of course, it isn't that important but close to it."

I had resigned from teaching and had gone back to slinging hash at the restaurant where Momma used to work.

I was a waitress at a restaurant during my second year out of high school and the first year past my failed teaching experience. I enjoyed being a waitress better than teaching.

"Every dog has its day, and this isn't your day," Momma said when she saw me moping around the house that summer.

I spent too many days crying and feeling sorry for myself. When a body's heart is broken, it is very easy to allow one to wallow in a pity party because of unkind events. After three years of going steady with a boy in Durham, he had suddenly broken off our understanding and abruptly married a girl in his town. All who knew us had assumed that we would be married in due time. I was nursing a broken heart and failing at that worse than I did at teaching.

Try as I might, I just couldn't shake the crying fits I had nearly every day. I had an almost unceasing, needy desire to slip back into some mournful place. There, I allowed my heart more time to release new torrents of pain deep into my soul. This desire kept me at a point where my heart wanted to rebel if I didn't feed its apparent hunger for pain. Mercifully, day by day, I started to recover. Then I would see a boy who looked like him or hear some music that reminded me of him, and the heartache would come calling. It was as fresh as a gushing waterfall, and tears were everywhere once again.

In late June, I came home from the restaurant and was lying on the bed. Soon the tears swelled and flushed out of my eyes, which led to some muffled sobs.

Momma's hands were soft against my back, and she patted me gently. She had evidently heard me crying and quietly slipped into the bedroom.

"Jessie, isn't it wonderful that God made our hearts as a muscle? It can stretch and adjust to accommodate all of its heartache," she whispered.

Even though I was nineteen, her touch gave me a sense of comfort. I rolled over and quickly reached up and put my arms

RANNY GRADY

around her neck. She held me close and rocked me as I allowed myself to cry.

"Momma, why? It hurts so bad," I moaned. Between my eyes and my running nose, I was an emotional and physical mess. "Why did God let this happen to me?"

Momma helped me dry my eyes and take care of my running nose. "God didn't cause this to happen. Jack"—Momma mentioned his name out loud, and it caused me to moan—"had free will, and he chose to break your heart."

"But he told me he loved me!" I yelled.

In a soft, almost apologizing manner, she said, "Evidently he didn't. I know you don't want to hear it, but it's time you put away your sack cloth and ashes and get on with living."

Momma got up off the bed and started to head out the door. She paused and said, "It has been my experience that when God closes a door, if you peek around the corner, often a window is open and you can crawl in. Our Tampa Rebels are playing Herington this weekend. Why don't you fix yourself up and go have some fun?"

Small farm towns, outside their high school sports teams, have little to brag about. Maybe that was why town baseball teams were so popular in my day. During the summer, before and after harvest time, each town had its team. There was a "big-to-do" each weekend when the teams traveled to play or were the host team for a baseball game. Tampa had a reputation for having a great team, year in and year out. It certainly was a source of pride for our town. As with any type of team competition, for various and unexplainable reasons, some teams became more hated, usually because they were such fierce competitors. Herington was the one team we hated the most. Seldom did a game pass without some sort of rhubarb breaking out; someone usually got a bloody nose. I'm not totally convinced that our townsfolk didn't attend the games to see the fights as much as the game itself.

Against my heart's better judgment, I heeded Momma's advice and went with some girlfriends to the game. My mood was so somber and bleak; nevertheless, I decided to wear a white and green gingham dress. *Maybe to help my eyes to sparkle and cover up my tired, puffy eyes,* I thought.

When we arrived at the ballpark, we got a bag of popcorn and a Coke. We decided to sit in the stands along the first-base side of the field. The game hadn't started yet, and we girls were busy chatting. The Herington Railroaders were still on the field taking their infield practice before the game started.

Carolyn Fike, one of the girls who came to the game with me, suddenly nudged me. "Do you see what I see?"

"What?" I asked.

She pointed out to the first baseman. At that instant, the ball was hit to the shortstop, and he fielded the ball and threw it to the first baseman. The throw was very low. The first baseman did a split and gracefully scooped up the ball as it took one bounce into his glove.

My, how graceful he is, I thought.

Carolyn stood up and clapped, which embarrassed all of us girls. "What a catch!" she yelled, and the first baseman turned and looked our way. He put his glove on his hip and gave us a big grin, which had a sheepish look to it. He waved his glove and returned to his business.

"He is so good looking," Carolyn said.

He was tall, lanky, and tanned from the sun. He had black hair. It was easy to see that he was a good player.

"Some boys are just given a gift," Momma once told me when she was explaining why some boys were better athletes or better liked by the girls. "I can't tell you how many women used to come up to me when your brother Howard was playing basketball, and they would tell me how they thought he was so graceful that it was worth coming to the games just to see him run."

After the third inning, it was apparent that the first baseman was deliberately flirting with us girls. He would tip his hat in our direction when he took his position each time he took the field after Herington had their turn at batting.

"I think he is trying to spark you," Carolyn said to me.

"You're talking like a crazy woman." I scoffed. "You don't think he is, do you?" I blushed a little at her suggestion.

"All I know is that he keeps looking our way, and I'd swear he is looking right at you. If he does the same thing the next inning, give him a little encouragement. You know, a great big smile, toss your hair a bit."

"I will not! Do you want him to think I'm some shameless hussy?"

When he came out to his position again, he tipped his hat and looked our way. His eyes seemed to lock on mine, and it gave me a funny feeling; it was a very exciting feeling, one I hadn't felt for a long time.

Tampa was leading the game. It was a hard-fought, contested game into the top of the ninth inning. The leadoff hitter drew a walk, and the next batter reached base on a fielding error by the third baseman. The next batter was the first baseman. When he came up as the on-deck hitter, he took a few swings with his bat; then he looked directly at me.

"Lefty! Pete! Pay attention for God's sake!" I heard his manager holler. His smile quickly vanished, and he abruptly turned away from where we girls were sitting. He worked the count to two and two, and then he lashed out with a mighty swing, like poetry in motion. The swing was filled with a force none of the other players exemplified; a sense of grace that one just wouldn't normally associate with hitting a baseball. When his bat met the ball, the crack of the bat caused the spectators to ooh and aah. It was a towering shot that soon passed the centerfield fence and disappeared out of sight. Even the Tampa fans recognized that they had witnessed something special and broke out in a mix of applause, groans, and boos. He trotted around the bases gracefully. I recalled what Momma had said: *Some boys are just given a gift.* His home run was the difference in the game. As he crossed home plate, he tipped his hat and smiled at me.

"Sure as brown sugar makes the best candy, that boy is sweet on you," Carolyn said. I looked at her and grinned.

When the game ended, we made our way out of the ballpark. Suddenly, the first baseman was standing in front of me.

I was inside the fence that protected the crowd, and he was on the outside.

"What's your name, pretty lady?" he asked.

I felt flushed and more than a bit embarrassed by his sudden approach and brashness. "I'm ... Jessie is my name," I halfway stuttered, and I flashed him a smile.

"A part of the James gang?"

His trite statement was only one of a million I had fielded in my lifetime about my name being associated with the famous Jesse James gang of outlaws from Missouri and Kansas. My demeanor changed.

"Hey, I was just fooling with you," he said as he quickly recognized that I didn't care for his attempt at humor at my expense. "I guess that pretty red hair comes with the territory?"

I looked directly at him for a few seconds; then I smiled. "What's your name?"

"I'm Pete," he said, and he was cut off in midsentence as his teammates started hollering for him to run and catch up with the bus that was leaving. "Do you dance?" he yelled as he started running for the slow-moving bus.

I watched him jump aboard. He turned and looked at me.

"Yes!" I yelled back. "Especially if the guy is as handsome as you," I sort of mumbled to myself.

"I'll meet you at the dance ... Saturday night," he hollered and waved at me then stepped all the way into the bus.

Romantic gossip travels faster than a miner staking the first claim on a gold mine.

"So, I hear that an interesting beau jumped through your window." Momma slyly intimated that she already knew about the new man on the peripheral of my life.

"Who told you? Mercy sakes, nothing is private, is it?"

"When it comes to love and romance, Jessie girl, mark my words, nothing is sacred." She laughed and raised her eyebrow, suggesting that she even knew more than she let on.

"It isn't a big deal." I did my best to discount the importance of any gossip she might have received about Pete.

"What's the boy's name?"

"He's not a boy, Momma. He's a man."

"Okay, what's the man's name?"

"His name is Pete."

"Pete what?"

I looked up at her. "I...I don't know his name, other than Pete."

"Where's he from?" She kept acting like she was in charge of internal affairs for Scotland Yard.

"Momma, he has to be from Herington since that was the team we played."

"Herington, huh. I certainly hope he isn't one of those Grady boys," she added. "I hear they are a real bunch of hell-raisers. All those boys want to do is get drunk, fight, and chase wild women."

"Oh, Momma, you can be so melodramatic sometimes. I'm sure he isn't one of them." I did my best to reassure her that the graceful, handsome man I had just met couldn't be any part of a hell-raising family.

"So, you're going to the dance next weekend?" Momma teased.

"I was intending to go anyway."

"Of course, sure you were." She winked at me. "Isn't it amazing how a new man in a girl's life can bring about miraculous healing to a broken heart?" she whispered as she left the room. She started to sing, "I saw Pete and Jessie sitting in a tree, K-I-S-S-I-N-G. First came love; second came marriage; then I saw Jessie pushing a baby carriage." She laughed loudly.

I threw my shoe at her retreating backside; it missed. "For a woman in advanced middle age, you can act so childish!" I hollered after her.

Even without the advent of Pete coming to Tampa on Saturday night for the dance, our community was abuzz because the famous Salina Moonshine Band was going to be playing. They had built up a reputation and were in great demand. The only reason a band of such high caliber ever came to Tampa was because the leader was a classmate of our newspaper's editor. Every year or so, the editor could persuade the bandleader to favor our small town with their great music. When the band showed up, people came from miles and miles to dance to their music. It was impossible to go anywhere in our town that week without seeing some type of advertisement for the band and the dance.

As was our family's usual custom, we all attended the dance together.

"Only the sweet sounds of a pure gospel hymn could beat the mellow sound of the Salina Moonshine Band," Momma said whenever they played in Tampa.

When my sisters and I were young, we stooped low enough to dance with our brothers, especially Howard. We seldom danced with Charlie, as he was too busy hustling someone for nickels. The one bright thing about dancing with Howard was that he was a fabulous dancer. He knew all of the newest dance steps, and he willingly taught them to us. Thus, we girls were never wallflowers because we could dance so well. The boys really appreciated our skill and our willingness to teach them.

Naomi chose to wear a red dress, and I chose a Kelly green dress to wear to the dance. While I never cared for the comparison, people often said that we looked like twins. I chose a dress with puffed sleeves and a flowing hemline, not too short, but allowing for some freedom of the legs.

Momma often said she thought I had good-looking gams. Naturally, I had to admit that I thought she was right. Momma told us girls, "Vanity is a second cousin to sin; but sloth is even worse." I had a hard time figuring out how those two had any chance of meeting in the middle. I knew I spent too much time preening in front of the mirror.

By the time our family finished with jobs and chores, we arrived at the dance fifteen minutes after the band had started playing.

"Now quit your fussing. Blame it all on me for our being

late," Momma said as she admonished us for bickering and fussing.

"But Momma, he may have come to the dance, and since he didn't see me, he may have left."

"Trust me, Jess. That boy will still be here. He took a notion to come, and that means he has a real hankering for you."

Keeping with our city fathers' tradition, the dance was free. The merchants provided the townsfolk with the band, either from their system of dues or philanthropy. It was deeply appreciated by all the people.

By the time we found a table for our family and had time to settle down a bit, I was a nervous wreck. I desperately wanted to find Pete at the dance, yet I hoped he wouldn't be there because I didn't know if I were ready to allow my heart to take a chance to be crushed again. Like a mirror broken into a thousand pieces, fitting those shattered parts back together so one's image could be clearly seen seemed nearly impossible. I sensed the precarious condition of my heart at that moment.

As I allowed my eyes to scan around the room, the band was playing a hot tune. The dancers on the floor were doing the Charleston. In a minute, most of the people on the dance floor stopped dancing and formed a circle. Soon they were applauding for the couple dancing. I quickly made my way to where all of the commotion was taking place. As I edged my way into the crowd and peeked around at the people, my breath quickened and my pulse raced. My heart was shocked. A flashy-looking blonde, who was firm and fully packed in all the right places, wearing a bright red dress, was high stepping in her high-heeled shoes. The man, with a very graceful gait, suddenly kicked his leg clear up over his head. That brought a chorus of oohs and aahs from the people. He smiled broadly and flashed his hands up and pointed them at the approving crowd. This dancer who was so amusing the crowd with his smart dance moves was Pete.

He quickly spied me at the edge of the crowd, and he smiled at me and gave me a wink. I was so unsettled by seeing him with that pretty blonde; I turned and went back to the table where the family was seated.

"What in tarnation is all the commotion?" Momma asked. "Why have the people stopped dancing?"

I put my hands on my hips and looked at her. "It's Pete and some hussy."

I could tell that Momma was having a hard time hiding a laugh.

"It isn't funny!"

The dance music changed, and the crowd of watchers soon dispersed and started dancing a slow dance.

It was just seconds until I heard a voice. "May I have this dance?"

I looked up, and it was Pete.

I didn't reply immediately.

"Perhaps this beautiful lady all decked out in red to your right would care to dance then?" he deftly said.

I realized that Pete wasn't a man to trifle with. "Excuse me, Pete," I said hurriedly, as I didn't want Momma to suffer from my bad manners. Most assuredly, I didn't want him to pay any attention to my sister Naomi. "Momma, this is Pete." I introduced him to my family.

Momma reached out her hand to shake his. He softly, elegantly picked it up and gallantly kissed her hand then clicked his heels together. "The honor is all mine."

Momma was a bit startled, and she looked over at me. "Well, Jess, for a boy that has no last name, this one just may be a keeper." She laughed and smiled at him.

Pete grinned in a shy way at Momma and let her know that he had deliberately put on a show for my benefit. "Paul Leo Grady at your service, madam," he boldly said.

I could see the sudden change in Momma's demeanor. I hoped Pete hadn't been able to detect it. Momma gave me a hard glance, and her eyes grew wider. I was positive I could see the wheels of her brain screaming, *The boy with no name is a hell-raiser.*

I quickly grabbed Pete's hand and halfway dragged him onto the dance floor. The band was playing "Silvery Moon," and I found myself in his arms. I immediately recognized how strong his body felt against mine. His hands were incredibly strong, and yet he held me with a feathery touch, as if I were fine china. We seemed to glide over the floor, and it was as if we both had wings and were floating on air.

He moved his head close to mine and whispered, "You're a great dancer."

His sudden movement close in my ear caused me to move slightly away from him.

"I'll bet you tell that to all the girls," I said, looking up at him.

We danced a few seconds in silence and savored the mood, the music, and the moment.

"Only the ones I want to get past first base with," he said softly.

I pulled away from him a little more and looked into his dreamy eyes. "More like a home run, right?"

My reply startled him some. "Now don't go confusing me for any one-time Johnny." He did his best to lay to rest any apprehension I might have concerning his intentions.

Just as suddenly, he pulled me very close. I was able to feel the outline of the unmistakable flask in his front coat pocket. "Are you a drinker?"

"Why do you ask?" He looked into my eyes. "I take a nip now and then. No harm in that, is there?"

The band switched to a fast number, and he motioned for me to catch the beat and start dancing the Charleston with him. In no time at all, we were the center of attention. The crowd soon stopped their dancing and watched Pete and me dance. At first I was very hesitant, but he kept coaxing me and encouraging me. Soon I found myself letting loose and enjoying the thrill of dancing with someone who made everything I did seem more elegant. I was as mesmerized as the rest of the crowd when he kicked his leg up over his head with such ease and grace. It was as if he never misstepped nor found himself out of balance. When the dance ended, we came together quickly. We found ourselves in a warm embrace. The sensual touching and the awareness of those feelings caused both of us to demonstrate a sense of unexpected withdrawal. We recognized there was a special spark of chemistry going off in our minds and hearts, and neither one had expected it, nor were we ready to handle it.

"Whoa, Nellie," he said. "Does your pretty red hair do that to all men?" Pete murmured in the midst of our embrace.

I was so emotionally undone, all I could do was look up at him and smile weakly.

"I need to find the little boys' room." He motioned for me to head back to our family's table. "I'll be back in a few minutes."

I was emotionally exhausted by what had just happened, and I was ready to take a seat.

"You and Pete cut quite a rug," Momma said as I took a seat. "Better be careful, Jess, that boy's like a magic elixir."

It was more than a few minutes before Pete made it back to our table. He motioned for me to take his hand, and we went to the dance floor. The band was playing "Harvest Moon," and I slid easily into his arms. He had the smell of liquor on his breath.

"You've been drinking." I gave him a disapproving look.

"Relax, doll." He took me in his arms and twirled me. "Just a tiny nip can't hurt, right?"

I pushed him away. "It seems to me you've had more than a tiny nip; it's more like a flask full." I started to return to my table.

"Come on, Jessie. Be reasonable," he pleaded as I walked away.

A rotund man in a white short-sleeved shirt appeared. He had a look of fear on his face and sweat running down his forehead. He reached out and tugged violently on Pete's coat sleeve.

"Come here." The man motioned to Pete. "Bill's about to meet his maker!" he shouted.

"Go tell him to screw himself," Pete lashed out.

"For God's sake, he's your brother," the man said as he yanked Pete's coat sleeve. At first Pete refused to leave, and he motioned for me to come back. "This time it's real bad! They said they were going to kill him," the man added with great urgency in his voice.

"Jessie, don't leave," Pete pleaded with me. "I … I have to go, but I'll be right back." He reluctantly moved in the direction his buddy had come from.

When we kids started staying out later at night on dates, it didn't take us too long to appreciate Momma's sage teaching about life.

"When whiskey and women mix with men, the only way to stay out of trouble is to become the pumpkin," Momma often warned us girls. "Midnight is the witching hour. If you are on your way home by then, seldom will trouble find you."

The only thing that spreads faster than juicy gossip is the announcement of an impending fight, usually between two drunks at a dance. While alcohol is forbidden on the premises of the dance hall, nothing keeps people from bringing their own to consume outside the hall. This happened every dance except the Christmas dance, which was more closely monitored.

I didn't want to allow myself to be drawn to that brutal arena where everyone was quickly moving in order to see the fight. I just couldn't stand the thought of not knowing whether Pete was a part of it. Worse, I was concerned that he was going to be harmed.

I struggled to fight my way so I could see what was happening. The hairs of my head stood up and tingled. I was filled with a mix of fear and the desire to see a fight. I can remember how horrible it made me feel that I was enticed with a sense of curious joy to be in the midst of any impending, brutal combat.

I saw Pete and his buddy step through the door, and the crowd quieted down. Pete's large frame was a dark silhouette in the doorframe against the light in the hall. Another man, already bloodied, his right eye swollen, was sitting up on the ground. Two large, bulky men were standing back just a few feet from the fallen man. The one man's fists were covered with blood.

I immediately recognized them. They were Neal and Curly Kowalski, the twin sons of Herman Kowalski, one of the area's richest wheat farmers. They were our town's biggest bullies and were once again causing mayhem. His two sons had terrorized people ever since they were in grade school. Their father was like a cheerleader for their brutal behavior. Mr. Kowalski a very prominent citizen; even the sheriff seldom bothered his family. They were Pollocks of the first degree; they fit all of the stereotypical profile. They were large, very strong, hardworking, hard drinking, and dumb as a box of rocks. Their forearms were as large as most men's legs, and they loved to fight.

When the man on the ground saw Pete, he struggled to his feet. He stood up, and his large chest heaved deeply. He spit out some blood, and he slurred his words. He took his right, beefy index finger and pointed it at the two men. Wiping some blood from his nose, he slurred: "Noowssh you ..." He spit some blood and let out a stream of expletives. "Noowssh youss," he bellowed. "Maybes you kickedsh my t-t-tail roundss like somes badsh mule trainersh, but now we'lls see what you cansh do with my bbrother and me." He spat out some more blood and expletives.

"Bill, will you shut your stinking mouth?" Pete commanded as he reached out and pulled his brother close to him. Pete's brother was drunk, and Pete's admonishment froze him for a few seconds. Pete patted him on the head and slowly moved him to the side so he leaned up against the building. He slowly walked up closer to the two men who had already given his brother a severe beating. His white sport coat stood out against the blackness of the night. It was framed by the illumination from the light coming from the dance hall and the outside light attached to the building. A cigarette was dangling from his mouth. Pete paused to take a drag and slowly blew a smoke ring, which was visible in the night air.

"Why have you given my brother a whipping?" he asked in a very even, almost unemotional tone of voice.

The larger of the two men took a step closer to where Pete moved, evidently to make sure he knew they weren't intimidated by his sudden presence. The one brother, who was standing just out of the direct light, said, "Oooh, better watch out, little brother; that fat boy we just beat up has a baby brother who's gonna kick your butt." He laughed in a derisive way.

The one who was standing closest to Pete turned his head

slightly and looked back at his brother. He started to shake his body, arms, and even his head deliberately.

"Can't you tell, I'm so, so scared; I'm liable to fill my pants." They both enjoyed laughter with a nasty sneer. "Your brother can't keep his hands off of another man's girl," he snapped as he deliberately spit a stream of tobacco at Pete's feet.

"Lets me shhut his mouthsh, little bbrothers," Bill pleaded in a drunken slur.

The one in the back said, "Doesn't he just put the fear of God in you?" He whispered for effect. "Just look at him; bet he weighs all of a hundred and something." He derided Pete's slender frame. They both enjoyed a loud laugh, as did the crowd.

"I've got farts stronger than he can handle," the one brother who was doing the most talking said through clenched teeth. This made the crowd howl with laughter. "Ash dark as he ish, he must b som D-dago-Whop; hell, hees might bes a n-nigger the ways he cans dance," the Kowalski brother in the background said drunkenly, and a lot of the gathered crowd laughed loudly.

In measured pace and tone of voice, Pete said, "Now, I will be the first one to agree that my brother is a bit of a moron from time to time, especially when he's had a few too many nips of ole Jim Beam." The crowd laughed again. "I agree; he probably needed a good whoopin'." The twin in front said, "This wuss is too wordy; let's kick the crap out of both of them. Then, maybe I'll just cut him and make him sound like a altar boy."

There was a collective sound that came from the gathered crowd that indicated that his brutal words had shocked them.

"Stop this!" I heard someone in the crowd scream. I quickly realized that it was my voice. I was embarrassed and sought to hide myself back in the large crowd.

Pete turned for just a second, and I know he recognized me out of the corner of his left eye. He slowly moved to where his body was about evenly placed between the two men.

"Maybe you're right," he said. And with almost the speed of a lightning strike, Pete fired off a left cross to the man standing closest to him. It was as if he were practicing quick thrusts on the dance floor. His full weight and strength were behind that punch. When Pete's fist exploded on the jaw of the closest man, he went down like a dead man falling from the hangman's noose. It happened so fast that most of the people never saw it happen. No sooner had the first man crumpled to the ground than Pete took a step back and did a half pirouette to face the other man. He just as suddenly let fly his left foot, as if he were trying to kick his leg up over his head as he did when he was out on the dance floor. His foot cracked the other man right square on his jaw; he too fell like a tall pine in a woodman's forest.

An immediate hush fell upon the cheering crowd. They were all too stunned to emotionally react to what they had just witnessed.

Pete stood over the two fallen bodies. With his hands, he made the sign of a cross, and he moved his hands, palms facing each other, and clicked them together. "And this shanty-tailed Irishman just punched your clock and rang your bell." He spit upon the faces of their prostrate bodies as he stepped back from them.

One day, our family discussed the value of boxing, and the importance of being the heavyweight champion of the world, like Jack Dempsey.

"Mr. Shakespeare said, 'All the world's a stage, and we all have a bit part' or something like that. I'm not sure about his wisdom, but all the world loves a gladiator," Momma assured us children.

Heaven help me, but in the midst of that brutal confrontation between Pete and those two men, I was torn in two directions. I wanted to pursue, by any means necessary, a way to stop the brutality. On the other hand, I was seeking a way to quench my thirst for bloodletting. I viewed and replayed in my mind each terrible, intoxicating second of that fight as it unfolded before my eyes. I found myself not being repulsed by the violence and blood but somehow drawn to its suggestive power.

Pete's brother, Bill, staggered over to the two men, both lying stonelike on the ground, and he raised his foot to stomp on their groins. Pete quickly grabbed him and twirled him around. He pulled him away.

"But they beat the hell out of me," Bill protested as he did his best to break away so they could punish the men who beat him.

Pete grabbed Bill and roughly manhandled him. "You drunken bum, one of these days I'm going to let you handle your own stuff."

Bill tried to break free and get to the two men still lying on the ground. Pete grabbed him and forced him up against the building's wall just to the right of the doorway. Pete grabbed him and hugged him, wiping his brother's bloody shirt on his coat.

"Let it go."

He struggled to calm him down, holding him by his shoulders and shook him more gently. "Let it go, just let it go." His voice was filled with command, yet a tone of nurturing was evident. Bill's shoulders slumped, indicating that he was accepting Pete's direction. Pete looked around at the crowd. "Party is over, folks. Let's get back to dancing." He quickly ushered his brother to their automobile. Pete forced Bill in and closed the door.

As the crowd dispersed, they were all talking about how Pete had just coldcocked those two guys in a split second. I lingered a bit to see if Pete would seek me out.

I was just inside the door when I felt a hand on my shoulder.

"I'm sorry about"—his hand made a motion toward the outside where the fight took place. "My sorry"—he stopped to keep from spewing profanity in front of her—"brother is a drunken lout. I'd like to brain him! I have to go."

I reached out and took his hands. I squeezed them tenderly. "I understand." I smiled.

"Jessie, can I see you again?" He was making his way to their car, and his brother was attempting to get out. "Get in the car or so help me God, I'll tie you to the bumper and drag you home," he hollered. He waved at me as he drove off.

"A leopard never changes his spots," Momma said the next day when we discussed that hell-raiser with whom I had become smitten. "Jessie, why would you want to get yourself tangled up with the likes of that boy? While I didn't traipse out to join in with all those hooligans who glory in seeing one man beat the other's brains out, I certainly heard enough about that Grady boy to know he is nothing but big trouble." She let out a loud sigh. "So vicious! It just makes my heart thump out of control with trembling and fears; do you hear me, Jessie? Great day in God's heaven! I understand that he nearly killed those two men with just one blow apiece." She threw up her hands and placed them on either side of her head. She rubbed them against her hair and head. "What if he loses his temper? What then?"

"Momma, you weren't there, so you don't really know what happened, do you?"

"Thank you, sweet Jesus, I wasn't a witness to such brutality. Mark my words, if you continue to see this … this lothario gladiator, one day I'll be visiting you in some hospital or, God forbid, some morgue."

Momma stopped in midsentence; she lifted up her hands to the ceiling, and she raised up her head and began to speak.

"I guess you taught me a good lesson this time, right, Lord? Be careful what you pray for, you just might get it. That's right, ole big mouth Lou opened up her big mouth and inserted foot, and on my knees no less. Here I'm wearing out my old, tired body just praying up a storm so some mopey-headed girl can see a little tiny bit of light at the end of the tunnel, broken heart and all. Of course you know all of that. And now you answer my prayers by having an axe murderer, well something near that, come a popping out of that window after you done closed the door." She was taking on something awful as she was doing her best to be sarcastically, overly dramatic.

"There is just no reasoning with you, Momma! Too often your ways, I might add, are not always God's ways. You operate like the proverb, 'Get rid of the rats by burning down the barn,' if you get my drift. I just went to the dance, and we danced a few times; that's all."

"A broken heart is so needy that it hasn't got the brains the good Lord gave to a goose," Momma said.

"You are acting like we are on the threshold of being married! I barely know his real name," I said.

"I never studied chemistry, in or out of school, but I have studied men and women, up close and very personal, for more years than I care to admit. You don't have to be Mr. Edison to know that if one threw a lit match into the midst of you and Pete, it would blow up half of Tampa."

I read somewhere that there are at least seven wonders of the world; where they are all located, I didn't know. But I was pretty sure that the next wonder of the world was 'God's ability to ignite the passions and emotions of two people, who only days before didn't know the other existed.

"You raise children, suckled from your breast, and you do all you can to see that they come out fit for humanity and are worthy to give God glory. A little girl grows into a woman, and she seems bright, witty, and precocious; then a boy shows up, and it all goes for naught." She glared at me.

"You can stop drilling for oil, Momma. That's a dry hole."

"I suppose I'm a little over the top, but you're too far gone to resort to just everyday, run-of-the-mill work. Jessie, by all that is holy in heaven, please promise me you won't see Pete anymore."

"Momma, when Poppa was alive, did you feel safe and secure?"

"Safe and secure in what way?"

"Well, I certainly didn't mean money! God help me, and I know it is a sin, but Momma, Pete took on those two drunken ruffians, and with just one strike of his mighty fist and one swift kick, he put them out and on the ground. He then got his brother, who started the whole mess, to turn away and not seek any revenge, as bloodied and battered as he was. He reminds me of some of the books I've read about knights in shining armor and heroes and such. Just the thought of being in his arms and knowing that he would and could protect me, even risk his life for mine, makes me feel secure with him. Didn't you feel safe and secure in the arms of Poppa? You know, emotionally more than anything else?"

Momma acted as if her thought pattern had been stopped in midstream. She looked deep into my eyes, and I became uncomfortable under the intensity of her stare. I thought, *It's like she is trying to see into the depths of my very soul; maybe it is her searching her own soul.*

With pent-up emotion in her voice, she slowly said, "When you put it that way, the truth be known, as God is my witness, and it hurts me so bad to say it, your poppa never gave me that."

"Well, Pete gives me that. Besides, didn't the preacher just preach a sermon about how God wants to treat us like frisky colts? You know, he doesn't want to break our spirits, but train us so we can handle the bit and win the race for ourselves. All the while, we help others win the race."

Momma gave me a knowing smile because she acknowledged that I had turned the biblical table over on her. "If the horse is drunk, it's mighty hard to win any race," Momma added. She left me standing in the kitchen.

Pete and I were some pair. I came from a family of twelve kids, and he came from a family of ten. Both of our mothers were widowed young, and both had to rely upon their kids to help them live. It was a hand-to-mouth living.

Pete was a section hand for the Rock Island Railroad headquartered in Herington. Though Herington wasn't a very large town, it was an important railway post. The section gang was also called gandy dancers. They maintained the rails that the trains ran on. When needed, they laid new rail. It was a back-breaking job in all kinds of weather. Nonetheless, he was thankful to have the job. Pete had two younger brothers and one older, the infamous Bill. Bill was irresponsible, and he spent his money on wine, women, and song. Even though he was the oldest son, his mother treated him with much favoritism; she covered his butt as much as possible. When it came to Pete, she demanded near fealty and obedience to her needs, real and imagined. Though Pete was known as a warrior amongst men, his soft heart allowed him to be manipulated by those who pretended to love him.

Since I knew how Momma felt about Pete, I just didn't push the idea of Momma and him spending much time together in any type of intimate environment. He came at Christmastime, and he shared a meal with our family the first year we went together.

To say the least, things didn't go too well. I must give the devil his due because Momma was on her best behavior. I'm sure she bit her lip a few times in order that peace and tranquility were flowing in our house, but they didn't last.

"So, Pete, Jessie tells me that you are a great baseball player, a first sacker or something." She attempted to make small talk.

He flashed a sly smile and nodded at me. "I reckon I am a fair country ballplayer." He took a bite out of a chicken leg.

Arthur, my baby brother, who was about ten, said, "Pete, are you good enough to play with the St. Louis Cardinals?"

Pete reached over to his left, where Arthur was seated, and he tousled his hair. He smiled at him. "Can't say for sure, but I probably could."

"Then why don't you?" Momma asked with just a hint of a challenge in her voice, indicating that she questioned the veracity of his answer.

I was thinking, *Momma, don't start something, please.*

Pete looked at Momma for a few seconds. It was easy to detect that he was aware of the true intent of her question. "I've thought about giving it a try. Shoot, the average player don't make any more than I do as a section hand. Besides, my family needs the money I earn at the railroad."

The rest of the meal went along without a hitch. Momma warmed up a mite to Pete and visited with him cordially, mostly about his sister, Lorain, who was a contestant for the Miss Kansas beauty pageant. I felt relieved. Momma had stopped trying to pick scabs off old wounds.

"The family will be going to a special Christmas service at

our church this weekend; we would be honored to have you join us."

Since Momma had made it crystal clear that she really didn't care for Pete, the idea of her inviting him to our church services was beyond anything I ever expected her to say that day. When I heard the invitation, I cringed and looked for a hole to crawl in. While I had shared a lot of information with Momma about Pete, there was one tiny, little thing I had chosen to keep from her: Pete's family was Roman Catholic.

Catholics and Protestants, especially at that time in history, were akin to how oil and water mix. Prejudice and bigotry were a part of the fabric of nearly every town in America. Pete and I had already had several heated arguments about his and my religions. If and when our relationship led us to a church to be married, we were going to be in a real quandary. Neither wanted to change our church worship.

"I can't do that," Pete told Momma in a blunt manner.

"Momma, can't we talk about something more interesting?" I did my best to steer this conversation away from the subject.

"Can't or won't?" Momma asked.

"Can't," he said, and he looked directly at me with a look of puzzlement on his face.

"Well, you're free, white, and twenty-one; why can't you?"

"The pope says I'm not to worship with people who don't follow our religion."

I could see the blood drain from Momma's face as his reply registered in her brain.

Momma, don't blow a fuse. It's not the end of the world, I thought, as I feared she would really ruin the day.

I could almost hear the sucking sound starting from the soles of her feet and rushing into a full-throttle scream coming out of her mouth. I'm sure she wanted to react very badly; all she could manage was a half-gurgled sound.

"I see. Jessie somehow failed to mention that detail." She gave me a look of controlled, inner rage. Thankfully, Momma wasn't allowed to openly show her anger because she was too much of a lady. Thank God!

"We're not good enough for the pope, huh?"

"Now, Jessie, tell your Momma not to be putting words in my mouth. Mrs. Crandal, I can't rightly say what is right and what is wrong. I can tell you that I don't go along with a lot of what our church says." He paused to collect his thoughts. "But I surely don't want to get excommunicated."

Momma, praise the Lord, chose not to continue that trend of discussion. She looked at me first and then directly at Pete. "I can see that you two have a day of reckoning in the days to come. Jessie, my dear, I suggest you become very familiar with Paul's second letter to the Corinthians, chapter six, verse fourteen." She slowly got up from the table. "Pete, can I interest you in a second piece of pumpkin pie?"

"What's that letter from that guy Paul?" Pete asked me.

That was the first time that I really came to grips with how different Pete and I were in the area of religion. Pete came to accept what was with his relationship with my momma; we had been dating for over a year before I finally met his mother and family. It happened only through my insistence.

"If my mother doesn't take to you right away, now don't allow yourself to get all worked up," Pete said as we approached his house.

I squeezed his hand. "Like my momma took to you?" We looked at each other and laughed.

"It could be worse." We laughed again nervously.

I had often spent time reflecting upon the age-old tradition of young adults making the obligatory and harrowing trek to meet the parents for the first time, and how much, if any, that meeting influenced the outcome of the relationship. I had allowed myself to conjure up a picture of how uncomfortable that time was. My imagination included everything from the medieval rack to the French guillotine. Biblically, I saw the couple being hoisted up and put into the fiery furnace with Shadrach, Meshach, and Abednego. I could see myself sitting in a chair, under searing, bright lights, enduring an inquisition

Pete's mother was tall and slender. She must have been nearly six feet tall. She had her hair up in a bun, and it was easy to see where Pete got his good looks.

"Mother, this is Jessie," Pete said, introducing me. "Jessie, this is my mother, Bessie." He smiled nervously at us.

I gingerly reached out my hand and shook hers. She squeezed mine very hard. I did my best to hide my wince from the pain. I smiled as best I knew how. "Pleased to meet you, Mrs. Grady. Pete has told me so much about you," I said in a nervous manner.

She looked directly into my eyes. "And he has told me so little about you." She looked at him with a disapproving look.

I had taken pains to make sure my hair was fixed up. I even wore a Kelly green ribbon in my hair, Pete's favorite color on me. He said it made my green eyes shine and my good-looking legs stand out. He was a leg man; however, I never could figure out how he associated those two together.

She stood there sizing me up for a few seconds. She turned to Pete. "Well, you said she had red hair, but I didn't think you meant *that* red of hair."

I looked at Pete, and his eyes were flashing like a bright light. *Ignore her rudeness,* I could almost hear him saying. I admit that my temper was ready to ignite the fuse. I swallowed my indignation and politely, passively, offered her a sweet smile. "That's what I've been telling God all my life."

Bessie wasn't prepared for my reply. I could tell that she expected me to react to her imprudent comment with like kind. She emitted a little laugh. "And she is so skinny." She stepped back and ushered us into the house.

"When did you meet my Petey?"

I looked over at him. "I guess it has been about a year and a half; is that right, hon? We first met at a baseball game, wasn't it, Pete?"

Pete's mother looked as if she had just spent two days trying to swallow a pig. I thought she was going to go into an apoplectic fit internally.

"Really," she said. "Pete failed to mention that he has known you for such a long time." She turned and looked at Pete. "Didn't you?"

His mother suddenly put her right hand to her forehead. She leaned back in the big, stuffed chair she was sitting in and swooned. I thought she had become ill. Pete immediately ran to the kitchen and fetched a cool drink of water. He handed her some form of medicine to swallow. She obliged his efforts and took the medicine. We sat there for a few minutes in silence. Pretty soon she sat up, and she seemed to have made a full recovery from whatever had ailed her a few minutes ago.

"Is you mother very ill?" I asked as I directed my comment to Pete.

"My constitution just weakens when I find myself under too much stress," Bessie said.

"Like meeting your future daughter-in-law?" I nervously laughed.

Bessie immediately reached for the glass of water and took a drink.

"Not *right now*...but in the future," Pete said.

"And when you get married, do you think Pete can afford to provide for you and my family?" She directed her question directly to me.

"Well, Mrs. Grady, Pete and I will certainly do all we can to help you. But when we have our own family, you will have to find a way to make it on your own, just like my widowed momma has since I was ten," I said.

His mother gave me such a stare. I felt that she wanted to reach out and scratch my eyes out. "Well, I suppose I will just find a way in a few years." She gave me a smug look. "Now, Jessie dear, tell me, how soon will you be converting?"

Her unsubtle reference was that Pete was a Catholic; all Catholics were forbidden to marry outside the church unless the Protestant was willing to convert.

My juices were ready to boil. She knew it, and she was enjoying it. Pete knew it too.

"Jessie and I have to be getting along." Pete interrupted the ongoing tête-à-tête between his mother and me.

"Oh yes, we do need to be going." I fell in with Pete's direction. *I really need to leave before I find myself saying things that will glaze the atmosphere, possibly permanently,* I thought.

From that moment on, I knew I had a worthy adversary for Pete's affection and devotion. Through fake heart attacks, unexpected dizzy spells, suicide threats (Bessie threatened to throw herself off the high railroad bridge if he married me), flat-out lies, and misdirection, Pete's momma found a way to keep us from being married for nearly four more years. This in no way displeased Momma!

I admit that there were many times I almost gave up and walked away from the love of my life because I was constantly on the horns of a dilemma. I wanted and expected Pete's total devotion. Yet, I knew full well that he just wasn't able to act in such a way if it displeased his conniving mother. Pete was a man's man in every way; however, when it came to standing up to his mother, he was just too kindhearted. This made him vulnerable to his mother's schemes. She used a great strength (a desire to please and shower her with unconditional love) of his to make him not only appear weak but to be weak. Deep down, it was a point of contention that I had to handle by myself all of our married life until his mother died. If I had chosen to make it an issue of contention in our relationship, he would have recognized the loss of respect for him in my eyes.

Before Pete and I finally were married, I reluctantly relented and agreed to meet with his priest. We spent time counseling, and we finally agreed that we would be married...outside the gate. This term was used when a non-Catholic married a member of that faith. I refused to the bitter end to agree that our children would have to be reared as Catholic.

In spite of Pete's reluctance to often make me feel as if I were first in his life until his mother died, he was the most loving man any woman could ever wish for. His five children thought he walked on water! He was funny and spent a lot of time entertaining our family with his quick wit. He frequently played the spoons or danced with his daughters as we all prepared to attend church services on Sunday morning. He was a staunch Democrat, and I was a Republican. We cancelled out each other's vote every election day. He was a simple man, mostly unlettered, and his children teased him because he lived all his life and never held a driver's license. He worked only for one company, the Rock Island Railroad, for forty-nine years.

He walked to work most of those years; even the people in the houses along the way where he walked looked forward to his melodic whistling. I know so because many of them mentioned it when they came to pay their respects at his huge funeral.

Oh, yes, when his oldest son was nine, Pete was baptized into the name of Jesus Christ at the First Christian Church's Christmas service, along with all of his family. Something had gone awry, and the baptismal water was like ice. Pete survived that ordeal, and none of our family got so much as a sniffle. We all laughed when he remarked, "At least the Catholics have the good sense to not be one of the frozen chosen just to get into Peter's gate."

My momma had already gone to be with the Lord. Pete's momma was living. Bessie didn't attend the new birth.

Crossing Jordan

Arthur James Crandal, in keeping with Momma's quest to give her sons names they would aspire to live up to, was named after the famous King Arthur of England.

He was the baby in a family of a dozen children; I guess he had a more difficult time finding his place in our brood's pecking order.

"I was always uninformed, too little, not old enough, regardless of the situation," he often lamented.

He was pampered and given a preferred place in our household. Momma didn't want him to grow up. Therefore, she lavished her loving on him, and he became her "love pillow," as Momma said. He was the last link to her being a momma, not just a woman with a lot of kids.

Arthur was average height, about five feet ten, and he was on the skinny side. He had reddish blond hair, very thick, which his sisters were jealous of, and a ruddy complexion helped define him as one of the Crandal clan. Girls thought he was handsome, and he charmed and disarmed them with a winsome smile. He had an outgoing personality that drew folks to him.

"That boy can charm snakes," Momma said. He was scrupulously honest, unlike his brother Charlie, the conman.

He was a magician with his hands, and he was an incredible carver of wood.

"Jess, someday I'm going to be a famous carver," he told me one day when we were playing at the park. He carried a Case Knife. He managed to earn enough money to buy it while he was working part-time at Tetson's Mercantile.

"The ladies love to have Arthur carry their packages to their cars or to their homes. He's such a dreamboat," I'd say. Like all of the Crandal clan, he embarrassed easily, and it showed.

He was very bright, and an excellent student, though not in the top ten percent of his class. He was a decent athlete but not gifted, and he played basketball and ran track like his big brother Howard.

"He puts out as much effort as Howard; he's just not as gifted," Momma said as she explained why he wasn't a big man on campus.

He was a part of the team, just not a star.

Momma's ruse with her trip to Kansas City with Hiram was uncovered, sadly. By the middle of 1937, Momma's rectal cancer had invaded her body and was setting up shop. She was doing her best to carry on. It was beginning to become a real struggle.

I never really knew why, but Momma began to talk about how worried she was that the war drums in Europe were beginning to stir. How she knew about Hitler and some of the political schemes he was maneuvering, I'll never know.

She was good friends with a German couple, Frank and Elsie Smith. Frank grew a special type of barley that he harvested and sold to breweries. They didn't speak English very well, but Momma and the Smiths managed to communicate despite the language barrier.

Perhaps they still had family in the homeland that sent them a newspaper or at least wrote them letters about the situation.

"You mark my word," Momma said often during that time, "Germany is fixing to go to war."

It didn't matter how much information someone tried to give her to totally discount such an outlandish suggestion, she remained convinced that the whole world was headed for a war.

"I don't care what Mr. Wilson said; the Big War wasn't the last one. Frank and Elsie are fearful for their kin. Frank said there were some crazy things going on over there. Just the other day, he said he had learned that Hitler was organizing young Germans into an elite society, and they were called the Brown Shirts. He said there were stories bandied about concerning open mistreatment of German Jewish citizens."

"Your favorite man, Mr. Roosevelt—" I teased her.

"He's not my man," Momma interrupted me. "I didn't vote for him! Giving people money for doing too little! Don't talk to me about that man."

"But you've got to admit he's helped thousands of families stay alive."

"If he had helped only the ones willing to help themselves! Mark my word, a day of reckoning is coming when we will have a nation full of people who expect the government to take care of them.

"Jessie, I've already spoken to the boys about this, but I want you to promise me you won't let Arthur join the army and run off to some godforsaken land and get himself killed."

"Momma, aren't you letting yourself get all worked up about something that is never going to happen? The idea of our country fighting another war in Europe is the kind of thinking that Chicken Little does. Besides, he's only going to be a sophomore in high school, and no one in his right mind would expect a high school boy to be in the army."

Regardless of Momma's near hallucinations about war, Arthur was bound and determined that he was going to one day join the army.

"One day, I'm going to be an officer," he said. "Whatever outfit the army has that is considered its best, I'm going to be a member of." He'd brag about his future achievements. "I'm going to test my mettle." He would put up his puny right arm and flex his muscle to show how strong he was. He laughed at himself, and then he gave Momma a hug and often sparred with her for a few seconds.

Our family really never gave his brash talk any real credence. With Momma, it was a different story; she worried all the time.

With the absolute clarity of 20/20 hindsight, Momma must have had a crystal ball hidden in our house. Her greatest fears about the war came true.

"Maybe she has some magical powers we never knew she had," Naomi suggested when history proved Momma right.

If Momma had any special powers, I wished she had used

them on herself. In the dark ages of cancer, any type, but especially rectal, ovarian, or breast, the death rate was nearly one hundred percent.

"The cancer isn't so bad," Momma said as it became her enemy. "It's just like sin. As the apostle Paul described it, 'He's like a roaring lion prowling around to see whom he can devour.'" She chuckled. "It's the living long enough to die; that is the hard part."

Under the oppressive and cruel dictatorship of Hitler, Germany invaded its neighbors and began to conquer and subjugate large countries and peoples. Our newspapers at first dismissed his brutal attacks.

"Germany was merely reacquiring the kingdoms they once ruled" was the often-heard comment as the appeasers in our country made excuses for Hitler's plan to conquer the world. After a while, two mind-sets began to show themselves in our country; most wanted a neutral position for the United States. Some others favored preparing for war.

The Smiths, who visited Momma when she was up to company, told her that they were trying to convince their kin to get out of Germany or any other occupied country Hitler had taken over since Poland was first invaded.

Arthur wanted to quit high school and join the army.

"You'll do no such thing as long as I'm alive," Momma announced to him and our family. "Until Hitler comes over here and sends a Howitzer down our throats, Arthur James Crandal will still live in Tampa, Kansas."

By this time in my momma's life, I was married and had moved away. Pete and I had grown so weary of all the acrimonious bickering between our mothers; we decided to elope, which we did. What I knew about all this information was given to me in her letters.

I never loved nor admired another living soul as I did my momma. Still, when she refused to accept my Pete into our family, it was difficult to gin up my desire to write letters to her. I realized much later that we were too much alike as women: headstrong, stubborn when we saw that our cause was just, unforgiving, and controlling.

In the mid- to late 1930s, medicine wasn't much more than a step or two away from "this is good for what ails you; take it. If it doesn't kill you, we'll know it works" philosophy. It wasn't far removed from the idea of writing on the death certificate, "Died of consumption," the be-all-and-end-all description of why a person expired from Planet Earth.

I never really knew too much about the cancer that took Momma's life.

The doctor said, "It started in her left ovary, and then, over time, slowly spread into her rectum."

My memory is seared like a hot branding iron as I watched Momma slowly change. She went from being the matriarch who somehow found a way to keep our family fed, regardless of difficult that task might be, to one who had to be fed to stay alive. She used to joke that she did it with bailing wire and a ball of string. She kept us clothed, motivated, and educated. From Momma we learned about God and all his creation and about the world we lived in each day. She wanted us to "show that you have more sense than God gave a goose," she'd say.

By this horrible time in Momma's life, I was a mother with my own daughter. Pete was working in Silvis, Illinois, for the Rock Island Railroad in its supply and storeroom department.

We lived from hand to mouth, and it was difficult to pay Momma a visit. Sometimes a person finds that it almost becomes a necessity to lie; Momma's illness did that to me. The truth be told, I was so devastated every time I paid Momma a visit, it took me more than a week to mentally recover from being in her presence and watching how she was dying.

Over time she became emaciated and wasted away to next to nothing. For years, I had fits of nightmares about the pads and all manner of gauze that were used to stem the stench, the urine, the pus, and the blood. My tears, mostly away from Momma, couldn't wash away the pain my heart was forced to endure. I wanted to pick her up and pull her so close that we could both melt into each other. I wanted all of her pain to be swept from her. Together we would beat this enemy to death and walk anew.

On my next to last visit to see Momma, she was unusually clear headed, and her countenance was better than it had been in years.

"Jessie," she said to me, "promise you won't tell anyone." Her voice cracked with emotion, and it possessed a hint of a whimper. "I'm a junkie," she whispered. "Can you believe it? Carrie Nation and Lou Crandal, the world's best teetotalers, died as a drug addicts." She moaned, and a few tears sprang to her eyes and ran down her cheeks.

What does a child, a grown woman, say to that? My mind was turned topsy-turvy. "Momma! No one is going to think that you are a drug addict."

"I don't remember much ... well, I never wanted to remember much about my father. But I do recall one thing very clearly. For some reason I was with him visiting an old man who was very ill. When we left, Jess, he said, 'If a man lives long enough, he'll be once a man and twice a child.' Look at me! I'm already dead, but my body just hasn't received the message." She chuckled. "Your momma is once a momma, twice a child." The pain wracked her body. She was ready for more morphine to help her live longer so she could die in an even more painful state.

"Life is only for the living," Momma said after we buried Poppa. When it came to my momma, there were times when I came to the prayerful conclusion that sometimes dying is preferred to living, especially when the person is a Christian.

My visit had been wonderful but very emotionally draining. In my lifetime I had witnessed several types of animals enduring pain. It always made me feel sick at my stomach; it shivered my heart and slivered my heart. Each sliver wracked my whole being with suffering and some type of internalized shame. Seeing my momma, lying there in her pain and abject misery, caused me to have those same feelings.

I bent down to kiss her and tell her how much I loved her.

"Jessie," she said, and I could tell that she was becoming emotional. Big saucer-sized tears were welling up in her eyes. "I have prayed that the Lord would allow me the time and the clarity to do this."

I looked at her with a puzzled look. "What is it, Momma? What's troubling you?"

"Oh, Jessie!" she said loudly. "I ... I've been such a fool." Her tears became heavy and started to get her gown wet. "I've asked the good Lord to forgive me. God only knows I don't want to show up in heaven with that sin."

I sat on the edge of her bed, and I gently picked up her hand and softly kissed it. "Momma, all your sins have been forgiven."

"Not if you don't seek repentance," she bellowed in the midst of her tears. "I've been a horrible momma," she moaned. "Why didn't the good Lord just sew my big mouth shut?"

I looked deep into her eyes, and even before she said it, I could tell she was attempting to apologize to me for her unreasonable behavior towards my Pete.

She tried to sit up; she was too weak.

"I ... I was so terribly wrong about Pete." Her tears streamed down her face. "He's a good man." She looked up at me with tears in her eyes. "He's a wonderful father, a wonderful husband and father."

I sat on the edge of her bed, and the tears came streaming down my face. My heart was bursting with joy.

I looked down at her. "I ... I know," I said in a soft tone of voice.

Suddenly we were hugging, and we showered each other with kisses. *"A word aptly spoken is like apples of gold in settings of silver,"* I thought. "Proverbs 25:11," I said, and then I repeated it to her.

"'Pleasant words are a honeycomb, sweet to the soul and healing to the bones,' Proverbs 16:34," Momma said as we exchanged some of her teachings.

"Momma, I have prayed for this day. You'll never know how much I prayed," I said, choking on my words.

I put my head down on her breast and lay there for some time. It had been a long time since I was physically close to Momma. Feeling her warmth run through my body sent my mind and body back to when I was a girl and she was providing me with succor.

"When you come again, will you bring Pete to see me?"

I didn't answer right away.

"If your momma doesn't love me, hell, even like me, there's noth-ing I can do about it." I could hear Pete's voice echoing in my mind. "I'll try," I said as my sobs distorted my answer.

"Jessie, if you can't, please, please, do your best to tell Pete how terribly sorry I am for misjudging him." She started to cry more. "I'd just die"—she started—"what am I saying? I am dying. I don't want to go to see my Maker knowing that Pete doesn't know my true heart about him."

Pete said he was willing to go and visit Momma. Unfortu-nately, he never had the opportunity to make that visit. Momma died before she and he had an earthly reconciliation.

The first week of December in 1940, I received word that I needed to get home as soon as I could; the doctor didn't think Momma would live another day. Pete arranged for me to take the train, and I arranged for my two babies to be taken care of while I went home.

"The old war horse isn't dead yet, but I'm getting ready to make that trip," Momma said as we kids all came home and gathered around her so we'd be with her when she died. All of us were there except Sammy. He had disappeared, and none of us knew if he was dead or alive.

I recall attending a funeral for an old man whom Momma cared for when I was just a girl. Vicariously experiencing how the family behaved puzzled me. I was under the impression that people mourned when they came to a funeral; this one was like a happy celebration in the midst of some tears.

"People can mourn and still enjoy a celebration of life," Momma said when I questioned why the man's family laughed and carried on so. "Funerals are really forced family reunions. It's a pity too; the reunion would have done a lot more good while the breathing was still going on."

Momma was still living, and we did our best to celebrate life.

Arthur graduated from high school that spring. He wanted to join the army, but he stayed because Momma was so sick.

All of us kids had made it home, and Momma had taken a turn for the best, in my eyes. The doctor told us he didn't think she'd live to see tomorrow. Momma wanted us girls to help her be as presentable as she could be under the circumstances. It was too much for her to get in and out of a gown, but when we cut it open and fixed it around her, our mission was accomplished. We cleaned her up and managed to get a new gown around her. She asked to have her pillows propped up even though it caused her more pain.

If I'm crossing over to Jordan, I want to be presentable to my Lord." She instructed us to do her bidding.

After she was presentable, she asked Napoleon to have the family gather around her bed. It was quite a feat to get that many grown bodies in that small room, but we managed.

"Children," Momma said, and just the sound of her voice caused tears to start coming in our eyes. "Your momma's reached the end of her journey; thank God for that."

One of the girls whispered loudly through her tears, "Momma, you're not going to die."

"*Shh,*" Momma said. "Don't waste your tears on me. Don't deny me my wish. I'm going home today!"

People talk about strange things happening before someone dies. Some are believable; some aren't. All I know is that suddenly, Momma acted as if she weren't sick at all. She didn't have cancer; she wasn't dying. Her pale, wasted, emaciated body seemed to glow with a healthy pink. Her eyes, glassed over from morphine, became clear. Her smile was bright and cheery. She pushed herself up, and we helped her prop herself up some.

We kids looked at each other, and we all had odd looks in our eyes. None of us spoke.

"Now, I'm ready for my heavenly choir. Girls, front and center," she ordered. "Sing your momma across Jordan."

We girls looked at each other to see what we should do in light of Momma's order. The sudden change in Momma's countenance led us to believe that God had miraculously touched

Momma. We were certain that Momma wasn't going to die. We grinned at her and at each other. The change in Momma was so wonderful; it was like we wanted to stop and have a group hug. We quickly assembled.

"What a sight you all are," she said as tears sprang to her eyes and ours. "No momma ever had it so good."

She blessed us with the most beautiful smile I ever recall in my life. "You truly were Lou's Dirty Dozen, a perfect number for Lou from God."

We all started blubbering.

"Sing my song, girls; boys, you come in on the chorus."

Pauline gave us a harmony key, and we began to serenade Momma. It was her most favorite hymn, the one she hummed the most when she was busy enjoying her life: "Rock of Ages."

Rock of Ages cleft for me, Let me hide myself in Thee;

Let the water and the blood, From Thy riven side which flowed,

Be of sin the double cure, Cleanse me from its guilt and pow'r.

Not the labors of my hands, can fulfill Thy law's demands;

Could any zeal no respite know, Could any tears forever flow,

All for sin could not atone; Thou must save and Thou alone.

"Nothing in my hand." Momma came in on our singing, and her voice was louder than ours. She sat up straighter in bed. Her voice grew stronger; she was smiling.

"I bring, simply to thy cross I cling; naked come to thee for dress, helpless, look to thee for grace; foul I to the fountain fly ..."

Momma's voice grew even louder.

"Wash me, Savior or I die!"

We girls did our best to catch up with Momma's singing; yet we only wanted to provide some harmony for her.

"While I draw this fleeting breath, when my eyes shall close to death." She said, "Praise Jesus." Her voice grew even stronger.

"When I soar to worlds unknown, see thee on thy judgment throne, rock of ages cleft for me, let me hide myself in thee."

Our family had gotten caught up in the singing and the celebrating. Watching Momma enjoy herself like she hadn't in years, my brothers joined in and added their male voices. It was like a heavenly choir.

As we finished the song, I shouted, "Momma, that was *so* ..." I gushed with glee.

Momma was sitting up in bed; her pillows propped her up. She had a smile on her face; she was dead. Somewhere in the last part of that song, God answered her prayer: she crossed Jordan.

We buried her on December 5, the year of our Lord 1940.

"Every man on earth has the choice to accept or reject the good Lord," I recalled her saying as I was mourning at her funeral. *"But when a baby is born or when a person dies, that's when the Creator is most powerful. He alone gives life, and he alone takes it. Man is only left to make a choice."* Her wisdom resonated and reverberated in my soul.

Shut up! I wanted to scream every time I heard someone laugh. *How could you be so thoughtless? Don't you know my momma just died? The greatest person who ever lived just died, and you see the need to act like it never happened!* My wearied, mourning, mentally anguished mind tormented me for a long time.

The first time I finally saw the Pacific Ocean and walked along the sandy beach, Momma's words came rushing to me. *"Sometimes, I think life is too much like the footprints a man makes when he walks along the seashore; it makes an indelible print for all the world to see. Come tide time, it is gone. It's as if the print had never existed."*

Hiram made arrangements to have a solitary red rose placed on Momma's grave every day while he was living. He died two years later of a massive stroke.

Just over a year and six months after Momma's death, they shipped her baby boy's body home to be buried with military honors. Arthur had enlisted the moment he heard about the attack on Pearl Harbor. He was killed by a sniper as he climbed aboard his ship. I can still close my eyes and hear those awful gun salutes going off; each one shook my inner core, and all I could do was weep.

Nine decades have come and gone in my life, and it won't be long before I get to join Momma up there in the heavenly choir. None of Momma's brood became famous. You'd have to go a far piece to find a family that enjoyed life more than we did. Momma was right; Lou's Dirty Dozen changed the world, one footprint at a time, if nowhere else than in our hearts.

My head must have fallen back far enough and my snoring, in spite of my dreaming, must have caused me to awaken. I caught my throat and tongue sort of fighting each other to get control inside my body. I swallowed a bit, and all seemed to get rebalanced. I looked at the clock that Ranny and Denny had given me, which glowed in the dark. It said 3:30.

My, my, I must have dozed off a long time, I thought. I slowly got up out of the rocker and made my way to the bed. I lay down and felt the softness of the mattress begin to contour my body. "Heavenly sleep, that's what this old woman needs. Heavenly sleep," I muttered under my breath.

Momma. I thought my dream had been so real that I could taste every morsel of its essence. I lay there in the silence and dark of the night; then tears started afflicting my eyes. My present and past memories flooded me. I felt goose bumps come afresh, and my bones were quaking.

I began to sing the words of my favorite hymn.

I would like to tell you what I think of Jesus

Since I found in Him a friend so strong and true;

I would tell you how He chang'd my life completely,

He did something that no other friend could do.

No one ever cared for me like Jesus,

There's no other friend as He;

No one else could take the sin and darkness from me

O how much he cared for me!

My self-entertainment seemed to comfort me.

"Therefore, since we are surrounded by such a great cloud of witnesses, let us throw off everything that hinders, and the sin that so easily entangles, and let us run with perseverance the race marked out for us. Let us fix our eyes on Jesus, the author and perfecter of our faith" (Hebrews 12:1–2). I thought, as I emitted a soft laugh, *And now playing first base for the Angel's team and batting fourth is Pete Grady. Will the loud-mouthed lady, Louise Mae Crandal, in the third row quit cheering so loudly? I can just hear the announcer say.*

"One way or another, by hook or by crook, Momma, you got to tell him, didn't you?" I laughed a little through my tears. I started to hum softly my momma's favorite hymn, and then I began to sing.

Rock of ages cleft for me, Let me hide myself in Thee;

Let the water and the blood, From Thy riven side which flowed,

Be of sin the double cure, Cleanse me from its guilt and pow'r.

"Momma, I'm coming home soon," I said softly. "Another one of Lou's Dirty Dozen is crossing Jordan. Soon, very soon."